MUSIC IN AMERICAN LIFE

A list of books in the series appears
at the end of this book.

Democracy at the Opera

Democracy at the Opera

Music, Theater, and Culture in New York City, 1815–60

Karen Ahlquist

University of Illinois Press

URBANA AND CHICAGO

Publication of this book was supported by grants from the
Henry and Edna Binkele Classical Music Fund, the George
Washington University, and the Sonneck Society.

This book is printed on acid-free paper.

Library of Congress Cataloging-in-Publication Data

Ahlquist, Karen Ethel.
    Democracy at the opera : music, theater, and culture in
New York City, 1815–60 / Karen Ahlquist.
       p.   cm. — (Music in American life)
    Includes bibliographical references and index.
    ISBN 0–252–02272–6 (cloth : alk. paper)
    1. Opera — New York (N.Y.) 2. Music — 19th century —
History and criticism. 3. Music and society. I. Title.
II. Series.
ML1711.8.N3A45   1997
306.4′84 — dc20

                                     96–4494
                                       CIP
                                       MN

On the mimic stage
idealities were realized.
The audience, as is usually the case,
was the better worth looking at
and studying of the two.

— *Walt Whitman*

Contents

Preface

Readers (or watchers) of *The Age of Innocence* know the scene: Edith Wharton's "set" at the opera—conspicuous wealth, the buzz of bored conversation, opera glasses panning the boxes opposite instead of the stage. We get the point without effort. Where else, after all, could a nineteenth-century New Yorker more surely have "arrived" than in a Gilded Age opera box?

Other New Yorkers before Wharton had drawn opera pictures, too. Like hers, their subjects were of the auditorium rather than the stage; in calling the audience "the better worth looking at and studying of the two," Walt Whitman expressed a midcentury preoccupation with theatrical settings.[1] Even Washington Irving, the city's gentlemanly "Jonathan Oldstyle" of the early nineteenth century, saw the old English plays-with-music that passed for "opera" at the Park Theatre. His audience concerns were more mundane than Wharton's: Would a so-called Gallery God in the house's upper balcony aim an unsavory missile at a performer and hit a dignified boxholder instead?

Despite the aura of inevitability Wharton's image emits, the distance traveled from Irving's experience to hers calls it into question. Her familiar elites did play a part in opera's early years in New York. But they did not play the expected star roles. On the contrary, opera's reach was broader. It had to be; simply put, there were not enough elites to go around. In fact, the "class character" descriptions of opera overstate a more subtle and interesting—and therefore more accurate—historical reality. Between the War of 1812 and the Civil War, it took New Yorkers from all parts of society—high, low, and in between—to establish opera in the city. From an ill-defined theater-with-music to a clear place in the city's entertainment world, opera's establishment took complex solutions to complex problems. Creating a repertoire, institution, and audience where there had been none required a careful balance among disparate elements at close range.

How, for example, could a musically sophisticated stage work be understood in a culture that both revered Shakespeare and thought of music as ornamental to the spoken word? How would opera's continental European origin play in an increasingly pro-American political climate? Would its high-culture reputation preclude attracting the audience needed to ensure success with the commercially oriented "common man" of the Jacksonian era? Could respectable Victorian ladies (a major target audience) be persuaded to accept plots that often failed the test of propriety expected, if not always achieved, in the theater? And finally, could opera's advocates and entrepreneurs solve the problem of production expenses beyond their experience or imaginations? Merely importing an opera troupe and expecting the city's public to understand, enjoy, and support its offerings would not bring success. As was said in the 1830s, opera would have to be "naturalized"—established as an institution, understood in terms of local culture and concerns, and enjoyed as entertainment by a paying audience.

Opera was successful in New York in spite of its European origin, rather than because of it. Unacceptable as "top-down" culture, it was not established by a social or intellectual elite bent on aping European culture or promoting the Western musical canon. Rather, it succeeded as a commercial endeavor, sold by entrepreneurs on the Barnum model and supported by a public that included the city's "aristocracy" but was open to much of the "democracy" as well. Opera was established in the city a full generation before the Metropolitan opened in 1883 and a dozen or so years before Wharton's *Age of Innocence* characters flirted and gossiped in the boxes at the Academy of Music. Its success had depended on a changing relationship between the stage and the house, between its substance and the audience it would attract, and between individual pieces and their receptions. Shakespeare's ideal of the theater as "the mirror up to nature" was taken seriously in the English (and hence, American) tradition. It mattered whether the production at hand was *The Beggar's Opera, Rigoletto,* or something in between, and changes in repertoire moved in tandem with changes in the institution and its public. But as Whitman and others recognized, the "mirror" between stage and house was always distorted. "On the *mimic* stage," he asserted, "*idealities* were realized."[2] Attractive new operas inspired attempts to encourage economic patronage and a respectable social setting, while increased public understanding of opera as separate from theater allowed a wider range of works to be accepted. Both kinds of changes were equally important. After all, for example, "ladies" in the audience would need "idealities" to mirror current notions of gentility. Without them, women's attendance would be discouraged as unseemly — and opera would fail for lack of customers.

From this perspective, attempts to understand opera's naturalization in New York in terms of fixed categories understate its ambivalent place in the social fabric. Observers didn't always get it right, and pictures such as Wharton's are drawn with a novelist's dramatic focus rather than a historian's colder but broader view. A theme of this study, then, is the disparity between events and their interpretation. One can trace an attitudinal tradition toward opera, especially among intellectuals and the press, that played as large a role in its reception as did the works themselves. Moreover, social attitudes influenced esthetic ones to no small degree. For example, the nineteenth-century press made no claims to objectivity or critical dispassion. Press writers in New York who disparaged opera as theatrical, elite, and crassly commercial can be found also unfavorably comparing Verdi to Mozart on purely musical terms.

Commentators on American culture have often reminded us that "New York is not America."[3] With regard to opera, the city's influence was broad but not infinite. Michael Broyles's work, for example, shows the genre playing only a small role in the linked social and musical changes in nineteenth-century Boston.[4] Yet this study does encompass issues that transcend the label "local." Through a close look at one case, it critiques some of the presuppositions that often underlie social accounts of the modern Western canon, seeking to confirm, modify, jettison, or at the least better understand them. In exploring relationships between a genre's place in society and attitudes toward individual works, it shows how responses to music are rooted in specific historical circumstances. The questions it answers support music scholars' increasingly made and, I believe, correct claim that music and broader cultural factors play legitimate and important roles in each other's history.

Finally, as students of New York's past have long known, such a story will never be dull. This tale in particular has surprises for nearly everyone, most prominently that of a musical genre in an unaccustomed lead role on the historical stage. Music participated in a social-cultural complex called "opera" of central artistic, social, and even political importance. New attitudes toward opera helped create a separate artistic sphere that in turn encouraged and marked a change in the social meaning of cultural activity. The vagaries of nineteenth-century reception show opera and its music off the pedestal, restored to a place in daily discourse that they enjoyed even as their elevated status was being considered. Some of the terms of debate may seem odd today. In part, the oddness is the point. By showing how one society selected and maintained works of art and artistic institutions and how a genre changed meaning (and hence usefulness to society) over time, it shows how meaning can bear as great a relationship to an environment different from either that of the original creators or from the present. In so doing, it reminds one that music can tolerate a wide variety of interpretations over time and can still be loved.

Acknowledgments

It is a pleasure to acknowledge and thank in print those who have encouraged and supported this book and whose input and work have improved it. Many of these people are librarians and curators who led me to useful material in their collections or workers who ordered, notified, fetched, carried, packaged, and mailed so I could have what I needed. I am particularly grateful to the staffs of the Microform Reading Room and the Interlibrary Loan Office at the Harlan Hatcher Graduate Library at the University of Michigan. The Interlibrary Loan staff in particular always had something new, including enormous nineteenth-century "blanket sheet" newspapers they had obtained at no cost to me. At the University of Wisconsin-Madison, Jean Bonin, project coordinator for the Tams-Witmark/Wisconsin Collection, spared no effort in giving me access to the collection and pointing out other relevant sources. I also thank staff members at the Music Library and William L. Clements Library (most recently Arlene Shy), University of Michigan, New York Public Library, New-York Historical Society, Museum of the City of New York, Library of Congress, Loeb Music Library at Harvard University, Harvard Theatre Collection, Newberry Library, Northern Illinois University Library, American Antiquarian Society, University of Pennsylvania Library, Olin Memorial Library at Wesleyan University, and Melvin Gelman Library at the George Washington University for their help.

Other sorts of aid have been simultaneously scholarly, practical, and more personal. Two individuals in particular made it possible for me to conceive of this project. Richard Crawford opened the whole area of nineteenth-century American music reception with a (seemingly) offhand remark that "the fundamental issues are only now being laid out." Raymond Grew asked questions that showed me layers of interpretative possibilities lurking beneath presumably innocent information. Once underway, I was aided by Katherine Preston's willingness to share her work in progress, Michael Broyles's thinking on issues his work and mine have in common, and Dale Cockrell's ideas about social class that helped me clarify my own. Friends—in particular Robin Armstrong, Barbara Dobbs Mackenzie, and Jeffrey Taylor—offered useful advice, willing ears, and encouragement, not to mention food and drink. Susan Cook and Kay Kaufman Shelemay offered invaluable collegiality and encouragement at a time of transition for this book and my career. Nancy B. Reich lent me her New York-area home and shared her musicological insight at a key point in my research. Strong words from Marilyn Butler and Adrienne Fried Block in Worcester, Massachusetts sped this book onto its present course. And I thank Bernice Ahlquist, Kristine Ahlquist, Nancy Ahlquist, and Paul Jakoubek for their hospitality during what must have seemed like my interminable research tours and for their attitudes of bemused tolerance worthy of Washington Irving.

More recently, I am grateful to colleagues at the George Washington University, especially Laura Youens, Catherine Pickar, and Madelyn Holmes, for their encouragement of this project and what I have to say in general. My department chair, Roy Guenther, gave me time and authorized staff resources to get it into shape. I cannot thank him enough. I have had cheerfully performed, eminently useful administrative, technical, and manuscript preparation help from Melisa Doherty, Steve Hilmy, Megan Oliver, and Jan Schuller. For financial support, I am grateful to the Horace H. Rackham School of Graduate Studies at the University of Michigan, the National Endowment for the Humanities for a summer stipend in support of revision, and the Columbian School of Arts and Sciences at the George Washington University for a publication subvention. I thank Mary Giles of the University of Illinois Press for sharp-eyed manuscript editing that led to many improvements in the text. And I am grateful to Judith McCulloh, also of the Press, not only for taking the book on but also for her generous and patient professional advice at every step. Working with Judy demystifies the publication process, providing a confidence-building knowledge in many ways as valuable as the book itself.

Finally, as a student of audiences, I am conscious of the role readers have played in shaping the book. They have told me, sometimes at length, what it is and means, and how to make it better. Some have told me a second time, having read it again. And two told the University of Illinois Press to publish it. I cannot imagine a better tryout audience than Robin Armstrong, Judith Becker, Richard Crawford, John Dizikes, Raymond Grew, Madelyn Holmes, James Manheim, Andrew Mead, Kathryn Oberdeck, David Scobey, and an anonymous reader. Thanks to them, I don't have to hit Broadway cold.

Democracy at the Opera

One

English Opera as Popular Culture:
The Beggar's Opera Tradition

*I*n the eighteenth century, *English opera* was a contradiction in terms. Although Italian opera was performed in London, even there many of the British preferred musical theater to be spoken and sung in English and steeped in the long-standing English tradition. English "opera" was not opera at all, but a play with musical pieces interpolated. Produced in the theater by the same performers and supported by the same financial structure, so-called operas were subject to the same critical and audience responses as spoken plays and other entertainment. The American theater followed the English practice, importing British plays and performers to New York, Philadelphia, and other eastern cities. The tradition was ill-suited to incorporating opera in its original form. Far from the modern "artistic" institution it became over the course of the nineteenth century, in 1825, when the first Italian opera performances were given in New York, the theater was by contrast commercial and popular. In virtually every respect — economic, social, political, and artistic — it could not prepare an audience for a continental European, musically based genre with an elitist reputation. Yet opera's story in New York begins in the city's English theater. There, even in an "opera," the play was the thing. Considering the energetic, eclectic, vigorous, and popular theater after the War of 1812, one wonders how the Italian upstart could even muster the support to reach the stage.

Could Italian opera succeed as commercial entertainment? It needed to. Doubtful as it may seem, the commercial theater was the only physical and economic structure remotely suited to opera performance. Moreover, the idea of "culture," in which wealthy, civic-minded citizens would support an artistic endeavor for the public good, did not exist. Like anything else, opera would have to sell, for selling a performance was the theater's bottom line.

The problems inherent in such a commercial venture are obvious, for the theater's need to survive financially determined its approach to the public. Even paying the rent was a problem; the managers of New York's Park Theatre paid landlords John K. Beekman and John Jacob Astor $13,000 a year from 1821 to 1828 and $18,000 thereafter to 1842.[1] Continuous profit was essential. Thus the Park tried to offer something for everyone in order to appeal to a heterogeneous audience. During the first years after the War of 1812, the days of specialized establishments catering to clearly defined categories of patrons were still in the future. Flexibility was important. To achieve it, theaters used a stock company of salaried actors who played the various common character types. The Park, for example, listed genteel comic, old woman, chambermaid, dancer, low comic, old man, old gentleman, tragedian, country boy, opera (i.e., lyric female singer), and vocalist (male only).[2] Because these players worked for salary, they were available as needed. Managers could then program a wide variety of theatrical pieces, changing the bill as often as necessary — usually nightly — to attract a repeat clientele. To this basic company was sometimes added a well-known performer billed as a star. The star's short engagement and reputation for high-quality performance helped the theater keep its audience coming back. In a small city with a potential audience of only a few thousand, the regular theatergoer was a sought-after customer.

The formula for an evening's entertainment varied little. The program opened with an overture and included a main piece (usually a drama, "opera," or genteel comedy) and an afterpiece (usually a farce, sometimes a short "opera"). In between appeared variety acts that depended on available performers. The programming may seem a jumble of incongruent elements, lacking a dramatic structure or a unity of mood or affect. But this mixture seems to have been what audiences found appealing; in one evening they could be moved to tears by tragedy or melodrama, dazzled by spectacle, kept laughing by comedy, amazed by athletic feats of dance or acrobatics, swept up by the power of a piece of music, and comforted by an old-favorite song. Moreover, the customer was always right. Audience members had the option — many would have said the responsibility — of responding immediately and decisively to each part of the performance. Individual acts came and went, sometimes in a single evening, because managers catered to audience response. These ultimate critics determined whether a novelty became the tried-and-true.

This sovereignty extended even to "classic" plays. As Lawrence Levine has noted, plays of Shakespeare or any other recognized author were produced and received on the same terms as any other part of the program. Distinctions between "art" and "entertainment," so obvious today, mattered little. "Greatness" would not be presumed; it had to be communicated on the spot. Thus, for example, preserving Shakespeare's text was not a priority; instead, versions of his plays were designed to appeal to nineteenth-century audiences. Universally recognized as monuments of the Anglo-American cultural heritage, night after night they were also subjected to the same tests of theatrical viability as works of lesser reputation. Shakespeare needed to "please" and sell; classic or not, his plays received no handicap.[3]

The theater's place in the humdrum of New York's city life was reflected in the building itself. Until the mid-1820s, New York's entertainment center was its only permanent theater, the Park. Known as "Old Drury" (after London's Drury Lane Theatre), it was nevertheless an ordinary building on an ordinary spot across from City Hall Park. A typical English or American theater of its day (1798–1848), it sat in the middle of a block of homes and shops on a comfortable street (figure 1). Unpretentious, blending in with the scenery, physically of rather than removed from its surroundings, and lacking any ostentation or even means of attracting attention the way modern public buildings do, the Park's exterior suggests that its builders saw theatergoing as belonging to the same order of the business of life as being at home, working, shopping, or visiting a tavern or eating place. In 1830 a newspaper even called its exterior "a plain, unsightly, 'shabby-looking affair.' "[4]

Its interior was divided into the three typical sections of an English theater auditorium (figure 2).[5] The divisions — pit, box, and gallery — allowed for what amounted to three separate audiences to be present at the same event, each enjoying the performance while easily avoid-

Figure 1. Park Row with the second Park Theatre (1821–48), lithograph by George Hayward. (Collection of The New-York Historical Society)

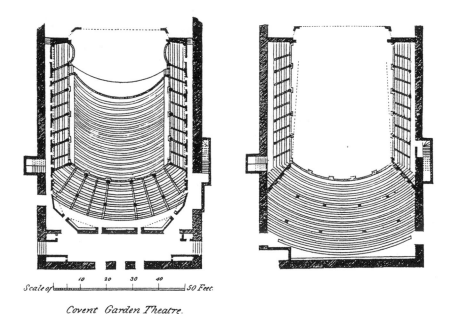

Scale of ⊢⊶⊶⊷⊷⊷⊷⊷⊷⊷⊷⊷⊣ 50 Feet.
   10   20   30   40

Covent Garden Theatre.

Figure 2. Covent Garden Theatre, London, interior diagram, from George Saunders, *A Treatise on Theatres* (London: the author, 1790), plate 10.

ing the others. The pit corresponds to the modern orchestra section, the boxes to the lower balcony or lower rings of boxes, and the gallery to the upper balcony. Each section had an outside entrance; people entered the Park according to where in the theater they would sit.[6] There was no common lobby and no physical connection among the three sections of the auditorium. The Park's interior allowed two opposing principles to be reconciled: The audience could reflect much of the social breadth of the city, thus enhancing income, while traditional distances among social groups could be maintained.

Contemporary comments on the audience link the physical layout to social distinctions among three clearly defined groups. Covering audience deportment, dress, and attitudes toward the other groups, they showed what went on in each section of the auditorium and prescribed allowable behavior. Although these groups corresponded roughly to social classes, they were not identical with them. Rather, the divisions in the auditorium mirrored the world of theatrical types on stage. Neither the types nor the divisions were realistic or subtle. But their long-term success shows that the audience considered the reflection to be in some manner accurate, entertaining, and worthwhile.

At the top in price and status, although not physically at the top of the theater, were the four tiers of box seats (figure 2, left). Beginning in the 1820s, box seats could be "secured" (reserved) in hopes of putting a premium on them. Secured seats meant that managers could allot a specific number of places for each box rather than cram as many people as possible onto the standard benches. Further, with advance sign-up for seats, it could be known ahead of time who would take them. The hope was that box seats would be taken by families, who otherwise would most likely have considered theater attendance, and certainly having to rush for seats, beneath their dignity. Moreover, on the performance evening servants usually held the places.[7] This practice excluded the servantless, who had no one to beat the crowd for them.

One tier of boxes—the third—was not suitable for families and others who considered themselves respectable and would ultimately become a problem for New York's advocates of European opera. In his study of prostitution in nineteenth-century New York, Timothy Gilfoyle points out the strong links between what he calls "sporting-male sexuality" and the theater.[8] In part, he refers to brothels in theatrical neighborhoods. But there is also evidence of prostitutes soliciting and even plying their trade from the third tier of boxes. This link between the theater and prostitution included the Park, which, as the number of theaters grew, was ostensibly the city's most high-toned. In 1838 the *Advocate of Moral Reform* reported that more than eighty prostitutes had roamed the Park's third tier during Tyrone Power's engagement.[9] In 1842 they were excluded during a production of a musical "sacred drama," *The Israelites in Egypt,* on the assumption that the audience for a biblical story would not patronize a theater infested with prostitutes. Despite the production's success, however, the prohibition was not extended, and by the end of the eighteen-night run it was back to business as usual.[10]

Below the boxes was the pit, the rows of benches on the floor level of the auditorium behind the orchestra and closest to the stage (figure 2, left). Contemporary accounts describe pit audiences as high-spirited, sometimes rowdy, and given to reacting forcefully and immediately to events onstage.[11] New York pit audiences were also usually all male. In 1826 the press, noting the appearance of some women in the pit of the Lafayette Theatre, remarked that "the presence of females . . . in the *pit* of a theatre, especially, it always insures a respectability which it would not otherwise obtain."[12] The influence of respectable women on male behavior was a continuous theme behind antebellum theatrical reform. Integrating the pit was seen as a logical, practical, and attainable goal.

At the top of the theater was the gallery. Above the lower boxes, it extended to the back of the auditorium (figure 2, right). Its inhabitants were literally as well as figuratively marginal. The gallery held men and women who could afford only inexpensive seats, along with blacks, who were further segregated into one section. But their marginality did not render them powerless. Like the so-called pit critics, the gallery gods were known as active participants in an evening's entertainment. As one observer commented, "The egg as a vehicle of dramatic criticism came into early use in this Continent."[13]

An often-quoted anecdote of Washington Irving shows how early-nineteenth-century observers viewed the theater audience. Like Irving, most commentators were boxholders who saw the rest of audience as colorful, even exotic. His story typifies the boxholders' attitude of bemused tolerance toward those in the gallery. It also shows why such an attitude may have been practical. One evening, Irving, seated in a box, was hit on the head by an apple thrown from the gallery. He was about to protest, but a neighbor told him "it was useless to threaten or expostulate." He soon learned the wisdom of that advice: "A stray thunder-bolt happened to light on the head of a little sharp-faced Frenchman. . . . Monsieur was terribly exasperated; he jumped upon his seat, shook his fist at the gallery, and swore violently in bad English. This was all nuts to his merry persecutors, their attention was wholly turned on him, and he formed their target for the rest of the evening."[14] That the victim of this mirth from the gallery was not American was significant. Irving surreptitiously reminded readers that the gallery gods had bought tickets and had the right to express their opinions. The "stray thunder-bolt" flew within the bounds of theatrical etiquette. The foreigner, ignorant of this subtilty, paid the price for ill-humored intolerance.

Finally, one more view of the Park, John Searle's painting of a November 1822 performance (figure 3), may also be read for its portrayal of the audience. The performance shown, three years before the first Italian opera season, was a civic event of sorts, the return of public life after a devastating yellow fever epidemic had all but shut the city down. The performance also marked the debut of the well-known English character actor Charles Mathews, the first star performer to appear after the theater reopened. Almost every individual in Searle's group portrait has been identified.[15] In Peter Buckley's characterization, the occupants of the pit and the boxes were "what contemporary Jeffersonians might have called the *Bon Ton* of the non-producing classes."[16] Searle's audience is composed of merchants, lawyers, doctors, and a few writers and newspaper editors, many of whom were among the civic, cultural, or business leaders of the day. Of the eighty-four persons who can be named, thirteen are women, twelve in boxes and one on the stage. But named individuals occupy the first two tiers only.[17] Women in the third tier sit facing the stage, while men (including one who seems to be leering) stand in the doorways behind them. The fourth tier is empty, while to its left a small portion of the gallery is shown crammed with spectators.

Although it is unlikely that so many of New York's prominent citizens would have been present on a given occasion, Searle's painting suggests that trend-setters considered the theater a worthwhile entertainment, and one primarily for men. Although the event shown onstage was a prominent one, it was also ordinary in many ways. The evening's star, Charles Mathews, played in a standard bill of a play,

Figure 3. John Searle, untitled water color of a Park Theatre audience, November 7, 1822. (Collection of The New-York Historical Society)

songs, and a farce. The tone of the painting — the city's elite shown proudly as a community — hints at the kind of pride that would burst forth with the completion of the Erie Canal in 1825 (chapter 3). But there is no hint of high culture; the merchants and doctors are shown enjoying the same entertainment as everyone else. Although the unnamed in the upper tiers and gallery could be ignored, the theater belonged to them, too.

Together, the three theater audiences and the stock company created an equilibrium between the world presented onstage and in the auditorium. Both worlds were well-ordered. Audiences of the pit, box, and gallery each had their place, status, etiquette, and individual liberties. To a degree, each had to tolerate the others, especially the behavior of one group that another found distasteful. The stage presented social and character types, with each actor presumably playing his or her type to that part of the audience that would enjoy it the most. Of course, the two worlds were not the same; the stage could and did focus attention on individuals (minorities and women, for example) who in the house were of little account or even absent. But the worlds were equally stable, at least in appearance. This stability — this *consonance* — seems to have been important, for, as the nineteenth century progressed motives for changing what went on onstage and in the hall were simultaneous and complementary.

The Searle painting is significant on one more account — Mathews and his partner, Ellen Johnson, seem to be doing a dance. Perhaps they are singing as well (Mathews, at least, was a vocalist). In any event, the Park's band, shown facing the stage, played every night, within plays and for overtures, entr'actes, and solo accompaniment. Nearly every play included music, and several musical pieces were part of every evening's entertainment. In this respect, the Park's practice was typical; before 1825 the difference between a play and an opera was one of degree rather than kind. From the theater's first establishment in eighteenth-century New York, music had been an important part of its offerings.[18] In England, the ratio of musical to nonmusical theater increased in the latter part of the century.[19] Many of these musical plays were exported to America, where, even in the nineteenth century, some of them remained in the repertoire (table 1).

In England and America, most of these so-called operas were sung largely by members of theatrical stock companies, which always included actors who could sing. When a musical star was available, he (no female stars performed in New York until the 1820s) sang the male lead. The other singing parts were distributed among the singing actors; if an actor could not sing, his or her songs were left out. This policy limited the technical difficulty that could be expected in a so-called opera. If scores are any indication, however, the actors were lyric singers. The parts are generally scored in soprano and tenor keys and include fioritura at cadences for men and women (ex. 3). Only as the nineteenth century progressed did the styles of popular musical theater and Italian opera become mutually exclusive.

One might not expect such a large amount of musical theater in the English tradition, for this repertoire is relatively little known today. Aside from an implicit assessment of its quality, its low profile may also reflect English attitudes toward music that have colored the Anglo-American musical theater since its inception. Although English musical culture was broad and pervasive, activity did not necessarily mean admiration or respect. On the contrary, English society has been ambivalent about music since the Renaissance. Again and again, essays, sermons, letters, and even poetry and painting have shown music to be a central topic of discourse, a major problem for the English regardless of individual taste or degree of interest. Reluctant to enjoy music for its own sake, English commentators sought on the one hand to apologize for it by carefully delineating its value and appropriate uses for various constituencies. On the other hand, they often ridiculed it as a meaningless, effeminate, and unintelligent pursuit. Ironically, perhaps, the negative attitude sometimes played itself out in the musical theater. As Richard Brinsley Sheridan's Don Jerome (a comic but sympathetic character) in the English opera *The Duenna* puts the complaint, "I'll suffer no more of these midnight [musical] incantations — these amorous orgies, that steal the senses in the hearing; as, they say, Egyptian embalmers serve mummies, extracting the brain through the ears."[20]

English writers on music routinely linked it with women. From the Renaissance on, male commentators either accepted women's practice of music as a solace or, more often, condemned it as dangerous. A woman musician (even more a dancer) could weaken men through her uncontrollable sexual allure.[21] By extension, males, especially of the upper classes, were advised against musical activity, for a man could not lead women if he in effect became one. In 1749, Philip Dormer Stanhope, Lord Chesterfield, advised his son that "fiddling . . .

puts a gentleman in a very frivolous, contemptible light; brings him into a great deal of bad company; and takes up a great deal of time, which might be much better employed." In another letter he averred, "I declare that I would rather be reckoned the best barber than the best fiddler in England."[22]

Chesterfield's admonitions, which were incorporated into an advice book based on his letters, are among dozens of similar remarks that document the English gentleman's pride in musical incompetence. The incompetence itself was in part a result of Puritan influence. The Puritans mandated plain vocal music in an unceremonious religious service. Fearing music's power to "ravish" the soul, they destroyed organs and other evidence of "Popish" musical practice.[23] During the Interregnum of 1640–60, music was little-taught, opening the way for an influx of performers and teachers from the Continent with the Restoration; thus, the much-mocked Italian music master and French dancing master resulted from a shortage of qualified English musicians.[24] In deriding music and musical training, English gentlemen made a virtue out of necessity.

As Richard Leppert notes, by the eighteenth century these musical bumblers "were the men who shaped English society and English culture."[25] And by then the controversies surrounding Italian opera in London included a new political element. Opera, performed by Italian companies in Italian and featuring the castrato hero, seemed to exaggerate foreignness at a time when Englishness was increasingly being defined in anticontinental terms.[26] Condemnation of opera was not universal, however, and its success with audiences for more than thirty years while its critics inveighed against it point to its clouded position in London's political culture. Opera and its advocates were usually linked with the Hanoverian monarchy and its Whig first minister, Robert Walpole. Lacking political clout, opera's critics aimed to enhance their position by out-Englishing the monarchial party. As Leppert observes, in 1711 one such critic, John Dennis, "virtually accuses English supporters of Italian opera of being enemies of the state":

> If they are so fond of the Italian Musick, why do they not take it from the Hay-Market [Theater] to their Houses, and hug it like their secret Sins there? . . . Is there not an implicit Contract between all the People of every Nation, to espouse one another's Interest against all Foreigners whatsoever? . . . Why . . . should they prefer Italian Sound to British Sense, Italian Nonsense to British Reason,

the Blockheads of Italy to their own Countrymen, who have Wit; and the Luxury, and Effeminacy of the most profligate Portion of the Globe to the British Virtue?[27]

The antagonism toward Italian opera in London fostered the growth of a self-consciously popular culture. For critics such as Joseph Addison, Richard Steele, Alexander Pope, and Jonathan Swift — all of them intelligent, literate, and sophisticated — denigrating official culture meant favoring music in which artistic complexity and power were stripped down or even mocked. Critical — and, ultimately, creative — axioms were based on political and social premises. Ronald Paulson discusses the growth of popular genres in eighteenth-century England in his interpretation of William Hogarth, whose work emphasized and sympathized with what Paulson calls "subculture marginality."[28] Paulson sees much of Hogarth's work as iconoclastic. The Harlot's Progress series of engravings (1732), for example, reduces classical and Christian stories to "popular retelling" and the great and abstract to mere physical presence.[29] Noting the reproducibility, cheapness, and therefore wide distribution of engravings, he sees this art as socially inclusive and readable on many levels. With the lower classes of London's marginal world better able to understand the multileveled images than their more protected betters, Hogarth "[elevated] this world of variety, liberty, and subculture above the old doctrines based on unity and order."[30]

Just as a Hogarth print challenged the idea of official notions of order with the disorder inherent in inclusion, so did the most popular musical theater piece of the eighteenth century, *The Beggar's Opera*. Created specifically as popular culture for the commercial theater, *The Beggar's Opera* was a foil for the accused official culture of the Italian opera and fostered the notion that sophisticated music belonged to a stuffy elite. Like opera's critics, its characters were out of favor, with an antihero, Macheath the highwayman, at the center. The thrust of the well-known story concerns Macheath pitting his two wives against each other as he waits in prison for execution. Like him, all of the characters are of the criminal underclass, all are humorous, and all (with the partial exception of Polly) present themselves in an ironic, flippant manner. For example, early in the story Polly's parents, the Peachums, suspect that she has married Macheath. In response, Peachum berates his wife, "You would not be so mad as have the wench marry him? Gamesters and highwaymen are generally very good to their mistresses, but they are very devils to their wives." Peachum's argument is consistent throughout: It would be acceptable for Polly to "toy" (his word) with Macheath, but to marry him would give him access to her family's ill-gotten fortune. His wife (they are not married) calls Polly immoral for having "as much pleasure in cheating a father and mother as in cheating at cards" and in a song calls her "a sad slut, nor heeds what we have taught her" (act 1, scene 1). The parents' response has all the rhetoric of the moral lesson; evil is identified and properly vilified. But the evil is marriage and the good dalliance. By turning the ideal of marriage on its head, the parents mock it as an object of genteel aspiration.

The songs in *The Beggar's Opera* are consonant with its plot and tone. Each consists of a new text on an old tune and takes the theme of multiple meanings into the musical realm. In the play's original setting (London, 1728) the multiple meanings were the point. The piece was understood as satire on the British government and Handel's Italian operas. The operatic satire was achieved in part through its structure — a comedy in spoken dialogue (analogous to recitative) interspersed with sixty-nine popular songs or ballads (analogous to arias). Yet *The Beggar's Opera* is not in Italian, but in English. Its story is not serious, but comic. And its characters are not great figures of mythology or history, but contemporary, Hogarthian lowlifes. *The Beggar's Opera* is blatantly not opera in some of that genre's most prominent respects. These negations are not satiric in and of themselves. Rather, the satire lies in calling the piece as a whole an opera, thereby evoking the contrast with the Italian works on the stage at the same time.

The piece is also a satire on the heroic character common in Italian opera. Although operatic heroes earn their success, Macheath does nothing to ensure his. As he is about to be hung, a rabble offstage shouts, "Reprieve!" and he is released. Macheath's reprieve subverts opera's moral and psychological logic and its dramatic structure. In winning success without merit, Macheath resembles England's first minister, Robert Walpole, who also had two "wives" and had recently been "reprieved" by George II shortly before *The Beggar's Opera* was performed. In Macheath, an individual of heroic proportion shows himself, unable even to keep his sex life out of the public arena. No longer to be taken seriously, he has become a mere object of titillation and gossip.[31]

Finally, with Macheath's triumph comes the triumph of an essentially antimusical musical style. Like the plot, the music is reductionist: as Macheath and the other characters reduce opera's heroes to lowlifes, the songs reduce music to satire of the operatic style. Yet the analogy is not exact, because music's esthetic qualities can undermine a drama's verbal message. Although a Hogarth print can mock everyone it shows, music in *The Beggar's Opera* tempers the satire's bite, granting the characters an appeal out of proportion to their attitudes. Regardless of its contribution to the play's political and social satire, the music also potentially distracted from it. *The Beggar's Opera* provided an attractive but limited style that kept musical complexity and esthetic effusiveness in check. Unable to incite unfocused rapture, music was no threat to reason, masculinity, or English nationality.

The Beggar's Opera represents a social and esthetic orientation tempered in the nineteenth century by Romanticism but still influential in England and the United States. The U.S. version was not a carbon copy. Polemics against music were fewer in English colonial America than in the mother country and came from fewer quarters. Although the Puritan critique (sometimes centered on instrumental music) was substantial, it did not reach far beyond the New England churches that had inherited the issue from the British.[32] There is evidence that eighteenth-century Americans pursued domestic music-making as a sign of genteel aspiration. Further, immediately after the Revolution growing concert life in northeastern cities included large-scale performances of European masterworks (notably those of Handel).[33]

Yet one can find evidence of an attitude that opposed gentility and included music among the signs of overrefinement rather than genuine good breeding. John Adams, for example, linked music with monarchy as against hardy republicanism: "A monarchy would probably, somehow or other make me rich, but it would produce so much Taste and Politeness, so much Elegance in Dress, Furniture, Equipage, so much Musick and Dancing, so much Fencing and Skaiting, so much Cards and Backgammon, so much Horse Racing and Cockfighting, so many Balls and Assemblies, so many Plays and Concerts that the very Imagination of them makes me feel vain, light, frivolous and insignificant."[34] An often-reported incident has a theater orchestra beginning an unfamiliar, "scientific" (i.e., complex) overture and the audience responding by calling for "Yankee Doodle."[35] The anecdote has as much to do with audience sovereignty and Americanism as with music. Indeed, it was often used to point out the "poor taste" of American audiences. But the fact that these same audiences would accept the powerful, complex verbal dramas of Shakespeare hints that music was considered essentially trivial, unintellectual, and unworthy of serious attention. And, in fact, Chesterfield, who singled out music and dancing for censure, went through dozens of American editions from the 1770s through the Civil War.[36]

Scholars have convincingly argued the case for American pursuit of cultivation in the eighteenth century.[37] But for the most part the idea of high or esthetically based culture was not extended to music. Signs of music as high culture, of its enhanced status as an art form, were relatively scarce, even in the urban Northeast. The two major sources of alarm in England, musical participation among the male gentry and Italian opera, were little (or in the latter case, not at all) in evidence. Music as foppish gentility was no threat to rationalism or nascent republicanism. Rather, music from the early republic's rapidly developing theater was becoming the mainstream American fare.[38]

This music was urban, popular, commercial entertainment in the tradition of *The Beggar's Opera*. As such it was neither cultivated nor vernacular, genteel nor folk. Its eclectic origin and position in the drama made it an ideal form of musical expression for the English and American theater. An English opera on *The Beggar's Opera* model served the theater's need for flexibility and immediate, broad audience appeal. Short enough to fit on a multiple bill, it helped the theater offer something for everyone and ensure success in a relatively small market. An evening at the Park Theatre in New York was a social event and, like the characters in *The Beggar's Opera*, members of the audience were thought of as social types. By the nineteenth century, the number of types on the stage had increased; as the English opera repertoire expanded, the onstage gallery gods of *The Beggar's Opera* increasingly gave way to pit and box characters. Yet other aspects of *The Beggar's Opera* legacy held fast, if modified, as the century turned. The piece linked relatively simple but attractive music to a verbally created social world viewed from a consciously nonaristocratic position. In so doing, it told its audience that elaborate music was undesirably upper class, that being common was a viable proposition, and, perhaps most important, that music could be limited in style, marginal in position, and yet integral to a production's appeal.

The Beggar's Opera was a landmark in eighteenth-century English culture. The social associations of its musical style affected the course of musical theater in Britain and the United States into the nineteenth century (some would say even into the twentieth). But its style was not the only one. Later operas from the English stage, influenced by *The Beggar's Opera* but musically more varied and complex, were better able to sustain themselves in a changing theatrical environment, for they were more consonant with it. The period following the end of the War of 1812 brought a growing dissatisfaction with the institution in which English opera had long been performed. Regardless of the dramatic material presented, the theater's social milieu was increasingly perceived as problematic. This perception, hardly new in the English tradition, was sometimes focused narrowly; the theme of boxholders putting up with the behavior of the rest of the audience runs throughout contemporary theatrical criticism. But the new critique was also broader, the result of an increasingly pervasive reformist impulse affecting American culture. The movement toward reform disturbed the comfortable equilibrium between the stage and the auditorium and undermined the social premises underlying the neat divisions in the house. It also enhanced the possibility of Italian opera's success in New York. At its inception, Italian opera was linked with the idea of reform. Its appearance shows that in the theater, as elsewhere, it was less and less acceptable to leave well enough alone.

Two

Nature's New Mirror:
English Opera and Theatrical Reform

*F*amous, popular, important, yet not unique — *The Beggar's Opera* shared the English stage with other ballad operas, along with masques, pantomimes, burlettas, pastorals, burlesques, so-called dialogue operas, a few all-sung operas in Italian style, and, finally, by the early nineteenth century, the newly emerging form of melodrama. This wealth of genres had its uses. Each offered its own social vision and a solution to the English "problem" of music in a dramatic production. Both the visions and the solutions changed over time. Although comedy continued to be an important mode of presentation, by the early nineteenth century the comedy had lost some of its bite and given way to more straightforward and serious treatment of a broadening range of themes. Meanwhile, the social and moral problems of the theater had already been well-articulated in England. Conversely, the theater's ability to aid in solving problems — theater as teacher — was simultaneously invoked as a way to justify its existence. Finally, from the late eighteenth century and into the nineteenth, music became more prominent in dramatic offerings and more varied in the styles and forms used. Although confirming rhetoric for the period is lacking, it seems that an abundantly *musical* theater enhanced stated goals for theatrical reform. In the theater, as in the larger urban society, a laissez-faire attitude was giving way to a stress on social and moral "improvement."

One usually thinks of a bawdy, satirical eighteenth century on a *Tom Jones* model giving way to a straitlaced and prudish nineteenth. In fact, the growth of the English bourgeois concern with politeness and propriety in public forums such as the theater can be documented from as early as the late seventeenth century. The Puritans had banned the theater outright. Although it was restored in 1660, an "anti-theatrical prejudice," as Jonas Barish has put it, persisted in Britain and America well into the nineteenth century.[1] At a time when the American theater was in its earliest stages of growth, moralist pressures persisted to close it down.

Although cosmopolitan New Yorkers inherited this strictness to a lesser degree than their New England neighbors, antitheatrical polemics were still voiced in the city. Most contrasted the theater's vices with Christian morality. The social ambiance of the theater was condemned as a corrupting influence. The morals of theater people were questioned, and associations with drink and prostitution were condemned. Live characters — good and evil — shown onstage could sway the innocent from a path of true virtue, rendering the theater dangerous. For religious objectors, the power of a play for the good was irrelevant, for plays were incapable of overcoming the inherent immorality of the institution. Even Harriet Beecher Stowe, whose purpose in writing *Uncle Tom's Cabin* was expressly didactic, at first objected to a staged version: "If the barrier which now keeps young people of religious families from theatrical entertainments is once broken down by the introduction of respectable and moral plays," she wrote, "they will then be open to all the temptations of those which are not such."[2]

Plays themselves also called forth objections. The deliberate representation of someone by someone else — acting — was suspect as inherent misrepresentation. This criticism was old. Tertullian had stated that "whatever is *born* is the work of God. Whatever . . . is *plastered on,* is the devil's work."[3] The argument was intensified by Puritan anti-Catholicism. As Barish has shown, Puritans disapproved of the theatricality of the Mass and liturgical drama. As the late-sixteenth-century critic John Rainolds put it, "In steede of *preaching the word,* they caused it to be played."[4]

The principal objection to acting was to its artificiality. Hobbes had distinguished between a "natural" person who represented himself and an "artificial" one, "considered as representing the words and actions of another."[5] To him, actors were professional liars. Jean-Christophe Agnew has argued that the rise of this view in Puritan times was paradoxical. In rejecting the theater, elaborate religious ritual, and artifice in dress and demeanor, the Puritans presented an image of a different sort, but as false as any other. And they were painfully aware of "spurious facsimilies of grace," insisting, as Agnew points out, "that the authenticity of religious experience be subjected to a grueling process of self-scrutiny and public witness."[6]

The question of authenticity versus artificiality was intensified in the nineteenth century. So was the paradox. Karen Halttunen has shown how much the "contagious moral leprosy" of the confidence man was feared.[7] Halttunen has studied advice literature addressed to young people in early-nineteenth-century America. At a time when social change, especially the rise of dangerous and anonymous cities, was creating a world of strangers, such literature represented an "effort to establish that it was possible to know something about the character of a stranger" by his outward presentation. This effort was doomed to failure, for the very *politesses* advisors recommended were the tools of the man who could lead an unsuspecting youth down the road to perdition.[8]

The theater demonstrated nightly how convincing an "artificial person" could be. It presented evil publicly in a genre created to entertain and allowed goodness to be played by people considered evil themselves. Such falsity rendered the theater impotent as an agent of moral reform. In blurring the distinction between false and true, it undermined the belief that outward appearances necessarily reflected inner character.

The success and popularity of the theater in early-nineteenth-century New York shows that this fundamental objection was not widespread. One may even wonder whether the theater's detractors did more than preach to the converted. At least one response to the city's critics questioned the competence of those who objected to the theater without ever having seen a play.[9] Closer to the realities of the theater were the many calls made for reform, bringing to the fore the question, as Kenneth Silverman puts it, of "whether [the United States] was obliged to purge its citizens of Old World corruption or to allow human nature unlimited expression."[10] Pressure for the former was strong and specific. Eliminating the grog shops and darkened third tiers would help make the theater acceptable to a respectable public. So would the moral improvement of actors and actresses themselves. So would the creation of clear and edifying plays and the judgment of the theater's offerings from a moral point of view. Incongruous as it may seem, given the institution's irregularities, a play's ability to instruct its audience in upright living formed much of the foundation on which its acceptability would rest.[11]

The argument behind a moral basis for judgment stated that although the stage could, as Shakespeare had put it, "hold the mirror up to nature," all of nature was not equally worthy of reflection.[12] Hamlet's advice to the players was well known and often quoted. Yet if people onstage were mirrors of nature, the reality they presented could be a force for either good or evil. To meet these objections, the theater's defenders called it a "school of morality" and tried to show how plays could provide moral lessons. Even classic plays faced morally based criticism. In 1817 Sheridan's *School for Scandal* was said to "lead to inferences unfriendly to morality."[13] Shakespeare's plays were often subjected to the test of the moral lesson and sometimes found wanting. Critics debated whether his text should be altered to clarify moral ambiguity or the poet's lines preserved at all costs, even when the lesson was left unclear.[14] As one critic put the argument in 1817, "A well regulated theatre may justly be regarded as a school of morality, literary taste and instruction, blended with innocent amusement."[15]

The role of the "moral drama" was not to show moral dilemma. Rather, it was to show good and evil as absolute by making distinctions between good and evil characters as clear as possible. By their actions, the characters would reap poetic justice; good would be rewarded and evil punished. While the good were to look as attractive and the bad as unattractive as possible, actors were also enjoined to make their characterizations "true to nature," as if a real person trod the stage. But truth to nature did not mean realism. Instead, exaggerated emotion was focused on the conflict so that audiences could not only understand but also, and more important, feel the tension and its ultimate resolution. Reason as a moral force was rejected in favor of the power of emotion to persuade.[16]

Thus actors such as the American Edwin Forrest, whose style was based on exaggeration, were popular. An incident involving Forrest illustrates the relationship between "nature," emotional power, and the moral imperative. Forrest was playing Iago one night when a man in the pit, overcome by his portrayal, stood up, shook his fist, and shouted, "You damned-lying scoundrel, I would like to get hold of you after the show and wring your infernal neck." The evening's Othello reportedly told Forrest that the man had paid him the highest compliment possible.[17] Forrest had used his emotional power to seem to be truly Iago, that is, a man who, after the show, would still be Iago — a "natural," not an "artificial," person and a "damned-lying scoundrel." By exaggerating, he could allow the "school of morality" to be seen as "the mirror up to nature" as well.

At the same time, it was hoped that moral plays would attract respectable audiences, making the theater simultaneously more respectful of moral scruples and more profitable for management. Tolerance of the variety of behavioral standards traditionally found in the theater was declining. The hope was that by making rowdyism, excessive drink, rioting, and prostitution unacceptable, the theater would attract respectable men and women — that is, ladies — both.[18] Although criticism generally came from beyond the theatrical establishment, reform came from within. As the city grew, individual theaters began to address smaller segments of the audience, each one developing its own balance between the traditional, commercially based practices and the reformist imperative.

Music was not the object of such efforts. Although still criticized for foppishness and irrelevance, with the decline of Puritanism it was less criticized for an ability to incite evil. On the contrary, the rise of instrumental and oratorio concerts in the post-Revolutionary era enhanced music's respectability and prestige. Lacking inherently objectionable content, it could help fulfill the mandate of the theater as "innocent amusement." Further, its ability to arouse a broad range of emotion was congruent with the new, more exaggerated style of acting. Yet any links between more positive attitudes toward music and an expanded musical theater in the same period are circumstantial and not well documented. In New York as elsewhere, the growth in musical theater took place within the established institution. Changes were evident, however. In the late teens, new operas, along with the first musical stars and substantial criticism, seemed to be absorbed without major adjustment. But all three — operas, stars, and critics — heightened the tension between the theater's standing traditions and the new reformist endeavor.

The period after the War of 1812 brought an expanded repertoire of English operas, many of which conformed to the new moral approach. Some, like the staple repertoire of plays, dated from the eighteenth century. These so-called operas (such as *Love in a Village*) were generally comic and indulged in satire of the theater's standard social types. But compared with *The Beggar's Opera*, the humor of later-eighteenth-century pieces was milder and more predictable. As Robert Hume puts it, "Potshots at long-established sitting ducks," along with a growing sentimental element, began to replace the biting satire and bawdy low comedy of *The Beggar's Opera* tradition.[19] Meanwhile, in London, the seating capacity of the two patent theaters was increased to cavernous proportions, presumably rendering them less suitable for subtle or sophisticated dialogue than in the earlier age.[20] Although confirming evidence is lacking, it may be that music could take up some of the burden of entertainment, highlight a social focus in characterization and plot, and lend the theater some of the new respectability of concerts.

One such opera, Thomas Arne's venerable *Love in a Village* (1762), links ballad opera in the *Beggar's Opera* tradition with the musically more elaborate genres of the late eighteenth and nineteenth centuries. Its tenure in New York, between 1768 and 1849, also shows how long an unoffensive, pleasant musical work could remain viable. Isaac Bickerstaffe, the librettist, borrowed its plot from a ballad opera, *The Village Opera* (1729). Arne compiled the score from a variety of sources, as had Christopher Pepusch for *The Beggar's Opera*. Like *The Beggar's Opera*, *Love in a Village* alternates spoken dialogue with songs that members of a theatrical stock company could sing. But while in the earlier work well-known music was given multiple meanings through new words, *Love in a Village* makes no explicit reference to earlier uses of musical material. Rather, its variety of musical sources and idioms categorizes in a straightforward manner the standard dramatic types found among the characters; the simple people sing simple music, while the songs of their betters are more complex. Like the social types created by the pit-box-gallery divisions in the auditorium, those on the stage agreeably presented what their audience presumably already knew.

These theatrical types are not equally important in the plot, but each has a place in the idealized English country village life that the opera presents. In fact, the story hinges on them; mistaken identities are corrected so that marriages between couples of equal social station can take place. Obstacles put in their paths are only diversions, for the village society is so well established that the characters' places in it are inevitable. No heavy or high-serious emotion impinges on the piece's reassuring simplicity. *Love in a Village* is comic opera, not in the sense that it makes one laugh (although it does that at times), but in its limited, generally positive emotional range.

The two couples who will marry are stereotypical box clientele: middle class, respectable, and polite. One of the young women, Rosetta, masquerades as the other's maid. Rosetta had known Lucinda at boarding school. When she needed a place to hide from her father, who had arranged an undesired marriage for her, Lucinda volunteered to take her in. Rosetta is supposed to marry, but has never met, Young Meadows, who has taken the same course. Having run away, he (a student at Oxford) finds himself employed as a gardener in the same household. He and Rosetta meet and are smitten with each other. But because each supposes the other to be a servant, a match is ostensibly impossible. At this point, the audience knows Rosetta's situation explicitly, but only knows that Young Meadows's identity as a gardener is a disguise.

Rosetta and Young Meadows attempt to dismiss each other in a duet, "Begone, I Agree" (ex. 1). The duet, one of the more elaborate pieces in *Love in a Village,* shows music linking the two characters socially (in spite of their disguises) and emotionally (in spite of misunderstanding each other's social position). Rosetta's opening arpeggiated quarter notes show her determined to put Young Meadows out of her mind (mm. 12–14, 16–18, 26–28, 30–32). But the ornamented melody that follows (mm. 34–42) conveys instead her ambivalence about the prospect, her ability as a singer, her social station, and a sense of what Young Meadows will lose by rejecting her. He, by contrast, is more transparent. Young Meadows's reply features a longer, more stepwise melody than Rosetta's first statement (mm. 52–64). He complains of "a trial so hard to be borne" with a melody whose plaintiveness contrasts with Rosetta's determination. They finish the duet together with material from the opening section, singing first lyrical material based on the passage that had cast doubt on Rosetta's resolve (mm. 94–101, taken from mm. 37–42). Then they sing in unison with each other and the orchestra one final statement in the style of

Example 1. "Begone, I Agree" (Rosetta and Young Meadows, *Love in a Village*), London: J. Dale, n.d.

Love in a Village.

Example 2. "Was Ever Poor Fellow" (Hodge, *Love in a Village*)

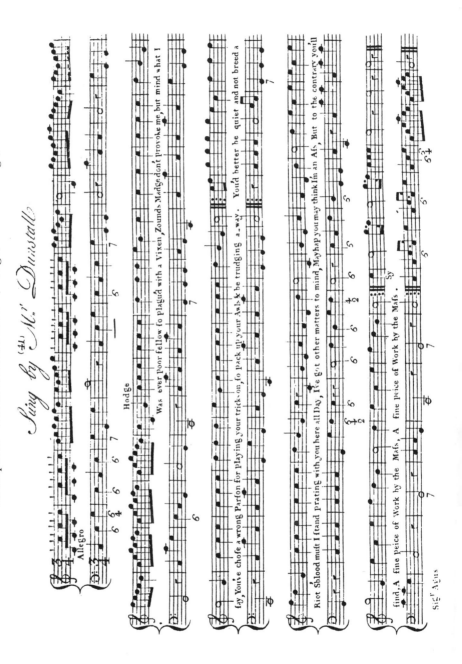

Rosetta's opening disjunct, quarter-note melody (mm. 101–5). The effect of the piece is delightful, and the end — "I banish you quite from my mind" — fools no one. Young Meadows's phrases notwithstanding, the duet's tone never allows the thought of banishment to be taken seriously.

Rosetta and Young Meadows form the upper end of the social scale in *Love in a Village*. At the other end, the two gallery characters, the servants Hodge and Madge, are equally what they seem. Hodge serves as a messenger between Lucinda and her lover, Eustace. Otherwise, he and Madge are superfluous to the plot, but they embody the sensibility of the village while putting their betters into perspective. In "Was Ever Poor Fellow," for example, Hodge simplemindedly mocks Madge for her distress at discovering she is pregnant (ex. 2). With its crude rhyme ("vixen" and "tricks on"), bland harmony, and unending series of quarter notes, Hodge's song presents a portrait of the rustic bumpkin, perhaps offensive to twentieth-century sensibilities but nevertheless a familiar figure on the stage of its day.

The song invites more than one interpretation. One can take Hodge's part, enjoy him, and laugh with him. One can note his simplemindedness, look down on him, and laugh at him. One can also, with Rosetta, be shocked. As she comes upon the two servants arguing, Rosetta is horrified at Hodge's attitude: "The brutality of that fellow shocks me!" She continues with a statement that, although it may sound feminist, was probably intended more as a social class commentary than a sexual one: "Oh, man, man — you are all alike — a bumpkin here, bred at the barn door; had he been brought up in a court, could he have been more fashionably vicious? Show me the lord, squire, colonel, or captain of them all, that can outdo him!"[21] Rosetta identifies proper morality as inherently middle class: Not only is the ill-bred country man abusive, but the "fashionable" as well. Being middle class saves women from the brutality and insensitivity perpetrated by the Hodges of the world and their upper-class counterparts. She also dismisses Madge with advice on the same standard: "Go your way, and be a good girl" (act 2, scene 11). For the pregnant servant, the implied solution — "Be a good girl, like me" — is no solution at all. In her own way, Rosetta is as insensitive as Hodge to the problem and distress of her social inferior.

Yet unlike her inferior, Rosetta gets her man. Young Meadows finally tells Rosetta that he is a gentleman and is delighted to find out that she is of the same station. But no one is truly surprised, for along with everyone else, Rosetta and Young Meadows have acted and sung their social positions throughout the opera.

The other characters in *Love in a Village* have their places and roles in the society the piece depicts. The rustic Hawthorn, a mature male, recognizable as a pit type, sings the well-known ballad "The River of Dee." Justice Woodcock, Lucinda's father, is a lecherous old man who sings a bawdy ballad (Rosetta does not approve of him). The young gentry sing music of greater complexity, some of it of Italian origin. Unlike Hawthorn, they would not have picked their pieces up in everyday situations; they would need to learn them and be trained to sing them. In "Begone, I Agree," for example, Rosetta and Meadows have to listen to internal ritornellos and count rests. The ballad singers do not.

Finally, in Justice Woodcock's sister, Deborah the shrew, the village has a character who does not sing at all. This last bit of "musical" portraiture is significant, for it points out music's purpose and limitations in the opera. The lighthearted, entertaining musical style of *Love in a Village* creates sympathy for all of the other characters, Hodge included. But it cannot portray a rude, meddlesome, envious, and unpleasant character without tempering the portrayal. Like operatic villains who do not sing (for example, Baron Toraldi in *The Devil's Bridge*), Deborah is denied the good feelings music creates.[22] In this way, the social portrayal of such a character is indirectly given a moral component.

The world *Love in a Village* presents is solid, traditional, and seemingly unchanging, like the world of the theater neatly divided into pit, boxes, and gallery. It allows its audience to enjoy the foibles of the human types it presents while (unlike *The Beggar's Opera*) favoring the respectable lovers, Rosetta and Young Meadows. The correction of their social misidentification is, if anything, the moral of the story, for it ends the tension created when some of the characters are not socially what they seem. The music anticipates the correction through its stylistic portrayal of the "real" Rosetta and Young Meadows. The songs are more than simple interpolations, for they pleasantly and seemingly innocently serve the opera's social statement.

The long tenure of *Love in a Village* in New York suggests that audiences found something satisfying about the solidity of the simple, romanticized rural society it depicts. For the most part, such operas, although not positively edifying, had been inoffensive to conventional moral standards. New operas that became popular after the War of 1812, however, were more explicitly didactic and had much to offer a theatrical profession trying to attract a reform-minded audience. As in melodrama, music in these works underlined emotion through placement at key points in the plot.[23] The highlighted emotion was, in turn, focused on a moral message. At the same time, opera plots grew more concerned with serious events, while the distinction between the serious and the comic (for the comic still held a place) increased in plot, character portrayal, and even musical style. This new thoughtfulness, together with a close emotional connection between plot incident and music, contributed as much to opera's new tone as did changes in the musical style itself.

The changes in the musical theater repertoire were accompanied by another change in its structure — the coming of the star. Although the star system in American theaters had been established since the turn of the century, only with the arrival of the musical stars of 1817 was more attention, and more *critical* attention, paid in the city to the quality of musical performance.[24] Stars provided variety (a way to attract repeat audiences) and reputed excellence. Seeing a star perform made a theatrical evening special; theater people complained ceaselessly that stars undermined the institution as a whole by creating a two-tiered performance schedule, pushing the stock company to poorly attended off nights.[25] More important from a manager's perspective, however, was a star's distinction from the usual roster of performers. Billed as an improvement on business as usual, a star provided evidence that a manager genuinely solicited the "best" clientele by offering the best talent available. Stars were to close the rift between quality and commercial motivation by making quality sell.

The stars of 1817 offered yet another novelty: Charles Incledon and Thomas Philipps were the first actors in New York to combine stardom, leading dramatic roles, and music. At fifty-four, Incledon (1763–1826) was a veteran of the London musical theater. Philipps (1774–1841) was somewhat younger but still well established. Together, their repertoires comprised most of the musical theater performed at the Park in the fall of 1817 and a considerable portion thereafter until Philipps's return to England in 1823. Together, they proved harbingers of a great expansion of musical theater in the city's near future. They also inspired more detailed press commentary than is available for earlier musical works. Their contrasting receptions shed light on changing attitudes toward the theater as a "mirror up to nature" and the role music was to play in clarifying its new image.

Although the two singers appeared in New York during the same season, a generation gap existed between their repertoires (tables 1 and 2). Incledon's repertoire included many pieces already well-worn on the New York stage. Philipps's offerings included many of the same works, and both brought the tried-and-true *Love in a Village*. But where Incledon sang Hawthorn, a mature male role, Philipps sang Young Meadows, the romantic juvenile lead. Moreover, Philipps's operas by Henry Bishop, himself a composer and arranger early in his career, place him in a later generation. Most significant for the future was Phillips's performance as Almaviva in Bishop's arrangement of Rossini's *The Barber of Seville*, the first adaptation from a Continental original with a singing male lead.[26] At forty-three, Philipps was apparently able to offer a verisimilitude in juvenile lead parts that the older man could not.

The differences in the two singers' repertoires affected their receptions. Initially, both performers' appearances were well publicized and attracted large audiences. Although stylistic differences between them were recognized, both were praised for their musicianship. But here the similarity ends. Like his repertoire, Philipps's reception an-

Table 1. Charles Incledon's New York Repertoire, 1817–18

First Performance	Title	New York Dates
1728	The Beggar's Opera	1750–1870
1762	*Love in a Village* (Hawthorn)	1768–1849
1765	*The Maid of the Mill*	1769–1821
1774	The Waterman	1793–1855
1775	*The Duenna*	1787–1835
1775	The Quaker	1794–1840
1779	The Turnpike Gate	1801–56
1780	The Lord of the Manor	1818–35
1783	*The Poor Soldier*	1785–1855
1782	The Castle of Andalusia	1797–1837
1782	Rosina	1786–1840
1791	The Woodman	1818 only

Note: Operas listed in italics were performed by both Incledon and Philipps (see table 2).

Table 2. Thomas Philipps's New York Repertoire, 1817–23

First Performance	Title	New York Dates
1762	*Love in a Village* (Young Meadows)	1768–1849
1765	*The Maid of the Mill*	1769–1821
1768	Lionel and Clarissa	1794–1828
1773	The Deserter	1798–1819
1775	*The Duenna*	1787–1835
1783	*The Poor Soldier*	1785–1855
1784	Fountainebleau	1797–1833
1788	The Highland Reel	1800–1837
1791	The Siege of Belgrade	1796–1840
1802	The Cabinet	1814–40
1803	The English Fleet in 1342	1819 only
1812	The Devil's Bridge	1815–40
1815	Brother and Sister	1816–63
1816	Guy Mannering	1816–77
1818	The Barber of Seville	1819–

Note: Operas listed in italics were performed by both Incledon and Philipps (see table 1).

ticipated that of singers yet to come to New York. For the first time, a star interested New Yorkers as a musician, a portrayer of characters, and a person. This threefold connection, linking music with characters and their impersonators and assigning moral value to all three, presaged the heyday of English opera in the 1830s. Its lineage can be traced to the receptions of these two early singing stars, for the response to Incledon's performance of *The Beggar's Opera* demonstrates what was newly expected — and hence newly missing — in his engagement.

Philipps's most popular offering was a two-year-old opera, Samuel James Arnold's *The Devil's Bridge,* with music by Charles Horn and John Braham. Philipps made a hit in the male lead, Count Belino, singing the role six times in 1817 while performing no other role more than twice. *The Devil's Bridge* was cut from different cloth than *Love in a Village.* In it, Philipps offered New Yorkers their first operatic melodrama and in Belino their first heroic and pathetic tenor. Although closer in spirit to the aristocratic castrato heroes of Handel than the antihero Macheath, Belino displays a heroism distinguished by virtue rather than birth. Marking for the first time the link between a popular new singing star and a successful new piece, *The Devil's*

Bridge offered the first close connection between music in a serious and affective style and a tension-filled, melodramatic plot.

An audience would be hard-pressed to miss the didactic intent of *The Devil's Bridge,* an eminently respectable good-versus-evil melodrama. The story takes place in the Italian Alps, where a young countess, Rosalvina, is being forced to marry the villain of the piece, Baron Toraldi. Neither partner is actually free to marry. Rosalvina has been secretly married to a young artist, Count Belino. For reasons not given, Belino has been exiled and is widely believed dead; his and Rosalvina's young son is being cared for by a couple who keep a nearby village inn. Toraldi is also married, but, unknown to everyone, he is keeping his wife prisoner in his castle dungeon even as he is forcing himself on Rosalvina.

The action concerns the rescue of Rosalvina from the clutches of Toraldi and the reunion of the young family. Rosalvina accomplishes the rescue herself by sneaking away from her own prewedding party. The innkeeper offers aid by hiding her in a cottage near the Devil's Bridge. Although Belino is virtue personified — youthful, noble, artistic, sensitive, loyal, gracious, loving, courageous, emotionally transparent, and morally upright — his part is largely bravado. Yet it is his moral uprightness that inspires the bravado, which in turn gets him into trouble.

Early in the plot, Belino arrives incognito at the inn. Toraldi is there as well, searching for the escaped Rosalvina. When Belino overhears Toraldi say that his wife is imprisoned and not dead, he is incensed. He boldly identifies himself to Toraldi, who has him imprisoned. When Toraldi offers him freedom if he will leave Piedmont forever, Belino says he would rather die. But as Toraldi's henchman is about to kill him, a hand is seen shooting the henchman. The body attached to the hand is never seen, but we know there is a mole in Toraldi's retinue, presumably the source of rescue. Belino escapes.

The bridge plays only a small role in the drama. At the opera's end, all of the good people are gathered on one side. As Toraldi's soldiers approach the other, the good people blow it up.[27]

At the New York opening, the plot of *The Devil's Bridge* received only cursory mention in the press. Rather more attention was paid to Philipps, the star. The writers' main interest was his portrayal of Belino, especially his use of John Braham's songs to delineate the character. Belino's songs (there are seven) are simple, lyric, and dignified settings that focus attention on the words. More than interpolations, they are carefully linked with the plot in order to intensify its dramatic situations. Yet the balance of power between spoken and sung words is carefully maintained. Belino's spoken style is self-consciously rhetorical. His lines use the good and evil polarity in the plot to set up emotionally charged moments that the songs intensify but do not overwhelm.

Early in act 2, for example, Belino is told that the inn where he is staying is close enough to Toraldi's castle that he can see it. This information sends him into a reverie in which he reminds himself, as he puts it, of "enraptured hours" with Rosalvina. This leads to a love song, "Is There a Heart?" addressed not to Rosalvina in particular, but to "woman" in general (ex. 3). Punish the man, he says, who remains unaffected by woman's sighs, tears, and smiles; to reject her is to reject virtue personified. The music adds its own emphases. In the third line of each verse — the one that describes man's punishment — the arpeggiated, chromatic accompaniment gives way to simple chords, focusing attention on the words. In the same line, the voice and accompaniment are in unison when Belino names the punishment: a "solitary cell."

Philipps's Belino made its point. In one song, wrote a New York critic, "the actor entirely disappeared for the moment, and nothing was seen but the young enthusiast giving vent to his impassioned feelings."[28] Belino was more than a fine job of acting and singing. Rather, Philipps actually seemed to become the young, passionate enthusiast and Romantic ideal. This he achieved principally in the songs, whose link with his "appropriate dignity of deportment" was recognized. "Listen to Philipps, as he sings . . . 'Is there a heart that never loved, nor felt soft woman's sigh?',", wrote a listener, "and the effect upon him, if he has one sensible fibre in his breast, will produce the same sort of conviction as that produced upon the philosopher who denied the power of motion when his opponent answered by getting up and walking across the room."[29] No longer merely a pleasant diversion, music could be understood as part of a play's verbal message. More than confirming a character's social position, music communicated personality traits and emotional states as well. Unlike operas such as *Love in a Village, The Devil's Bridge* argued for the value of a broader, more romantic musical style and an enhanced role for music in a dramatic work.

Example 3. John Braham, "Is There a Heart?" (Horn and Braham, *The Devil's Bridge*), London: Goulding, d'Almaine, and Potter, n.d.

mark unmov'd dear Woman's tearful eye _ _ Oh! bear him to some distant shore, Or

so _ _ li _ _ ta _ _ ry cell, Where none but savage mons _ ters roar, Where

Love _ _ _ _ _ _ ne'er deign'd to dwell.

2

For there's a charm in Woman's eye,
　A language in her tear,
A spell in every sacred sigh
　　To Man _ to Virtue dear:
And he who can resist her smiles,
　　With Brutes alone should live,
Nor taste that joy which care beguiles,
　　That joy her Virtues give.

Philipps's Belino was both a "mirror up to nature" and a "school of morality." His convincing portrayal made Belino seem like a real person. At the same time, his personification of the good in a conflict with evil made him a model of an attractive, upright male. The fact that Belino is literally too good to be true was irrelevant; by seeming to become Belino, Philipps made the moral ideal seem attainable. Moreover, as "those ladies and gentlemen among us who lay claims to some proficiency in the practical part of music" were enjoined to "improve their taste by the performances of this gentleman."[30] In so doing, they could internalize and relive musically the values and personality his character displayed. The songs, emotionally transparent and technically accessible, were in a sense souvenirs of the piece's message. Through music, the opera could bring the message home through the ear to the heart in ways no nonmusical play could.

One more contemporary remark on *The Devil's Bridge* merits comment. In a report on Philipps's third performance as Belino, a writer bragged, "The boxes of the lower tier made a shew of ladies such as we have not seen in the theater for many years."[31] Such reporting was designed to inform potential audience members, especially but not exclusively women, that the content of the theatrical offering had proved itself respectable enough for their attendance. Women ("ladies") were understood as raising the tone of an evening's performance. Their mere presence was considered able to inhibit unruly behavior in their male companions, altering not only the makeup of the audience but its code of etiquette as well. In return, they were entitled to entertainment that neither offended their sensibilities nor tarnished their reputations. Noticing the presence or absence of women in the audience later became a common feature of theater reporting. Here, however, was the first link between a musical star and large numbers of women willing to enter a theater to hear him. The report heralds the many times in the future when a writer would make a similar remark about an opera performance, anticipating the documentation (and encouragement) of women as a large proportion of the opera audience.

The Devil's Bridge raised the rhetorical and didactic level of opera. The integration of music into the piece's emotional character linked music with this new dramatic focus without requiring major changes in the musical style itself. The use of stars in 1817 suggests that music was being taken more seriously and considered more integral to musical drama than had previously been the case. Quality was becoming an issue; just any performer would not do. The success of *The Devil's Bridge* and of Philipps's engagement as a whole suggests that audiences were receptive to the new emotional tone and emphasis on music the opera presented. A star such as Philipps playing a character such as Belino could assure audiences that business was not always as usual in the city's theater.

The failure of *The Beggar's Opera* in the same year as *The Devil's Bridge* was the converse of the latter's success. Like *Love in a Village*, *The Devil's Bridge* was composed for the kind of heterogeneous audience found at the Park Theatre. The characters and music of both works distinguished between the polite and the popular. Moreover, *The Devil's Bridge* was romantic, rhetorically "elevated," and didactic. Even *Love in a Village*, with its stereotypical English country gentry, could be taken as romantic by an American city audience. On all of these counts, *The Beggar's Opera* failed. The story of Macheath the highwayman who, while waiting in prison for his execution, plays his two wives against each other, has no characters even remotely equivalent to the "good" people of *The Devil's Bridge*. There is no room for a conflict between good and evil or for Belino's brand of sincerity and conviction. To make matters worse in terms of a moral message, Macheath gets off in the end. Virtue goes unrewarded and evil unpunished. Belino could be accepted as "real"; Macheath could not.

Nor does *The Beggar's Opera* display seriousness or sentimentality. There are no middle-class characters to sing elaborate music and disapprove of (while enjoying) the antics of the lower-class comics. Moreover, it is doubtful that the beggar's prologue and epilogue (which tip the audience off that the whole play is satirical and multileveled) were performed in New York on October 29, 1817, with Incledon as Macheath.[32] The frame that surrounds the piece, pointing out its essential unreality and the source of its double meanings, was probably missing. Without it, *The Beggar's Opera* could seem to mock poetic justice and music as an object of respectable aspiration. Nineteenth-century New Yorkers had no idea of either Italian opera or the Walpole government. The piece had to stand judgment on its text alone.

That it failed is no surprise. Rather more startling is that before the evening was out the audience had expressed its sovereignty by nearly rioting in the theater. *The Beggar's Opera* itself did not literally cause the riot. The audience hissed the piece and became violent when Incledon would not accede to its request for an encore. Editorial comment on the incident was unanimous.[33] *The Beggar's Opera* was judged as substandard theatrical fare, deserving of its hostile reception. One writer censured "its want of morality and its loose characters." Another described the members of the audience as "quite offended and disgusted, which they were at no pains to conceal." A third commented, "Such . . . was the disgust produced by the representation of this vulgar and licentious burletta, that the curtain dropt amidst the hisses of the audience."[34] Of the four reports available on the incident, only one even mentioned the music, calling it the piece's "only recommendation."[35] Finally, a reporter commented that Incledon should have been willing to sing an encore, "since so respectable a house had been disappointed in the play."[36]

Given that the performer himself was not considered at fault, how seriously do we take these remarks in the press? Was this really a more "respectable" audience — one that would be genuinely offended by the plot and the words — than usual? Or was the hissing of *The Beggar's Opera* a casual affair, a statement of audience power like the penchant for demanding "Yankee Doodle" from the band? Were the comments about the piece's morality thus so much fluff, the most obvious excuse for the actions of an unruly crowd? Could it be that the audience just did not like the music?

It is impossible to tell absolutely. Certainly, *The Beggar's Opera* lacked the connection among music, emotion, and plot of *The Devil's Bridge*, and the audience may have missed an emotional kick rather than a moral lesson. Yet Incledon played other roles that lacked the emotional power of *The Devil's Bridge*, for example Patrick in the musical farce *The Poor Soldier*. Incledon's pieces were essentially lightweight entertainment, each as pleasant and unimpeachable as *Love in a Village*. Yet they did not offend, and no other opera he performed was rejected.

Here, however, the audience *was* offended. *The Beggar's Opera* featured a cast full of Hodges and Madges, with no one to look down on them and cluck at their indiscretions and crude behavior. It showed a hero who, unlike Belino, mirrored that part of nature antithetical to the stage as a model for moral living. It exposed moral irregularity as a source of amusement. And it also presented fine music. But in 1817 fine music well performed may have been part of the problem. If music was highly valued (as it was) and if the music of *The Beggar's Opera* was enjoyable and enjoyed (which it was), then using music to make an objectionable story palatable would in itself offend.

The Beggar's Opera had graced the London stage every season from its premiere in 1728 and had been produced frequently in New York since 1751. That it would create such a stir now, when the piece itself was essentially the same, shows how much the public attitude toward the theater had changed. A commentator explained the connection between heightened expectations and the piece's rejection:

> Those especially [in the audience] who did not know the history of the piece, so absurdly mis-named, but came with expectations of seeing something entirely different, were quite offended and disgusted; which they were at no pains to conceal. A well regulated theatre may justly be regarded as a school of morality, literary taste and instruction, blended with innocent amusement. . . . When, therefore, a piece is presented, which militates in the most important of these particulars, it reflects credit on the audience, that they bestow unequivocal marks of their disapprobation, such as they testified on Monday evening.[37]

In placing the "school of morality" at the head of the new theatrical ideal, this writer spoke for reform. He also defended an audience response that in other circumstances might have reflected discredit on its members. The audience "came with expectations of seeing something entirely different," apparently because the piece was called an opera. Meeting these expectations was essential to treating the audience fairly and living up to the theater's side of a bargain. If the theater presented itself as "improved" entertainment, it had better fulfill its promise.

In the operas new to New York in the late teens, music supported dramas that served the prevailing moral ideology. With music able to enhance moral power and uplift, opera brought a new seriousness to the theater. Except on the issue of performance quality, however, the heightened expectations had no esthetic component; the new pieces were expected to be emotionally powerful, but their esthetic merit was not judged. If anything, the kind of musical complexity now often taken as a sign of esthetic excellence would have defeated their purpose. Despite their romanticism, they spoke to their audience in terms readily understood.

With the advent of Italian opera in 1825, these expectations began to change. In the abstract, Italian opera seemed the natural extension of this newly serious musical theater and was initially presented as the ultimate in theatrical improvement. In actuality, however, it gave New Yorkers more than they bargained for. In trying to create a "refined" social setting in the theater, opera's proponents created a controversial one. In presenting a new genre, the Park Theatre's management brought a novel, not immediately accessible, musical style. Accepting original-language opera took thirty years. It required reassessing the relationship between words and music in musical drama, understanding a performance genre of Continental rather than Anglo-American ancestry, creating a social setting acceptable as "democratic" rather than exclusive, rethinking the link between music's emotional power and moral reform, attracting a steady audience by enticing large numbers of women into the theater, and learning how to meet unprecedented expenses without a patronage tradition. Perhaps most of all, Italian opera's arrival increased the already growing tension between the frank commercialism and "democratic" audience behavior of the theater and the movement toward reform independent of monetary concerns. Italian opera — unanglicized from its original European form — brought artistic, social, and even political tensions as New Yorkers considered why, for whom, and on what terms it should be accepted. These tensions affected opera's course of development and reception as the city grew.

Three

Culture and Commerce:
The First Opera Nights in New York

*P*ostrevolutionary American theater was not unique to New York. On the contrary, theaters throughout the urban northeast established stock companies and presented the same stars as were seen in the city. Italian opera, however, was a different story. In 1825 and 1826, the first company to visit New York performed at the Park Theatre, recruited, financed, and promoted by the city's movers and shakers. With Italian opera, New York began to promote itself as a unique cultural center. In so doing, New Yorkers began to articulate the notion of culture itself. Their rhetoric of social and moral improvement reached beyond the theater to embrace the idea of culture as a shaper of society. Music's position in this endeavor was at first ambivalent, for the new values stood opposed to received notions of music's inherent low worth and to much of the unpretentious music heard in the theater. With its plots and stage action to aid comprehension, however, Italian opera was well suited to enhancing the understanding needed to raise music's position. But its intense musical power obscured the links with improvement culture's advocates wished to make. If a genre such as opera, in which music was central to meaning, was to be developed as culture, the relationship between musical beauty and social and moral worth would need to be made clear.

In the meantime, opera could try to make it in the market-based commercial theater. Although English operas had been successful for many years, Italian opera was an unknown quantity. Thus the idea of actually selling culture — selling opera as an object of social, moral, and esthetic aspiration along with fashion and social panache — made good sense. Luring an audience (necessary for an entrepreneurial venture) meant addressing potential operagoers in terms they could already understand.

The Garcia company stood at the forefront of these efforts. Arriving in New York in November of 1825, the troupe headed by tenor Manuel Garcia and consisting mainly of his family brought a tug of war between old and new, Anglo-American and continental. It was the first in a series of original-language opera companies and singing stars whose performances intermittently opposed steady productions of opera in English. A few continental performances in the post-Garcia era were in French, and occasionally local and visiting performers mounted an opera in German. But the bulk of continental opera heard in the city between 1825 and the Civil War was Italian. With Rossini's *Il barbiere di Siviglia* and Mozart's *Don Giovanni,* the Garcia company began to create a standard operatic repertoire that is still in evidence.

The Garcias performed at the Park Theatre for almost a year, from November of 1825 to September of 1826. Their influence, however, was felt for another two generations. When a singer performed well, she was compared to Maria Garcia. When a company sang badly, it was said to fail to meet the Garcias' standard. When a new opera house was proposed, the hope was to attract a company as fine as they had been. Their performances, especially Maria's, presented opera as refined and elegant. But refinement and elegance were not universally accepted theatrical goals. Importing a staged genre from a "foreign" culture and asking the public to rise to the occasion in accepting it was bound to rankle republican sensibilities.

Italian opera's novelty extended to its music as well, and understanding opera's conventions would be a central factor in its acceptance. Understandably, however, some commentators tried to interpret the Garcias' performances within the familiar conventions of drama. As drama in the English musical theater had provided a framework for a simple musical style, so it did for the more complex Italian idiom. But the reverse also began to take place: As commentators began to make musical sense of a piece, opera's reception began to include interpreting the drama—especially its emotional content—from the standpoint of the music. This reversal in priority developed slowly, largely independent of the social, economic, moral, and political issues opera raised. Ultimately, however, music and external issues met head-on. The Garcias' performances began a process whereby opera's music effectively trumped its opposition.

The first opera performances in New York came hard on the heels of the completion of the Erie Canal. The relationship between a technological and commercial achievement and a new theatrical genre may not be immediately apparent. Yet in the 1820s they were understood as two sides of the same coin, a "spirit of improvement," said to permeate many facets of society and culture. This spirit was not new. "Prophecies of imminent American cultural greatness" date from the mid-eighteenth century—prophecies based on the assumption that economic growth would produce the wealth necessary for culture to flower, while political freedom would unleash creativity.[1]

In New York, the relationship between economic growth and cultural flowering was more explicit than for the nation as a whole. As the country's chief port, providing manufactured goods from abroad and exporting raw materials, New York grew in size and prosperity as the hinterland developed. The city's potential as a commercial center was manifestly apparent to its leaders. In 1824, Erie Canal Commissioner De Witt Clinton (1769–1828) predicted that New York would become "the granary of the western world" and that the canal's income would "realize a vast fund applicable to all the objects of human improvement, upon intellectual and moral cultivation."[2] Reflecting a widespread belief in Clinton's vision, in November 1825 the city celebrated the canal's opening.

The festivities were elaborate. Clinton himself led a ceremonial mingling of water from Lake Erie with the Atlantic. The maritime community paraded tall ships, barges, and even some new paddle-wheel steamers. Workers paraded through the city arranged by professions and crafts, each with a banner or float. With them marched the benevolent organizations, the fire department, the military, the societies—artistic, historical, literary, and scientific—members of the bar, Columbia College, and the corporation of the city, all accompanied by the city's bands. Even the British shipboard bands played "Yankee Doodle" in respectful response to American renditions of "God Save the King." On the evening of November 4, public buildings and theaters were illuminated, and fireworks lit up the sky. The whole celebration closed on the seventh with a grand ball.[3]

As a cultural event honoring a technological achievement whose benefit would be economic, the canal festivities epitomized the close ties among commerce, technology, and culture in the city. The canal was described in almost esthetic terms as "a work alike useful and magnificent."[4] At the same time, as Mary Ryan has pointed out, the canal celebration parade was the last major parade in nineteenth-century New York in which people from many walks of life participated.[5] So did a vast and varied audience: "There were . . . probably near *100,000* lookers-on, of every age and description, from puling infancy, to spectacled old age, countrymen and citizens, gentle and simple — and among them all . . . we saw not a single instance of drunkenness, no quarrel, no riot, no confusion."[6] A committee of civic leaders working with the Common Council had produced the kind of well-ordered world shown in the theater. Each group had its place in line. All cooperated, seeming to recognize that all New Yorkers were entitled to a share in civic pride in the canal's completion, stood to benefit by the economic growth promised, and were happy to have a good time.

The canal celebration may have been a watershed in New York's sociocultural life. On the one hand, its inclusiveness, like that of the theater, showed the city as a unified community in which the interests of one segment of the population seemed to complement and reinforce those of the others. On the other hand, its organization by leaders who were either merchants themselves or beneficiaries of mercantile profits pointed to a growing civic culture, self-consciously being developed "from above" as an "ornament" to business-based material progress and prosperity.[7] This culture was organized independent of the marketplace with its commercial constraints. Unlike the theater, it had no need to offer "something for everyone." Organized from the top, its downward reach was limited.

Like the canal celebration, civic culture was infused with a New York chauvinism that Thomas Bender sees as an attempt to make up for the city's loss of the national capital in 1790.[8] Nineteenth-century histories of the city list with pride leaders who contributed to New York's progress rather than the nation's and whose achievements were either not political, or if political, of the city rather than the nation as a whole. The object of this "multifunctional elite," as Bender calls these men, was to create a self-fulfilling prophecy: If freedom and economic liberalism could produce prosperity, it could produce a viable — and visible — culture as well.

Most of these prominent New Yorkers were not creators themselves. Rather, they were organizers who built an infrastructure on which creative work and hence cultural progress could rest.[9] Chief among them was Clinton himself, both mayor of the city and governor of the state, a founding member of the New-York Historical Society, the Literary and Philosophical Society, and the American Bible Society, president of the American Academy of Fine Arts, a member of the Free School Society (precursor of the city's public school system), and commissioner of the Erie Canal (known as "Clinton's Ditch") during its construction.[10] Another was Samuel L. Mitchill (1764–1831) — physician, chemist, and geologist, principal founder of the Lyceum of Natural History, and author of New York's first guidebook.[11]

The variety of these leaders' activities suggests that their cultural vision for the city was broad and ambitious. Referring to the canal, De Witt Clinton had spoken of "cultivation." *Webster's Dictionary* defined culture and cultivation as synonymous: "The act of tilling and preparing the earth for crops; . . . the application of labor or other means of improvement."[12] New Yorkers were not tilling the soil, but they were producing wealth from commerce to fill the same need that farmers filled literally. The mental step to producing other sorts of improvement was not a large one: Any activity or commodity that required work and could bring about evidence of achievement was desirable on these terms. European high culture was an ideal candidate. Not readily available, it consisted of activities or products that required work to produce and knowledge to appreciate. By the 1820s, the connection among material wealth, the idea of improvement, and the arts was already being made. An 1827 city guidebook called New York the "London of America" for "its rapid growth, commercial character, and unrivalled prosperity." But the author, James Hardie, then suggested that "it is now high time to change the appelation." New York should be known as the "Paris of the New World" for its "extensive patronage afforded to the liberal arts, and works of taste."[13] Cultivating the arts would be a new kind of improvement, worthy of a new model to replace an old one. In spite of the links between culture and commerce and the relationship of both to wealth, the separate spheres of commercial and cultural activity were beginning to be defined.

Civic culture included music. Two musical enterprises, the Philharmonic Society (immediate predecessor of the present Philharmonic, founded in 1842) and the New York Choral Society, were products of the mid-1820s. Like the city's other societies, the Philharmonic and the Choral Society were participatory. Members joined to take part in an activity, whether it be scientific, benevolent, or musical. Like the intellectual societies, the musical organizations were private and elite-governed. The Choral Society's conductor, James H. Swindells, was organist at St. George's Episcopal Church, while the Philharmonic's board of governors reads like a who's who of the city's male upper class.[14]

Membership in these organizations was carefully organized. For example, the Philharmonic's governors contributed $50 initially and $5 per year; the board of directors was chosen from among them. There were two other membership categories. Contributors gave $25 initially and $5 per year, while professional musicians, called associates, paid nothing, performed for free, and were barred from governing activities. Associates could earn survivors' benefits by attending all rehearsals and performances; the longer a musician served the society, the more his family would receive if he died while a member. However, if the musician "should, by immoral or improper conduct, render himself obnoxious to the Society, he shall cease to derive any benefit." All members were admitted by ballot—two black balls excluded a candidate.[15]

The Philharmonic allowed professionals and amateurs to play and provided for financial support for the organization from within the membership. Thus it was essentially a closed society; although it performed two public concerts a year, it had little need to attract a paying audience. Governors were allowed to bring two "ladies" to each concert and contributors one, providing an audience of at least several dozen, if not a few hundred. An ostensibly public institution was public in name only.

The Philharmonic and the Choral Society were dedicated to disseminating "good" music through performance. They fulfilled Clinton's prediction that New York would soon realize "objects of human improvement, . . . intellectual and moral cultivation." The societies' aim was to present music as high art in a concert setting free from commercial interests and acceptable to a respectable audience. Such music was to be a civilizing force. One writer even invoked a technological metaphor, calling it "moral electricity." Because music was believed to possess the esthetic power to improve an individual's social and moral temper, elevating a community's musical taste could enhance the progress of civilization toward universal rationality and refinement. Taste was thus a sign of morality. A person with good taste was a moral person; one who made the effort to develop good taste would be assured of becoming one; and a musical nation had less to fear from the forces of evil.[16]

The Choral Society's Swindells stated this argument in his opening editorial in *The Lyre,* a short-lived magazine given largely to news of musical societies. "If it be true," he wrote, "that 'Music has charms to soothe the savage breast,' it is equally so, that when exhibited in its purity, it has a powerful tendency to refine the bosom of civilization. That both remarks are founded in fact, appears from the attentive observation and deep experience of ages. Some in all nations, have, by the harmony of sounds, been preserved from vice: others have been reclaimed. . . . Good music exerts an influence the most benign." Swindells also linked commerce and culture and indulged in the standard New York chauvinism: "We desire to see New-York as distinguished for her culture of this noble science, this divine art, as she already is for her commercial enterprise, her public spirit, her enlarged philanthropy, her attachment to the ordinances of God's house, and her astonishingly increasing importance." Finally, he expressed the hope that his own efforts would have a wide impact: "When we contemplate the vast benefits in an intellectual and spiritual point of view, resulting from a sedulous and persevering attention, judiciously directed to vocal and instrumental music, we cannot but indulge the hope, that our humble efforts in the good cause, will meet with due encouragement."[17]

This last statement represents an Enlightenment tenet invoked by many New York organizations, including (and perhaps especially) ones established by members of the city's elite. Organizing "from above" would benefit everyone. Just as commercial progress was understood as an advantage to all New Yorkers, cultural organizations, coupled with "sedulous and persevering attention," would bring their benefits to anyone who would make an effort to receive them. The material benefits of commerce and the moral benefits of culture were linked in a rhetoric that was optimistic and energetic. That the broader public might be inaccessible, indifferent, or even hostile to these efforts was not to be taken seriously.

As manifestations of culture, the musical organizations did not grow from New Yorkers' common experience, and no writers referred to work songs, dances, hymns, theater songs, patriotic songs, or other music that grows from it. Rather, they attempted to organize music as a separate, high-cultural practice — as Swindells put it, "exhibited in its purity." Despite rhetoric encouraging music's dissemination to a broader public, the two musical societies were supported from within, and they created a category of music whose availability was limited. Commerce had begun to build a pedestal on which "art" music could stand, free of economic exigencies and therefore seemingly free of artistic compromise.

Italian opera could not stand on this pedestal. An opera society could not be established on the same terms as the Choral Society or the Philharmonic; although elite governance was available, musical talent and training were not. Simply put, there was no one to sing operatic roles in hopes of earning survivors' benefits. Instead, opera's establishment as an institution would depend on a partnership between elite encouragement in the "spirit of improvement" and the organizational structure and commercial interests of the established theater. Its high cost brought economic necessities to the fore. Like the theater, it relied on a ticket-buying public. Unlike the Philharmonic and the Choral Society, opera could not represent culture as pure, unsullied by the marketplace, and free of any overt connection with the commerce that supported it.

Of all performance genres available for public support, opera most clearly reflected the interdependence of culture and commerce. As a lavish public entertainment, opera needed the participation of a network of individuals and groups, including its audience, each with a contribution to make toward its success. In New York, the need for strong financial backing was constantly brought before the public. From the first announcement of opera performances in 1825, audiences were continually reminded that their attendance was a form of support. Later, as opera's high cost was better understood, the press issued calls to the wealthy, who had benefited from New York's commercial growth, to sustain it.[18] Through patronage, New Yorkers could participate in an art form by offering money rather than talent, training, or even understanding.

The civic pride that permeates the announcements and reviews of Italian opera's first season in New York echoes the prophesies about the Erie Canal's impact and the celebrations of its completion. Like the canal, Italian opera was a dream come true. But while all New Yorkers could potentially benefit from the canal, opera played to a narrower clientele. When Maria Garcia stepped onto the stage at the Park Theatre on November 29, 1825 and began her opening cavatina in Rossini's opera *Il barbiere de Siviglia,* her appearance marked a fundamental cultural irony in New York. As a sign of civic pride — *American* pride — New Yorkers were being asked to support a continental European form of public culture. As culture — "the application of labor or other means of improvement" — the content of the Garcias' performances was not at issue. Opera as culture put the Garcias' audience on trial: Could they appreciate this new, refined entertainment? But as theater — as commerce — it allowed the audience its sovereignty. And it created a different question: Could opera please an audience on a nightly basis and pay the management?

The symbolic power of the canal notwithstanding, the debut of Italian opera on the heels of its opening probably had more to do with the Park Theatre management's willingness to take a chance on an unknown genre. The Garcias were recruited by Dominick Lynch, a gentleman of the New York bon ton and the city's best known musical amateur, who acted as agent for the Park's talent manager, Stephen Price. The family had been performing at the King's Theatre, London's Italian opera house. A professional with a long career already behind him, Manuel Garcia (1775–1832) had created the role of Almaviva in the original production of *Il barbiere di Siviglia* under Rossini's direction in Rome (1816) and had repeated the role (also under Rossini) in London in 1824 and 1825. The company that performed in New York included his wife, soprano Joaquina Briones, their children Manuel, a baritone, and Maria, a contralto, bass Felix Angrisani, basso buffo Paolo Rosich, and tenor Giovanni Crivelli. In December of 1825, they were joined in New York by Madame Barbiere (or Barbieri), a soprano from Paris.[19]

The exact financial terms on which the Garcias performed are not known. It is possible, however, to understand some of the steps the

Park took to ensure against loss. Price was used to offering lucrative contracts to English stars. Presumably, a novelty such as opera would garner at least the usual level of compensation. Hence, the Garcias were probably well paid. Moreover, the English set the precedent of paying singers well, and foreign singers (including the Garcias) especially well. In these circumstances, Garcia and his colleagues were offering their services to new buyers in a seller's market.[20]

As artistic director of the company, Garcia was in charge of programming, casting, and rehearsals, filling more of a managerial role than did the usual visiting star. Advertisements for opera performances state that "Signor Garcia . . . has made arrangements with the managers of the New-York Theatre [i.e., the Park], to have the house on Tuesdays and Saturdays."[21] Having brought most of his cast, he seems to have subcontracted for the theater in a manner common by midcentury but unique in New York at the time. In February 1826, a newspaper reported financial troubles: "[Garcia has] scarcely been paid for the salaries of the other performers and his own necessary expenses, receiving little or no compensation for his own services and those of his family."[22] If this is true, his income must have depended at least in part on the theater's receipts — a substantial risk with an untried audience.

Whatever Garcia's stake, the Park had also taken a risk in giving up the theater for two nights a week. Edmund Simpson, the operations manager, had to pay the stock company members, whether or not they performed. Accustomed to making last-minute program changes to increase attendance, he was hampered in his ability to ensure a profit. To meet expenses, the managers raised prices on opera nights from $1 to $2 for a box seat and from 50 cents to $1 for a pit seat.[23] Gallery seats, on the other hand, were "issued for the accommodation of the frequenters of that part of the Theatre, at the original price of 25 cents."[24] The managers probably thought that respectable audience members would pay increased prices for the boxes and pit, but that the gallery audience could or would not. Keeping the lowest price unchanged avoided pricing anyone out of the theater entirely.

Advertisements show that box seats could be reserved ("secured"), a standard theatrical practice, and so could seats in the pit, which was new.[25] The change had two effects. If the boxes were sold out, one could still reserve a seat in the pit. Second, if the house was crowded, the holder of a secured seat in the pit would be guaranteed a place, alleviating the rush when seats were offered on a first-come-first-served basis. Although evidence is lacking, it may also be that secured seats in the pit encouraged escorted women to sit there if the boxes were full.

Selling season tickets was also new. Box tickets for each "season" the Garcias offered were sold at the theater's box office.[26] The seats were sold individually, or someone could reserve an entire box, the first choice being given to "the applicants for the longest term and the greatest number of seats."[27] Season tickets guaranteed buyers a place at an event that might prove popular. They also guaranteed them a location near other season ticket holders, hence identifying themselves as members of the opera audience. Season tickets thus fostered an atmosphere more like a large private entertainment than an anonymous public event, an entertainment admitting those who paid in advance for thirty performances at $2 per place.

Season tickets had advantages for the theater as well. Those who subscribed to two season tickets brought $120 into the till at a time when expenses for scenery and maintenance of the company were highest. Subscriptions helped to indicate the size of the audience, which aided in planning. They also guaranteed an income for what turned out to be a limited repertory: The advertised thirty performances of the first season (November through March) included only four different operas. The management likely did not know before the season opened that so few pieces would be produced. In any event, the Park gained a tremendous advantage by soliciting subscriptions before the public knew how often the same operas would be given.

It is difficult to assess the Garcias' effect on the Park's financial situation. The first season of three months was extended five times, continuing with only minor interruptions from the November premiere through the following September — a extraordinarily long "star" engagement. The extensions suggest that opera "pleased" and the Park thought it could handle the financial burden. But they became progressively shorter, as if the theater were willing to take less of a chance as time went on. Prices for the third and fourth tiers of boxes were also lowered from $2 to $1, suggesting either initial miscalculation or trouble.[28] Total receipts for the season were $56,685; the opening night took in $2,980 and the smallest house $250.[29] But we do not know how much was paid out for the singers, the augmented orchestra, and overhead expenses.

That the Park Theatre had taken a chance on the Garcias was obvious to all. An entire company being employed rather than just one star, and a genre previously unknown in New York was being performed. Moreover, the Garcias' performance in a theater was problematic. Potential patrons would need to be convinced that such events were respectable, and because productions usually succeeded or failed immediately, opera needed to be an instant hit.

Thus the press, which in general supported opera's success but knew nothing of its substance, sold instead what it knew—fashion and local pride. Opera was called a "source of rational and refined enjoyment" and "ranked as the most elegant and refined among the amusements of the higher classes of the old world."[30] The *Mirror* gleefully reported that Americans' developing musical taste had upset the English: "Our taste for music increases with a rapidity that our Faux-friends on the other side of the Atlantic would call 'truly alarming.' . . . We are informed that the Johnny Bulls would not credit the report that Mr. Price had engaged the whole company of the Italian opera house to come to America. . . . We hope the public will convince them that the manager of our theatre does not misplace his confidence when he relies upon the support of a New-York audience."[31]

Trumping the English was a logical ploy. Ironically, however, despite the mocking reference to "our Faux-friends" and "the Johnny Bulls," local civic pride depended on answering to them for their "taste for music." If the opera failed, New Yorkers would be exposed as the provincials the English accused them of being. In order to show themselves as "advanced" in taste as Londoners, they had to meet the Londoners' terms by imitating them.

New Yorkers were expected to do so in dress as well, thus exposing another irony: In order to show their good breeding, a quality considered timeless, people were to adhere to a dress code that was in a state of flux. One writer urged "the Managers to establish rules for those visiting the lower boxes," asserting that "no truly well-bred people will withhold their support in consequence."[32] Another writer, "Cinderella," noted that "in this republican country it would not be altogether consistent with the character of the manager, should he either require or request such a thing [as a dress code]." She suggested voluntary compliance, noting that "on the part of the ladies, the difficulty will be found trifling, for their good taste will immediately suggest how far superior the appearance of the theatre will be, should they comply with the wishes (of the, I will not say, writer alone) but of society in general."[33]

In this manner, compliance with fashion was presented as a goal for individuals and "society in general." Although a few articles did tell people what an opera was like, none asserted that opera would be enjoyable on its merits. Rather, the press urged the public to attend in order to create yet another New York achievement. If people of good breeding would follow the rules, the theater would appear "superior." A uniformly elegant audience would replace the usual motley assortment of types, and a well-behaved audience would free ladies from fear of hurled objects, painted women in the third tier, or riots. In this audience an "improved" society would be displayed — one more uniform and less inclusive than at the theater.

The campaign was successful. On November 29, 1825, New Yorkers could celebrate yet again their ability to achieve anything they set out to do. *Imagine!* a commentator crowed, *Italian opera* "in a country where, two centuries before, the only music which was heard was the howl of the wolf and the yell of the savage."[34] Reports praised the audience at length: "Never before within the walls of the Park Theatre has such an audience been assembled, and never before have they resounded to such music. By eight o'clock (the hour at which the curtain rose) the pit and boxes were filled to overflowing — the lower and second circles were occupied chiefly by elegant and well-dressed females."[35] Opera was an instant hit, "fully and fashionably attended." Writers noted the late starting time that allowed for a longer dinner hour. They mentioned the large number of women, whose presence set and confirmed a respectable tone. That they were "elegant and well-dressed" meant that opera had been deemed fashionable as well.

The audience was also described as attentive and respectful of the performers: "When the orchestra began the overture, a most gratifying silence was immediately produced. . . . The attention was constant, intelligent, and eminently flattering to the artists who were the objects of it."[36] This behavior departed from the theatrical standard, especially the reception given Edmund Kean only two weeks before. Kean, an English tragedian of the first rank, had been dogged by American disapproval of his sex life (he had been convicted of adultery in England) and his alleged anti-American attitudes. On November 14, as he appeared as Richard III, the audience rioted, shouting him down and pelting him with rotten fruit. Refusing to allow him to apologize, they eventually damaged furnishings in the theater.[37] Kean pled for mercy in print: "I make an appeal to that country famed for hospitality to the stranger, and mercy to the conquered. Allow me to say, Sirs, whatever are my offences, I disclaim all intention of offering any thing in the shape of disrespect toward the inhabitants of New York. . . . That I have committed an error, appears too evident from the all-decisive voice of the public."[38] Kean may not have believed that he deserved such treatment, but he was compelled to apologize in order to regain public respect. Like the *Beggar's Opera* riot, the Kean riot shows a sovereign audience communicating its dissatisfaction and forcing an acknowledgment of "the all-decisive voice of the public" from the theatrical profession.

The Garcias' audience was no longer sovereign. On the contrary, their performances tested it for compliance with a code of behavior and subservience to the performance as given. Its submission was its triumph. Although New York theater audiences rioted sporadically throughout the second quarter of the century, no opera audience ever did. Indeed, the idea would have been laughable. Yet the audience's lowered status had its compensations. The high value placed on attendance and attention to the performance may have given New Yorkers the patience with Italian opera they would need for it to take hold. Over the long term, its survival could be divorced from the theatrical imperative of the instant hit.

On the basis of the opening night's attendance, a writer in the *Evening Post* considered "the question [of] whether the American taste will bear the Italian Opera as now settled" and predicted that "it will never hereafter dispense with it."[39] Over the long term, the writer was correct; from the Garcias' year on, New Yorkers have always been willing to attend opera performances and support opera houses. In the short run, however, the question of "whether the American taste will bear" it remained unsettled, for as opera became routine, the momentum leading to the debut could not be sustained.

The Garcias' engagement allowed New Yorkers to explore opera's artistic and social meaning and consider who was its appropriate audience. The campaign that led to opening night brought the issue of audience to the fore, for it hinted at social exclusiveness. Subscriptions allowed the wealthy, who could put more money up front than others, to choose seats for several performances at once. Moreover, a dress code would exclude those who, by social sanction if not by law, could or would not comply. As years passed, opera's "aristocratic" social setting became a standard "democratic" criticism. But at the Park in 1825 opera was available to ordinary theatergoers. The "gods" of the gallery were needed; the theater's management could ill-afford to lose part of its regular audience.

As long as ordinary New Yorkers had access to performances, the question of how the audience would be defined remained open. Although the notion of opera as fashionable circulated around the city, some were untouched or unimpressed by the idea of opera as an icon of civic pride. For them, it was simply another theatrical evening. As in the theater, the show itself needed to please. If "the American taste" was to "bear the Italian Opera," common understanding and sympathy were needed between the action onstage and the audience. Although bases for such understanding did exist, response to the Garcias' performances shows that they were not always self-evident.

The Garcias' departures from the traditions of the American stage were obvious. The troupe brought the city's first European-trained opera cast, performing the first Italian operas sung complete and in their original language rather than adapted to the Anglo-American theater tradition. They brought the first dialogue sung in recitative rather than spoken and a wider range of singing characters, especially men. They brought the first staged performances in the style of a single composer. In Maria Garcia, they brought the city's first female singing star who, at seventeen, performed roles that would make her famous as Maria Malibran. The Garcias also brought the first theatrical single bills, main performances — three hours of Italian opera — without additional entertainment. They brought the first performance genre sold to a public that had no firsthand knowledge of it. The Garcias inspired a new public ritual and even instructions in the press on proper dress and deportment at the opera. And they inspired arguments about the meaning, use, and financial implications of this expensive new European import.

All was not new, however. The Garcias gave nine operas in seventy-nine performances. Two, Rossini's *Il barbiere di Siviglia* and Mozart's *Don Giovanni*, had been performed in New York in English adaptations and account for thirty-one performances. The stories of three others, Rossini's *Otello* and *Cenerentola* and Zingarelli's *Romeo e Giulietta*, were well known. The other four works were entirely new to New Yorkers: Rossini's *Tancredi* and *Il Turco in Italia* and two operas by

Table 3. The Garcias' Repertoire

Composer and Title	Premiere	Number of Performances
Rossini, *Il barbiere di Siviglia*	November 29, 1825	21
Garcia, *L'amante astuto*	December 17, 1825	4
Rossini, *Tancredi*	December 31, 1825	16
Rossini, *Otello*	February 7, 1826	10
Rossini, *Il Turco in Italia*	March 14, 1826	4
Garcia, *La figlia dell'aria*	April 25, 1826	6
Mozart, *Don Giovanni*	May 23, 1826	10
Rossini, *La Cenerentola*	June 27, 1826	5
Zingarelli, *Romeo e Giulietta*	July 26, 1826	3

Garcia himself, *L'amante astuto* and *La figlia dell'aria*. The Garcias' repertoire is given chronologically in table 3.[40]

In the face of so many firsts, it took the familiar aspects of most of the performances to provide a common understanding between the stage and the audience. As comedies, most of the operas fit into the standing theatrical tradition. *Il barbiere di Siviglia* was the most accessible to an audience new to the genre, and one may safely assume that the Garcias chose it for their debut with the hope of making the best possible first impression. With music built into the plot, the opera could be understood to some degree as a play with music. Probably more important, however, the story and some of the music were known in New York through an arrangement by Henry Bishop and Thomas Philipps popular since 1819.

The plot of *Il barbiere* fit into the standing comic tradition: A clever servant (Figaro) helps his noble employer (Count Almaviva) win the lady of his choice (Rosina), rescuing her from the clutches of her lecherous old guardian (Bartolo). A simple set — a balcony for Rosina with Figaro and the count on the stage floor — could clarify this situation immediately. The opera offers opportunities for musical character-drawing along with pantomime, exaggeration, and plain silliness — including a classic music lesson scene (familiar from *Love in a Village*), based on the privileged access music teachers had to young women.[41] Figaro, the servant, is the hero throughout. Consistent with the republican rhetoric of the day, he proves himself more capable than the aristocratic but helpless count.

Rossini's music was likewise accessible. Although his style was more elaborate and varied than that of English opera, it was built on essentially the same musical syntax while offering nothing purposefully complex or esoteric. One commentator called the music "the sort which is almost immediately appreciated by the most unpractised ear (provided it be naturally a good one) and fixes itself firmly in the least retentive memory."[42] The description probably overstates its accessibility, yet given the expectation of something "rational and refined," something more dignified than the antics of a flirt and a drunken count, one can imagine, for example, "Di tanti palpiti" from Rossini's *Tancredi* (ex. 4) making a convincing case for Italian opera as simultaneously exquisite and easily understood.

"Di tanti palpiti" was Maria Garcia's most popular Italian aria. She sang it in the opera itself and as a separate number during other performances. As such, it offered a "pure" musical experience, allowing audiences to experience bel canto singing for its own sake. It was an astute choice. More than "Una voce poco fa," Garcia's other "favorite" aria (ex. 5), "Di tanti palpiti" fulfilled the ideal of music that can "melt us at once into a dream of pity or of love."[43] Both arias provide a patterned accompaniment subservient to the vocal line, allowing Garcia's audiences to follow the structure by following the melody. But the characters of the two arias are fundamentally different. "Di tanti palpiti" substitutes for the comic, coquettish virtuosity of "Una voce" a simple delicacy that is best heard in the even rhythm and repeated notes of the opening. The melodic range is narrow. Where "Una voce" spans more than two octaves, "Di tanti palpiti" spans an octave and a fourth, most of it lying within the fifth F-C. It also offers a "melting" moment, a deceptive resolution of the dominant (mm. 16–17) slipped unpretentiously into the middle of a phrase.

The aria is formally simple. The opening repeated notes form a "hook," a short, melodic motive identified with a text. The hook is heard twice at the outset (mm. 1–2 and 5–6) and marks the return to opening, clarifying the structure (mm. 29–30 and 33–34). As in an English opera piece (e.g., "Begone, I Agree" [ex. 1]), the hook identifies the piece melodically. Although the aria offered a tasteful simplicity and musical beauty that the English pieces did not, its structural basis was essentially the same. "Di tanti palpiti" introduced the idea of an Italian operatic "gem," popular either within or removed from its

Example 4. Rossini, "Di tanti palpiti" (*Tancredi*, act 1, no. 7), Paris: Pacini, n.d.

dramatic context. In so doing, it enhanced New Yorkers' understanding of the Italian musical style while holding the music up as an esthetic experience to be enjoyed for its own sake.

Finally, "Di tanti palpiti" introduced an important new kind of musical role. A character such as Rosina in *Il barbiere di Siviglia* needed careful portrayal to limit the sexual implications of her youthful, slightly flippant exuberance. By contrast, the personality implied by "Di tanti palpiti" cannot be so played. Rather, she is a new model for operatic characters, the pure, chaste, lyric-coloratura bel canto soprano or mezzo-soprano. Her sweetness and refinement are unassailable, even as her music gives her a depth beyond the stereotype of the vulnerable ingenue. The directness of the vocal line (especially the opening) reminds one that the original character she plays, Tancredi, is male. But the singer at the Park Theatre was female (the role was composed as a cross-dress or "pants" role), one whose success as this new kind of character was significant for her audience.

As Mary Ryan has shown, during the 1820s women were accepted in public in symbolic form (i.e., allegorical figures modeled on the French Marianne, prototypes of the Statue of Liberty). But actual women were considered inherently corrupting by attraction.[44] Maria Garcia—specifically her performance of "Di tanti palpiti"—broke this pattern. Garcia was not a symbol, she was real and a personality to be enjoyed. The aria was straightforward, interesting, and, perhaps most important, not comic. Garcia could project a seriousness and dignity as a performer and a woman that could enhance the status of the women in her audience, for they were as real as she, present at a theatrical performance on terms more or less equal with their male escorts. The men had given something up in sexually integrating the theater for two nights a week, agreeing to dress well and refraining from ill-behavior. Seeing only potentially corrupting characters onstage would have been incongruous with this program. "Di tanti palpiti" helped establish a relationship between the stage as a manifestation of culture and a new, consciously respectable audience.

In this manner, "Di tanti palpiti" gave New Yorkers a glimpse of opera's future. So did Rossini's *Otello,* especially the character of Desdemona, the city's first operatic heroine-victim. This was a glimpse farther down the road. The first opera with an unhappy ending produced in New York, *Otello* anticipated the tension, horror, and death common on the operatic stage from the 1840s on. It brought other firsts as well. A violent event, Otello's murder of Desdemona, was interpreted musically. Audiences heard serious, evil male characters sing, which in English opera they did not. They also heard Shakespeare's *Othello,* a well-known, powerful text, recreated as an opera.

It is hard to imagine a response to musical theater that is not essentially a response to the music. Except for *The Beggar's Opera,* however, *Otello* was the first piece heard in New York that suggested a response either as music or as drama but not as both at the same time. A comparison with *The Beggar's Opera* in this regard is less bizarre than it may seem. As Macheath's music lessened the impact of an unsavory character, so the music of *Otello* replaces Shakespeare's psychological complexity with Rossini's musical complexity, rendering the story more abstract. Music's ability to diffuse painful emotion in favor of an equally intense musical beauty allowed its association with evil to be accepted. Although evil comic characters, for example, Don Giovanni, Macheath, and Fra Diavolo, sometimes sang in English opera, a singing Iago was a contradiction, his very "unnaturalness" undermining a "school of morality" interpretation of the opera. Instead, the music adds a second, simultaneous layer of meaning not necessarily congruent with a conventional dramatic interpretation.

Available evidence suggests that *Otello* was successful as a drama, its musical substance accepted in terms of the familiar story. Knowing the plot allowed one to follow the drama without understanding every word — or, for that matter, *any* word. Moreover, the play seems to have been interpreted as much in visual as in verbal terms. In 1824, for example, a commentator on William Augustus Conway's portrayal of Othello remarked how "the gigantic figure of the Moor, bent down in the act of plunging the dagger into Desdemona's bosom . . . almost deprived the spectators of breath, and we heard many shrieks from different parts of the house."[45] Here was no prettified *Othello.* On the contrary, its horror was shown in graphic terms as the physical act riveted the audience's attention. No commentator left an equivalent description of Manuel Garcia's portrayal. Links were made between it and the play, however. One reviewer noted "how near of kin the opera is to the drama" and called Garcia "the best representative of the Moor that we have ever seen."[46] More telling, however, is the story of an intermission encounter between Garcia and Edmund Kean, who was to play Othello the following night. Kean "introduced himself as he said, for the satisfaction of expressing his admiration at the excellent manner in which the part of Othello had been represented [by Garcia], and of complimenting the artist who had so well delineated a most difficult character."[47]

The dramatic actor approving his competitor, the musician, was remarkable. Kean knew the story intimately and was equipped to understand a portrayal across the gap between the two media, if such understanding was possible. The commentator's point was that the gap could be bridged, a point effective regardless of what Kean said to Garcia — if anything. "This opera serves to show how music may affect the feelings in tragic composition," the writer asserted. Like physical action, music communicated directly, affecting the feelings without mediation by the analytical or rationalizing tendency of words. Having Kean support Garcia asserted for music an ability to contribute to meaning, even in a work long successful in verbal and visual terms. In fact, given the use of background music in contemporary plays (probably including *Othello*), Kean's reported comment that the play and the opera had much in common probably represents an accurate assessment from an audience's point of view.

The commentary on *Otello*, sparse as it is, begins to acknowledge music's role in opera. Acceptance, however, was slow; on the short term, such fundamental rethinking was not possible. For some of the Garcias' commentators, musical and verbal sources of meaning were opposed. Given the theatrical tradition of keeping the music simple and ornamental, using it to create meaning in a dramatic work brought support, puzzlement, and even hostility. The debate centered on first principles. One writer, for example, supported the place of music in drama, calling a melody in Manuel Garcia's *L'amante astuto* "the very language of tenderest entreaty" and asserting that "the plaintive tones of an exquisite contralto, successfully exerting all the wonderful power which voices of that quality have above all others of moving the affections, made upon the minds of the whole audience a deep and indelible impression, such as the drama, we seriously believe, without the aid of music, could never have produced."[48] The writer was impressed by Maria Garcia's physical actions and performance style in ways he believed the drama alone could not achieve. He dignified the link between music and a specific emotion by referring to music as a language. Even the sound of Garcia's voice could "move the affections," making an audience feel what the singer conveyed. The effect was profound. But it was only an "impression." The writer was willing to forgo the interpretative richness words offer for the less specific but, to him, even more "wonderful power" of Garcia's voice alone.

Other commentators, however, argued that the Italian style was too complex to reach most of its audience. It succeeded only as a virtuosic tour-de-force, and its emotional impact was sometimes denied. "So powerful, at one time, was [music's] influence considered in the formation of character," wrote one, "that no system of education was deemed complete without music for its basis." This power required music that "speaks to the heart, not to the head": "We would have tears issue from the eyes, not 'bravos' from the lips — crying, not criticizing." The commentator wanted a simple, impressive, easily communicative style: "Which, we would ask, is the greater victory, to tickle a knot of connoisseurs, or to make a whole audience feel as one man?"[49]

Communicative ability was paramount in the words as well. Whenever Maria Garcia sang in English, which she often did in the music lesson scene in *Il barbiere di Siviglia,* someone would remind readers what they were missing in Italian. One witness told of how, after singing a "favourite Scotch song with great feeling and effect," she "rose from the piano amid the plaudits of all," and then "cheerfully and gracefully she seated herself again, and sang 'Home, sweet home,' with more science and effect than we have ever heard it before." His point was clear: "These two songs made us deeply lament that the other parts of her performance were both in song [style] and language so unintelligible to us." Only such simple music sung in the vernacular would be so well received. The writer ignored the possibility that the audience was honored to hear Garcia sing in their language and the fact that "Home, Sweet Home," only three years old, was already a popular standard. He believed that such a piece could communicate in ways that a Rossini opera could not. And in admitting his inability to grasp Rossini's musical meaning, he denied that perhaps others could.[50] Yet in using the word *science,* the writer also acknowledged the Italian style even as he wrote it off as "unintelligible." The musical style he advocated, that of "Home, Sweet Home," was purposefully "unscientific," to be sung without technical training and communicated without virtuosity. But in appreciating the trained singer and her "science," he contradicted his inference that Garcia's Italian repertoire could not be understood.

As these excerpts show, the first responses to opera as a musical genre were mixed, with the positive tempered and hesitant and the negative forthright and clear. The pattern remained throughout the Garcias' season. In fact, hostility was common, as some writers disparaged and trivialized opera's music and its audience. Although drama "represents the actions and passions of men as we see them in the world at large," the argument ran, opera presents so much music as to overshadow the words, which naturally bear a drama's message. It is not genuine art but merely a technical gimmick to show off a performer's skill, and those who purport to understand it may need someone to call their bluff:

> Is the false Italian school of opera natural? What man ever *sung* out his fit of passion? Who in jealousy, ambition, or revenge, ever vented his feelings in song? No man: on the contrary, these passions always destroy the harmony of the mind, and often choke the utterance. The style of singing now introduced is, in a measure, new in this country, and the science they display, wonderful. For ourselves (ignoramuses that we are!) we do not relish the music, because we do not understand the Italian. There are those, no doubt, who can, or pretend, to follow the composer through all his passages, even without a syllable of language: we have not so much skill, and never delight in vocal music without the words.[51]

Here was the classic anti-opera attitude in the English tradition: ignorant, literalist, and proud of both. As the writer stated, people do not sing all of the time, therefore opera cannot be "true to nature." This is, of course, fact. But the writer also denied music even the ability to enhance emotion. Without understanding the words, one cannot tell what emotion is being represented. The letter of this last objection could be answered by the fact that librettos were available at the Garcias' performances. But the spirit is a fundamental one. Music's beauty could not replace words as a bearer of meaning. Nor could the notion that it could bear a significant independent meaning. Simply put, some people saw opera as bad theater rather than an independent genre.

To a degree, such insistence made sense. A central problem of opera reception for the two decades following the Garcias' season was that music, as long as words were considered bearers of essential meaning, would remain in some quarters an overelaborate distraction. Shifting the burden of meaning to the music required more experience with opera than audiences possessed. Eventually, as New Yorkers learned to "follow the composer through all his passages, even without a syllable of language," Italian opera could be taken as "natural." Once they understood how a "fit of passion" could be sung, plot details would recede in importance. Only then would opera be assimilated on all counts.

Finally, this early critic was proud of his ignorance. Despite calling the "science" of the new style "wonderful," he nevertheless saw it as an empty technical exercise, lacking the richness of the spoken drama. He hinted that if he did not understand the music, it was not worth understanding; those claiming to "follow the composer through all his passages" were only pretending to do so. He, on the other hand, would remain independent, unwilling to accept opera on another's authority or pretend to enjoy what he could not.

The issue of pretense was the last major theme of early opera criticism. Writers who mocked music they did not understand mocked what they saw as the purely social interest of its audience. As in England and the early United States, critics such as this writer in the *Literary Gazette* disdained fashion and the fashionable, distinguishing between pursuers of a "reasonless phantom" and the truly wellbred: "There is no object on earth so vapidly disagreeable as your superlative man of fashion, encounter him under any circumstances. I do not mean the well-bred gentleman, but him of the spurious breed, who is the reverse in character — yet is at the *acme* of exalted life."[52] The man of fashion admired physical weakness and effeminacy: "I have heard a healthy brawny fellow, habited in the pink of the mode, declare his envy of a hobbling beau, equally high dressed, because he bore emaciated legs and a mealy visage, expressive of ill health from long dissipation, which threw over his gait a modish langour, exactly squaring with certain *bizarre* ideas of the most exquisite of fashion's masterpieces. . . . Rough and coarse on the coach-box, when in the drawing-room he is so delicately essenced, he looks as if he might be 'brained with his lady's fan' — *si il a en.*" Above all, he had to be intellectually and even morally no more than à la mode: "Life, with the man of fashion, evaporates in essences and perfumes. Knowledge, except its outscourings, is the butt of all such, and reason has no place in their vocabulary. Natural impulses must be limited, and never transgress set forms and customary ordinances. Honesty, virtue, or talent, are of no avail in a circle of fashion, if the air of the *ton* be wanting — it is well they have better supporters."

To this writer, there was nothing honest about fashion or the fashionable. He saw his values, taken as the genuine ones, subverted to the necessity of following its dictates. The fashionable lacked independence of thought, an especially severe indictment of the fashionable male in the republican United States. The writer even hinted that a male who could "declare his envy of a hobbling beau" was not a real man. Covering his point with feeble French, he accused the man of fashion of being unable to defend himself from "his lady's fan," or even lacking enough interest in women to have a lady at all.

Only in the 1830s and 1840s was the critique of opera as merely fashion applied with full force. Even in the Garcias' season, however, writers had great fun ridiculing opera and its audience for musical and social pretensions. Noting an increase in the number of women in the theater, they focused as often on the upper-class, gullible woman as on her eviscerated male companion. In January 1826, the *Mirror* told of a merchant who had imported a bundle of women's silk cloaks that no one would buy. But after "Signor Garcia and the Italian company set themselves down among us and began *una voc*-ing and *poco fa*-ing until everyone's head was turned," he advertised them as opera cloaks — "a *bran new* importation" — and sold them out to "Blue-eye" and other "fair creatures" in a day.[53] Later in the season, a widely circulated comment by Thomas Cooper, an actor, attributed the poor attendance at his benefit performance to "two influenzas," one laying people low physically, the other keeping them away only from the theater: "The one [influenza] is of foreign growth, the other of domestic origin — the one barks, barks, and the other *una voces una voces,* the one is allied to heaven, the other to the fogs of Pandemonium. The one, said Cooper, is a mental mania — the other a nasal twang; the one is composed of shakers, trills, and quavers — the other made up of coughs, spitting, and fevers, the one the vocables of Italy, the other the consonants of Greenland."[54]

Thus began a long history of ridicule — some amusing, some envious, some merely rude — aimed at opera and operagoing. Cooper, fearing for his livelihood, mocked what opera seemed to be doing to his theater. His barbs — against music, Italians, and fashion — became thematic as writers conflated the genre with attempts to create a polite social setting for it. Opera was described as a "forced and unnatural bantling," inferior to old English drama. The Garcias could be dismissed with the statement that it was merely "fashionable to witness their representations," while the extent of their success confirmed the fashionable world's interest in appearances over substance.[55]

The sources of this criticism were mixed and included populists who disdained aristocratic pretense in Americans, intellectuals who mistrusted music's power over people, moralists for whom a foreign-language genre could not contribute to theatrical reform, romantic conservatives who wanted to hold onto the "palmy days" of the legitimate stage, and self-proclaimed outsiders who disparaged the wealth and social prestige that attendance at the opera was seen to represent. The myth of the blue-eyed fashionable was originated in part by people who had never been to an opera performance. On the other side, opera had been identified as a means of showing good taste and breeding before it could be judged. Both interpretations allowed people who held a fixed position with regard to opera—either in or out of its audience—to rationalize that position in social and artistic terms. For better or worse, accurately or not, the Garcias were often portrayed as playing only to an elite.

Given the content-orientation of much twentieth-century opera criticism, these writers' interest in their audience seems remarkable. Both writers who enjoyed the Garcias' performances and those who wished for a simpler style claimed that audience responses backed up their points. Writers who granted opera no value, however, mocked audiences who seemed to accept it. These critical distinctions blended the social with the philosophical. Critics who voiced an objection to opera's loss of meaning with respect to drama wrote from an older, rationalist perspective. For them, meaning meant knowing what the story was about via words. Musical beauty could not compensate for this loss. Nor could any prior value placed on music compensate for the primacy of the theatrical experience. In the theater, you had to please or your patrons would not come back. Exaggerated claims made for opera could not compensate for its need to satisfy its audience nightly. And those who seemed to be pleased with it needed to be rationalized away.

Other critics wrote from a later, romantic perspective more sensitive to music as a bearer of significant meaning. They saw appreciative audiences not as elites to be mocked from below, but as audiences improving themselves with new social codes and an influx of

for other women: "Let the opportunity, while it lasts, be improved by our ladies improving their taste and powers by her example."[60] Presenting a theatrical figure in this manner was extraordinary. If anything, people went to the theater despite its problems rather than because of its virtues. Garcia's youth, accomplishment, attractiveness, and ladylike demeanor made her an ideal vehicle for effecting changes in public attitudes toward the stage, changes that would eventually prove essential to opera's success. These characteristics, rather than her talent and accomplishment, gave her permission to appear onstage and were the basis for her acceptance.

Thus Garcia's outside life mattered as well — an actress as role model had to convince offstage as well as on. An announcement of her first benefit performance asserts that she was entitled to a benefit "not less by her talents as an artist, than her graceful and becoming conduct in private life." She was portrayed as a dutiful daughter, giving a benefit for "the remuneration of parents who have done so much for her, and [who,] by assiduously cultivating [her] fine natural parts, have made her what she is."[61] The idea could be expected to play well. Garcia could come across as anxious to make up for potential losses due to her marriage and possible retirement from the stage, reconciling the feminine ideal with the mercenary practice of a benefit.

But Garcia was more than just a feminine icon. She also entertained. Such was the appeal of her Rosina in *Il barbiere di Siviglia* that some disappointed operagoers went home when Manuel Garcia's illness forced the substitution of *Tancredi* at her benefit.[62] Rosina was enjoyed as a character and a singer. The role allowed the Signorina to be charming and humorous as well as ladylike, and audiences appreciated Garcia's spirited acting in the part. For example, in the scene in which her guardian, Bartolo, discovers ink on her fingers after she has written to her suitor, Count Almaviva, they recognized a female stereotype that they could accept and with whom they could identify: "The ingenuity of Rosina's excuses, and the account she gives of the suspicious circumstances; the perfectly natural, playful, feminine — guile — must we call it — by which in all times, damsels in love have been in possession of the privilege to cheat their Argus-eyed tutors, could not have been rendered with greater effect, or more grace."[63]

Rosina is well-to-do youth in bloom and in a situation her emulators could envy. Moreover, she wins the man of her choice through old ploys involving surreptious intelligence. Compared with Garcia's other roles, this one most closely resembled such long-familiar female stock characters as Rosetta in *Love in a Village*. The changes in language and musical style brought by the Italian production were effected on a familiar foundation. The role allowed Rosina to be accepted as "natural" even as the artificiality of opera itself was debated.

New Yorkers also enjoyed Garcia's singing. She took advantage of the music lesson scene, for example, to perform British ballads and "Home, Sweet Home." The scene allowed *Il barbiere* to present the widest stylistic range of any opera given; operagoers did not have to choose between the new Italian idiom and the familiar Anglo-American. Seated at the piano in the onstage parlor, Garcia could look and sound as much like a female member of her audience as she ever would.

By achieving a feminine ideal nightly onstage, Garcia challenged the women in her audience to use music to do the same. The men of New York had built the Erie Canal; the women — considered more naturally musical — could reach an equivalent goal by successfully emulating the Signorina as Rosina. This notion of emulation worked on two levels — that of the opera character and of the singer. For Garcia's feminine audience, mere attendance was not enough, nor was singing her English pieces alone. If Rosina was recognizable to her auditors, if her story was an appealing fairy tale, she showed that by "improving their taste and powers" the young ladies in the audience could meet both her and Garcia on their own ground and bring the fairy tale a step closer to reality.

The favorite Italian piece in *Il barbiere di Siviglia* was "Una voce poco fa," Rosina's opening cavatina (ex. 5), which could be performed from a sheet-music edition published in New York and advertised as "sung by Signorina Garcia."[64] Compared with the dignified "Di tanti palpiti," "Una voce poco fa" is a spirited, virtuosic tour-de-force that makes no technical concessions to the musical amateur. Garcia's emulators were challenged to meet her in an area of her own greatest strength by performing Rossini's wide-ranging and rhythmically complex vocal line intact.[65] Moreover, they were challenged to perform it as she did, with skill, taste, and ease, "as if without the smallest effort."[66]

Singers learning the piece from the New York edition had only one choice of text language: Italian. Garcia, whose native language was probably French, was admired for her linguistic skills.[67] Like her, wealthy young New York women of the 1820s were expected to acquire modern languages, or, as a critic complained in 1826, at least "a smattering of French and Italian . . . more for the sake of singing the songs of these nations, and in the present era, for understanding the Opera, than for any lasting benefit."[68] The remark deprecates music and languages as trivial feminine accomplishments, but Garcia showed them as valuable and appealing. She also showed that it was possible to perform convincingly in languages not one's own. In this respect, the edition of "Una voce" gave her admirers another chance to meet her on her own ground.

Finally, the commentary on Garcia's performances provided operagoers with an understanding of her musical and dramatic interpretation. In this way it provides a clue about the interpretative ideal to which performers of "Una voce" could aspire. Rosina has two distinct sides to her personality, one sweet and innocent, the other cunning and full of guile. The sweet Rosina sings of her love for Lindoro (the name by which she knows her suitor, Almaviva), whereas the cunning Rosina is determined to win him, no matter what it takes. Given the musical style, the task for Garcia and other performers of "Una voce" was to keep the cunning side from exceeding the bounds of conventional femininity.

That Garcia balanced the two sides of Rosina's character to the satisfaction of at least some auditors is suggested by the one detailed press comment available on her interpretation of "Una voce": "Among the innumerable fine points of Mademoiselle Garcia's singing, we beg leave to mention . . . the change of tone and manner at the word *ma* towards the conclusion of the air; (we may observe, by the way, that Mlle Garcia's action and expression of the *sentiment* of this air are inimitably beautiful)."[69] The text to which the reviewer refers is that of the second half of the cavatina. This text has two verses (verses A and B) divided at the word "*ma*—but:"

Verse A

Io sono docile	I am docile,
Son rispettosa	I am respectful,
Son ubbidiente	I am obedient,
Dolce amorosa,	Sweetly loving;
Mi lascio reggere,	I let myself be ruled
Mi fo guidar.	and guided.

Verse B

Ma se mi toccano	But if they touch me
Dov'è il mio debole	at my weak spot,
Sarò una vipera,	I become a viper,
E cento trappole	And a hundred traps
Prima di cedere	before giving up
Farò giocar.	I will lay.

The word *ma* divides the sweet and innocent Rosina (verse A) from the spirited and cunning Rosina (verse B). She sings both texts twice (i.e., verses A and B, then A and B again), so that *ma* is heard twice. But the music does not alternate between expressing the two sides of Rosina's personality. Although the music for verse B is the same both times, the music for verse A is not (i.e., the text form is ABAB, whereas the musical form is ABCB). Rosina's musical personality is not quite the same as her verbal one.

In the musical setting, Rosina's "verse B" personality overshadows her "verse A" personality. The first verse A setting is as placid as its words. Rosina begins with a balanced musical period of four phrases, each two measures long (ex. 5a). Each one simply and sweetly lists a character trait, including docility, respect, and obedience. Together, the four phrases make a textual unit (one sentence) and a musical one (one period).

At this point, Rosina has another textual sentence to sing, the last one before *ma*. She begins on the model of the first period — two lines of text, sweetly, to four measures of music (ex. 5b, first four mm.). If she were to continue on the model of the first period, she would have to sing another four measures. But she does not. At *ma* she begins a whole new section — the B text, sung in a higher range, in faster notes, with a bass line that moves twice as fast as in the previous section (ex. 5b, after the fermata). This B section interrupts the as-yet unfinished second period of the A section; listeners following her discourse would find *ma* a fresh beginning. Rosina has not only changed her tune, but she has also made a point of disturbing the formal design that she has set up. Respectful? Obedient? Probably not. More likely, listeners will hear "determined" and, thanks to the virtuosity, "eminently capable."

The setting of *ma* that caught the reviewer's attention in 1825 was most likely the one just described. Once Rosina has asserted the "B" side of her personality, she never returns to her former docile self, even though she repeats the A text. There is no "change of tone and manner" at the second *ma*. If anything, Rosina seems to have forgotten her "A" personality; when she repeats the A text, she merely accompanies the orchestra. The violins continue the exuberant bravura passage with which she had finished the previous B section, keeping the B mood going until she has exhausted the A text and can begin it again at *ma* (ex. 5c).

"Una foce poco fa" is rife with possibilities for exaggeration in performance. It expresses the extremes of Rosina's character. It is vocally virtuosic and rhythmically energetic; its "oom-pah" rhythm between the bass and the upper strings (ex. 5b and c) could easily degenerate into a cancan. Maria Garcia would need talent and will to appear "perfectly natural, playful, [and] feminine" to her audience, for it was essential that the *sentiment* be right.[70] Rosina could appear cunning and spirited, self-aware, intelligent, and motivated (of course, by a quintessentially feminine goal). She need not be boring. But at the same time, she could not appear common or cheap. Perhaps because of her youth, Garcia managed to avoid crossing the essential line between spirit and vulgarity. Her acting displayed "a most remarkable chasteness and propriety, never violating good taste nor exceeding the bounds of female decorum."[71]

In *Il barbiere di Siviglia*, Garcia played not one character but three: Rosina, a "typical" young woman in the audience, and herself. The accolades she received suggest that she succeeded in all three roles. Her Rosina was recognizable as a female type of the right sort. She herself was accomplished yet modest and proper. Along with her interpreters in the press, she helped establish opera as the one genre that could codify and express onstage its audience's good taste, social standing, respectability, and cosmopolitanism.

Maria Garcia's performances had the broadest appeal of any aspect of New York's first opera season. The conventionality of her charm helped her auditors accept a suspect musical virtuosity. At the same time, she honored them with music both familiar and beloved, most notably "Home, Sweet Home." Garcia bridged the gap between a repertoire that was to be respected, appreciated, and enjoyed in a dignified way and music that immediately spoke to its audience without benefit of acquired tastes.

Her success at the Bowery Theatre in 1827 speaks to the same

Example 5a. Rossini, "Una voce poco fa" (*Il barbiere di Siviglia*), New York: Dubois and Stodart [1826]

Example 5b. "Una voce poco fa."

Example 5c. "Una voce poco fa."

theme. Having married Eugene Malibran in New York in March of 1826, Maria Garcia remained behind when her family left for Mexico in November of the same year. By the following January, the couple needed money, and she was back in the theater at $500 a night, performing mainly in English. Even at that high pay, she earned a profit for the Bowery's management.[72]

Interest in Garcia even increased after her family's departure. "Storms cannot deprive her of an audience," wrote one commentator.[73] The image of a delicate young woman left in a foreign city with a husband unable to support her was irresistible. Garcia was broke, and everyone knew it. Pleas for public attendance at her benefits are full of poignant euphemisms: "a youthful female, and one so gifted, cannot in her own person, and *from a motive so touching*, make an appeal in vain," and "there are strong and nameless reasons why her benefit should be most generously patronized."[74]

Writers also emphasized human interest vignettes. Garcia did an

Irish brogue so well that "Keene [her costar], himself an Irishman, presented to her a sprig of shamrock [onstage]."[75] At her farewell performance on October 29, 1827, she and the audience were described as overcome with emotion, "struggling with feelings that ill suited the mimicry of acting." At last, the actress and the young woman appeared at odds, as Garcia honored her patrons by appearing overwhelmed at the thought of her imminent departure. Seeing her unable to "be the player before those to whom she was about to bid a final adieu" confirmed her audience's high estimation not of her talent but of her character: "The audience entered fully into [her] feelings," and "her voice found an echo in every bosom."[76] Garcia even finished the evening with a "farewell song" of her own composition on a text by Keene. Overcome with emotion, she was unable to accompany herself on the harp, and the pianist had to step in.[77]

Somewhere in New York there may have been a hint of cynicism about all of this, but not a word of it appeared in the press. Garcia was a great unifier, "admired by all ranks and all classes" — evidence that opera was not just for the fashionable few.[78] Her willingness to turn her artistry on a wide range of music contributed to her popularity, as did her character and personality. Her emotional farewell was a sign of a femininity that transcended her profession, and her success was a sign that the feminine ideal she embodied was recognized across a broad social spectrum. One commentator encapsulized the set of traits essential to Garcia's success by observing that "she seemed to belong less to the theatre than to the friendly circle." Yet "when she quitted the one [circle] to dazzle and delight in the other, it was not so much a thing of profession, as from a desire to gratify the world by her exquisite talents, and to shew that the most splendid theatrical endowments were not incompatible with the most amiable and gentle domestic virtues."[79] Despite her professional career and her foreign origin, New Yorkers could be made to see Garcia as one of them.

That Garcia might have been ambitious or mercenary was not to be considered. Thinking of her as professional rather than merely generous would have degraded her, as would mentioning her publicly displayed independence, which reached far beyond the current feminine norm. On the contrary, Garcia's "domestic virtues" were essential to her acceptance as a model for women in public, as was the hint that she softened and domesticized the theater itself. That she was successful — that New Yorkers could identify with her — kept the link strong between the stage and the world beyond. This link — the notion that drama could provide models for living — was central to the theater's hope of justifying its existence. Garcia could not be just a musical conduit to be admired from afar. Indeed, she was not. Rather, she enabled Italian opera to reach people looking first for entertainment that they could enjoy as well as those concerned with opera as culture. Her Italian and English performances were equally refined. Yet as long as opera in New York meant the Signorina, refinement could transcend the clichés of fashionable aspiration to be widely enjoyed on its own terms.

Maria Garcia Malibran left New York and her husband for Europe, fame, and fortune at the age of nineteen. From that time on, her life was a whirlwind that ended only with her death in 1836, at the age of twenty-eight.

◊ ◊ ◊

The Garcias' engagement changed the meaning of the word *opera* in New York. What had been known as opera before 1825 was now called *English opera.* The Garcias performed *Italian opera,* which New Yorkers quickly recognized as opera of a different sort. Italian and English opera coexisted in New York for the next thirty years, by which time English opera had begun to give way to other kinds of English-language dramatic entertainment with music. By that time, Italian opera (along with French and German) had replaced English musical theater as simply opera. What had begun as an experimental, controversial novelty when performed by the Garcias had become the norm.

In introducing Italian opera to New York, the Garcias inspired two kinds of response to the issue of words and music and the function of musical beauty in opera. For some, opera's musical style was said to influence the taste and demeanor of its auditors. For others, music's pervasiveness was said to distract the mind from the words, the true bearers of the drama's message. Together, these opposing perspectives set terms for debate on the substance of opera that would last until midcentury, even as the genre underwent major changes. Social and economic considerations aside, the essence of opera was music. Over time, musical sound, virtuosity, and emotional power would give New Yorkers a new understanding of opera as a dramatic genre, which in turn would foster its acceptance.

While the Garcias brought the new genre to New York, New Yorkers themselves began to build an audience for it. Park Theatre manager Simpson did not renew the Garcias' engagement in 1826 despite some public pressure to do so.[80] Accustomed to billing what pleased, he may have found the audience for Italian opera too small to meet expenses. But he continued to mount English opera and in the summer of 1827 engaged a French-language opera and theater company from New Orleans for a two-month season. The Park's repeated testing of the waters made opera available sporadically until stronger support could keep it going on a regular basis.

Other New Yorkers, however, saw opera as culture, "the application of labor or other means to improve good qualities in, or growth." An attempt at institutionalized support came from patrons who tried to organize an opera company in March of 1826. As reported in the *Evening Post,* Dominick Lynch chaired a public meeting of the "friends of the *Italian Opera*," called to organize a New-York Opera Company that would solicit subscriptions for the permanent establishment of opera in the city. The report does not tell what action the company would take. For example, would it subsidize opera at the Park or build an opera house? Moreover, the scheme seems to have been abandoned for lack of support ($100,000 was to be raised in shares of $250, requiring four hundred shareholders at one share per person).[81] But the meeting shows that a few individuals (the report names a nine-member steering committee) understood that opera was going to take more money than the theater could provide and were willing to consider subsidizing it themselves.

Opera had much to offer a business-oriented patron. It was logistically and financially challenging, therefore suited to the skills of successful merchants. It was highly regarded esthetically. It was nonparticipatory; patrons could leave the actual doing of the music to trained professionals. It was attached to an established institution, the theater. As a musical genre, it was considered innately attractive and appropriate for women, who could be expected to form a larger proportion of the audience than in the theater, thereby raising its level of decorum and refinement.

The patrons of 1826 established a pattern of support for opera that endured into the twentieth century. Wealthy individuals would band together as an opera company, build an opera house, and hire a manager or impresario to run the actual productions. Company stock-

Table 4. Opera Houses in New York before 1860[a]

Name	Years as Opera House[b]
Italian Opera House	1833–35
Palmo's Opera House	1844–47
Astor Place Opera House	1847–52
Academy of Music	1854–84

[a]The list includes only locations built explicitly for opera, thus excluding theaters and other venues for opera performances.
[b]Other musical and theatrical genres were performed at the opera houses at various times. It is not always clear when each building ceased to be an opera house, however.

holders would maintain financial and, indirectly, artistic control.[82] Unwilling to let opera succeed or fail on the open market, these early patrons maintained in a published resolution that Italian opera was "a source of rational and refined pleasure, imparting a purer character to public amusements, and elevating the public taste," that it was "an admirable school of instruction in the science of music, . . . exciting a taste and forming a style which could not without it be accomplished by the efforts of professional instruction," that it would "aid the public morals, counteracting the influence of less innocent pleasure," and that it would "attract to this city the best professional talent . . . [and] make this city the centre and capital of the liberal and elegant arts."[83] Builders of New York opera houses throughout the century made similar claims in their own resolutions. By removing Italian opera performances from the commercial theaters, patrons acted on the belief that they deserved a more elevated social setting, which could only be achieved through organized, nonentrepreneurial effort. Beginning in 1826, patrons devoted energy and financial resources to establishing and maintaining a series of opera houses designed to provide such a setting (table 4).

Opera as culture — an object of aspiration, removed from the humdrum of everyday life — required advocates who would focus more on its distinctive qualities than its familiar ones. The debates on its performance language, musical style, and social setting centered on the worth of a new kind of culture. If opera was inherently "rational and refined," as its proponents asserted, then appreciating it on its own terms was a desirable form of self-improvement. If, on the other hand, it was not entitled to such respect, then in order to succeed it would have to be understood by, and meet the expectations of, an audience wide enough to support it in the marketplace.

Opera's performance in the theater probably exacerbated the debate. Unlike the Philharmonic and the Choral Society, which were new institutions, opera began its career on territory that others had already claimed. Thomas Cooper complained about the opera not only out of professional jealousy, but also in response to the pressure opera put on the theater to change its ways. Despite some critics' belief that it needed reform, however, the theater was at least familiar. Opera's requirements, especially the elaborate, European-derived, "unrepublican" social ritual said to surround it, meant that accurately or not, opera and its social setting were publicly linked.

Like opera's patrons, the press considered Italian opera a genre separate from musical theater. From the beginning of the Garcias' engagement, the press influenced New Yorkers' understanding of it. Although esthetically based taste as a criterion for judging a play or theatrical production was known, the theater still aimed first to please an audience. Opera, on the other hand, was not only to be tasteful but also to *elevate* taste. Although a tasteful opera could please, pleasure was no longer a first principle. The issues on which critics would later base their judgments—style and quality of performance, style and quality of the music itself, and fidelity to an original text—were hardly in evidence. Nevertheless, with the development of new criteria for judgment began the evolution of reporters into critics, the standard for success from pleasure to excellence, and the standards of judgment based on individual rather than collective response.

It was midcentury, however, before commentary began to focus primarily on individual works. Of greater interest, and probably within the bounds of journalists' expertise, were the social, economic, and even political issues surrounding opera as a form of public culture. More than any other performance genre, opera as presented by the Garcias raised the question of what sorts of entertainment were appropriate for what sorts of people and why. The question had two sides, both based on an understanding of opera as "rational and refined." It was argued that opera would elevate the taste and even the morals of those who made the effort to appreciate it. Therefore, its support would lead audiences to these benefits. It was also argued that opera was appropriate only for those who already had the means, leisure, and inclination to be connoisseurs. Therefore, it was essential to provide a way for the few to appreciate it free of the many. Finally, it was argued that opera was too expensive, foreign, aristocratic, and artificial to take root in republican America. And those who wanted to cultivate it from above were hindering citizens from exercising their right of free choice. Opera's arrival in New York advanced the perception that individual segments of the population might enjoy different performance genres and styles. The days when the city's elite would gather in the Park Theatre to enjoy the same mixed bill as everyone else were drawing to a close.

Over the next thirty years, opera established itself in fits and starts. Institutionally, the Garcias' legacy branched out in two directions. While the bon ton was building opera houses that priced most theatergoers out of the market, entrepreneurs (including the Park's Simpson at the end of his career) were engaging opera companies or even putting Italian troupes together at prices theatergoers could afford. Until the 1850s, the opera houses failed quickly. English opera in the theater, on the other hand, enjoyed a series of resounding successes. These English adaptations formed the other branch of opera's development, giving audiences Italian music with English words—the best of both worlds and an opportunity to come to terms with the new style. Ultimately, Italian opera's success in its original form depended on New Yorkers' experience with this mixed genre. Opera's connection with the theater—with commerce, entrepreneurship, and marketing—was a major component of its saving grace.

English opera's heyday during the 1830s linked the idea of a respectable social setting with that of music as an agent of moral reform. Even in the theater, an opera night was to be something special—serious but enjoyable, a privilege to attend, and, above all, not to be taken for granted. The Garcias' legacy of a "rational and refined" entertainment performed by the best talent available for an audience capable of appreciating it had survived intact.

"Directly from the Heart":
English Opera and the Power of Music in the Age of Sentiment

The Garcias' New York engagement was called a stunning success and a miserable failure. It was, of course, both. The Garcias
succeeded with audiences who came to know Italian opera through
their performances. But in the years following their departure, they
were accused of failing by New Yorkers who expected them to inspire
opera's quick establishment in the city. Building an institution and an
audience for opera was harder than it seemed at first. From the time of
Andrew Jackson's election in 1828, the ideal of Italian opera as a
refining, Europeanizing influence over its audience clashed with the
commercial imperative of reaching a broad, popular clientele. By the
1830s, some New Yorkers, increasingly pro-American in their outlook,
likewise mocked cultural genres such as opera as "aristocratic" (a
common term of derision) and therefore reprehensible to populist
sentiment. The quick failure of the city's first opera house, built in
1833 (chapter 5), attests to opera's inability to transcend this part of its
reputation.

Italian opera succeeded in New York in spite of its European origin
rather than because of it. It did so of necessity; a society consciously
distancing itself from its European roots would have to reinterpret —
perhaps even recreate — a European genre on its own terms. New
Yorkers "naturalized" opera by solving its two big problems. They

created and learned to sustain a new institution, the opera house, in which respectability and cosmopolitanism could be distinguished from exclusivity. They also came to terms with opera as a musical event — not a drama with musical accompaniment, but its reverse, a musical work that told a story. The process took thirty years of trial, error, frustration, interim success, and compromise among conflicting elements — culture and commerce, respectability and access, and music and drama.

Throughout the 1830s, as the new Italian Opera House opened and quickly closed, New Yorkers flocked to the Park and other theaters, where British singing stars could be heard in English-language adaptations of continental originals. These English operas (named for their language of performance) proved to be an ideal compromise between the old plays with music and the Garcias' repertoire. Many of them also played on the idea of using music to make the stage a tool of moral reform, glorifying female sexual propriety through roles in which young, innocent women triumphed over threats to their virtue. This theme was central to the repertoire's acceptance. Featuring women prominently in such roles answered the objection that the stage held evil up to be admired. In one case especially, identifying a singing actress with the characters she played could also answer the objection that theater people were morally corrupt. Women could take places in the theater audience without hurting their reputations, contributing to the increasingly female cast of the opera public.

By incorporating Italian music, English opera allowed New Yorkers to continue assimilating the Italian style. Where understanding an Italian opera in the Garcias' day had been aided by familiar stories, now all of the stories could be familiar. Through English opera, audiences could learn Italian musical conventions — music for characters and situations recognizable from the English theater. By the end of the 1830s, with English opera triumphant, New Yorkers' growing understanding of Italian music through English opera sowed the seeds of the latter's ultimate defeat.

English opera was a hybrid product, usually an arrangement from a continental original, performed in English in theaters throughout the English-speaking world. As a theater piece it was the successor to such eighteenth-century English operas as *The Beggar's Opera* and *Love in a Village*. But unlike these earlier works, the new English opera offered a release from the old constraints on the place of music in drama. In the years following the Garcias' engagement, it offered the perfect balance between music and words, for its gave New Yorkers the verbally based drama they wanted and music in the new Italian musical style. Much of their knowledge of Italian music came from these versions; English opera performances allowed audiences to understand it in terms of dramatic conventions they already knew. The performances also provided a rich sensory experience without the social and educational barrier of the Italian language. The sound, shape, emotional clarity, and depth of the style enhanced — eventually, even created — the power of the drama's message. By the 1830s, English opera was an idea whose time had come.

This prevailing musical tide brought dozens of operas to New York and to the height of popularity for many years. Charles Hamm has called Italian operatic music "a powerful new strain [that] began flowing into the stream of popular song in America," leaving it "changed and enriched."[1] Hamm uses the word *popular* advisedly. In New York as elsewhere, Italian operatic music was not just for the bon ton but for everyone. Throughout the antebellum period, operatic melodies were heard on the Italian, English, burlesque, and concert stages, in the city's parlors, outdoors (performed by bands or organ grinders), and even (to the disgust of the conservative) in church. Arguments about opera's social setting aside, there was nothing "aristocratic" about the music.

The proliferation of opera was part of a larger trend. In Europe and North America, the nineteenth century was a great age of musical participation. In public, massed choruses, huge concert halls, and opera houses allowed people to hear or even help perform large, elaborate, and powerful compositions. In private, small groups gathered around pianos in parlors and salons for intimate renderings of musical miniatures. Whether this activity represented a net increase over that of previous centuries cannot be known. In any event, the nineteenth century did bring a new awareness of music coupled with a faith in its positive value. Music was an excellent choice as an ideological tool; it could be simultaneously a force for the good and "the thing to do."

As elsewhere, New Yorkers found value in music's emotional power, its ability to "speak to the heart, not to the head." Without need of intervening knowledge or reason, it could reach even those with limited education and have an immediate effect on all listeners. For reformers, music's ability to "speak to the heart" was the source of its value. A critic of the Garcias had declared that "these [musical] passions always destroy the harmony of the mind."[2] Others, however, put the idea that music lacked intellectual content in a positive light. Music need not inform the intellect if it could speak to "feeling." Thus it played a major part in American sentimentalized — or, as Ann Douglas calls it, "feminized" — culture. As Douglas argues, nineteenth-century Protestantism sought to bring multitudes to virtue by replacing theology with emotion.[3] In like manner, music, supposedly lacking an intellectual component equivalent to theology, could quite naturally achieve the same end.[4]

The unmediated quality of music was especially valued for its isolation from ordinary day-to-day activity and thinking. "There are moments when we are unfit for strict application," "Apollo" informed the readers of the *Ladies' Companion* in 1834, "when we are unfit for rational discourse." At such times, he recommended, music is the perfect palliative, "capable of producing emotions nearly approaching to the sublimity of moral and heroic actions." He also acknowledged its ability to give pleasure by calling it an "indulgence." Music was separated from the rational world, valued as therapeutic, and recommended for being simultaneously pleasant and helpful.[5]

But music was more than just a palliative; it could also affect its hearers' lives. Its connection with life was twofold, through memory and sentiment. Music could recall pleasant associations from the past — "a favorite tune of a departed friend or relation — an air that we first heard — perhaps, in the company of those we love, and who are absent, can never be heard without exciting those affections which purify the heart."[6] In this scenario, music is catalytic, evoking important memories that could replace interfering improper thoughts. The link among music, memory, and virtue was a common theme in sentimental fiction. In John Howard Payne's opera *Clari* (with music by Henry Bishop), the heroine has been lured away to the estate of a wealthy nobleman by the promise of marriage. One evening a play is performed in which the female protagonist's situation mirrors her own. The woman onstage evokes Clari's lost happiness by singing "Home, Sweet Home." Clari is overcome with emotion and immediately flees the noble household for her own village. In a similar example (a short story by Lydia Maria Child), an upright family man takes to drink, loses his job, and abuses his family. He is brought to his senses only when his young daughter sings him the favorite song he had often sung to her before losing his virtue. There are many other such stories, each illustrating the same relationship. One music magazine, the *American Musical Journal*, even based its whole reason for being on such associations. "Music is at present so entwined with our feelings," the editor wrote, "and so associated with objects on which the mind sets the highest value, as almost to be necessary to our existence."[7]

Music's effect on feelings depended on the key concept of sentiment. Sentiment included what is commonly derided as sentimental, but it was not limited to it. In 1835 *Webster's Dictionary* called sentiment "the sense, thought or opinion contained in words, but considered as distinct from them." In drama, sentiment was a emotional or affective quality created at a given point by the words.[8] In music, it was a specific meaning derived from the combination of musical affect and a text or reference of an explicit character. Sentiment conceptually linked words and notes, with words central to understanding. In 1834 a writer for *Knickerbocker* spelled out the value of words in creating musical sentiment:

> Sounds . . . produced [by singing] become the audible signs of real emotions, and on this principle, expression in music is based. It will readily be perceived, therefore, that some classes of general emotions may be thus expressed, but that particular passions and feelings — such, for instance, as love or hatred — cannot be expressed by sounds, without the aid of words. Poetry, therefore, is joined to music, to enlarge the sphere of its operations, by becoming its interpreter. On this account, vocal is superior to instrumental music. It has a wider range of application, and exerts a more direct influence upon sentiment and passion. It is only, however, when both are judiciously combined, that the full force and effect of musical sounds can be appreciated.[9]

Words, then, provided referents for music's "audible signs," allowing music to serve the same emotions found in verbal genres. The ability of words to interpret music was essential to music's task of influencing sentiment and enabled listeners to know what a piece or passage was "about." Although the writer did not so state, his argument favored English over Italian opera; for his purposes, words in a foreign language were hardly better than no words at all.

But music was not linked to all sentiments equally. As the *American*

Musical Journal's writer argued, music evoked *lofty* sentiments — "associated with objects on which the mind sets the highest value." Words acted as quality control, assuring a performer or listener that a piece was sufficiently elevated in character. A piece such as "Home, Sweet Home" could elicit thoughts considered pleasant and elevating, although its sounds alone could not. Despite the role of the words, however, musical style was an important aspect of sentiment. In "Home, Sweet Home," for example, the style does not overwhelm the words. The song has a clear melodic profile, straightforward harmony, and a subservient accompaniment, all of which link melody and words. Although the melody itself has no strongly affective character, neither does it detract from or contradict the text. Easy understanding was the key to sentiment, irony its antithesis.

This mechanism of association had operated in such English pieces from the teens as *The Devil's Bridge*. It continued to operate as musical style became more elaborate in the Italianate English operas of the 1830s. Music valued for lofty sentiment did not have to be bland in order to be understood. In fact, as the operas of Bellini and his British counterparts became known, objections to Italian musical complexity decreased. An elaborate or pathetic melody that intensified an elevated emotion could be appreciated for its esthetic quality and sentiment at the same time. The range of understandable musical styles was wide, and sentiment was not at odds with esthetic value. Listeners could enjoy beautiful music while allowing its sentiment to act as a moral purifier.

These beliefs about the sources of music's meaning and value affected the reception of Italian and English opera in New York. Italian opera was "culture," its tasteful music and polite social setting said to refine and civilize its audience. In English opera, on the other hand, words revealed the sentiment and allowed the music to serve goodness and virtue. Both sets of beliefs served the ideals of progress and social and moral reform. The new English operas of the 1830s took a form the general public could recognize, but with its "rational and refined" musical style intact. As the city's theaters assimilated the genre into their own tradition, its success increased. English opera at the Park Theatre and later at the National allowed New Yorkers to have their sentimental ideal, play on Italian opera's elegant social setting, and support a genre that could support itself.

The heyday of English opera in New York extended from the first performances at the Park Theatre in 1833 of Mary Ann and Joseph Wood, a well-known English soprano and tenor, to the mid-1840s. Published income records from before the Panic of 1837 show that with an average weekly income of over $3,000, the Park could easily pay its $18,000 annual rent and turn a profit. These same records show that the Woods drew as well as the stars of the legitimate drama.[10] English opera also supported the new National Theatre and helped keep the Park going after the panic. It even played at the Olympic, a tiny theater with no social pretentions and known for burlesque and spoofs of city life. In the late 1830s, observers called the public "opera mad."

The Park and the National brought in singers described in the press as first rate. Besides the Woods, the Park offered Elizabeth Austin (before the Woods), Maria Caradori-Allan, and Charles Horn, the latter composing for the theater as well as performing. The National offered Jane Shirreff, John Wilson, and Anne and Edward Seguin. Most of these singers are unknown today. But they were the stars of their time. They toured, their activities were reported in the press, they introduced pieces that received critical attention, and their names and faces graced sheet-music editions of their repertoire.

The repertoire itself was eclectic. It included, first, eighteenth-century comic operas that still drew an audience, for example, *Love in a Village, The Waterman* (the New York premiere was in 1793), *The Quaker* (1794), and *The Duenna* (1787); second, English melodramatic operas from the teens and 1820s, such as *The Devil's Bridge* and Bishop's *Clari* (1823); third, new English operas from continental originals such as Rophino Lacy's *Cinderella* (1831, after Rossini's *La Cenerentola*), his *Maid of Judah* (1832, a Rossini pastiche on Scott's *Ivanhoe*), and Bellini's *La sonnambula* (1835); and, fourth, operas in Italian style by British composers, for example, Michael William Balfe's *The Bohemian Girl* (1844) and William Michael Rooke's *Amilie* (1838).

"Englished" opera (the third category) was the most successful type. These adaptations, many by Henry Bishop, had played in New York since the teens. Among the most popular early examples were *The Libertine* (1817, after *Don Giovanni*), *The Barber of Seville* (1819), and *The Marriage of Figaro* (1823). Adaptation "for the English stage" consisted of deleting some of the music, substituting spoken dialogue for recitative, translating the texts into English, and sometimes inserting ballads, glees, or dance music. Although Bishop's *Barber of Seville* included some of Rossini's elaborate ensembles, in general the early adaptations were stripped-down versions of the originals.[11] By the 1830s, however, this was becoming less the case. Librettos from productions of this period show music directors treating the English arrangements as loosely as the arrangers had treated the originals. With scores more readily available, it was possible to restore music Bishop or another arranger had omitted. Englished opera, along with newly composed operas by British composers, was beginning to resemble its Italian counterpart in musical structure and style.[12]

The new operas served the ideal of edification through musical sentiment. While the plots of the earlier English pieces had often dealt with conflicts between good and evil men, the operas of the 1830s often featured female protagonists being tested for purity, virtue, and innocence. For example, Mary Ann Wood sang title roles in *Cinderella, La sonnambula, Clari, The Maid of Judah, The Mountain Sylph,* and *The Jewess,* the oldest of which (*Clari*) dated only from 1823. With narrative emphasis shifted toward women as a force for the good, a female singer could counter her link with the evils of the stage. Able to confirm a theater piece's moral value by communicating "appropriate thoughts in appropriate dress," she could implicitly answer objections to the theater through a convincing performance of suitable repertoire.[13] Operas such as *Cinderella, La sonnambula,* and *Amilie* all feature leading female characters in serious situations. If they include comic action (*Cinderella* is largely comic), the heroine takes no part in it, but remains above, dignified, idealized, and sentimental. Each of these operas was introduced by a popular prima donna; all three became the singers' signature-pieces.[14] Enjoyable as they were, all three were also eminently respectable: Opera, presented in high-quality performances by singers in didactic roles, gave New Yorkers new ways to understand and value it, along with a new avenue into the Italian style.

This change in focus, together with the Italian style's wider expressive range, allowed all opera characters to sing. In fact, music's growing role in English opera slowly forced characters to sing. The musical style of the teens had not been varied enough to allow characters like Baron Toraldi of *The Devil's Bridge* to express their villainy. The new pieces solved the problem through their plots: They needed no singing Toraldis or Iagos because evil, rather than being personified, appeared instead as error or the absence of positive good. Villains were replaced by a variety of singing men, each given his own musical style. Guy Mannering, for example, a nonsinging title character in Henry Bishop's opera after Walter Scott, has several successors—Alidoro in *Cinderella,* the counts in *La sonnambula* and *Amilie,* and Auber's Fra Diavolo. These roles are all mature, attractive men who are foils for juvenile leads. But unlike Guy, the later roles required singers. Had Guy been created in the 1830s instead of the teens, he would probably have been a baritone.

Despite music's increased role, however, English opera of the 1830s still put theater first. These pieces were not "in music" throughout; therefore, they depended on their spoken portions for dramatic structure and meaning. Because they were performed in English, New Yorkers could grasp that meaning without filtering it through a foreign language. More important, the music, no matter how elaborate, nearly always supported an opera's textual meaning. Rather than follow its own agenda, thereby undermining or critiquing the words, the music reliably heightened the libretto's effect. Taken together, the emotional, high-toned, didactic librettos set to attractive music fitting their sentiments produced a genre that met the standard for the well-regulated theater: "a school of morality, literary taste and instruction, blended with innocent amusement."[15]

At a time when any musical production on the New York stage had a good chance of success, two pieces stand out as the most spectacular, and in one case long-lasting, hits. *La sonnambula* came from Italy via London and was still in the city's English opera repertoire as late as the 1870s. In 1838 *Amilie* repeated its Covent Garden success in New York, but after the return to England of its star, Jane Shirreff, the opera was only occasionally produced (its last New York performance was in 1853).[16] The stories of both operas focus on the theme of feminine virtue rewarded. Both use either Italian or Italianate music to link emotional and esthetic enjoyment with a moral ideal and communicate that link to a diverse audience. Both featured a performer said to personify the ideal herself. Finally, the success of both shows how compelling the combined power of music, emotion, and belief could be.

Both new operas put their female protagonists into dire straits as they face threats to either their reputations or virtue. Thus both make use of the dramatic scena and aria for soprano. As a "true woman" feels, she will show her audience the range of her emotion in a desperate situation.[17] The scena-aria combination increasingly filled a dramatic need, the free, text-based structure of the scena showing the character's thought process, and the tighter musical form of the aria allowing her to vent powerful emotion. In adapting Rossini's *Il barbiere di Siviglia* for performance in English, for example, Henry Bishop added a scena and aria for Rosina's (mistaken) discovery that Almaviva was not an honest lover.[18] Bishop's Rosina is not a totally comic character, but one who uses a "serious" form, along with virtuosity, to communicate her distress. *Amilie* and *La sonnambula* go farther in the new direction. Both title characters stand at the center of smaller casts than in earlier operas. In both, a young woman earns the man of her choice by proving her moral worth. In both, her music confirms to the other characters and the audience the depth of her conviction. In these operas, the scena-aria asserts the moral acceptability of the main character and the power of music to argue her case.

Amilie, for example, offers a variant on the classic moral lesson, its subtitle, *The Love Test,* making the point for the slow-witted. Amilie is a peasant villager. Her fiancé, Anderl, has gone to war, and she does not know when he will return. Meanwhile, she is being courted by a young hunter, José. Unknown to her, however, a distinguished count visiting her village is Anderl's father. He had been displeased with his son's choice of a wife. But he had agreed to approve the marriage if Anderl refrained from communicating with Amilie for a year and she remained loyal to him. This task is the love test. The count has now come to find out whether she has passed.

That Amilie will be successful is apparent early in the opera, where she sings a scena and aria ("Oh Love, Thou'rt Absent" and "O Love, Thou'rt Near Me") addressed, in her imagination, to Anderl. The scena and aria communicate her complex emotional state, in which she overcomes ambivalence with determination, spirit, and plain good cheer. The two pieces are emotionally and psychologically contrasting. The scena shows Amilie's struggle to deal with her pain at Anderl's absence, while the aria shows her keeping her spirits up even in the face of the unknown. The musical settings enhance the contrast between the two sentiments, allowing Amilie to communicate her strength of character.

In the scena (ex. 6), Amilie tells the imagined Anderl how music reminds her of him. Although the words evoke the sentimental link

Example 6. Rooke, "Oh Love, Thou'rt Absent" (*Amilie*), London: Duff and Hodgson, n.d.

between music and memory, the setting reveals her as ambivalent and troubled. The piece begins with a standard opening dramatic gesture — three chords in the orchestra (m. 1) that announce the key (C♯ minor) and the dynamic level (soft). Amilie echoes the mood and the musical substance of the orchestra. She states her problem, "Oh love, thour't absent," by spelling out the orchestra's chord a cappella (mm. 1–2). But immediately she shifts perspective — "Yet thou'rt near" (mm. 2–3). Her melodic gesture reverses the first as well. Where she had previously sung a broken chord, here she sings a scale that ascends to a second set of chords, this time in the more "relaxed" key of B major, in the orchestra. By undoing in the second gesture what has been done in the first, the first phrase of the scena shows Amilie expressing uncertainty, distress, and hope.

The scena continues in the same vein. Amilie's second phrase ("For the song you lov'd comes on mine ear," mm. 3–7) consists mainly of a repeated B, the repetitions creating tension over the orchestra's harmonic progression. As the tension is released at the resolution (m. 6, downbeat), Amilie seems to relax as well. The orchestra cuts back to two chords, allowing her room for a wide-ranging melody that leads to the final cadence of the phrase (mm. 6–7). As before, Amilie's second gesture has reversed the first. But where in the first phrase she had contradicted herself verbally and musically, here she sings the same words twice. The music does the contradicting alone. Her repetitive melody at the beginning of the phrase had created tension between what she said and what she sang, but her cadential melody unites the two. Where the tension had evoked questioning, its release evokes confidence. The confidence is inspired by the link between music and memory; as she sings about "the song you lov'd," Amilie reasserts and holds onto her faith in Anderl.

But the faith is still shaky; in the third phrase (mm. 7–15), Amilie reverses herself yet again. Longer and more dissonant than the second, its basic structure is the same. Amilie sings a melody of only two notes while the orchestra creates harmonic tension below. Again she breaks the tension and leads the phrase melodically to a tonic cadence, this one in C major (mm. 11–13). In tonal terms, however, C major is the wrong key; as her text says, it is literally "far away." Because the first two phrases have ended in B major, C major cannot produce the stable resolution needed to end the phrase. Instead, the C triad acquires a B♭, and the phrase winds down into a half cadence

Example 7. Rooke, "Oh! Love, Thou'rt Near Me," opening (*Amilie*)

on B as Amilie repeats, this time plaintively, "Thou'rt far away" (mm. 13–15). This third phrase, the longest of the scena, is open-ended; Amilie has not resolved the distress of her situation. The word painting of "far" (m. 14) on the highest note of the scena, coupled with a slow cadential descent to the end, suggests that the music she imagines has been unable to banish the pain of Anderl's absence.

There is a musical resolution for the open-endedness, however, in the energetic and buoyant aria that follows the scena (ex. 7). The scena had finished on B major as dominant; the aria resolves it conventionally to a tonic on E. Here Amilie the virtuoso takes over; all of her effort and energy are poured into banishing the thought that Anderl is gone. "Oh! Love, Thou'rt Near Me" takes a full ABA form to triumph over the effect of the scena. The aria uses agility, stamina, breath control, and a two-octave range, as Amilie repeats over and over the text "oh love, thou'rt near me, near me still, / tho' waves divide, tho' dangers part." The melody of this text is disjunct throughout, each subphrase (i.e., each measure) spanning an octave or more. The melodic disjunction expresses the two lines of text in different ways. It literally paints the second line: As Amilie sings "tho' waves divide, tho' dangers part" again and again, the melody rises and falls with wavelike motion, dividing the vocal line into one-measure fragments (mm. 9–17). This rising, falling, and fragmentation may seem to undermine the impact of the first line. If wavelike motion expresses division, how can it also show togetherness? In a literal sense, it cannot. Instead, each subphrase ends on its highest note, as Amilie sings, "Oh! Love, thou'rt near *me*, near me *still*" (mm. 9–10, 13–14).

The aria is straightforward and convincing. Compared with the scena, its musical language is simple and unvarying. Its level of harmonic tension is low, giving no hint of a thought process. The orchestra remains in the background, providing a rhythmic and harmonic underpinning for the vocal line but little more. Moreover, the music is relentlessly cheerful. As hard as the singer may have to work, the aria is unabashed, uncomplicated, and naive, all qualities hard to destroy. The required vocal energy pushes Amilie beyond cheer toward triumph, letting the audience know that her faith will carry her through. This knowledge holds the listener in good stead in act 2, when she is given a forged letter telling her falsely that Anderl is married. Indeed, it is hard to imagine a singer performing this aria in act 1 and not ending the opera triumphant.

"Oh Love, Thou'rt Near Me" is "singer's music," composed to show off its performer's vocal talent. Like Rossini's "Una voce poco fa," it highlights its singer's character and personality. Like Rosina, Amilie is young and energetic, and her music is virtuosic. But Rosina sings of laying traps to get her man, using music to play the coquette. Amilie, on the other hand, uses virtuosity as a statement of faith. Incapable of coquetry or any other artifice, she commands a sincerity that allows her to pass the love test. This sincerity is most tellingly displayed in the contrast between the scena and the aria. By letting her audience hear her mixed feelings, Amilie comes across as emotionally more substantial than Rosina. Although the earlier character shows more than one level of thought (in "Una voce poco fa"), her point of departure — coquettish determination — never deserts her. Amilie's loyalty almost does; she has to work mightily to overcome the urge to give herself over to despair. Her struggle, to which the scena-aria format lends itself, completes her triumph and makes her emotion more convincing. She idealizes the feminine stereotype, acknowledges the difficulties in achieving it, and communicates its value and the rewards awaiting a successful struggle.

Amilie's aria hints at a newly developing type of musical-dramatic expression in opera, but one still dependent in New York on performance in English. In *Otello*, audiences had heard a beautiful score whose style could seem to overwhelm the drama. Here, on the other hand, they heard an operatic scene begin (ever so slightly) to pull music away from dependence on words for its meaning. Amilie gave her audiences a character whose musical ability was properly focused on moral didacticism. Her emotional struggle and triumph established her as a woman "true to nature" and fit for the stage. But in the scena she also gave them more than they bargained for — a hint of music meaning something beyond reflecting the words it set. Amilie couched that hint in a performance of virtuosity and consonant musical and dramatic elements. Then she presented it to a public listening for joy and truth. From here, one can imagine acceptance of truth offered by sound alone, leaving verbal layers of meaning behind.

Thus the way was opened for musical sound to be understood as imparting the ultimate truth about a drama and its characters. As music could place characters socially even when they were disguised, so a more emotionally explicit style could tell emotional truths in spite of surface appearances. Hence the growth of fine-tuned librettos that included mad scenes for prima-donna characters. The mad scene was (and is) the ultimate emotional license. And, of course, it is a musical license as well, allowing a composer to push syntax close to the line that separates music from incoherent sound.[19] Madness had many advantages for the creators of female roles. Given stereotypes of women as emotional beings, it was an acceptable response for a female character under duress. It took advantage of music's unmediated quality, allowing for virtuosic flights of fancy that would have risked being derided in male characters. In showing a woman emotionally out of control, it allowed her audience to experience her essential irrationality; she could do more than tell you she was mad, she could make you feel it.

She could make the other characters feel it as well. *Amilie* and *La sonnambula* include mad scenes of sorts, and the title character's emotional extremes are central to the plot in both operas. Also central is a more complex interaction between words and music than the alternation between spoken dialogue and song traditional in the older English works. The case of Amina in *La sonnambula* is the more striking example. As the music follows the course of her madness, its sound, along with stage action, communicates the opera's didactic point.

La sonnambula was New York's sentimental hit of the decade. Direct in story and musical style, from its premiere in 1835 it allowed New Yorkers to imagine a world in which an innocent and guileless country virgin could prove the value of virtue and the joy that comes as it reaps its reward. *La sonnambula* was — or was represented to be — "true to nature." This truth was based on ease of understanding. Like Bellini's other operas, *La sonnambula* is simpler in style than Rossini's works, a difference originating in their librettos.[20] Rossini's are longer. They include more conversation, thus more recitative. *Il barbiere di Siviglia, Cenerentola,* and *Otello* are complex stories with verbal exchanges needed for plot development. Even *Cenerentola,* whose narrative thrust is a straightforward girl-gets-boy, establishes familial relationships and distinctions between true and false identities. In *La sonnambula,* on the other hand, the plot's action is exactly that — action. The key events are performed in pantomime: Amina is seen sleepwalking in a stranger's bedroom, which enrages her jealous fiancé. At the end of the opera, she is again seen sleepwalking, dreaming of the fiancé, which vindicates her. This simplicity adapted more easily in translation, was more immediately accessible than dialogue-oriented dramas and allowed the composer to give more attention to setting text in arias and ensembles than in recitative.

Bellini's musical style is likewise simpler than Rossini's. It may even be called more "popular," if such a statement is understood as nonjudgmental. In the 1830s Italian opera was beginning to offer New Yorkers music in a new lyric style that allowed a whole series of musical-dramatic conventions to come into focus. With its bel canto style, emotional clarity, and moral didacticism, *La sonnambula* epitomized the idea of music as a civilizing force.

The story of the opera takes place in an idealized Swiss peasant village. Amina is a villager, naive and guileless like her neighbors. She is about to be married to a young farmer, Elvino. Amid the preparatory celebrations, a lone, unnamed rider arrives. He is attracted to Amina. She is flattered by his attention, and Elvino is jealous. The party soon ends, however, as Teresa (Amina's mother) warns everyone about the frightening night-wandering phantom. The visitor scoffs at the idea but soon realizes his mistake when the "phantom" appears outside the french doors of his hotel room. Unlike the villagers, he recognizes Amina, who is sleepwalking.

By this time, word has circulated that the visitor is the count of the nearby castle, returned after many years. The villagers come to his room to greet him, but instead find Amina alone, asleep on his bed. They are aghast, and Elvino is enraged. He rejects Amina, who awakes, not knowing why he has done so or how she has come to the count's room. The villagers are less quick to condemn. The next day, they ask the count about Amina's presence in his room. He tries to explain about somnambulism, but they have never heard of it and refuse to believe him. Then Teresa cautions them: Quiet, please. After such a trauma, Amina has finally managed to sleep. And asleep she appears, a somnambulist. The villagers watch in horror as she steps across a rickety bridge over the mill stream rapids. It creaks, but she manages to reach the other side safely. Then, still asleep, she sings poignantly of her love for Elvino and her distress at his rejection. Elvino realizes that his jealousy is misplaced; Amina is as innocent as she and the count have asserted. He replaces the ring he had removed from her finger the night before and wakes her. Again, Amina does not know why she is back in his favor. But no matter. Under the eye of the wise count, the celebrations begin again.

La sonnambula appeals to a sense of justice while tugging at the heartstrings. Not only is Amina innocent and virtuous, but through most of the opera she also stands falsely accused of sexual impropriety. An audience probably shocked at finding a young woman in the bed of a noble stranger must endure the additional tension that the incorrect interpretation creates. But like Elvino, the opera's plot refuses to give Amina the benefit of the doubt. Although she is falsely accused, she is left responsible for her own defense. Thus she undergoes a trial by fire, establishing her innocence by negotiating the dangerous bridge while asleep. One is expected to hope for her success and release from physical danger, but one is not expected to see Elvino's attitude as unreasonable. Amina's adherence to the sexual code could be questioned at any time, regardless of her companions' prior knowledge of and respect for her.

Moreover, crossing the bridge is not enough. Amina's real test is to convince the others of her honesty and virtue as she responds to a series of events and attitudes over which she has no control. The linchpin of her success occurs at the end of the opera, after she has crossed the bridge. Figuratively, if not literally, a mad scene, this scena and aria (the scena excerpted in ex. 8 in a translation used by Jane Shirreff in the late 1830s) show the "true" Amina, one unfettered by rational consciousness, control, or artifice. As much as the bridge crossing, her music tests whether her protestations of innocence should be believed. Even unconscious, she must seem incapable of feint and modest, even as she puts herself on display. There is no room for even a hint of the confidence man or of virtuosity for its own sake.

The scene begins with a slow introduction in the orchestra as Amina proceeds from the bridge to center stage (ex. 8a). She has the attention of Elvino, the count, the village, and the audience. The introduction sets the stage for her revelation. Utterly simple, it begins with a two-measure disjunct melody of only four notes accompanied by tonic and dominant harmonies over a tonic pedal. The phrase is repeated three times, finally ending on a long tonic in F major followed by a pause as we wait to hear the truth. Amina begins the scena in the same spirit as the introduction, low in her range, with short, largely unaccompanied phrases. She proceeds in a stream-of-consciousness manner, speaking each line as she thinks it. As she relives the past in her dream, we relive it as well, taking the same emotional journey and,

Example 8a. Bellini, *La sonnambula,* act 3, scene 2 (finale)

like her assembled friends and family, understanding the situation from her perspective.

The key to that understanding is musical memory. Three times in the scena, the orchestra brings to Amina's mind a fragment of music that reminds her and the audience of a prior situation (ex. 8b). The first recalls her previous sleepwalk, in which she dreamed of arriving at church to marry Elvino. Here, however, she overlays the sprightly melody from the past with a plaintive counterpoint in the present (mm. 2–9). Finally, the melody breaks off (on the dominant) as Amina reverts to recitative to assert her innocence (mm. 9–11). She finishes on C, and Elvino and the villagers echo with their comment in a mournful C minor (m. 12). So far, Amina has been convincing.

The next two evocations of the past follow quickly (ex. 8c). The first takes Amina back to Elvino's gift of an engagement ring (mm. 1–2). The melody is Elvino's as he offers her the ring, and again it breaks off as Amina remembers (in recitative) that he has taken it back (mm. 2–7). But here she shows that she still loves him; as she evokes his "dear image," she brings on the last musical evocation from the past (mm. 7–11). This fragment comes from a love duet in which she, not El-

women. In part, opera's long-term success depended on this second perspective becoming the mainstream. The process would take time, for the charge of elitism from the other side was vigorous and long-sustained. Throughout the century, iconoclastic, hostile critics continued to write off enthusiastic responses to opera as ignorant and socially motivated. But they could not row against a prevailing tide that eventually replaced widespread puzzlement with understanding and enjoyment.

The tide began to turn early. Although commentators disagreed on whether Italian opera was an asset to their city, they all agreed on one aspect of it: Everyone adored "the Signorina," seventeen-year-old Maria Garcia. The first female product of the theatrical star system, this "admirable creature" whose voice worked "witching wonders" was not only a star among stars but also one of an entirely new sort.[56] Never had a teenaged girl appeared in New York and enchanted her audience with so much talent. Never had youth, innocence, and skill gone so far to help legitimate the stage for a new public. If opera's respectability was not questioned seriously, if it managed to expand the theater's clientele even slightly, Maria Garcia was due credit. As long as she performed in New York, opera stood a chance of acceptance.

Garcia's later career (under the name Maria Malibran) suggests that New York writers were justified in the effusive praise they lavished on her. One suspects that praise for the other singers in the company was conditioned in part by writers' inexperience with opera and their interest in showing how it had met the public's expectations. Praise for the Signorina, on the other hand, never reads as if the writer were putting the best face on an uneven situation. The accolades heaped on her were as "refined" as the opera itself. She was praised for good taste, dignity of deportment, lack of exaggeration, charm, simplicity, ease, and grace.[57] Her acting showed "a remarkable chasteness and propriety, never violating good taste nor exceeding the bounds of female decorum."[58] At the same time (this from the writer who called opera a "forced and unnatural bantling"), "with great science and execution, she is modest and unostentatious, . . . delicate and unassuming."[59]

Commentary on Garcia blended personal traits with remarks on her singing and acting. This interest in the Signorina herself was new in theatrical reporting; Garcia was the first woman of the stage presented to the public as respectable. She was even held up as a model

Example 8b. Bellini, *La sonnambula,* act 3, scene 2 (Amina)

Example 8c. Bellini, *La sonnambula*, act 3, scene 2 (Amina)

vino, had sung the first verse. And at last she allows a melody from the past to complete itself on the tonic. She waits, then, breaking the line with breath, swears fidelity to Elvino (mm. 12–14).

The contrast between the tantalizing bits of orchestral melody from Amina's past and the thin, sad lines of her present is striking. The orchestra brings back her happier times and visions. It also brings us old texts and their associated emotions — as a listener in the 1830s would say, old sentiments. At the same time, the scena's broken structure ties listeners to each present moment. It exposes a mental state unadorned by the artifice and momentum of a set musical structure and helps convince Amina's listeners of her sincerity.

But the first of the three evocations brings rather more. The text inserted between the treble and the bass of the grand staff in examples 8b and c, which gives the words as sung in their original places in the opera, shows that most of the melody in the first flashback was originally instrumental. The only verbal line attached to it is the count's statement of belief in Amina's innocence (ex. 8b, mm. 7–9). Although in the earlier scene Amina had sung a brief counterpoint as she does in the bridge scene, the affective and persuasive burden, which had originally convinced the count, had been carried by the orchestra. The point is hardly noticeable to a modern listener. In the English theater, however, where a drama's message was traditionally carried by the words, and in which music was often ornamental or even irrelevant, the passage would have been significant for its dependence on almost purely musical communication. As Amina has said, "The soft confession you can *feel* in every *tone*" (ex. 8c, andante, emphasis added).

This musical independence comes precisely when Amina's future hinges on being believed. Asleep, she can only tell the profoundest truth. The dramatic situation produces an inherently irrational moment; by analogy, her music can only do the same. Had she been awake and for some reason tried to lie, the music would have found her out. New Yorkers, of course, had no way of knowing this, and the rhetoric of the day still linked music's elevated sentiment to a text. But in treasuring a piece like *La sonnambula,* in which music all but saves a character's life, they edged slowly toward accepting pieces in which musical truth was the only truth they needed to acknowledge.

The recitative is followed by an aria, "Yes, for Thee Time's Sad Power" ("Ah, non credea"), in which Amina, still asleep, convinces Elvino of her honesty and inspires him to return his ring. Her full vocal strength, however, she saves for the end of the opera, when the villagers have finally awakened her and she realizes that she is back in Elvino's favor. Here Amina the virtuoso emerges. Although she has sung florid passages before, only in "Ah! Don't Mingle" ("Ah, non giunge," ex. 9) does she do so at a brisk tempo, with the orchestral accompaniment in energetic eighths rather than the more usual, sedate quarter notes. It is as if her entire musical persona doubles time as she kicks up her heels with joy at the realization that Elvino is hers again. The juxtaposition of the most poignant and the most jubilant moments in the opera gives the latter a boost of energy as Amina finally shows the audience what she can do.

Given the story, and given this final musical juxtaposition in which she has convinced everyone of her innocence, Amina's virtuosity is hardly empty rhetoric. In linking music and virtue, the scena and aria confirm in a joyous, emotionally satisfying way that this wonderful singer deserves the reward she is so happy to have. They also point to music's role in Amina's self-defense. Asleep, Amina is as out of control as a madwoman. She has the license to show as much anger, bitterness, or hysteria as exists in her deepest unconscious. But she shows none; if anything, her music when she is unconscious is more restrained than the final aria rather than less. As in the rest of the piece, the music and the story reinforce each other in offering what a contemporary writer called music's "highest purpose," to provide "appropriate thoughts in appropriate dress." That accomplished, the opera could offer "participation in joy" without reservation.[21]

Response to *La sonnambula* in New York shows that it made its point immediately. Amina's emotional roller coaster inspired the same in her audience: "When Amina invites us to weep, we know not how to refrain from weeping, or from sharing the anguish of her innocent soul in the pitiful bewilderment of her dreams; nor can we repress our tears of joy upon her sudden awaking from despair to happiness."[22] Amina's triumph had its lessons as well. Not simply a personal conflict, her plight was linked to a moral tone that added righteous satisfaction to the joy her success inspired. The music's style was a key factor in communicating the opera's message. The self-consciously popular idiom of *The Beggar's Opera* would not do, nor would Rossini's dignified style found in "Di tanti palpiti" or his virtuosic but comic idiom of "Una voce poco fa." Rather, it took a style that could be called *holy* and *divine,* along with Amina's innocence, transparent

Example 9. Bellini, "Ah! Don't Mingle," opening ("Ah, non giunge," *La sonnambula*)

emotion, and carefully directed virtuosity, to cajol her audience into finding joy in a more upright life. As one reviewer put it, "We should think the heart of that man as hard as 'the nether mill-stone,' who, after having listened to 'La Sonnambula,' could pass his enemy without proffering the friendly grasp; or who, till the world had again worn away the soft impression, could entertain any sentiment less holy than one of universal kindness and good-will. The soul which is filled with music so divine can breathe only harmonious thoughts."[23]

The didactic purpose of *Amilie* and *La sonnambula* is by now obvious, as it was in the 1830s. The operas confirmed a link between music and a respectable but profound theatrical genre. They played out the Platonic notion that music's power could and should be a force for the good. They taught New Yorkers a new musical style, enabling them to enjoy a broad new repertoire in which elaborate musical structures were no longer reduced to simple ballad forms but could be understood on their own terms. They idealized music, the emotions it could elicit, and the moral lesson it could be used to teach. No longer ornamentation of the spoken text, music was becoming central to an opera's message. Extreme dramatic situations provoking overwhelming emotion lent themselves to musical, rather than verbal, display. In this way, the settings hinted at a new independence of music from text. By meaning more than its text, and in Amilie's scena meaning slightly other than its text, the music of these operas fosters essentially musical communication, even in a verbally based genre. By requiring its audience to integrate music into an opera's message, they tipped the balance of power between words and music in music's favor.

Of course, the Garcias' repertoire had done this as well. But their performances had made audiences aware of the differences between English and Italian opera — the foreign language, the domination by music, the attention paid to the social setting, and the expense. Here some of the former problems no longer existed. The musical idiom had become better known, the performances were in English, the social setting was familiar and becoming more acceptable to middle-class, sexually mixed audiences, and the prices of admission were reasonable. Moreover, the stories were exemplary in their idealization of feminine virtue — at this point the path to an emerging, respectable theater. No longer criticized for meaningless "scientific" virtuosity unsuitable for a popular audience, music was becoming not only acceptable but also central to opera's perceived attraction and worth. Emotion and beauty served moral value. Although New Yorkers had not yet resolved the issue of musical value independent of a moral message, they did not yet need to do so, for such operas as *La sonnambula* and *Amilie* served both at the same time.

With such heavy didacticism in the plots, it may seem excessive to expect the singers to serve moral value as well. But like Maria Garcia, opera stars of the 1830s were scrutinized as performers and people of the stage. The most successful in this regard was the English singer Jane Shirreff, who introduced *Amilie* to New York and sang Amina as well. With her colleagues Edward and Anne Seguin and John Wilson, she dominated the city's opera scene from December of 1838 through May of 1840.[24] Shirreff was New York's foremost performer of sentimental opera and the singer who best personified the idealized women being portrayed. Presenting virtue in a respectable but entertaining form, she helped establish the theater as an appropriate performance genre for women as well as men. Her reception marked a high point in the link among music, beauty, and virtue in opera and between respectability and popular appeal.

By the time Shirreff first appeared in New York as Amina in 1838, the role had already been interpreted in the city by two highly regarded sopranos, Mary Ann Wood and Maria Caradori-Allan. With the role well known, Shirreff's reviewers focused most often on her character portrayal. Describing the scene in *La sonnambula* where Elvino forcibly removes his ring from Amina's finger, one praised her "impassioned expression and truth to nature, exhibiting a delineation of frantic despair seldom seen in the most accomplished tragic actress."[25] Commenting on the same scene, another compared her favorably to Mary Ann Wood, criticizing "the violence of [Wood's] tones and gestures . . . making the performance more like the exhibition of a Bedlamite, than of one overwhelmed with grief and dismay." Shirreff, on the other hand, deserved praise for her "discretion, never overstepping the modesty of nature, or losing sight of the feminine delicacy which gives such graceful effect to the performance."[26] Wood may have been a wonderful singer, but Shirreff, through her modesty and feminine delicacy, was truer to the expected convention.

Occasionally, Shirreff was also faulted on the same terms: "In some parts of Amina . . . we are inclined to say MISS SHIRREFF does not fully realize the character. In the first act is there not a little too much cause given for Elvino's jealousy? In the conclusion of the second act, is not the struggle to detain her lover a little too robust? . . . Is it therefore proper for Amina to catch at every expression of [Elvino's] tenderness as if there was hope that all would yet be well?"[27] The writer knew the piece well, knew what he wanted to see and hear, and sustained his case in detail. Paradoxically, Shirreff did not fully realize the role by overplaying it; the writer found more individuality and strength of character than he wanted. Perhaps the objection was essentially that she paid too much attention to detail at the expense of the whole. But the writer also seemed to want a blander, more delicate Amina—one more dependent on Elvino's love, less capable of an effort to keep him, and, most of all, less likely to give the count a reason for his interest. In showing herself attractive to a man at first glance, Shirreff's Amina hinted at a sexuality and a self-worth independent of Elvino's judgment. The writer blamed Shirreff for not quite proving Amina innocent of impropriety.

This point of view was not common. More typically, another reviewer (of *Amilie*) described the "female character" Shirreff depicted and praised her for personifying it. In doing so, he named a whole series of characteristics he believed personified womanhood:

> Miss Shirreff is, beyond all comparison, in our humble opinion, the most chaste and accurate in her conceptions of the elevated and enobling traits of the female character, and the happiest delineation of them in any lady whose performances we ever witnessed. There is a delightful purity and naivette in her acting wholly unalloyed by rant or effort for *points,* which commends her to the praise of the judicious and the discriminating. The modesty of her audience is never outraged, nor their patience with levity taxed by exhibitions of coarse demeanor or sentiment, and even the indelicacy of the author is not infrequently rebuked by her concealment or rejection of passages obnoxious to such an objection.[28]

Shirreff was seen to present a convention rather than an individual. She accurately showed the "elevated and enobling traits of the female character" and, more important, made no attempt to focus the audience's attention on herself. As clever as she undoubtedly was, Shirreff's job was to make her artless young women seem real and avoid suggesting that purity and naiveté could be feigned. The specialist in artifice must suggest that artifice does not exist.

Shirreff also needed to convey a congruence between her nature and her roles. By seeming to play herself, she received much of the credit for the innocence of her characters. As long as the roles were interpreted in terms of a feminine ideal, and as long as the actress was seen as the character herself, writers' willingness to credit the actress for proper portrayal was essential to her success. Playing an ideal meant making it seem inevitable. Cleverness and artifice, although necessary, must be hidden, for they would dispel the myth that Shirreff's characterizations were anything but truth.

Any perceived discrepancy between Shirreff's roles and her life would do the same thing. If the stage was to represent an idealized "truth to nature," only proper women belonged on it. Praise of Shirreff's character and deportment began early, with a report of a shipboard toast to "a lady who sustains amidst the points of a trying profession, the dignity of her sex and the modesty and grace of those virtues which belong to woman in the most secluded and guarded of those stations to which she may be called in the very recesses of private life." As in the quotation on the female character, the speaker referred to *woman*—the abstraction to which Shirreff was seen as adhering despite her chosen profession. More remarkable, however, is the reference to women as bearer of sexual responsibility, as keeper of "those virtues which belong to woman" even situations that in public would only be mentioned euphemistically. Amina and Amilie were held responsible for seemingly compromising situations; one finds in neither the librettos nor the criticism of the two operas any hint that the Count's charm or José's persistence might excuse them. By contrast, Shirreff's admirer at least admitted that keeping womanly virtue might be difficult "amidst the points of a trying profession."

He spoke on other issues as well, notably making a metaphor between music and virtue by speaking of "the melody of a voice which seems entirely in tune with the graceful harmony of her virtues." Finally, he predicted Shirreff's American reception in glowing terms: "Is it not therefore the office at once of both hospitality and chivalry to assure her of her warm, respectful and friendly reception that awaits her in a country where it is the sacred sentiment of manhood that a woman, and a stranger, shall never want a champion, protector and friend."[29] Although the text of this toast may have been apocryphal, its sentiment rang true. Its placement in a newspaper on the day of Jane Shirreff's debut assured the public that she merited acceptance for the correct reasons and appealed to Americans' sense of fairness in giving her the reception she deserved. For men, this last idea placed attending Shirreff's performances in the framework of the myth — or, as the writer said, the "sacred sentiment" — that, among other things, women needed men's protection. By buying a ticket, a man could become her personal "champion, protector and friend." Moreover, the report as a whole let men and women know that Shirreff could be trusted to validate the female character on the stage, essential to her respectability as a woman on public display.

Through the texts provided for Amilie and Amina, Shirreff appeared to personify the characters she played. She managed this "truth to nature" and to the "female character" as a musician as well. Just as a Tyrolean peasant girl might, Jane Shirreff the singer delighted her listeners. But she neither awed nor astonished them. One listener wrote, "With a clear *soprano* voice managed with skill — delightful, yet not startling — pleasing, yet not great, she became instantly the favourite of the whole house, and we are much mistaken if in other pieces less difficult of execution, and yet more melodious — in simple ballads, she will not make a more powerful impression."[30] "Her voice," wrote another, "yields to that of Mrs. Wood's in power, . . . nor does it compare with Caradori's in clear, flute-like roundness of tone." But she made up for these deficiencies with sincerity, "every word she speaks, or note she utters, coming directly from the heart."[31] A favorite in part for not being great, Shirreff was considered best in music her audience could understand and sing. Even in competition with virtuosity, her genuineness was valued. It "appeals to the best feelings of the listener with eloquence quite irresistible, and cheats him of that applause which he is wont to bestow only upon the most elaborate display of scientific skill."[32]

Like Maria Garcia before her, Jane Shirreff presented roles interpreted in terms of a feminine ideal. She also showed how much the ideal had changed since 1825. Where Garcia's Rosina could be remarked upon for cunning and guile, for humor and an acceptably feminine intelligence, Amilie and Amina were valued primarily for their virtue. Charm was no longer a major source of attraction, nor was virtuosity (itself a form of cunning) especially important. Cinderella, played by Garcia but not Shirreff, played a transitional role, introducing the noncomic, sentimental heroine but retaining a degree of virtuosity that Shirreff did not reach. Yet ironically perhaps,

Amilie and Amina were more dependent on music for their success than Rosina (or Cinderella or Zerlina) had been. With the comic element (with its potential for multileveled stories) eliminated from the roles, these newer characters conveyed instead a series of individual emotions, each based on a musical affect. Shirreff's women used music in a direct and spontaneous emotional response to events impinging on their lives, a response that showed propriety as their most active and distinctive trait.

Shirreff caused a furor in New York. She seems to have delighted everyone. Just looking at her was pleasant. One writer noted that she was not pretty, but "when her countenance is lighted up with smiles, and every feature beams with exultation and delight, and she pours forth in heavenly strains, 'joy, rapturous joy,' then is she positively beautiful."[33] She even inspired poetry. The daily *Atlas* claimed to have received dozens of poems. It printed three and announced that henceforth it would print only those of "exceptional merit."[34] She also inspired the inevitable puns on the "Shirreff" holding people under "arrest."

Throughout Shirreff's engagement, the press praised the performers and audiences for a gratifying mutual relationship. Admiring the opera audience reinforced the idea that the operas were more than entertainment and would bring listeners to a higher plane of civility and virtue. As one writer put it, "There breathes [in these works] a spirit of subliminity above the mere productions of art."[35] The tone is self-congratulatory: "Their reception [that of Shirreff, John Wilson, and Edward Seguin] was such as did honor to the American character," wrote one reporter after the premiere of *Amilie*. Writers praised New Yorkers for filling the theater, for their warm welcome of the newcomers, for their heavy patronage of benefit performances, and (most often) for the significant numbers of women in the audience. They praised Shirreff and her colleagues for "receiving . . . evidences of approbation with profound respect," a comment probably designed to reassure Americans that the foreign performers properly appreciated their American public.[36] Finally, they praised the National Theatre's manager, James William Wallack, for his "zeal and enterprise in making the American stage what it should be — perfect in all its parts."[37]

Of all the accolades, the last may be the most telling, for it recalls the notion of opera as an ideal, an object of aspiration. By successfully mounting an opera season, Wallack used the power of music and its ability to draw respectable audiences to achieve the long-wished-for goal of theatrical improvement. By offering stories glorifying conventional femininity enhanced by powerful music and performed by an appealing leading lady, he entertained everyone while offending no one. The joy Jane Shirreff's characters found in proving their adherence to the sexual code allowed these operas to realize an ideal not possible in earlier days — that of moral purifier. Although the women Shirreff played were undoubtedly not everyone's ideal even in 1838, they were least unobjectionable. As long as she remained a prima donna, this ideal remained fundamental to the way she was judged.

Amilie and *La sonnambula* were serious operas and taken as such. They gave New Yorkers the best of both worlds — emotionally satisfying, unthreatening, clean, moral stories and beautiful music. They did not yet force the issue of a balance of power between words and music; instead, each was more effective through a reciprocal relationship with the other. Moreover, by supporting the feminine ideal of innocence and goodness, the operas solved the problem of whether the theater was a fit place for ladies. Like films advertised now as G rated, they freed audiences from worry that they might see a side of life the respectable mainstream did not wish to acknowledge in public. Thus they fit the goals of the "well-regulated theatre" defined when *The Beggar's Opera* had been rejected twenty years previously — "a school of morality, literary taste and instruction, blended with innocent amusement."[38]

The press regulars at Shirreff's performances also made an observation about the audience that surprised them. The members of the bon ton were conspicuously absent.[39] Shirreff and her colleagues had been successful without the patronage of the upper-class Italian Opera House clientele. This was an exciting development that contrasted to the failure (ironically, in the same building) of the opera house only three years before (chapter 5). Wallack's productions had been appreciated without the leadership and support of the city's upper class and without deserting the theater for the opera house. Moreover, the performances had been financially successful without exorbitant admission charges. Having grown out of the popular theater, they had been enjoyed without the novelty of the opera house social setting. Like any theatrical offering that had to sink or swim on merit, Shirreff's performances spoke to contemporary concerns and fears, making clear statements about issues affecting their hearers' lives. And, like the longstanding English operas from the eighteenth century, they seemed to offer a reflection of the audience—a consonance between the stage and the house—that put the audience in its best light.

Opera at the opera house had not been able to do so. Yet the actual musical differences between the accepted and rejected genres were relatively small—the style of Rossini, Bellini, and even some of Rooke in English at the National Theatre was virtually the same as in Italian at the opera house. Divorced from associations branded aristocratic, the music had taken on an international cast compatible with American rhetoric. This is not to say that stylistic differences between this repertoire and the ballad tradition were not recognized. They were. Nor does it mean that all segments of the population accepted these works as their own—the success of the Bowery Theatre in the 1830s (chapter 5) shows that they did not. But presented in a form audiences could understand and enjoy, the style's origin was not a socially divisive issue. Opera in English was *English* opera and, as such, a part of New York's local popular culture.

This acceptance of the style was critical to the growth of Italian opera in the city. As natural as Jane Shirreff was held to be, she helped New Yorkers assimilate a refined and artificial idiom. By showing them how this idiom could convincingly express emotions common among her audience, she undermined the longstanding assumption that words were the primary source of meaning even in a piece of musical theater. Although the English operas of the 1830s were still considered primarily drama, they taught New Yorkers the style that, when performed in Italian, would eventually be taken primarily as music. Such a shift in emphasis was consistent with the contemporary understanding of music's purpose. Music was, as a magazine writer put it, being "cultivated for its control over the peculiarities of the age."[40] As long as opera continued to be performed in institutions open (nominally, at least) to all, and as long as it continued to be considered unobjectionable and attractive, then its cultivation as an inherently improving genre could continue. And its association with an elite of virtue and respectability, rather than one of wealth and social status, could be maintained.

The Failure That Flourished:
Early New York Opera Houses

*E*nglish opera's success in the 1830s did its Italian competition no good. It must have galled Italian opera's supporters who insisted an opera house was essential to New York to watch English opera's string of hits in the commercial theater. But the 1830s were not the right time for a compromise between commerce and culture. Jacksonian social polarities were too strong for a "democratic" opera house to be anything other than a contradiction in terms. The terms themselves — social, economic, political, and esthetic — on which an opera house could succeed in an American city were as yet unknown.

Max Maretzek, a prominent conductor and impresario who immigrated to New York in 1848, called Italian opera during the Jacksonian era "an establishment whose 'failure' has flourished for the last five and twenty years."[1] As Maretzek suggested, the three opera house failures that preceded the Academy of Music's success in 1854 were in some ways successes as well. Contemporary accounts describe many fine, well-attended performances. And the quick replacement of each failed opera house by a new attempt shows a determination to succeed among organizers and the public. Those in charge, however, were slow to understand that Italian opera companies could neither be bought cheaply nor imposed on the public at will. It took years to distinguish between an opera house failure of "public taste" from fiscal naiveté or mismanagement.

Competing attitudes toward opera hindered efforts to establish opera houses in the city. From the first attempt at an opera company in 1826, its success or failure was often treated as a referendum on New Yorkers' ability to appreciate it. But the interpretation of the opera house as a haven for the wealthy and ostentatious persisted as well. The expectation that opera could and should reach a wide population competed with accounts of its social exclusiveness. The incongruity between the two attitudes brought the same kinds of questions with every new opera house endeavor. Could opera survive financially at prices the public could pay? What were the rights and obligations of the wealthy in opera patronage? Is opera meaningful only to a refined minority or can the "democracy" understand and enjoy it as well?

From the 1830s on, Italian opera's success was linked to the success of opera houses. Its early years were rough, as organizers and entrepreneurs slowly learned how to run an opera company, sell the performances, and pay the bills. At the same time, the principles of audience sovereignty and capitalism, both central to notions of American democracy in the Jacksonian era, clashed with those of respectability, esthetic value, and social and moral improvement. As the success of English opera in the theaters would show, respectability was essential to building a sexually mixed audience willing to assimilate the new Italian style. In English opera the two sets of principles were compatible, but in the opera house they were not; respectability alone could not overcome the stigma of Italian opera's European origin and seeming exclusiveness. The question of whether Italian opera could maintain its integrity and still be sold to a sovereign American audience remained open for thirty years.

Although English opera in the 1830s and 1840s was the stronger genre, the Italian managed showy maneuvers that anticipated the character of its ultimate triumph. In 1826 an attempted opera company had tried and failed to muster a critical mass of support (chapter 3). By contrast, in 1832 an Italian Opera Association did better, building an opera house and maintaining it with a resident troupe from 1833 to 1835. Independent of the commercial theaters, the Italian Opera House was built, supported, and managed by a group of New York's business and civic leaders. In setting up their enterprise, the opera house's founders worked under the premise that such a self-named group could establish an institution that would be accepted by a public broad enough to support it. In so doing, they created a setting as elegant and refined as opera's reputation. In fact, the new opera house audience successfully competed for public attention with the performances themselves. But public attitudes toward such enterprises had changed since the Garcias' departure, and much of the notice was unfavorable. Some of the practices designed to attract a respectable clientele were interpreted as ostentatious and exclusive. Perhaps understandably in Jacksonian America, "democratic" hatred of anything smacking of "aristocracy" hurt opera's chance at financial success.

Americans, of course, did not inherit titles; literally speaking, there were no American aristocrats. But the term was often used to express a growing negative attitude toward New York's upper class. Students of American social classes, including Stuart Blumin, Gary Nash, and Edward Pessen, have explored how elites distinguished themselves from the rest of society. Nash argues that in the eighteenth century, close quarters in northern cities made conspicuous signs of an individual's position essential for social stability. Blumin names signs of high rank, including attendance at exclusive balls, holding an expensive church pew, and membership in private social organizations. He also describes "traditional constraints against dressing above or below one's station."[2]

By the nineteenth century, especially in the years following the Erie Canal's opening, mercantile growth had rapidly increased the numbers of New York's wealthy citizens. Pessen has identified these people, assessed their wealth, and described their lives. By examining New York's tax records, he found fifty-nine city residents in 1828 worth more than $100,000, including two worth more than $500,000 — John Jacob Astor, the Park Theatre's landlord, and John G. Coster, whose family supported the Italian Opera House. For 1845 (the recent economic downturn notwithstanding), Pessen found 295 men worth more than $100,000, this time including eleven half-millionaires.[3] Many of these men were members of what he calls "Philip Hone's set," named for the merchant, civic leader, gentleman about town, and diarist. Pessen describes the former mayor's associates and social equals as being guided by "ideals of exclusiveness" in their social connections and activities. For example, the charter of the St. Nicholas Club (1835), of which Hone was a member, opened it to men of "respectable standing in society" whose families had lived in New York State before 1775. In listing the membership in this and other clubs, Pessen repeats the same names again and again, finding them on his lists of the wealthy as well.[4]

Whether this elite activity represents a net increase over former times is unclear. By the 1830s, however, it was widely noticed; at times, the Jacksonian press seemed obsessed with aristocracy and fashion. Where a writer in the *Literary Gazette* had criticized fashion in 1825 as a social aspiration, by the 1830s the critique had become inflammatory and the picture of the bon ton painted in extremes. Many examples illustrate the new tone. In 1834 the Democratic *Evening Post* issued a jab at the rival *American* "and other great organs of our mushroom aristocracy, [who] are still harping about our *'leading the way in a crusade of the poor against the rich.'* "Not so, the *Post* retorted, "We did not lead the way; nor is it a crusade of the poor against the rich, but of the rich against the poor, that we are calling on the latter to put down, by the exercise of their constitutional right, at the polls." The same issue includes an article by "A Plebeian," maintaining that women are even more aristocratic then men. As participants in government, men must at least pay lip service to the republican ideal. Women, excluded from political life, need not.[5] Just before the year's election, the *Evening Post* listed a long series of "aristocratic" assertions, for example, that a working man "is incapable of self-government, and thus [aristocracy] degrades him below the level of animals; for even brutes, in their natural state, are left to their own discretion and self-government."[6] Finally, in 1841, the *Herald*, the leading paper of the new and burgeoning penny press, ridiculed the wealthy with a front-page cartoon of monocled "specimens of the supreme bon ton," maintaining that "every candidate for admission into the new *noblesse* must be dressed and pressed into these forms and figures."[7]

The emblem of theatrical democracy, the Bowery Theatre, played on this view. Founded in 1826 as an alternative to the Park, with its cornerstone laid by Mayor Hone, the Bowery had presented Maria Garcia's successful English opera season in 1827. From 1830, however, under manager Thomas Hamblin, it began to court what was essentially a pit audience. Using spectacle, melodrama, and "native talent" (American, rather than British performers), Hamblin attracted a clientele of young men, generally working-class and strongly pro-American. In his later years, Walt Whitman remembered the Bowery: "Recalling from that period the occasion of either [Edwin] Forrest or [Junius Brutus] Booth [the elder], any good night at the Old

Bowery, pack'd from ceiling to pit[,] . . . the whole crowded auditorium . . . bursting forth in one of those long-kept-up tempests of hand-clapping, peculiar to the Bowery—no dainty kid-glove business, but electric force and muscle from perhaps 2,000 full-sinew'd men."[8]

The Bowery specialized in presenting the "Bowery b'hoy," by the 1840s part of the city's lore. The subject of stories, plays, and press reports, the b'hoy dressed sharply, strutted the streets at night, and brooked no nonsense. Shown onstage in the character of Mose the fireman, with his girl friend Lize, the Bowery b'hoy was the antithesis of gentility. Like other antebellum stage Americans, including the Yankee Jonathan, Metamora the Indian, and Jumpin' Jim Crow, Mose was a caricature. But he allowed audience members to see their social milieu validated through a popular form of public culture.[9]

The Bowery's biggest star in the 1830s and 1840s was Philadelphia-born Forrest, as famous for his patriotism as for his acting. In 1833 the *Evening Post* described a furor over Forrest's appearance in John Augustus Stone's *Metamora,* presenting the essence of a Bowery event:

> As early as five o'clock in the afternoon a numerous multitude had assembled round the doors, which were opened much sooner than usual, though with considerable difficulty, owing to the pressure of the dense throng. Every part of the theatre was soon filled to excess. . . . The manager was desirous of staying the sale of tickets, when the number which the house is calculated to accommodate had been disposed of; but the people would take no denial, and those who could not obtain tickets were pressed forward by the crowd behind, and obliged to be admitted for their money at the door. . . . Tickets and money were freely returned to those who, gaining admission, and finding that they could not obtain even a glimpse of the stage, were desirous to withdraw; and although the number of these were very considerable, yet their departure did not occasion any perceptible diminution of the multitude.[10]

This press of humanity was as much a part of the event as Forrest's performance. Without subscriptions or reserved seats, the Bowery's policy was first-come-first-served. Thus a popular offering such as Forrest playing Metamora usually brought a rush for seats, and shoving at the door and jostling for a good place were part of democratic theater. Everyone had an equal chance, aggressiveness was rewarded, the people determined the etiquette, and the management treated them fairly and with respect. Shouting down a performer, throwing things, and even rioting would be acceptable. Self-consciously anti-genteel, the Bowery's social setting was consonant with the culture of its neighborhood.

Evidence of Forrest's success was central to this news report, for it showed the audience passing judgment and the crowd as an active participant. It also showed distinctions from Italian opera that would characterize the genres socially. Like the reporters who praised the Garcias' audiences, this writer believed in audience sovereignty. But where some of the Garcias' commentators had questioned the genuineness of Italian opera's success, here there was no such issue. Popular success was genuine success; at least as important as the kind of audience that had approved Forrest was its strength. Popularity, democratic and hence American, was inherently the correct basis for judgment.

All commentators, however, were not so sanguine about the Bowery. While some observers had looked up "from below" and mocked the "aristocracy," others looked down at the Bowery and its clientele with disdain. In the early 1830s the *Mirror* began to tell a story of decline, rowdyism, and disreputable characters unfit for polite company (Whitman's "full-sinew'd men," no doubt).[11] Around 1830, Frances Trollope, the most famous transatlantic observer of American life before Tocqueville, called the Bowery "infinitely superior [to the Park] in beauty; it is indeed as pretty a theatre as I ever entered, perfect as to size and proportion." However, she reported, "It is not the fashion."[12] Philip Hone concurred. In 1838 he remarked of his Bowery cornerstone-laying of 1826, "No act of my public life cost me so many friends."[13] This attitude was a far cry from Washington Irving's bemused tolerance of pit critics and gallery gods recorded in the century's first decade. As Peter Buckley has observed, the changes in the city's theatrical structure "do not account, in themselves, for the urgency with which [they were] registered."[14]

Yet despite its social setting, and despite accusations to the contrary, the Bowery's repertoire was in many ways similar to the Park's.[15] Distinct settings did not automatically bring distinct offerings. In addition to Forrest, another of the Bowery's stars was Junius Brutus Booth, also a tragedian. Both actors' Shakespeare performances were considered legitimate alternatives to those given at the Park. In 1833 a daily theatrical newsletter, *Figaro,* pro-Italian opera and pro-opera house, recommended the Bowery's legitimate drama over the Park's, just as it recommended opera at the Italian Opera House over the Park's Joseph and Mary Ann Wood.[16] Two middle-class weeklies, the *Albion* and the *Spirit of the Times,* reported on Bowery performances. Its stock company was considered excellent; indeed, its productions attracted favorable commentary even as its clientele was seen as less and less respectable.[17] Worthwhile offerings and exclusiveness did not go hand in hand. A Shakespeare play could be produced equally well for a common audience as for an elite.

So could opera. Hone's remark that his role in the Bowery's establishment cost him friends hints at the social, rather than esthetic, rationale behind the need for an opera house. The Bowery had declined precipitously in the minds of the city's leaders; Hone's friends (and he had many) found it unfit for their presence. This ill-fitness was proven literally. In 1832 an Italian opera company under Giocomo Montresor performed a short season at the Richmond Hill Theatre. In 1833 it moved to the Bowery. Despite the latter's physical and acoustic superiority, the season was a failure. By its end, the performers were "almost literally playing to empty benches."[18]

Would New Yorkers attend Italian opera performances at a proper opera house? Hone's friends seem to have thought so. The Italian Opera House was more than just a new performance locale. In building it, its organizers condemned not just the Bowery but the theater in general. The new name said much, for it linked a performance genre with a new institution, a link seen as necessary to its success. Moving opera from the theater gave the opera house's builders control over its manner of presentation. They could create their own establishment; location, design, decor, prices, management policies, personnel, and customs would be their choices. There need be no crowding, no impoliteness, and no compromise.

Starting from scratch gave them other choices as well. They could build essentially a private club, an ostensibly public institution for their own set that would put their wealth on display for others to admire from afar. They could extend the notion of high culture in the city by patronizing New Yorkers' access to European music. Or they could found a business — one that would attract customers as in the theater and pay its own way. Evidence suggests that the builders' motives were mixed and probably not well thought-out. In any event, however, the opera house's reception was tempered by the social climate of the day. An expensive, European-derived genre in an era of "native talent" was not destined for success.

By removing opera from the city's theatrical establishment, its organizers freed themselves from the theater's traditions. But they also lost its supportive infrastructure. Thus they faced problems more difficult than the Garcias' managers at the Park — how to attract an audience to a new location and assure that this audience would be respectable (a motive behind abandoning the theater) and still allow the enterprise to break even. In 1832 the Italian Opera Association was formed to support the project.[19] The association's minutes do not mention Montresor's opera company at the Richmond Hill and Bowery theaters. That company was probably its first project, however. A Committee of the Italian Opera was credited with advancing a "large sum of money" for the Montresor venture at the behest of Lorenzo Da Ponte, Mozart's former librettist, now an elderly New Yorker.[20] In March of 1833, Montresor protested to the association when he was replaced as the company director by the Chevalier Vincenzo de Rivafinoli.[21]

In the meantime, the opera house was being built. Contracts and minutes of the association show that it was carefully planned. By 1833 twenty proprietors' boxes (the Park had two) had been sold to members at $6,000 and $4,000.[22] This outlay entitled members to privileges that put severe constraints on the management. The lessee (Rivafinoli for the first season) was to meet expenses from the sale of tickets for the rest of the auditorium.[23] In lieu of receiving rent, the members of the association could use their boxes without additional payment. They could lock them up or lend them out; the management had no access to them. This policy resulted in 116 free seats being given out at every performance that was not a benefit. In addition, the association members reserved the right to collect rent instead of receiving free tickets. In that case, however, they would still keep exclusive use of their boxes and would pay only for performances they attended.[24] As one observer estimated, "the manager's money making part" held about $1,200 — "too small."[25]

The proprietors' boxes, which took up the second tier of the horseshoe-shaped theater, were flanked by a private lobby reached via its own entrance from the street. The boxes were awarded to members of the association by lot (fig. 4), and their holders were entitled to decorate them, presumably at their own expense.[26] One can imagine the

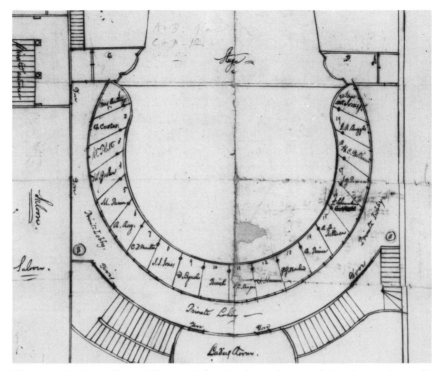

Figure 4. Italian Opera House (1833), plan of second tier (proprietors')
boxes. (Collection of The New-York Historical Society)

view from below—a motley row of memorials to American individual-
ism, "good taste," and financial well-being described by a journalist
visiting the opera house before its opening:

> Box No. 1. Upholsterers at work, covering the wall with silk of a
> pale delicate straw colour and the floor with Brussels carpeting.
> Box No. 2. Interior lined with gros de Naples silk, fluted, Wilton
> carpeting, taleurets, gilt moulding, &c. Unfinished.
> Box No. 3. Proprietors box—door closed—the only remaining
> private box unsold in the Opera House—price only $6000.
> Box No. 4. No ostentatious display in this box—plain Windsor
> chairs, ingrain carpeting, walls whitewashed and colored blue.

◊ ◊ ◊

> Box No. 8 [Philip Hone had a one-third share in this box]. Walls
> beautifully panelled, with rich stripes of gilt moulding—a move-

able cushioned seat in the back part of the box, for the accommodation of casual visitors.[27]

The rest of the auditorium's decor was not quite as extravagant, but it was elegant nonetheless. The fronts of the private boxes were "richly hung with silken curtains of crimson, festooned with gold knots." The floor was carpeted, and the seats in the pit were mahogany-backed (theater seats usually had no backs at all).[28] The auditorium's decor was as eclectic as that of the boxes. The ceiling was covered with classical images — paintings of Apollo, the Muses, and the Genii of history, music, and poetry. The two stage curtains showed a chariot race and a rural dance. The proscenium was decorated with "the everglorious American Eagle, surrounded by Fame and Victory."[29]

Such opulence did not come cheap. The land had cost $39,000, and in 1833 the association authorized $42,000 for construction and decoration. A year later, with the house open, unpaid bills came to $68,500.[30] Although it is not known who, if anyone, took up the slack, there is no evidence that the Italian Opera Association contributed additional funds. Rather, it seems that the $6,000 boxholders were not patrons; they contributed nothing to supporting the house or its company. The association members heard the performances themselves free of charge.

Nonmembers, on the other hand, paid the highest admission prices yet seen in New York. Reaching beyond the traditional pit-box-gallery seating distinctions, the auditorium was divided into new categories of seats, each designed to attract a given clientele and priced accordingly. Sofa seats in the first tier of boxes were $2. Projecting out from this tier was a balcony "for the accommodation of those who are not with a party." Its seats were $1.50. So were box seats that were not sofas in the first and third tiers, as well as seats in private, nonproprietor's boxes (stalls) on each side of the pit. Pit seats were $1, and gallery seats were 75 cents. All were available for a single evening or by subscription.[31]

Given the expenses incurred, the top prices are no surprise. More unusual, however, is the 75 cent gallery seat when both the Park and the Bowery were charging 25 cents. During the Garcias' engagement the Park had left the gallery price untouched, raising only the box and pit prices. For Maria Garcia's engagement in 1827, the Bowery had done the same. Thus the Italian Opera House policy was new.

Raising prices at the high end could conceivably move some audience members from a box or pit seat to the gallery. Raising them at the low end would price the traditional gallery audience out of the opera house altogether. The fact that during the summer of 1834 the gallery was eliminated suggests that its high price had left it without much clientele at all.[32]

Despite high prices and free seats, the opera house took in money. In March of 1835, Rivafinoli made public a summary of his 1833–34 account books. They show that his main category of income — almost $16,000 — was single-ticket sales during the first season of forty performances. After that came twenty benefits, which brought in more than $10,000 from the proprietors as well as the public.[33] The company performed two subscription seasons in New York and one in Philadelphia. Subscriptions for the three seasons brought in $11,000, but sales at the door earned more in all three. Together, New Yorkers and Philadelphians paid almost $52,000 to hear the opera company.[34]

Yet as income mounted, so did expenses. Rivafinoli listed $81,000 worth, including $36,000 in eight-month contracts for singers and orchestra members. He spelled out the rest as well: extra singers and players, cashiers, police, box-keepers, gas men, hairdressers, tailors, servants, travel expenses (including fourteen company members from Paris, six from Italy, and all to and from Philadelphia), gas, coal, oil, candles, carpenters, other workers in Philadelphia, coaches, printing and posting, agents, stage extras, cleaning people, painters, scenery cloth, a machinist, properties, costumes, music, copy paper, house furniture, house expenses, petty cash, "etc." These expenses produced a $29,000 deficit. To them would be added insurance, taxes, and a licensing fee in 1834–35, all of which had been paid for the first year by the association.[35] The *American Musical Journal* reported that although Rivafinoli paid no rent on the opera house, his unrealized income on the free, transferable tickets in the second tier provided to the patrons had amounted to $15,776. It also noted that "there being no fourth tier in the house, the third was of little or no profit to the manager."[36]

By the end of the first season, the opera was dying of "lingering consumption."[37] After two seasons under two managements, the Italian Opera Association gave up the ghost. "Every one must have forseen this result who looked at the boxes during the last engagement," one commentator remarked.[38] The association had looked at them as well. In October 1835 the members advertised the building for sale.[39] In the meantime, it stood empty, the first but not the last New York opera house to be deserted by its patrons. In December 1836 the building was sold to Oroondates Mauran, one of the original association members, and James Henry Hackett, the well-known American actor and sometime theater manager.[40] Association members received 20 cents for every dollar of their original investment.[41] In the meantime, the opera house had reopened as the National Theatre, where it soon distinguished itself as the home of the legitimate drama and, ironically perhaps, English opera.

Was the Italian Opera House essentially a place to extend European culture to the city's residents? Was it an exclusive club? Or was it a business? Contemporary interpretations hint at all three. As during the Garcias' engagement, opera was held up to the public as good music presented in a polite social setting. According to the *Mirror*, opera would do "more to truly civilize and refine [its audience], than all the other luxuries which can minister to the senses of an opulent and expanding nation."[42] More surprisingly perhaps, similar rhetoric appeared in the *Evening Post,* which habitually derided the city's upper class.[43] As the Jacksonian era progressed, opera as a staged presentation was at least sometimes distinguished from the opulent institution of the opera house.

But in other quarters, opera's social setting was seen as a fatal flaw. For example, the *Spirit of the Times* mocked Montresor's unsuccessful season:

> Another circumstance has created some talk with the gossips. . . . The Opera House was not *crammed* on Monday night. Those not initiated into the mysteries of the *ton* cannot conceive the sensation such an event creates in "good society." What! The patrons of the Opera to suffer the mortification of not rendering popular to any extent, what their judgment approves? Are the *elite* to be told that MISS KEMBLE is more attractive than PEDROTTI? Defend us[,] good angels — we dare not intimate that such is the case. . . . "Mum's the word" for the present. Yet we cannot resist the temptation of whispering in your ear, kind reader, that some folks are getting a little tired of some folks.[44]

In the 1820s, "some folks" would have been treated more respectfully. The *Spirit of the Times* rejected opera as inherently civilizing and took delight in the failure of an enterprise organized and sanctioned by elites.[45] Further, it hinted that the bon ton was either too naive or arrogant to notice that its tastes did not suit all New Yorkers. Unlike the *Post,* the *Spirit* equated opera's social setting with the genre and rejected the latter on account of the former.

So did the bon ton's spokesman, Philip Hone. As the holder of two shares (one-third of a box), Hone's financial stake in the enterprise was low. He did not particularly care for music; rather, he seems to have supported the opera house out of a belief that New York should have one. His diary entry on the proprietors' boxes shows his finger on the pulse of the times: "They cost $6,000 each, to be sure, and the use of them is all that the proprietors get for their money; but it forms a sort of aristocratical distinction. Many people do not choose to occupy seats [i.e., the standard benches]. . . while others recline upon satin cushions, and rest their elbows upon armchairs, albeit they are bought with their own money. . . . I like this spirit of independence which refuses its countenance to anything exclusive."[46] As a participant in many exclusive activities, Hone may have been somewhat disingenuous in his interpretation of the opera's failure. And where the *American Musical Journal* noted how much income was lost by providing the stockholders with free seats, Hone saw instead the stockholders' great outlay for little return. But he seems at least to have been sensitive to non-elite New Yorkers' intolerance of an activity that so sharply and publicly distinguished among its participants by social rank.

Hone may also have understood that non-elite New Yorkers would be needed to make opera succeed. The association had built the opera house but could not support it. In 1835 a writer for the *American Musical Journal,* one of opera's strongest advocates, summarized the tension between opera as private, elite entertainment and its need for a broader public: "If the proprietors of the House are determined to keep it for their own amusement, as a sort of private establishment, it is incumbent on them to assume the entire management and the whole responsibility. No one will have any right to complain of such a course. But if, on the contrary, they really wish to establish permanently the Opera in this city, then such changes in the present arrangement as experience indicate to be necessary to effect this object should be disinterestedly and at once adopted."[47] In either case, the association had miscalculated, and much of the blame for opera's failure could be laid on financial mismanagement.[48] Italian opera, expensive and seen as exclusive, could not be made to pay in a purportedly egalitarian society.

How naive were the businessmen who built the opera house? Did they think the public would bow to their example and follow them to the opera? Were they indifferent to the increasingly polarized social climate of the 1830s? Did they overestimate the market for the kind of culture they were offering? Or did they deliberately try to exclude the broader public while overestimating the size and commitment of their own set? They may have been trying to prove that they were cultured gentlemen by engaging in their usual kinds of business activity in support of a cultural form that required no direct participation. Or they may have actually thought they could turn a profit.

The last possibility may seem the most startling. Given modern knowledge of high culture's cost, it seems absurd to suggest that the Italian Opera Association actually hoped to make money. Yet these men were wealthy because they knew how to do so. Their activities— organizing, incorporating, contracting, hiring, advertising, and keeping books—normally produced a profit. The original association articles provided for an annual meeting during which the trustees would show the stockholders the books "and divide the surplus rents if any."[49] Moreover, they abandoned the project after only two years, suggesting that their commitments to opera and the idea of patronage were shallow. In their view, opera seems to have been a potentially profitable European import, like so many successfully marketed material goods. Like any other speculation, it carried the possibility of failure. As with any failure, the association cut its losses and unloaded its liability. Rhetoric about opera's value notwithstanding, these sponsors did not treat it as culture divorced from New York's economic life.

In one respect, however, the opera house's failure was beyond the association's control. Although some press reports evaluated the two companies positively, in general the performances were received without enthusiasm. The female performers seem to have been weaker then the men. Although all acknowledged that another Maria Garcia Malibran would be hard to find, none of the women impressed, charmed, or delighted her audience as had been hoped. One writer called the second company (of 1834–35) "the most destitute of vocal talent of any that has essayed the performance of Italian Opera in this country."[50] The opera house offered novelty, elegance, and respectability, yet the performances seem to have offered little of interest or value to their audience. Especially revealing of the situation is the expressed hope that the current performers be supported in hopes of getting better ones in the future. Some New Yorkers feared that opera would be written off as unsupportable, thus discouraging other companies from taking a chance on the city.[51] This kind of long-term patronage may have been acceptable to a music advocate or an "aristocrat," but an audience member investing in an evening's entertainment seems to have expected a quicker return.

The Italian Opera House's troubles affected its contribution to the city's musical life. It offered mainly works not previously heard in New York, such as Rossini's *La gazza ladra, La donna del lago,* and *Mathilde di Shabran,* Cimarosa's *Il matrimonio segreto,* and Pacini's *Gli Arabi nelle Gallie.* It also produced Rossini's *Cenerentola* and *Il Turco in Italia,* both already heard in New York, as well as the ever-popular *Il barbiere di Siviglia.* Of the new pieces, only *La gazza ladra* entered the repertoire. And while the first Bellini operas heard in New York, *Il pirata* and *La straniera,* were performed at the opera house, it took the successful English adaptation of *La sonnambula* to establish his works in the city.

Not surprisingly, another opera house was not tried in New York for nearly a decade. Yet musical growth continued unabated. Aside from opera, the 1840s brought the founding of the New York Philharmonic and the first blackface minstrel performances (both in 1842). Criticized as vulgar in all respectable media, minstrelsy was successful in various settings that among them encompassed much of the social spectrum. The Philharmonic, on the other hand, played to a narrower clientele. Its membership included many of the growing number of German immigrants in the city, and its repertoire was largely German. Indeed, the encroaching German influence in New York's musical life was first felt in the 1840s. Aside from the Philharmonic, a short German opera season was produced in 1845, and in 1848 the renowned Germania Orchestra arrived on a leg of the tour that evolved into a group immigration. (For German music's influence on attitudes toward Italian opera, see chapter 7.)

The musical growth of the 1840s included Italian opera. The economic distress that followed the Panic of 1837 made such an enterprise even riskier than usual. But beginning in 1843, attempts to revive it were repeated until, with the Academy of Music of 1854, an opera house was finally successful. As the genre's advocates put it, opera was being "naturalized" — made a part of the local culture — in its original state. Yet it was still controversial, and the opera house's economic, social, and political character was reinterpreted more than once during the period. As the Jacksonian era progressed, censure of anything deemed aristocratic and foreign increased. Democratization — creating a social setting in which non-elites could feel comfortable and a price structure they would consider a good value — was critical to opera's success. New Yorkers seemed ready to accept opera if the institution would accept them.

Of all the antebellum opera houses, the next, Palmo's, drew the least criticism for social ostentation. Perhaps for that reason, it was better able to foster opera's establishment in New York. Like the 1833 opera house, it was a short-lived venture — only three years.[52] Yet by the time Palmo's produced its last opera, the seventy-member Havana Opera Company had performed at the Park Theatre, four operas of Verdi had been heard (the first, *I Lombardi,* at Palmo's), and the next patron-sponsored opera house, the Astor Place, was under construction. Palmo's opened in 1844. From that date until the present, New York has always had a theater available for opera.[53]

The Italian Opera House closed in 1835; with the theater in general suffering from the economic downturn, for the next few years New Yorkers heard only occasional Italian opera performances. Income figures for the Park, for example, show how close to the edge it was working in the early 1840s. In 1834 and 1835, the Woods had brought in $3,000 to $5,000 a week. But by 1842 weekly income ran between $1,000 and $1,500, with some performances bringing in less than $100.[54] These figures confirm Charles Dickens's 1842 observation that the Park and Bowery theaters were "generally deserted."[55]

Italian opera's revival in 1843 shows that someone, at least, thought the depression had bottomed out. As it turned out, William Niblo, proprietor of Niblo's Garden and arguably the city's shrewdest theatrical entrepreneur, was right. He produced a seven-night season in his newly enclosed "garden" theater with a touring company from Havana. Admission was his standard 50 cents for all seats. Three works were given: Bellini's *Norma* and Donizetti's *Gemma di Vergy* and *Lucia di Lammermoor.* All three were Italian premieres; only *Norma* had been performed in English.[56] Although the performances were reportedly poor and the last was disrupted by a fire in the theater, opera's brief run at a popular price helped bring into focus the terms on which it could be successfully established.

Perhaps inspired by Niblo's success, a second entrepreneur had a similar idea. Ferdinando Palmo, an Italian immigrant, successful restaurateur, and opera lover, opened his opera house on February 3, 1844, on Chambers Street near his restaurant. Unlike the Italian Opera House, Palmo's was financed solely by its proprietor. This financial structure had one advantage: It was controlled, at first, by Palmo himself. All income went toward maintaining the company rather than toward rent. And because there were no stockholders, "free list" (the press) excepted, all admissions were paid.

The *Herald* called Palmo's "a little *bijou* of a theater."[57] Indeed, at about eight hundred places, the opera house was smaller than the city's standard; only William Mitchell's Olympic was as much noticed for its small size. Its physical structure was part opera house, part theater. For the first time, a New York theater had a sloped parquette instead of a pit. Palmo's parquette was connected to the lower tier of boxes, none of which was private. Further, with only two tiers, "no part of this house [was] devoted to purposes of assignation."[58] But all the seats, as in the theaters, were benches; no sofas or armchairs were provided. The backs of the benches were numbered to save non-subscribers from having to arrive early or rush for places if the house was crowded. The slope of each tier was sufficient to allow a good view of the stage from anywhere in the auditorium.[59] And the price structure was egalitarian; all seats were $1.

Palmo failed as quickly as had the Italian Opera House. His first season left him so short of funds that he organized a benefit for himself at $3 a ticket.[60] His second season, in the fall of 1844, came to an abrupt halt on October 14, when most of the company struck for want of salary.[61] By December the policy of pricing all seats equally had given way to a three-tiered scale. Seats in the first tier and parquette went for the original price of $1, second-tier seats for 50 cents, and newly built private boxes, each seating four, cost $6.[62] Presumably the new structure would broaden the audience base, allowing for those who could not afford $1 as well as for those who insisted on a private box.

By 1847, however, the opera house's problem was size — it was too small. In January a new company opened, and New Yorkers flocked to hear its performances. Press reports derided "the shabby smallness of the house," maintaining that more people would have attended had there been room for them.[63] Finally, two events precipitated Palmo's demise. A long-awaited, reportedly excellent opera company from Havana arrived, setting up first in the Park Theatre and then, in the summer, at Castle Garden in the Battery.[64] Had Palmo's been large enough for a company of more than seventy it would have been the natural choice. Then, in November of 1847, the Astor Place Opera House opened, its company drawing on Palmo's singers. Palmo's was abandoned as an opera house. In 1848 it was sold to the comedian William Burton, who opened it as Burton's Theatre. Like the Italian Opera House before it, Palmo's continued to play a role in city life, but one a theater of its size could support.

Despite its short career, Palmo's legacy was significant, for it hinted at practical solutions to opera's problems. Where the Italian Opera House had seemed too exclusive, Palmo's at first seemed not exclusive enough. Hence the new boxes allowed for greater privacy from the general audience. On a more mundane level, Palmo's small size also pointed to an untapped source of revenue — more operagoers. Turning people away would have to become unnecessary — hence the growth in auditorium size with each newly built venue that followed.

Palmo's was even more important in another respect. Unlike at the Italian Opera House, operas produced at Palmo's helped establish New York's standard operatic repertoire. Audiences were learning opera from Italian originals rather than from English adaptations. This trend would continue. Slowly, the Italian versions established themselves as definitive, reducing the adaptations to mere variants. Opera was being "naturalized" in New York in its original state.

Between the opening of Palmo's in 1844 and the opening of the Academy of Music ten years later, opera's establishment in New York was completed. But it was still not a simple matter of progress toward a goal of cultural improvement. Opera, a complex, elegant, and expensive continental genre with an elitist reputation, was taking hold at a time of great social tension. Polarizations in the close quarters of the burgeoning city — the "Upper Ten Thousand" (also called the codfish aristocracy) versus "the Million," Americans versus foreigners, city- versus country-born, the virtuous versus sinners, white versus black, Protestant versus Catholic, capital versus labor, and Whig versus Democrat — fostered an atmosphere in which mutual antagonism was, as in Jackson's day, still taken as the norm.[65] An opera house could be seen as a place where the wealthy lounged in opulent, public comfort while their neighbors starved. Built in 1847, the infamous Italian Opera House, Astor Place, was so taken. In keeping with the age in which opera took root, its infamy and disastrous history were opera's last great setback.

From the first, the Astor Place took center stage in New York's public culture. It quickly acquired nicknames — Upper Row House in Disaster Place, Uproar House, and Astor Palace in Massacre Place. Of all the opera houses before the Metropolitan, this one was, and is, the best known — the site of the Astor Place riots of May 7 and 10, 1849, which left twenty-two dead and dozens wounded. It was also the opera house around which the issue of aristocratic snobbery was finally brought into the open. Even before it opened on November 22, 1847, the Astor Place had generated controversy in its management, offerings, and social ambiance. The controversy focused public attention on opera as essentially its social setting. Along with the riots, it completed a link between the opera house and a hated upper class.

The Astor Place was located in a newly developing uptown neighborhood and set in a courtyard formed by the intersection of Broadway, Astor Place, and Eighth Street (fig. 5). The courtyard setting was a new environment for a theater (an exception, the Richmond Hill, had been converted from a private mansion). The opera house was neither inserted between neighboring buildings nor flush with the street (compare the Park's setting, fig. 1). For the first time, a newly built theater was not blended in with shops, homes, and other ordinary-use buildings. Instead, it was separated by space on three sides that made it prominent in the landscape, even from a distance. In the increasingly crowded city, the opera house's surrounding space marked it as special. In 1849 the space also made it vulnerable to attack.

The interior of the house was likewise innovative. The auditorium had two tiers of boxes (no "guilty third tier"). The front portions were balconies, designed to "invite repose or display" and foster recognition across the auditorium.[66] The advantage of this arrangement was immediately apparent; as "a pleasant rendezvous to meet friends and exchange greetings" the opera house's clublike atmosphere was welcome.[67]

Like the Italian Opera House, the Astor Place was run by a committee of wealthy patrons. Although details of the organization are un-

Figure 5. Astor Place Opera House (1847–52), from Henry Hoff, *Views of New York*, 1850. (Collection of The New-York Historical Society)

available, some information is found in the press. The Astor Place was built by soliciting two hundred subscriptions at $75 per year for five years. As at the 1833 opera house, the subscribers would attend performances free. But the managers would pay them no rent and were allowed to rent the house on non-opera nights as they saw fit.[68]

The committee made changes in standard management practice. The free list, whereby the press and the theatrical profession were admitted without charge, was abolished, a policy that annoyed the press corps. Editorials pointed out that because earlier opera houses had been unsuccessful, the Astor Place would need all the publicity it could get.[69] One- and five-year subscriptions were available, with seats assigned by a complex lottery system that guaranteed five-year subscribers the same seats throughout the period.[70] Subscription tickets, each with a blank for its holder's name, were not transferable.[71] All seats cost $1 except those in the amphitheater (gallery), which cost 50 cents. Although the advertising does not so state, probably only amphitheater seats were sold to nonsubscribers. To discourage prostitutes, unaccompanied women were not admitted.[72]

The opera house was opened on November 22, 1847 with Verdi's *Ernani*. Although the auditorium seated between 1,500 and 1,800 persons, by opening night only 500 had subscribed.[73] The house was not a success. In its remarks, the press took the part of the nonsubscribers at the top of the auditorium. The amphitheater, "a large, steep, open, cold-looking place," was unappealing and potentially dangerous if a quick exit was needed.[74] The lighting was also criticized: A large chandelier blocked the view of the stage from many amphitheater seats.[75] Only two days after the opening, the *Tribune* expressed the need to "restore a feeling of confidence in the enterprise which has been seriously shaken." After a week of performances, a writer for the *Sunday Age* noted non-elites in the amphitheater audience.[76] Yet on December 4, when a nonsubscription night offered all seats first-come-first-served, only about three hundred attended.[77]

The Astor Place's poor showing led to editorializing on the obligations of the subscribers as opposed to those of the rest of the public. As at the Italian Opera House of 1833, subscribers had put a good deal of money up front. Thus, the argument went, it was unfair to expect more from them. Moreover, it was unfair that the public got so much for little; if people wanted opera, they would have to pay enough to keep the opera house alive. But it was also clear that current public support could not meet expenses. The remedy suggested was increased public attendance. After all, opera could not be established without steady support, regardless of the appeal of its nightly offerings.[78]

The opera house's troubles also inspired a variety of social comment. Only three weeks after its opening, the irrepressible William Mitchell of the Olympic Theatre produced William K. Northall's *Upper Row House in Disaster Place*.[79] The playbill describes the fashionable dramatis personae as parodies of members of the Upper Ten Thousand. The leading couple were "A la mode — King of the realm of Fashion, a gentleman who does not wear his clothes but lets his clothes wear him" and "Lutestring — A lady of many airs, anxious to strike a blow."[80] The male lead was played by Frank Chanfrau, whose forte was the working-class Bowery b'hoy, usually Mose the fireman. The chorus consisted of "Fairies, Ladies of Upper Ten-Dom, Courtiers, Mechanics, etc." In his studies of the Olympic, David Rinear has surmised that *Upper Row House* "concerned itself with the attempt of three people to found a fashionably elite opera house and closely paralleled the actual events which had caused the 'disaster' in Astor Place." No script or evidence of the music used survives.[81]

The relationship between the spoof and the "disaster" was evident, and the spoof was a success. Mitchell was praised for tact in dealing with such a delicate social issue, and the *Spirit of the Times* predicted he would "reap a harvest from public dissensions, and will at the same time contribute much to the restoration of good humor."[82] On the short term, the *Spirit*'s writer may have had a point about good humor. But ultimately the class distinctions were no joke; the social setting Mitchell had burlesqued had hit a raw nerve. The *Home Journal* nicknamed the Astor Place the Dress Opera, the Up-Town Opera, and the Excelsior Opera, calling it a place for "the out-of-sight-out-of-mind fashionables [to] . . . remedy . . . the calamitous miscellaneousness of their condition." The paper continued, "The public has, somehow, by universal consent, looked upon the whole Astor-place project as a *movement of the Aristocracy.*"[83]

This kind of attack quickly became a cliché. It was probably also an overstatement. Indeed, some of the commentary is neither dispassionate nor, like Mitchell's play, good-humored, but thoughtless and inflammatory. It even brought the specter of death: The *Times and Messenger* evoked the spirits of the Upper Ten Thousand's artisan ancestors. In a vision, they return from the grave through traps in the stage to "glare at [the operagoers] mournfully, shaking their heads at the folly of their position, and pointing in derision with their skinny fingers to the golden fretwork, painted dome, and richly-colored panels, dedicated to an amusement and in a language neither of which they understood."[84]

The operas of what was called the modern Italian school played a role in the Astor Place's ill-success. The operatic upsurge of 1847 (Palmo's, the Havana company, and the opera house) brought the first Verdi operas to New York — *I Lombardi, Ernani,* and *I due Foscari.* With Verdi, whose works were being heard in the city near the beginning of his career, each new opera could be judged with a view toward establishing his reputation. Although the first, *I Lombardi,* had been produced at Palmo's, the Astor Place's opening quickly linked the opera house social setting with the new composer. Critics' responses to the composer and the setting moved in tandem. For most, neither lived up to the old ideal: a balanced communion between a refined, elevating performance genre and an audience of taste and virtue.

Beginnings of this change in attitude toward opera may be seen in the reaction to *I Lombardi*, performed on March 3, 1847. On the long term, Verdi's operas became popular staples of the repertoire. On the short term, however, Verdi was the first composer subjected to deliberate fault-finding in New York. His success in Italy and Paris entitled him to a hearing, but New York critics asserted their autonomy by disparaging European audiences: "Tinsel, glare, and music fascinate the Parisians. Many a heavy opera is carried safely through on the back of gorgeous processions."[85] By looking for negative traits in a European success, the critics could assert an American perspective.

Reviewers noted the differences between Verdi's operas and those of his bel canto predecessors, finding three problems with his style. Verdi's operas were noisy; some suggested he was merely covering poverty of invention with sound. The music was overworked; the melodies lacked ease, grace, and memorability. Finally, through relentless musical ambition, Verdi disturbed the stereotype of the emotional, unintellectual Italian. To some critics' surprise, his chiaroscuro — the orchestral light and dark — was intentional. Verdi was not merely creating a flow of melodies with "the controlled abandon of the Italian school," but was actually thinking about what he was doing.[86]

Here Verdi was compared with Bellini, Donizetti, and Mozart. Writers suggested that by trying too hard Verdi failed to achieve the sweet lightness of bel canto. A comment from the *Albion* is typical: "The melodies do not possess the catching, popular qualities of a Bellini, or a Donizetti, but they are very similar in character and construction. . . . They seem to us as though they were written under restraint [constraint], that is, as though they were composed under the most impressive remembrances of the masters of his school who have gone before him." The orchestration, on the other hand, suggested that Verdi aspired to Mozart's musical heights. The same review continued: "This love of noise is the curse of our modern writers: with the Italians it is mere noise without substance. It will be a happy day for the cause of music, when writers will return to Mozart's simplicity! His music always had meaning, always bore the impress of the mind; he needed not the aid of drums and trumpets to cover up the want of thought."[87]

The comparison with Mozart is especially telling — an early critical comparison between a contemporary opera composer and a revered master on musical terms. Unlike the relatively young Verdi, Mozart was long-dead, his music beginning to symbolize an eternal truth of musical excellence distinguished from an ephemeral modishness. Verdi had yet to prove himself. Thus he offered critics an opportunity to distinguish between quality and fashion and between critically ordained truth and ignorant fads among the public: "If there were a body of learned musicians in the country who could withstand this Verdi inundation, or any other — who could oppose the ephemeral, . . . the influence of false music would not be so bad. The composer would be ranked at once according to his real merits by this tribunal; and those who then persisted in admiring him, would do it of their own free will, as preferring to be fashionable rather than musical."[88] That Verdi could seem an aspirant to musical excellence threatened the interpretation of opera as amusement and social ostentation. A critic who disparaged opera as fashion would more likely deprecate its newest composer. In contrast, one who advocated opera's permanent establishment would more likely seek out his merits.

The first path was more often taken. With Verdi, opera was losing esthetic status and a link with the sentimental ideal. As one writer put it, "The days of Rossini, Bellini and the others are numbered. There is no just appreciation of their great labors. Taste, or rather a want of taste, prevails, and new composers became the public rage."[89] The public could no longer be edified if the new operas were inferior. Nor could audiences be praised for enjoying music that lacked the refinement Rossini and Bellini had created through "their great labors." With Verdi, bursting on the scene with a new style just as opera's elitist reputation seemed to become fixed, the link between the decline of "taste" with the rise of "aristocracy" could be made.

The completion of the Astor Place furthered the connection. At its opening, the *Albion*'s Henry Watson expressed disgust with the composer while asserting that the opera house's patrons were not true cognoscenti: "We have awarded him [Verdi] some praise upon certain points, but of this the favourite opera with our Italian singers [*Ernani*], we can hardly say a civil word — it is noise, noise, noise! a perfect row-de row, with one or two exceptions. But if the subscribers *will* this sort of performance, who shall gainsay them? They have a perfect right to do what they like with their own, but we should be sorry to take this class of music as a standard of the taste in that delightful art of our educated citizens."[90] This link had developed since the time of the Italian Opera House. In 1833 criticism of opera's exclusiveness did not diminish the high value usually placed on the genre. Now, however, the operas and the audience were bound together. That subscribers would actually prefer such music contradicted the notion of simultaneous esthetic and social superiority. Rather, the bonds between esthetic and social distinction were slowly loosening as many critics increasingly turned inward, favoring composer-oriented esthetic issues that wrote most of the opera audience off as incompetent and philistine (chapter 7).

By May of 1848 the *Spirit of the Times* could state accurately that "the opera has failed."[91] The paper gave the usual reasons — bad management, repetitive repertoire, poor productions, and singers' wars. The *Democratic Review* added the operas themselves to the list of problems: "instead of Rossini we have been stunned with Verdi" and many of the new operas were ill-received.[92] In June the opera house was leased to theatrical entrepreneur William Niblo, whose popular resort and theater, Niblo's Garden, had burned in 1846 and was not rebuilt until 1849. Dramatic productions continued until November of 1848, when opera was resumed under the management of Edward P. Fry.

Like the first year, the second was a financial failure. In March of 1849 Fry bowed out due to insufficient subscriptions for a new season. After a brief nonsubscription season under Max Maretzek, the house was again leased out for dramatic performances. It was under these circumstances that William Charles Macready performed on May 7 and 10, 1849, the nights of the bloody Astor Place Opera House riots.

The riots were touched off by a feud between Macready, who was British, and Edwin Forrest. Forrest had booed a Macready performance and defended his right as an audience member to do so. The incident (along with others) sparked animosity between the two stars. Their differences were aggravated by Forrest's American patriotism, his broader acting style, and his popularity with working-class audiences at the Bowery Theatre. When Macready was billed for the Astor Place in the same role Forrest was playing elsewhere in the city the makings of a riot were in place.

The first night's events took the usual theater riot format. The all-male audience booed Macready as he appeared, showering him with objects brought for that purpose. Macready resolved not to perform again but a committee of literary and "gentleman" supporters urged him in a newspaper advertisement to continue the engagement. He acquiesced, and on May 10 his audience included supporters and adversaries. But this time, contrary to custom, thousands of his opponents had gathered outside the opera house. People from beyond its uptown, upper-class neighborhood tried to press their way in. The police fired on the crowd.

Sean Wilentz argues that the police action exacerbated the class interpretation of the conflict. Death, after all, was not in the script of a theater riot.[93] Accounts gave sharply different interpretations of the incident. From one perspective, the police were needed to keep public order. From the other, they represented the forces of aristocracy keeping "the people" at bay. Connections with opera were also made. In June, the *Herald* proclaimed that "the Italian Opera, and all that concerns it, has been growing dreadfully unpopular during the last two years; and the late tragic events in that neighborhood have not by any means diminished the unpopularity."[94]

Although opera played no direct role in the conflict, Macready's performance at the opera house aggravated the riot's class interpretation. The riots placed a stigma on the Astor Place from which it never recovered. The opera house did not last beyond the five seasons guaranteed by its original supporters. It limped along until 1852 with occasional success, its last performers a troupe of trained dogs and monkeys.[95] The following year the opera house's contents were auctioned, and the building was sold to the Mercantile Library Association.[96] Its demise brought a spate of commentary. *Putnam's Magazine* published a long evaluation of the enterprise, part sentimental and part mocking, attributing its downfall to social isolation, mediocre productions, and a catering to fashion over substance: "The little world of Astor Place rolled on: in the boxes flirtation, on the stage indifferent singing and tremendous feuds, and in the treasury a doleful raven sitting over the door, and the funds 'flitting, flitting, evermore.' "[97] The *Musical Review* published a poem in Upper Ten Thousand dialect, "The Last Kick of Fops' Alley," and asserted that the Astor Place's exclusiveness had "merited the unqualified condemnation of all true American citizens."[98] Opera house supporters had been slow to learn this lesson. In the riots, others had paid the price.

In contributing to the Astor Place's demise, the riots and their aftermath undermined the assertion that opera was inherently worthy of establishment. But the opera house's failure did not kill opera or even the idea of giving it a home of its own. Even as the Astor Place was going under, a new effort on the same model was taking shape. In May of 1852 — before the animals had taken the stage — a prospectus offered shares in an opera house under a new name: the New York Academy of Music.[99] The failure was going to flourish in spite of itself.

By all accounts the Astor Place was a failure, lasting longer than the Italian Opera House and Palmo's only because five years of subscriptions had been bought. It had, after all, been rented out as a legitimate theater as early as 1848, bringing Macready there in May of 1849. But as the Astor Place foundered, other houses, not built exclusively for opera, stepped into the breach. If Niblo's, Castle Garden, and the Broadway Theatre did not fill their treasuries with Italian opera profits, they at least held their own. There is also evidence that their most popular performances attracted large audiences. Despite disdain for opera's social setting aggravated by the Astor Place, and despite criticism of the repertoire and the performances, opera had survived; the pundits who had extended the riots' class interpretation to opera were off the mark. It was not yet known whether a demand existed for reasonably priced performances independent of the trappings of the Upper Ten Thousand mocked by the middle-class press. But if it did, entrepreneurs would fill it and in so doing reap a profit.

Performance venues for such enterprises already existed in the city. Two, the popular "gardens," were well established and profitable. Neither Castle Garden nor Niblo's Garden had originated as a theater, but were mixed-use facilities — summer resorts and sometime concert halls. The gardens were considered clean and family-oriented, free from the rowdyism and immorality of the theaters. When they included Italian opera among their offerings, they provided opera performers with a ready-made audience. In them, Italian opera finally had a venue where it could sink or swim on its own merits.

The gardens' management situations were also more flexible than those of the theaters. Committed to a permanent stock company, a theater that imported an opera troupe put its resident actors out of work. Without this commitment, the gardens' proprietors could book short-term engagements with less risk than theater managers. At Castle Garden, organizations such as opera companies sometimes paid the proprietors rent, assuring them an income regardless of attendance. At Niblo's, individual dramatic engagements lasted only a few weeks. With this flexibility, neither garden depended on the success of a particular kind of theatrical offering; if needed, opera could be supported in part by cheaper productions.

Figure 6. Castle Garden. The landfill on which the shell of Castle Clinton (Castle Garden) now sits was begun in 1854. (Collection of The New-York Historical Society)

The histories of the two gardens have much in common. Castle Garden, first (and again today) known as Castle Clinton, had been built as a fortress for the War of 1812 (fig. 6).[100] It jutted out from the Battery into New York harbor to protect the city from a British invasion that never came. Unnecessary as a fortress, Castle Clinton was given to the city in 1822 and converted into a summer (later year-round) resort with a promenade, refreshment stands, floating rafts for swimming, and a roofed-over pavilion.[101] In 1824 the Marquis de Lafayette disembarked at Castle Garden on his commemorative return to the United States. From then on, the garden was a favorite landing spot for famous visitors. Beginning in 1838, early steamship sightings drew crowds.[102] During the winter of 1844–45 the pavilion was converted into a fully equipped theater. Sunday concerts were particularly profitable, and balls were also held.[103] By midcentury, Castle Garden had become one of the city's best-known landmarks; Jenny Lind sang her first concert there on September 11, 1850.

Niblo's Garden was acquiring a similar status at the same time.[104] William Niblo, an Irish-born entrepreneur and amateur horticulturist, had built his first garden in 1828 in a rural northern part of the city. As at Castle Garden, the attractions at Niblo's were healthful air, food and drink, a variety of entertainment, and the same low admission price for everyone. On this basis, both offered refreshing summer alternatives to hot, stuffy theaters. By midcentury both gardens had incorporated theaters equipped for opera. More important, both were in a financial position to take a chance on Italian opera without fear of disaster.

Italian opera's easy success at Castle Garden mitigated the social problems lingering from the Astor Place debacle. The first productions at Castle Garden had been heard in 1847. The Marty company from Havana had performed at the Park Theatre in June and early July. By August, the Park was closed for renovation, and the company had to perform where it could get a place.[105] The choice of Castle Garden proved prophetic. Again in 1850, 1851, 1853, and 1854, the Garden doubled as an opera house. At the height of its popularity, it provided Italian opera with a setting both attractive and, before the twentieth-century performances in Central Park, arguably the most widely accessible in the city's history.

By all accounts, the 1850 Havana company performances were the most successful. Maretzek suggested, probably accurately, that only the wealthy Marty could afford to offer opera performances at 50 cents a ticket. A surviving Castle Garden account book shows that at first the company paid the proprietors $529 a week for rent, which was lowered to $300 after six weeks.[106] Whether the rent was tied to attendance is unknown. In any case, the opera company had essentially underwritten the Garden for two months.

Because the rent constituted Castle Garden's income for opera performances, the account book shows no attendance figures or amounts taken in at the door. It does include comments on attendance at each performance, however. For example, a performance of *Lucrezia Borgia* brought a "slim house — evening shower." *I Puritani* brought a "first rate house — over three thousand present." Finally, late in the season, *Lucia di Lammermoor* inspired not only a "first rate house" but "thundering applause" as well. These notes are confirmed by press accounts. At Castle Garden, Italian opera reached its first mass audience in New York.[107] These operagoers were not members of the Upper Ten Thousand. Rather, opera was available to all comers in a familiar, unobjectionable setting. For all of the disparagement of the Astor

Place as aristocratic and exclusive, opera, when it was well priced and well placed, attracted the public at large.

Being a summer enterprise, opera at Castle Garden faced no competition. At Niblo's, however, it usually did. In the winter of 1852 it competed with the last season at the Astor Place, and through the spring of 1854 it competed with companies set up at the Broadway Theatre. Finally, beginning in 1854, it competed with the Academy of Music. The competition increased the press's tendency to interpret the rivals in social terms. Invariably, opera at Niblo's was the "people's opera."

The label was well founded. Niblo's had a long-standing pricing policy of "50 cents to all parts of the house." Moreover, it had mounted no subscription series, which were usually branded aristocratic. In 1852 it even had its own company, a cooperative troupe calling itself the American Artists' Union (it included no Americans), whose members had broken off from Maretzek's troupe at the Astor Place and opened at Niblo's, with Luigi Arditi of the Havana company as conductor. New York now had two full opera companies — two sets of leading singers, two orchestras, and two prominent conductors. In early February, New Yorkers could even choose between two operas with large casts, Meyerbeer's *Robert le diable* and Mozart's *Don Giovanni,* on the same evening.

Opening prices at Niblo's were $1, second-row boxes were 50 cents, private boxes were $6, and children under ten were charged half price. A storm of protest arose as people demanded a return to "old prices," the term borrowed from the London "old price" (O.P.) riots of 1809. Prices were reduced to 50 cents, with no extra charge for a reserved seat. The press cheered, and the public flocked to the performances. The *Times* commented, "[They] have now resolved upon what they should have done at first, CHEAP ADMISSIONS."[108]

The differences between the two opera houses went beyond price. The *Albion*'s Richard Storrs Willis analyzed them socially:

> From the tone of feeling displayed, it is said that the one party [i.e., one opera troupe] represents the aristocracy, the other the democracy of the city; each appealing to these two supposed classes in the community. In point of plurality the democrats will of course have it, as has been shown by the truly mass-audiences at Niblo's. . . . The houses at the Astor Place, have been — as was to be expected with

the old price of tickets [i.e., old, high opera house prices] — not over large. We observe, however, that the fashionables still keep their seats, and show no wavering of fidelity to the favourite locality and leader [Maretzek].[109]

This interpretation was hardly new. Now, however, the Astor Place management was sensitive to it. Niblo's low prices forced Maretzek's hand. He had begun his winter season charging the same prices as the previous fall: box and parquette were $1, with 50 cents extra for a reserved seat and 50 cents for the amphitheater. On February 2, 1852, he announced a new nonsubscription season with all seats priced at 50 cents except in the amphitheater, which were 25 cents. Thus the cheapest seats at the Astor Place were actually cheaper than at Niblo's.[110]

Opera at the Astor Place for 25 cents? The press expressed delight at such prices, along with the performance quality and the attendance at both houses. *"The Opera* in Astor Place drew a ruinously-full house last evening," one commentator, typically, observed. "The seats, the passage-ways and every nook and cranny within the theatre were occupied by the closely-packed audience, which[,] not content with crowding to suffocation all the available space within the walls, actually protruded into the lobbies, which were occupied around the doors by those who stood, with eager eyes and ears, perched upon chairs."[111]

The "people's opera" had arrived, hailed "as the auguing of the Millennium of Cheapness, Genius and Music, which, we trust, is only just before us, in the shape of a permanently low-priced opera."[112] The bargain prices had brought the opera house an audience. The aristocratic label fell away in the face of the opportunity to see a splendid production of Meyerbeer's *Robert le diable* for 25 or 50 cents. As the *Tribune* put the issue, "As the *people* must support the Opera here, there must be the people's price, or the thing will be an inefficient imitation of something altogether foreign."[113] Foreign (aristocratic) opera was expensive, admitting only the wealthy. In the tradition of the theater, American (democratic) opera was open to — and by all appearances dependent on — the public at large.

But the Millennium of Cheapness brought on by competition was short-lived. As soon as Niblo's company ended its season in mid-February, Maretzek raised his top price to $1.[114] His season ended in early March, leaving the city without Italian opera for nearly a year. In early

1853 rival companies again sprang up, performing at Niblo's and the Broadway Theatre, each with a newly imported European prima donna. But "people's opera" prices were gone. Hearing soprano Henriette Sontag at Niblo's cost $2 top, and tickets to hear contralto Marietta Alboni at the Broadway cost $1.50.[115]

Nevertheless, the dream of high-quality performances at moderate cost continued. The key was the size of the house. If the public would not pay high prices, a large auditorium could hold enough people to meet expenses at a lower rate. With seeming unquenchable optimism, the *Tribune* reasoned, "If the united audiences at Astor-place and Niblo's were assembled at a reasonable price in a spacious house, the proceeds would cover the necessary expenses, with a balance in the manager's favor."[116] This dream had a chance; in October 1854 the spacious Academy of Music was opened to the public.

The story of the aristocratic opera house versus the democratic gardens shows midcentury New Yorkers' sensitivity to issues of nationality and social class. Aristocratic opera was expensive and seen as foreign-oriented; in 1852 the *Herald* called the Astor Place's subscription system the "European Plan."[117] The "people's opera," free of aristocratic associations, could treat the broader public with "American" equality. In both cases, however, the performance was the same — musical theater composed by Europeans and sung in its original language by a European-trained cast. At a time of nativist awareness and activity, neither the appropriateness of Italian opera's substance for a mass audience of Americans nor the loss in meaning resulting from the foreign language was questioned. Underlying the hoopla over opera's social setting, economics, and politics was an unremarked movement toward tolerance. Any controversy the works might have engendered had been eclipsed while the free publicity aided their acceptance.

From this perspective, New York still needed an opera house to replace the failed Astor Place. The discarded opera house had major faults, but by the time it closed a venue designed for opera performances had become indispensable. Building the Academy of Music allowed New Yorkers to work yet again on the institution's social and economic problems. This time they achieved a substantial improvement. Commercial methods and a wide audience pool at the Academy provided opera with a sturdy financial base, giving it a steady chance at success.

Compared with its predecessors, the Academy, located at Fourteenth Street and Irving Place, was a success. It offered opera performances for thirty years from its opening in 1854 until being succeeded by the Metropolitan Opera in the 1880s. Unlike the Astor Place, the Academy's organization and physical structure at least paid lip service to broad public patronage. The auditorium was large; at its opening it seated 4,600 people (compared with the current Metropolitan's 3,900). Moreover, its name change signaled a new function. As the term *opera house* countered the stigma of the theater, the term *academy* countered the stigma of the opera house. Focused on opera as music, the Academy was chartered by New York State to offer music instruction and composition prizes.[118] And, finally, while the moral rectitude of opera houses in the city had not been questioned, the Academy management heralded its respectability by renaming the third tier of boxes (where in the theaters prostitutes had long plied their trade) the "family circle." Audience members were invited to bring their children to what had been the most notorious part of the hall.

But like the Astor Place, the Academy was organized by a stock company that leased the building to managers who paid production expenses and rent. Subscriptions were offered, and the opening admission price of $3 was among the highest charged in the city. Many seats in the amphitheater (the lowest-price seats) afforded no view of the stage.[119] The Academy came under the same criticism as its predecessors. It opened on October 2, 1854, with the renowned singers Giulia Grisi and Giovanni Mario in *Norma*. Grisi and Mario had already performed at Castle Garden, at prices considered exorbitantly high, with only moderate success. One periodical even called the engagement "opera-giving on the humbug system," a poor imitation of P. T. Barnum's handling of Jenny Lind.[120] Their manager, James Henry Hackett, was an old theater hand and probably knew better than to try the same trick again. But he did. And the results were the same: "The ill success of the opening nights of the new Opera-House was undoubtedly owing to the indiscreet scale of prices of admission established, and the consequent alienation of the popular sympathies from the enterprise."[121] The name, Academy of Music, "is not merely a mistake, it is a deception, for it is not in any sense an Academy, unless the public are to be regarded as pupils, who take occasional instructions in operatic singing, at the rather expensive rate of three dollars a lesson."[122] Observers also criticized a financial structure that required a manager to pay rent to the stockholders as well as admit them free. The *Musical Review* calculated an annual market rate of $78,000 for these two payments combined and commented, "No wonder Mr. Hackett could not succeed; and yet these [stockholders] are called *patrons* of the music drama."[123]

Older readers of these comments must have recognized a familiar story; the press praised moderate prices and "democratic" management policies and condemned the opposite.[124] They could not yet know, however, that this chapter would be the last, as later managements answered criticism by experimenting with prices and improving the physical layout of the auditorium. Moreover, the Academy was benefiting from Italian opera's long history in the city. The opera house story assured the Academy a reputation for elegance. To it was added the gardens' openness and freedom from the excesses of the theater. The managers' task was to maximize the twin advantages of elegance and access. Enough potential audience members needed to feel comfortable with the opera house and its rituals to allow it to break even, for the large Academy auditorium could accommodate everyone the management could entice inside.

An important example of this new approach to the public can be found in the Academy's first marketing triumph, the fall 1858 season under Bernard Ullman's management. The star of the season was twenty-four-year-old Marietta Piccolomini, a belle of the London opera stage and that city's first Violetta in Verdi's *La traviata*. Critics differed about her artistic merits (chapter 6), but all marveled at Ullman's ability to use her to draw a crowd, keep the crowd returning, and even turn a handsome profit.

Ullman had honed his marketing skill promoting performers such as the pianist and composer Louis Moreau Gottschalk.[125] His Piccolomini strategy was comprehensive. Ullman created demand for tickets by offering them at reasonable prices while seeming to limit the supply. He announced that by contract with Benjamin Lumley in London Piccolomini would play only twelve evening performances. When advertising her first matinee, he claimed it would be her only one.[126] In fact, Piccolomini gave nineteen evening performances, four matinees, and two performances in Brooklyn.[127]

Ullman also created competition for good seats. He advertised eighty new private boxes, a remodeling of the auditorium's first tier.

Taking advantage of complaints about poor sight lines, he announced that all boxes offered "A FULL VIEW OF THE STAGE." He reminded readers that the remodeling had cost the Academy hundreds of seats. Moreover, no advance orders for these boxes would be honored; they would be sold on a first-come-first-served basis at the box office. The top prices were high: A private box seating four cost $10, and a reserved seat in the parquette or one of the old proscenium boxes cost $2. But an unreserved seat in a box or the parquette cost $1, and seats in the family circle (the old "guilty third tier") and amphitheater sold for a reasonable 50 cents and 25 cents, respectively.[128]

Like the number of performances, however, the prices were not quite what they seemed. Scalpers sold tickets at other locations at high premiums. Ullman apologized, pleaded innocent, and announced that only persons known to the box office personnel would be allowed to buy more than six tickets. The scalping continued. Finally, he decided to beat the scalpers at their own game by offering tickets for the first performance of *Don Giovanni* at auction, with premiums realized going to charity. The strategy seems to have deterred the scalpers, for the complaints stopped. But comments from editors, correspondents, readers, and Ullman himself during the first two weeks of Piccolomini's engagement suggest that the best seats may have been unavailable at the stated prices, at least at first.[129] In any event, the free publicity kept Ullman's campaign before the public.

Advertising, which increased markedly under Ullman, served the same purpose. In this practice he was not alone. The amount of advertising of all sorts in, for example, the *Times* of 1858 had more than doubled from its first year (1851–52). But Ullman also had more to say than his predecessor Maretzek. The latter had advertised his programs and performers in detail. Ullman, however, gave readers full columns announcing upcoming performances. Programs were varied and featured new artists. Each had its own set of prices, along with the date that tickets were available and the procedure for obtaining them. In giving readers information needed to obtain a seat, Ullman produced advertisements that required attention and study, again marking opera as an object of aspiration.

Finally, Ullman delivered a creditable product. Marketing techniques aside, he was appreciated for making good on his promises. He was praised for the strength of the casts, for the high-quality orchestra, sets, and costumes, and for his attention to production detail.[130]

He offered his star in a variety of roles, including Lucrezia Borgia, a character considered unsuitable for a young woman with a light voice. He offered *Don Giovanni* with a second prima donna, Marietta Gazzaniga, who had already impressed the city's public as Violetta. For the same opera, he played on Barnumesque gigantism by advertising "THREE DISTINCT ORCHESTRAS" while augmenting Mozart's three ensembles to "upwards of ONE HUNDRED MUSICIANS." He offered Piccolomini in a new role (Lucia di Lammermoor) on her closing night, when a large house was already virtually guaranteed.[131] He offered two connections with charity—contributions from the *Don Giovanni* ticket auction and chorus members from the Academy's newly established free music school. He even offered performances without Piccolomini at all, including *Il barbiere di Siviglia, Norma, Robert le diable,* and *Les Huguenots.*[132] As the *Herald* noted, although Ullman's lease required him to give forty performances in a year, he had given nearly thirty in six weeks.[133]

The public responded. On the first day of ticket sales, the *Herald* reported, "So great was the 'outside pressure' that when the doors were opened it was found necessary to exercise a little gentle restraining authority, and a *queue,* after the manner of the French theatres, was formed."[134] Once inside, most of the public and press were charmed. Every performance was reported as crowded. Even the *Spirit of the Times,* whose critic was "utterly disappointed with the fair Italian," admitted that "an immense house greeted Piccolomini."[135] After her last performance, Piccolomini was honored by both the Upper Ten Thousand and the Million. The Academy's board of directors gave her a diamond-studded bracelet, and the city's uniformed fire fighters, escorting her by torchlight to her hotel, "manifested the most boisterous enthusiasm for her."[136]

Both Ullman's techniques and the response they inspired recall P. T. Barnum's marketing of Jenny Lind. Like Lind, who did not sing opera roles in the United States, Piccolomini was a celebrity, one of the most widely known in New York. The ceremonies on her departure suggest the breadth of her appeal. Like Lind, she had the affection of the fire fighters, symbols of the city's hearty, "full-sinewed" denizens of the Bowery idealized by Walt Whitman. But unlike Lind, Piccolomini also enchanted the boxholders. Her own role in her success belongs in the next chapter; the point here is her acceptance by a broad public. Young, pretty, and charming she undoubtedly was, yet she was still a woman of the stage. That Ullman, who had his choice of genres to market, gambled on an opera singer and won shows how far opera had come toward winning an audience.

Ullman based his marketing techniques on dealing with a mass public. The Academy building, along with opera's history in the city, assured it a reputation for respectability, taste, and cosmopolitanism. Equally respectable, the two gardens had also welcomed a broad audience. Ullman drew from both traditions, exploiting opera's reputation while ensuring inclusiveness. His success confirmed that inclusiveness could bring higher profits. Presumably the stockholders got their free admissions (it is hard to know; the press reports little about them at this point). But the evidence points to Ullman as the policymaker; the power of a narrow group to organize on its own terms had been eclipsed by mass-market strategies devised by a daring entrepreneur working from an underdog position. Likewise, the vestiges of an Astor Place-style private party atmosphere were gone. The presence of scalpers shows that good seats could be sold to persons unknown. The new private boxes allowed for socializing, but "Fifth Avenue belles" besieged the box office for them along with everyone else. The Astor Place's social elegance had been seen as exclusive; at the Academy, Ullman allowed anyone to have it for a price.

On the presence of fire fighters and the like in the 25 cent seats there is little evidence.[137] However, soon after Piccolomini's departure, the *Times* estimated that "the poorer classes of mechanics, laborers, &c." spent $3,600 a week "in the galleries of the first-class theatres and the opera-house."[138] The Academy's clientele probably lacked the proportion of workers found at the Park Theatre in 1822. Workers' theaters in the 1850s entertained many men who did not attend the opera but probably would have visited New York's only theater in the 1820s. But to some extent, all the old constituencies of the theater still took places in the opera audience, along with vast numbers of women. The city's theaters traditionally offered something for everyone in order to attract a broad clientele. Ullman managed to retain much of this clientele even while offering everyone the *same* thing.

In 1852 the Astor Place and Niblo's had represented opposing social settings and economic foundations. But by 1858 the two approaches were combined at the Academy of Music. The merger of elite patronage and entrepreneurial skill had supported the institution and sold its product. A long-sought goal had been achieved: Commerce had built a pedestal on which a cultural offering could stand.

But with success came a loss of status on the old moral terms. Because elites could no longer assume the respect of the rest of society, the opera house was no longer considered inherently worthy of support. The term *aristocratic* was still pejorative, and, as at the Astor Place, critical cheap shots were tempting. They usually hit their mark. In 1855 (a hard winter for the city's poor), the *Herald* published a satirical article entitled "Hard Times, the Codfish Aristocracy and the Italian Opera." Rather than sympathize with those whose distress "has been in some degree relieved by souphouses, charitable subscriptions, calico balls, and other eleemosynary shifts," it shed crocodile tears over a social class "whose sufferings have been entirely overlooked in the sympathetic and charitable movements that have distinguished our community. We allude to that select, refined, intellectual and highly ornate section of society which . . . goes by the title . . . of the codfish aristocracy." The article explained that the source of the aristocracy's distress was "the ill success that has hitherto attended their efforts to establish upon a prosperous and permanent basis that noble, intellectual and useful institution, so necessary to the progress of Western civilization — the Italian Opera."[139]

Two years later, Dion Boucicault's popular melodrama *The Poor of New York* played on the same theme. In adapting Brisbarre and Nus's *Les pauvres de Paris,* Boucicault sought to "localize it for each town, and hit the public between the eyes."[140] In doing so, he used the Academy of Music to represent the rich. Mark Livingstone, a gentleman of impeccable lineage but recently ruined financially, opens act 2 trying to sell his coat. He describes his situation this way: "Three months ago, I stood there the fashionable Mark Livingstone, owner of the Waterwitch Yacht, one of the original stock-holders in the Academy of Music, and now, burst up, sold out, and reduced to breakfast off this coat." To recoup his fortunes, he takes up with Alida Bloodgood, daughter of an unscrupulous banker snubbed by society because of his ill-gotten gains. As the two emerge from the Academy, dressed to the nines, an old, long-lost friend of Mark's appears as a beggar. Alida dismisses him: "I wonder they permit such vagabonds to hang about the opera."[141] Mark, true to his melodramatic "good" character, recognizes his friend and rushes to help him.

The opera also became a staple of "city mysteries" literature. In novels, magazines, cartoons, and other popular genres, it was subjected to the same exaggerated, often sensationalized critiques as other aspects of city life. In this literature, the upper-class stuffed-shirt was a recognizable type and an object of social satire. He and his family were often shown at the opera.[142] But by the 1850s the mocking tone of Jacksonian-era criticism had given way to a lighter, less derisive style that implicitly accepted the social order described. Walt Whitman's journalism in the 1850s is a case in point. In 1855 a report on the Academy for the nationwide readers of *Life Illustrated* shows him fascinated by the social ritual:

> It is nearly eight o'clock, and the arrivals are full and hurried. . . . Look at that woman just stepping to the pavement! . . . A half-indifferent look she gave to the crowd, every one of whom renders to her his mute admiration, and then she passed on. The gentleman, her husband, is a mean-looking man, forty-five or fifty years old, a very rich banker and capitalist. She was of poor family, and married him for his wealth, and has no love or respect for him. You can see many such couples at the opera. . . . It shines here — it is rich — but somehow do we not feel cold, estranged, mocked? Are we not in this place as in a heartless place? Would not a commoner gathering of every-day people, with friendship, and jokes, and plenty of fun and laughter, be more of a satisfaction?[143]

For Whitman, opera's setting was a fait accompli and to be pitied rather than resented. Despite his negative judgment of elite opera-goers, he saw them as worth his interest. He suggested that out-of-town readers were free to come have a look for themselves. Despite opera's exclusive reputation, the wealthy were actually part of the show. Moreover, seeing how the other half lived could teach them a lesson in valuing their own "common gatherings" over the heartless ritual at the opera.

Whitman's readers could afford to come. Opera's elegant atmosphere did not make it exclusive. The key to accessibility was price, and accessibility and profit went hand in hand (table 5). Efforts between 1847 and 1858 to find a profitable price scale eventually produced the most inclusive policy: The most expensive seats were priced high, and the cheapest only slightly more than at the theaters. This policy was developed as managers responded to competition and calls for more democratic prices. The press insisted that without govern-

Table 5. Italian Opera Prices, 1847–58

Date	Theater	Event, Manager (Performer)	High	Low
3/3/47	Palmo's	*Lombardi* premiere	1.50	.50
11/22/47	Astor Place	opening	1.00	.50
12/15/48	Astor Place	Fry company (Maretzek)	1.00	.50
3/19/49	Astor Place	Maretzek	1.00	.50
11/1/49	Astor Place	Maretzek	1.50	.25
summer 1850	Castle Garden	Havana company	.50	.50
10/21/50	Astor Place	Maretzek	1.50	.25
fall 1850	Astor Place	Maretzek (Parodi only)	2.50	.25
1/19/52	Niblo's	American Artists' Union	1.00	.50
1/20/52	Astor Place	Maretzek	1.50	.50
1/20/52	Niblo's	American Artists' Union	.50	.50
2/2/52	Astor Place	Maretzek	.50	.25
2/21/52	Astor Place	Maretzek	1.00	.25
1/3/53	Broadway	(Alboni)	1.50	.25
1/10/53	Niblo's	(Sontag)	2.00	1.00
8/7/54	Castle Garden	Maretzek	1.00	1.00
9/4/54	Castle Garden	(Grisi and Mario)	5.00	3.00
9/7/54	Castle Garden	(Grisi and Mario)	3.00	1.00
10/2/54	Academy of Music	opening (Grisi and Mario)	3.00	.50
10/5/54	Academy of Music	(Grisi and Mario)	2.00	.50
2/17/55	Metropolitan Theatre	(Grisi and Mario)	1.50	1.00
2/19/55	Academy of Music	Bull/Maretzek (*Rigoletto*)	1.50	.25
10/4/58	Academy of Music	Maretzek ("regular price")	1.50	.25
10/7/58	Academy of Music	Maretzek ("cheap night")	.50	.50
10/18/58	Academy of Music	Ullman (Piccolomini)	2.50	.25
11/6/58	Academy of Music	*Don Giovanni* (Piccolomini)	2.50	.50
12/7/58	Academy of Music	Piccolomini farewell benefit	2.50	.25
12/8/58	Academy of Music	Ullman matinee	1.00	1.00

ment support, opera in America must appeal to a broad public in order to survive.[144] Price experimentation—a series of up-and-down shifts of the structure as a whole—reflects responses by opera's controlling interests. As long as it remained unclear whether an elite or a broad-based audience would bring in more money, prices fluctuated. Once managers learned that high price scales deprived them of needed income, experimentation stopped.

The Academy also used two new settings to bring in spectators. "Cheap night" audiences were nonsubscribers who either could not afford high prices or disparaged the "aristocratic" atmosphere on subscription nights. Saturday matinees were also nonsubscription. Like cheap nights, they opened the best box seats to all comers, attracting unaccompanied women, their children, and suburbanites.

Attitudes toward matinees reflect opera's evolving social status. As with other public venues, women's presence in the matinee audiences was controversial. In 1860 the *Times* printed a long editorial arguing that matinee attendance undermined the proper relationship between a "lady" and the men in her life. Such a shift was found degrading: "The female world of New-York and all other large cities is divided unfortunately into two classes: those who have domestic and social duties during the day, and who look to fathers, husbands or brothers as the providers and protectors of their evening amusements; and secondly, those with whom the day has no duties, and who would fly to the ends of the earth rather than allow father, brother, or husband to witness their degradation."[145] Two days later, the paper printed a rebuttal from "a mother," who was offended at the idea of the opera matinee as degrading and used American free-country rhetoric to defend her attendance: "It is an invasion against the rights of the female portion of society in our City, to wish to deprive them of these legitimate and high-toned amusements, by endeavoring to throw slurs on the character of those who patronize them, and force our society to take the same tone as in Europe, where no woman is safe from insult, even in the street, without a gentleman accompanies her."[146]

The *Times*'s attitude toward opera is hardly admiring. Likening an unaccompanied woman at a matinee to a degraded one (i.e., a prostitute) demonstrates that no positive value was being placed on it. Rather, a woman attending a matinee was seen as neglecting more important work. It was no longer part of her duty to improve herself in "taste and refinement" at the opera. Indeed, the woman who wrote to the *Times* had defended daytime performances as "legitimate and high-toned"; the *Times* had called them a "dangerous resort."

Without the encouraging rhetoric that had supported the Garcias' engagement and the Italian Opera House of 1833, opera had managed to establish itself in New York. By the time writers considered the Academy of Music in 1854, their stake in opera as a goal had declined. The Academy's weak initial showing brought no calls for increased patronage of the sort even the Astor Place had inspired. Instead, commentators argued that an opera house designed as a toy of the wealthy would fail without regrets from the rest of society. Similarly, Piccolomini was seen as an engaging singing actress and a commercial success. As successful as her performances were in entrepreneurial terms, they were not seen as evidence of artistic or cultural progress.

Marketplace success had long sustained stage entertainments critics had judged immoral, vulgar, or cheap. Although performed in a polite setting, opera had likewise lost status as a civilizing force. Opera as culture, "the application of labor or other means of improvement," had been a tripartite endeavor. It was to provide a polite social setting able to refine the hard edges of American manners. It was to elevate its audience's musical taste. And it was to promote the theater's social and moral reform through music's ability to enhance an elevating sentiment. Opera's establishment met none of these goals. Instead, the union among social, esthetic, and moral progress dissolved as each went its own way.

Creating an acceptably democratic institution meant downplaying or abandoning some of the practices initially calculated to encourage a polite atmosphere — management by committee, subscriptions, high prices, out-of-the-way locations, and dress and behavior codes. Profit-orientation undermined these customs. An impresario needing to break even cared less about the kind of people he brought in than about how many. Commercialization widened the audience base through publicity along with admission policies seen as democratic and thus American. The press applauded. By noting the lack of state subsidy, commentators emphasized the commercial system's fairness. Managements cannot cater to only a few, writers argued, for the opera house is not underwritten. Aristocratic management practices will cost opera the public at large, ultimately bringing on its failure.

Opera's commercial success confirmed its naturalization on American soil. By the 1850s opera as a commodity was a source of pride for many commentators in the city's press and contradicted the perception of opera as elite entertainment. Its accessibility, particularly its availability at reasonable prices, was hailed as a distinction between operatic practice in New York and London. In 1858, for example, the *Musical Review* asserted that in London, "there are thousands of well-to-do people . . . who have never entered [an opera house] . . . on account of the exorbitant price of admission." In New York, however, "whoever is willing to pay fifty cents for operatic enjoyment has certainly been to the Academy" where "the Italians do the thing better" than the English.[147] Admission by payment rather than by membership in a select, perhaps inherited, group meant that opera was truly public — hence, truly democratic. Without aristocratic or government patronage, the argument went, opera had to be supported by the public or it would not survive. As in the theater, commercial success was equated with audience sovereignty, which in turn determined value in American terms. Naturalization had replaced an ideology of cultivation directed from above with one of access, entrepreneurship, and freedom of choice. As market forces had been severed from the stigma of the theater, merit had lost its link with elite control.

With these changes, other practices, originally conceived as improvement but disparaged in the 1840s as ostentation, were now admired as social panache. Members of the city's "middling classes," attracted by opera's elegance and by their longstanding interest in music, could either use opera to mark their social position with the Upper Ten Thousand or, as Whitman suggested, at least have a good look. Music's civilizing power no longer formed an ideological basis for opera's social value. Instead, as a form of public culture accessible through the (moderate) price of a ticket, opera could serve social mobility or, as critics in the 1850s argued, social climbing. Thirty years after the Garcias, using opera as an object of aspiration had become a marketing strategy that was paying off.

Opera's institutional establishment had failed to give it the respect that early proponents expected. Audiences that had responded to the sentimental operas of the 1830s had acquired social status and moral uplift. Since then, however, many of the most successful operas had undermined rather than supported the moral ideal, thus seeming to counter old links between virtue and social success. The decline of the moral message reopened the question of the bases on which opera would be respected and judged. How, for example, would New Yorkers deal with such pieces as *Rigoletto* and *La traviata*? Could they face the moral issues (as opposed to absolutes) these operas raise? How could they deal with powerful emotion that no longer supported an elevated sentiment? Is there evidence of opera's rejection in some quarters on moral grounds, or was the link severed among verbal content, meaning, and value? New Yorkers were offered many musical genres during and after the 1850s. Which among them — the Jenny Lind concert series or, more likely, the Philharmonic — could inherit the ideal of music as esthetic refinement and moral uplift? Or had the belief in music's all-encompassing value to an individual or a society been permanently destroyed?

The New Italian Opera and
Its Reception

*A*fter years of uncertainty, the failure had finally flourished. At last, New Yorkers could take a critical look at opera itself. As in Europe, nineteenth-century opera was a repertoire in formation; new works by Verdi, Wagner, Meyerbeer, and other composers were tested for public and critical approval. New Yorkers heard these operas at the Astor Place Opera House, Castle Garden, Niblo's, occasionally the Broadway Theatre, and finally the Academy of Music. Many were successful, and from the 1850s on New York audiences shared the task of creating the now-standard repertoire with their counterparts in London, Paris, Milan, and other cities. After all the attention paid to the institution and the social setting, opera's substance — its music, drama, performance quality, and message — was finally the center of attention. It was called into question as well. With its entrepreneurial foundations laid out before the public and its success defined in commercial terms, opera could no longer be accepted as inherently elevating, deserving of support regardless of its onstage success. The old theatrical dictum of please-or-fail remained in force.

Meanwhile, the style of opera that finally established itself in New York had changed radically. Steady performances over the years had created a growing repertoire of operas that would hold the stage for much of the century. Regular operagoers, including commentators on the city's musical scene, knew dozens of works, ranging from Rossini's lighthearted *Barbiere* to the latest blood-and-thunder production of Verdi. Few of these works had been composed, not to mention heard in New York, in the 1820s. Although in many ways resembling the successes of the 1830s, the operas of the so-called modern Italian school were a far cry from the Rossini pieces held up as "rational and refined" in 1825. Further, they were incompatible with, and untransferable to, the tradition of adaptation for the English and American theater. The vocal styles, especially for the men, outpaced the training undertaken by many English and American singer-actors. More important, sentimentality and (with a few exceptions) comedy were being replaced by unresolvable conflict, sometimes horror, and death. Operatic death had been seen in New York as early as the Garcias' performance of Rossini's *Otello* in 1826. But by the 1840s it had become the rule. As a writer on Donizetti's *Anna Bolena* snidely commented in 1850, "We heard it remarked . . . that the attendance on the Opera was chiefly regulated by the number of characters killed in the plot. One death by dagger on the stage insures a fair attendance; and the treasury gains just in proportion to the increase of the slaughter."[1]

Although the English operas of the 1830s had supported links between opera and moral didacticism, most of the Italian works were introduced in the 1840s and thereafter did not. Along with opera's commercial basis, the decline of sentimental themes undermined the view of music as a civilizing force. The new operas affected the way the genre could be promoted and on what terms audiences could accept it. Opera could neither be held up as "innocent amusement" nor its music as elevating. Neither the civic culture rhetoric from the Garcias' season nor the moral ideology that had served the successes of the 1830s would do. Few of the new operas would have been acceptable, much less pleasurable, to audiences enchanted with *La sonnambula* in its early years. Moreover, with opera no longer considered inherently worthy of acceptance, attempts to promote its "progress" through laudatory reviews like those of the 1820s and 1830s would no longer be effective. Dealing with a fait accompli, midcentury writers on the city's operatic scene saw themselves as judges, aiming at independent, dispassionate accounts of a piece or performance. As reviewers cast a jaundiced eye on a genre that had lost some of its luster, opera's establishment fostered its first serious critical scrutiny in New York.

At center stage in this reassessment stood the operas of Verdi, especially the three major operas of the so-called middle period, *Rigoletto, Il trovatore,* and *La traviata.* Although these works share much with their bel canto predecessors, their stylistic range is wider, more clearly reflecting individual characters and dramatic situations. Verdi began to call more sparingly upon lyric beauty, mixing it with either the dark and brooding or the brash and cheap. This new blend of styles brought opera's dramatic content to the fore, but it cost opera some of the appeal that had previously fostered its acceptance in New York. In middle-period Verdi, musical beauty no longer tempered the horror's effect or supported moral conventionality or uplift.

The new operas finally forced the moral issue. Opera's social and institutional upheaval had not buried the old question of the theater's didactic purpose. Thus in 1855 *Rigoletto*'s critics struggled with its horror, its lack of poetic justice, and its seemingly misplaced musical beauty. Nearly two years later, *La traviata* retold in music the story of Alexandre Dumas *fils*' successful new play, *Camille.* In contrast with *Rigoletto*'s reception, its immediate triumph shows a new set of values in force. The name of the new opera house, Academy of Music, reflected and highlighted the change — a new understanding of the relative importance of opera's music and plot. No longer a drama with musical accompaniment, opera had become a piece of music that told a story. Reversing the priority between musical and dramatic understanding distanced opera from the link between esthetic and moral value. With *La traviata,* it finally became possible to face the moral implications of an opera plot from a more musically oriented perspective. Opera could be judged as a musical, emotional, and dramatic performance independent of the traditional idealities of the stage.

That *Rigoletto* would set this process in motion is unremarkable, for the opera undermines with irony every principle central to the theater as a school of morality. Its method is simple and obvious: The three main characters turn on their heads the conventional relationships among long-familiar vocal and character types. *Rigoletto* shared the prima donna lyric-coloratura soprano, the tenor (seemingly) in love with her, and the fatherly baritone with earlier bel canto and English operas. Like the heroines of the 1830s, the prima donna, Gilda, is tested for virtue. But unlike them, she fails to uphold standards achieved by such characters as Amina and Amilie. Worse still, her father, the baritone Rigoletto, fails to save his daughter's virtue from the profligate, arrogant, evil, but charming duke. The duke has seduced, abducted, and raped her. Rigoletto, the court jester, plots to kill him in revenge. But Gilda manages to place herself in the duke's place as murder victim, thus sacrificing her own life to save her lover's. The scene at the end of the opera in which the father finds his daughter near death in a body bag is as shocking as anything yet seen on the opera stage. Thus *Rigoletto* undermined the conventional social contract in which a woman places herself in the care of a father or husband in exchange for protection from physical, psychological, or moral harm. Together, Rigoletto and Gilda show viewers exactly what respectable Victorian ideology wanted to hide: how easily a "good" girl, everyman's daughter, could go wrong.

The duke, however, was the linchpin of the message. In him, *Rigoletto* showed how easily a consummate actor could overcome everything the good girl had been taught. As ardent a tenor as New Yorkers had seen, the duke was nevertheless, as one critic put it, "a most vacillating and unaccountable ruffian." Yet he "sings gaily to the last," unstoppable in his conquest despite having caused misery and death.[2] Critics at the New York premiere in 1855 recognized how important the duke's music was to his charm and appeal as a character and identified his jaunty "La donna è mobile" (ex. 10) as the "gem" of the opera. It "would alone save the piece from a fiasco," wrote one critic.[3] Another called it "equal to anything of the kind Verdi has ever written."[4] A third found "something — I don't know what — young, fresh, and galant that commands bravos."[5] This comment is exactly right — the duke's song is calculated to make a hit. With its clear melodic profile, buoyant rhythm, and simple accompaniment, when delivered by a tenor whose voice is equal to its demands, "La donna è mobile" seems to sing itself. Written in a consciously popular idiom, it is easily remembered when it returns. And its irony — the lying, promiscuous duke accusing women of being "changeable as a feather in the wind" — is all the more powerful for being irrelevant to its attraction.

The duke and his tune are robust, "muscular and manly." Yet applauding them in the name of musical enjoyment meant applauding the confidence man, the ultimate artificial person and one of the types most evil to the reformist sensibility. At a time when good versus evil was considered a fundamental human distinction, especially onstage, a seemingly upright deceiver, in particular a successful one, was particularly feared. By seducing Gilda, the duke shows how easily virtue and candor can be faked — especially by a wealthy aristocrat. Iron-

Example 10. "La donna è mobile" (*Rigoletto*), Boston: Oliver Ditson, 1853, excerpt.

ically, however, through the music he seduces the audience as well. The character plays on the by-now standard persona of the operatic tenor — vocally powerful, sincere, and a fervent lover (as, for example, Elvino in *La sonnambula*). In "La donna è mobile," this vocal power is mixed with bravado, glibness, charm, amorality, and joie de vivre. Its reprise at the end of the opera announces the duke's victory over the brooding Rigoletto, who, hearing him sing, learns that the paid assassin has failed to kill him. The reviewers who applauded the duke for musical reasons likewise applauded the source of the plot's horror and the arrogance with which he trumpets injustice. In so doing, they accepted the unacceptable on musical grounds, privileging the musical over the verbal as the primary source of meaning in opera.

The link between music and didacticism, so successful in the 1830s, was breaking. The days when evil men did not even sing at all in an opera were gone, replaced by sophisticated, multileveled, often ironic characters incompatible with the old one-to-one correspondence between sound and sentiment. One is reminded that the early English adaptations of *Don Giovanni* (first performed in New York in 1819) featured the seduction song, "La ci darem la mano," sung not by the evil don, as Da Ponte and Mozart wrote it, but by Zerlina's legitimate lover, Masetto. By midcentury, of course, the song was instead sung onstage in New York by the confidence man and seducer.

With so much to confuse or offend the public, *Rigoletto* inspired an ambivalent response from critics and only modest success with audiences. Although some reviews of both the premiere and subsequent productions are positive, none is enthusiastic. Most suggest that writers struggled to reconcile conventional expectations with the opera's seeming strangeness. For some commentators, the piece's horror was the triumph of the evil duke over the innocent Rigoletto: one critic called Rigoletto "a very ill-used gentleman" and noted that "the Duke sings gaily to the last, albeit a most vacillating and unaccountable ruffian. There is no justice, poetic or otherwise; nothing but horrors, horrors."[6] Others, however, defended the story, arguing that an opera needed such a heavy plot to inspire the composer. The *Tribune*'s William Henry Fry put the connection in abstract terms: "The merits of an opera, as a composition, are two-fold — the interest of the work as a drama with good situations, exciting the genius of the composer, . . . and next, the value of the music."[7] Another writer was more specific: "The story of Rigoletto is as horrible as any Italian librettist could conceive, but as it gives occasion for several highly dramatic scenes, which can be effectively worked up by the composer, it is rendered not merely endurable but attractive."[8]

Like the laudatory comments on the music of "La donna è mobile," interpreting the plot as grist for the composer's mill allowed a critic to avoid facing the opera's failure in traditional moral terms. There was, of course, much to face. As in contemporary popular melodrama, *Rigoletto* shows the underside of life as not only out of control but also understandable as a sequence of events. The opera's most beautiful music, such as Gilda's "Caro nome," in which she sings to the "dear name" of the duke (who has lied about his identity), makes those events convincing. As Verdi's listeners feel her emotion through the music, they understand how a sweet girl and devoted daughter could indeed succumb to such temptation. The possibilities for real-life interpretation were clear, especially at a time when prevailing male-female stereotypes pictured young, innocent women as incapable of surviving without men's protection.

The standard melodramatic interpretation of *Rigoletto* would have been a warning to unwary virgins that seemingly well-intentioned young men often bore dishonorable intentions and that women and their protectors needed to be vigilant for evil designs.[9] This interpretation plays on a genuine nineteenth-century fear. Opera was not the usual public forum for that fear to be exposed, however. A real-life interpretation of *Rigoletto* would have contradicted the very notion of opera as an elevated art form. Moreover, with the most popular tune sung by an attractive villain, the music became an agent of the view of life expressed by the plot. *Rigoletto*'s reviewers were forced to deal with a frightening story where they least wanted it. In the opera house, the story of the confidence man overpowering the precious daughter of an outcast may have hit too close to home. From this perspective, the reviewers' ambivalence is understandable. The question is not whether New Yorkers were able to appreciate *Rigoletto* as a work of art, but whether, given its departures from standard operatic fare, they could have been expected to come to terms with it at all.

Amid the ambivalence, one journal—the *Musical World: A Journal for "Heavenly Music's Earthly Friends"*—did condemn the plot outright. Its editor, Richard Storrs Willis, had kept to the "school of morality" approach to criticism: "The exhibition of crime when the guilty suffer, as in Mozart's *Don Juan*, may impart sometimes, and at certain stages

of life, a useful lesson. But when crime . . . is depicted, and the innocent suffer, while the guilty escape, the plot we consider objectionable." This much had been noticed by others. But Willis went further,
referring to Gilda's "infidelity" and "ingratitude" to her father — the
only 1855 response to *Rigoletto* that blamed Gilda for anything. Willis
also condemned the "great latent power and an intense (too intense)
appeal to the feelings" in the plot: "Shakesperian suffering ('sharper
than a serpent's tooth'). . . dwindles in comparison."[10]

In his condemnation, Willis took the opposite perspective from Fry,
for whom the "intense appeal to the feelings" in the plot was needed
to inspire the composer. Willis understood and feared that the strong
emotion could have an appeal of its own independent of a moral
message. In condemning *Rigoletto,* he did not expressly state this fear.
He did so elsewhere in the *Musical World,* however. In a long article
titled simply "Music" he insisted that "the modern opera . . . [does
not] square with our endeavor to prove the exclusive value of music as
the only one of the arts exempt from the trail of the serpent. There
are some recent operas that do not give this theory somewhat of a lie;
not only in the pomp and vanity of their luxurious accessories, but in a
suspicious fascination in the music itself, leaving impressions on the
mind that we have been rather listening to the Syrens from the Isle of
Calypso than to the Muses of Mount Olympus."[11] Willis recognized
the power of music in the "modern opera." He understood that its
"suspicious fascination" could undermine the moral control he still
expected music to exert. Its style fit the new plots and the "intense . . .
appeal to the feelings" too well to be a source of uplift. In condemning *Rigoletto*'s plot and the new operatic style, Willis perceived that
music was being pried loose from its didactic moorings. His concern
was to reestablish conditions under which it could still keep hold.

As Willis showed, the sentimental standard was not yet completely
ignored, and as the 1850s progressed a current of moral debate on
opera not only continued but also increased. While *Rigoletto* had inspired an ambivalent and poorly articulated exchange, *La traviata,* a
classic prima donna opera, brought these issues to center stage. The
opera, premiered in New York on December 3, 1856, was debated
both before and after it appeared. The propriety of treating a morally
unconventional character sympathetically was questioned, focusing
attention on the conflict between didactic and esthetic value in a stage
work. In the face of such controversy, the opera was a hit. In establish-

ing the modern Italian school on its own terms, charm succeeded where direct assault had failed. Despite debate, its immediate success clarified new assumptions about the terms on which a stage work could be accepted and its role in the lives of its audience. While *Rigoletto* had forced its audience to take it seriously, *La traviata,* aided by a succession of appealing prima donnas, beguiled New Yorkers to the same end.

At the time of its premiere, *La traviata* was known in the city on two accounts. Its source, Dumas's *Camille,* had been produced several times from December 1853, and efforts to have the opera removed from the London stage were reported in New York. The early careers of *Camille* and *La traviata* in New York were similar. The first performance of *Camille* was widely applauded, but because the star, Jean Davenport, was at the end of her engagement, the play was not repeated. Later performances attracted favorable attention, however, and within five years city audiences had seen seven actresses, ranging from amateur to star, in the role. *La traviata* opened with Anna de Lagrange as Violetta. Again, the reception was favorable, but the company was on its way to Havana, so the opera was not widely heard. Within five years, however, New Yorkers had seen seven Violettas, including Marietta Piccolomini, who had created a sensation in the role in London, and, in 1860, seventeen-year-old Adelina Patti.

Both works were successful in spite of (or more probably in part because of) arguments about their morality. *Camille* is the story of a woman of the Parisian demimonde who falls in love for the first time but is forced to sacrifice her love because of her checkered past. Camille's lover, Armand, is of a respectable provincial family that includes a father and a sister. The sister is about to be married, but her fiancé's family disapproves of the marriage because of Armand's liaison with Camille. Armand's father convinces Camille that if she truly loves Armand she must give him up for the good of his family. To do less would be to only to play at love for pleasure, a pastime for which she is already well known. Camille acquiesces, leaves Armand, and throws herself back into her old life. Her frenetic activity strains her consumptive constitution. At the last moment, the devastated Armand learns of her sacrifice and arrives in time for Camille to forgive him as she dies.

Dumas's plot was criticized on moral grounds. When in 1857 the Unitarian pastor Henry W. Bellows shocked the religious community by stating that under some circumstances the theater could be considered acceptable, he advocated reform by eliminating objectionable plays such as "the late alarmingly popular 'Camille.'"[12] Dumas was dismissed as "utterly devoid . . . of either a high moral nature or beauty of conception or thought" and the play's Parisian success was attributed to "pandering to some passion of the hour."[13] In 1856 the actress Laura Keene even tried to answer objections by having "all the incidents . . . transpire in the course of a dream." Thus, "the heroine who goes to sleep virtuous awakes in the same happy condition."[14]

In one respect the criticism of *Camille* was on the mark. The play is primarily about morality — about an impossible liaison between a man of respectable past and prospects and a woman who has lived outside conventional expectations. Camille understands her place in society. She has doubts about Armand because of his background, understands before he does that his father will disapprove of their relationship, tells Armand that he must "remember who I am and what I am," and finally sacrifices her own happiness so that his sister can marry. These issues are treated with care in the play. But responses to *Camille* suggest that in some quarters morality was still a given and an absolute. Camille's past made her unacceptable as a companion for Armand and unfit for the stage.

Yet, like Armand's father, the New York public was won over by Camille's character and personality. Writers found *Camille* (as they often said) *interesting* and its dramatic situations powerful. Containing "scarcely a wearisome word," *Camille* held its audience's attention for five acts devoted to the struggle between love and convention.[15] Throughout, the spotlight is on Camille. The opening party scene's frivolous banter shows her the woman of the world who, by her own admission, has never loved anyone: "Thank God!" she says (act 1, scene 12). We see Armand slowly penetrate her shell with the offer of love; she calls him sentimental (act 1 scene 10), but she is listening closely. We hear her debate and finally give in, all the while suspecting that her happiness will come at a price. We see Armand's father corner her in debate and her failed attempt to tell Armand that she does not love him. We see her try to play her old self at a party where Armand publicly insults her. We see her frantic attempt to dissuade Armand from dueling with her escort on her account. Finally, we see her listless on her deathbed, having heard from Armand's father that Armand now knows the truth and is coming to beg forgiveness. We see her joy at his arrival, her sudden urge to live, and its futility as she spends her last breath urging him to marry but still revere her memory.

Camille forced the New York critics to distinguish between moral and artistic value and face the success of an objectionable play with a respectable public. Because none related the play's emotional power to its moral dilemma, approval required separating emotion from morality. The *Albion*'s "Hamilton," who detested *Camille* on moral grounds, nevertheless appreciated Laura Keene as "an impassioned, brilliant, and effective Camille."[16] By 1857, when Matilda Heron's performance in the role brought both critics and public to their knees, he admitted that "conceding the play as fit to be played at all, we must admit that the part of Camille is eminently adapted to develop all the resources of emotion, intensity, finesse and pathos which an actress may possess." Of Heron, he expected a lesson, but not a moral one: "I shall be disappointed indeed if she does not stay with us long enough . . . to teach our people in their turn, how marvelous a virtue lies in the artistic spirit." The critic's use of the word *virtue* is telling. Not associated with the character she was playing, Heron's virtue was artistic and her role a vehicle for "emotion, intensity, finesse and pathos."[17]

The response to *Camille* influenced reactions to *La traviata*. The opera's origin in the play was well known, as was the debate about both in the London press.[18] The debate on the opera took place in New York as well. The New York reporter for *Dwight's Journal of Music* summarized the city's press on the moral issue: "Mr. Seymour, the critic of the *Times,* treats the contested point of the immorality of the opera in his usual light, facetious style, considering it as of no special moment. Mr. Fry of the *Tribune* ignores the suggestions of the story altogether. The critics of the *Courier* and *Evening Mirror* apologize for the opera, attribut[ing] any disapprobation to excessive and false prudery, while the *Post, Express,* and *Day Book* condemn the work as unfit for public presentation." The writer went on to make his own case: "Certainly the career of a prostitute is not a fit subject to be brought into public notoriety, and especially in a manner that arouses for the guilty creature not merely pity, but a lively sympathy."[19]

Dwight's critic spoke for the music journals as a whole. As in the case of *Rigoletto,* the music magazines still held to the ideal of music as morally uplifting and the role of words in creating a properly elevated sentiment. According to the *Musical Review, La traviata* showed "a world which has all the appearance of the most noble society without its respectability, and even that little purity of sentiment and character which it can still claim as its own." Verdi, it claimed, was thus a suitable composer for the libretto: "he shares . . . the fate of most modern artists, who instead of elevating the spirits, of ennobling the minds, of strengthening them by the purest artistic efforts, by means of the grand and the beautiful, stoop down to its lowest understanding and its lowest passions."[20] The *Musical World,* on the other hand, declined to review *La traviata* at all, preferring only to print the drinking song from act 1 with an innocuous text, "Gaily through life we wander," substituted for the original.[21]

Given the reception of *Camille* in New York and *La traviata* in London, this sort of comment is not surprising. But held against New York's opera reception alone, it belongs to an emerging train of thought. Taking a historical perspective on the issue for the first time, some critics of *La traviata* remarked that other "immoral" women, such as "Mrs. Norma [and] Mrs. Borgia," had long been seen without objection in successful operas.[22] With such operatic precedents, they argued, writers had no business linking *La traviata* with *Camille,* for doing so would produce objections "quite untenable when taken up against the 'Traviata' alone":

> If it be wrong to produce any representation of unlawful passion, or of immoral life upon the stage, then it is clear that we must make almost as clean a sweep of both the dramatic and operatic *repertoire,* as the flames made lately at Covent Garden. The interest of "Norma" is not founded on relations such as a right-minded gentleman would wish to see established between his bosom friend and the ladies of his immediate family: the heroine of "La Favorita" does not occupy a social position to which a respectable young lady would be encouraged by her mother and her pastor to aspire; and yet these Operas have been performed, one dares not think how many times, before the most proper and even Puritanical audiences to be found in America, without exciting one word of comment and remonstrance, from the pulpit or the press, while the cry of terror and tribulation sent up in London, and echoed from Dublin, has been re-echoed from Boston and from New York, against the production of an Opera of which the hero is a vastly better-behaved and more magnanimous person than Pollione [in *Norma*], while the

heroine of it stoops to no conduct so degrading as that by which the royal "Favorita" brings down upon her hapless head the unerring justice of the stage.[23]

Surprisingly perhaps, the writer had a point; the watchdogs of the public stage had been napping unnoticed for more than ten years. Moreover, he considered the status quo acceptable. Given that *Norma, La favorita,* and similar operas had been accepted, it would be hypocritical to base judgment of *La traviata* on a higher moral standard merely for being based on an objectionable play. In rejecting a moral basis for judgment of an opera, the critic affirmed that the opera stage had abandoned a standard to which the theater was still expected to aspire.

The abandonment of the fixed moral requirement affected the response to Marietta Piccolomini, who played Violetta in 1858. Piccolomini benefited from the fact that the role had already passed muster, for her auditors could unproblematically enjoy the star in her own vehicle. Thus it opened the way for a flood of performer-oriented criticism that considered both Piccolomini's musical and dramatic merits. Despite cuts, the plot of *La traviata* follows the play closely. Like Camille, Violetta was known as an "acting role," one in which a performer could easily communicate a character to her audience. Dramatic reasons for this interpretation are obvious. The leading female character takes the stage early and is the center of attention throughout. Violetta herself is fully formed — young, vibrant, and personable, surely a welcome change from the morose Rigoletto or the quartet from the tuneful but horror-filled *Trovatore.* During Marietta Piccolomini's engagement, both *La traviata* and Violetta were sometimes even called "charming."[24]

Violetta is also honest; the other characters and the audience know what she is. Nor is she idealized; although many bel canto leading women (Desdemona, Norma, Lucrezia Borgia, and Lucia di Lammermoor among them) are given elaborate orchestral introductions, Violetta has none. Instead, she appears at the outset, mingling with the other characters, playing party hostess. Nor is her musical style particularly refined. When she is joyful, her music is virtuosic, but she sings no ornament for its own sake. Although her vocal range reaches high C, the tessitura is closer to that of a Rossini mezzo-soprano such as Rosina or Cenerentola than that of later sopranos. This range, coupled with an active, agitated accompaniment in the orchestra, gives Violetta a forceful vocal quality suitable to a nonconventional character, especially a woman with a life and mind of her own.

Marietta Piccolomini seems to have understood Violetta well. Her portrayal had initiated her London success and was her first offering in New York. Although reviewers admitted that she was not the best singer they had ever heard, many thought that her realization of the character overcame her vocal deficiencies. Piccolomini was an engaging young woman, graceful and pretty, who played mostly ingenue roles. Like Maria Garcia Malibran and Jane Shirreff, she sang both comic and serious parts. But she had little repertoire in common with them — only Zerlina, which both she and Malibran sang. Piccolomini sang neither Bellini nor Rossini and no sentimental heroines such as Amina, Donizetti's Linda di Chamounix, or Giselda in Verdi's *I Lombardi*. Instead, her operas were mostly new and popular (*La traviata* and *Il trovatore*) or old but new to New York (Mozart's *Le nozze di Figaro* and Pergolesi's *La serva padrona*).

Of these works, *La traviata* allowed Piccolomini the best opportunity to minimize her vocal limitations while emphasizing her acting talent. She shared this strategy with Jane Shirreff. But where in 1838 Shirreff's lack of virtuosity was taken as a sign of her "truth to nature," in 1858 Piccolomini's hearers addressed her deficiencies directly. Again the New York correspondent for *Dwight's* summed up:

> Piccolomini is by no means a great singer — her voice, though somewhat sympathetic, is not powerful, and can scarcely be heard in the concerted pieces. Her execution is smooth, though not facile; and a difficult chromatic passage she will turn off into something else that is easier. . . . The critics are very just and unanimous in their estimate of her abilities. While awarding to the young prima donna much praise for her finished and touching style of acting, and for her sympathetic singing, they all acknowledge that she is not a first-class opera singer.[25]

This new attitude resulted in part from raised performance standards and from knowledge of the opera, including its difficulties. Unlike Shirreff's audience, Piccolomini's expected acceptable sound and technique on purely musical terms, and its spokesmen knew precisely how and when she failed to meet it. Despite her acting ability, an agreed-on fault was given the last word: She was not a great opera *singer.*

The response to Piccolomini also reflected a new notion of what an actress was actually doing onstage. Her ability to realize a character in a direct, seemingly spontaneous, unmannered style was admired. Unlike Shirreff, however, she was no longer expected to represent reality, that is, a feminine ideal. Praised for her charm in the first act and pathos in the second, she could not be praised for portraying an elevated sentiment, for she presented a kind of reality seldom spoken of in polite company. Like the critics of Matilda Heron in *Camille,* commentators on Piccolomini's Violetta were impressed by her emotional power and intensity. But they failed to temper their enthusiasm for her portrayal of a sympathetic but immoral woman. A reviewer of the original production even defended Violetta's mixture of the noble and the depraved. "A perfectly pure being does not interest us — Why?" he asked. "Because," he replied, "it does not awaken any fellow feeling . . . in our hearts." He then reminded "the Scribes of Grace Church, and innumerable other graceful churches, that mankind's best friend was also the friend and defender of Mary Magdalene."[26] A look back shows how much had changed. Maria Garcia had evoked "fellow feeling" — common understanding and sympathy between the stage and the audience — with her lighthearted, delicate but spirited portrayal of the coquette Rosina. Jane Shirreff had done it by seeming to become the artless innocents Amina and Amilie, who imparted their most profound truths from beyond the rational intellect. Ironically perhaps, Marietta Piccolomini did it by persuading her audience to accept an opera character who would remind them of the Bible's best-known prostitute.

With this approach to an opera plot came a new perspective on Verdi's music. One critic wrote, "[With Verdi], vocal gymnastics gave place to declamation, and earnest realism displaced artistic finish and gave a greater vitality to opera than it had ever reached before." This situation, he continued, was a two-edged sword, with a new kind of excellence replacing the old: "While Verdi's music calls equally upon the genius of the singer, it asks less of the mechanical education than that of his predecessors. Consequently, while his works will inevitably tend to the early development of the *genius* of the vocal student, they will also bring before the world a legion of unfinished artists — that is, artists unable to render acceptably the compositions of other and more ornate composers."[27] As heard in *La traviata,* Verdi's vocal style had clarified the difference between opera as an elevated, refined musical art and the course it had actually taken. The change was not necessarily an improvement. Singers unstudied in bel canto were sometimes condemned for not being true artists. "Voice and individuality are the elements of the modern school of operatic singing in Italy," wrote one critic.[28] But for others, musical "earnest realism" meant as much a dramatic gain as a musical loss. Without the burden of edification, opera could allow its audience to face the powerful but unidealized emotions to which the new style was suited.

Walt Whitman's change of attitude toward opera is a case in point. In his 1845 manifesto "Art-Singing and Heart-Singing," Whitman had criticized opera's social character and its music.[29] "The subtlest spirit of a nation is expressed through its music," he maintained, "but nearly every nation has its peculiarities and its idioms, . . . so that hardly any thing which comes to us in the music and songs of the Old World is strictly good and fitting to our own nation." Whitman objected to "the stale, second-hand, foreign method, with its flourishes, its ridiculous sentimentality, its anti-republican spirit, and its sycophantic influence, tainting the young taste of the republic" and preferred the "elegant simplicity" of the Cheney family, "something original and beautiful in the way of American musical execution."[30]

Eventually he changed his mind. In "Art-Singing," Whitman had advocated music that "appeals to the throbbings of the great heart of humanity itself—pictures love, hope, or mirth in their comprehensive aspect." He came to see opera as having such appeal, allowing it to transcend national and class boundaries. Verdi's music, no longer tainted by un-American, "ridiculous sentimentality," could even cancel his negative social interpretation of the Academy:

> The orchestra is full . . . and at the signal of the leader they begin. . . .
> The Opera-house, with all its contents, drops rapidly away. The crowded tiers—the gas-lights—the rich and novel spectacle—the beautiful women—vanish from your eyes and thoughts with the first beat of the drum. It is the stormy music of Giuseppe Verdi; it is the noble opera of Ernani. With the rise of the curtain you are transported afar—such power has music. . . . A new world—a liquid world—rushes like a torrent through you. If you have the true musical feeling in you, from this night you date a new era in your

development, and, for the first time, receive your ideas of what the divine art of music really is.[31]

Whitman's enthusiasm for Verdi shows how deeply Italian opera had penetrated the American democracy. It also gives us an alternative to the critics' perspective on the genre. By the 1850s the idea of beginning "a new era in your development" with an opera performance was conservative. Critics no longer conceded to opera the power to initiate such development. Acceptance of the new style had brought a new attitude toward music's influence. In the 1830s music had been advocated for its ameliorative properties and "control over the peculiarities of the age."[32] It had been promoted as a shaper of culture — an artistic activity that could improve the moral tone of society. By the 1850s, however, it seemed merely to reflect instead of influence its time. "The intense and passionate music of Verdi," remarked a critic, "although sometimes exaggerated and vulgar, is more in accordance with the energy and velocity of our time [than Rossini's]."[33] *La traviata*'s setting, style, and sensibilities were modern. They were accepted as such, in spite of their imperfections, with neither adulation nor disparagement. Enjoying and appreciating the opera on its own terms — as drama, as entertainment, as a star vehicle, as elegant social event, and as musical involvement — showed that the age in which promoting music (or perhaps any activity) in hopes of reforming society was drawing to a close.

The reception of *La traviata* marked a low point in opera's status as a didactic art form in New York. The enthusiasm caused by a singer acknowledged as mediocre undermined opera's link with progress. So did the success of musical power in an unedifying dramatic vehicle. Yet the press's attention to moral issues suggests that *La traviata* had at the same time made a strong impression on its audience. Opera was more than fashion and social climbing. No longer elevating, yet serious enough to transcend entertainment, it brought human imperfections to the fore while tempering their impact through music. In so doing, it was freed of the illusions of piety, virtue, and poetic justice that had constituted the theatrical ideal. But it also weakened — perhaps broke — the ideological links between refined taste and moral uprightness and between music and social or moral reform.

The decline in moral idealism left room for other avenues of reception. As Walt Whitman urged his fellow audience members to gawk at the social elite at the opera, so did events onstage inspire an pleasurable disdain of the "not us." Voyeurism, born of this attitude, acknowledged the less-than-refined aspects of the new operas while rationalizing enjoyment of such characters as Violetta, who required at least lip-service condemnation. An early critic who took this approach was Richard Grant White of the New York *Courier and Enquirer*. Further, the social origin of his reviews may shed light on the growing cleavages between holders of distinct points of view toward opera's substance. The *Courier* was one of the few influential papers left of the old mercantile press. Expensive, sold by subscription, and conservative, it served a clientele of wealthy Astor Place Opera House supporters.[34] White's articles on opera included no opera house descriptions, disdainful remarks about the Upper Ten Thousand or the codfish aristocracy, and no social analysis. Unlike most of his journalist colleagues, White wrote "from within."

From this position, White could approach opera's substance more freely. The most striking example of his style may be an 1848 review of Donizetti's *Lucrezia Borgia*. The review, twelve paragraphs on the first page, is remarkable not only for its willingness to face new issues but also for its author's appreciation of a horrible plot: A Renaissance murderess poisons a gang of young men who have offended her, only to find she has poisoned her son as well. White made no concessions to audience fastidiousness. Nor did he attempt to ameliorate the opera's horror with any claim that music is edifying or compensatory. Instead, he told the story in the style of a popular sensationalist writer, treating the plot and its emotional impact, describing the performers' success in connecting the two, and taking delight in both. His view of the final murderous scene recalls the 1825 *Othello* reviewer's horrified delight at "the act of plunging the dagger into Desdemona's bosom":

> With the impression of the second [act] yet occupying the mind, we anticipate the doings of the third as we would the coming of a threatened tempest, and with shrinking expectation long for the lifting of the curtain which hides [Lucrezia] from us, and as it rises we are awed by her presence and feel that she is the *Lucrezia Borgia* whom she claims to be. — With the gesture of a queen and the expression of a beautiful demon she motions her victims away to die, but the appearance of [her son] *Gennaro* among them dethrones the queen and exorcises the demon, and she is again the frantic mother. *Gennaro* refuses his own life and threatens hers. *"Preparati!"*

he exclaims in a tone hoarse and oppressed with fury, and at this fearful moment she gasps out the long concealed confession, *"Son tue madre!"* The tone in which these exclamations are uttered by the two artists, and the action with which they are accompanied make the scene thrilling, painfully exciting. The knife drops from his palsied grasp and his arms remain raised in horror while she couches before him with her hands hard clasped hard upon her knees and her head bent down upon them in abasement. Both are crushed, he with the shameful thought that he is a Borgia, she with the consciousness that she is the author of that shame. We have never seen, nor can we imagine an attitude more beautiful or more pregnant with expression than that of TRUFFI [the singer], as she thus bends before *Gennaro.* — But the castrophe hastens, the poison is finishing its work and *Gennaro* writhing in agony clings to his guilty mother, and true to the pursuit of his existence forgets her guilt and breathes his last breath upon the bosom of her from whom he received both his life and his death. He falls heavily from her arms and she casts herself a living corpse by his side, the victim of contending passions.[35]

White minced no words. He expected his reader to see the death scene (anew or for the first time) as he painted it. Rather than offering "participation in joy," as a writer had done in the 1830s, he called the scene "thrilling, painfully exciting." Far from deemphasizing its horror, he found beauty in its emotional power. White detailed Lucrezia's "contending passions" without expecting her to have taken any other action. He recognized that she was no longer the idealized virgin of the operas popular in English in the 1830s, yet he passed no judgment. "We speak of the characters of the opera as realities," he wrote, "and the events of the scene as facts." According to White, Lucrezia and the others represented nothing beyond themselves; they simply *were.*

For White, the strong emotion that the bel canto musical style elicited was still a powerful draw. But it was no longer dependent on a stereotype that elevated a middle-class ideal of sexual purity. Instead, it presented someone else's stereotype. White's quotations from the libretto (without translation) reminded his readers that he had heard *Italian* opera. Performed by "foreigners" and depicting a far-off time and place, *Lucrezia* could show New Yorkers — in particular his upper-class readership — a reality that they could safely assume was not their own.

Calling the characters realities acknowledged a side of life not often articulated in polite company, especially in public. But at midcentury, the "underside" of society was of intense interest. Making sense of an increasingly diverse population in New York brought a proliferation of racial and ethnic stereotypes and unabashed voyeurism. The plot of *Lucrezia Borgia* was the stuff of "city mystery" literature, books with titles like *New York in Slices, by an Experienced Carver*, a type of pseudo-nonfiction purporting to expose the "full truth" of urban life while emphasizing (and undoubtedly exaggerating) its seamy side.[36] White played on the genre. Without irony he used a sensational style associated with marginal rather than conventional society. This style was well known in the city, as was the marginal world it conjured up — a world reformers were trying to eliminate or at least hide but that could be viewed from afar through "yellow covered" pamphlets, in the press, or from the safety of an opera box. White's style tacitly accepts what David S. Reynolds calls subversive culture as if it were orthodox, fails to speak from a morally conventional point of view, and betrays a code of reticence and gentility in writing on music.[37]

Nor were reticence and gentility always applied to performers. The stereotype of Italians as charming, overemotional, oversexed, and unfit to be taken seriously extended beyond opera, and at least one observer noted the discrepancy between the Anglo-American respect for Italian culture (i.e., the classical heritage) and disparagement of Italians themselves.[38] Female opera singers were fair game, subject to veiled sexual commentary that would have been considered disrespectful of earlier stars such as Maria Garcia or Jane Shirreff or even the upper-class Marietta Piccolomini. There was no need to present these opera singers as role models or even as respectable women. Thus eighteen-year-old Clotilda Barili was described as "picked, like fruit under-sun in the garden of Italy, to finish ripening in another clime."[39] Teresa Parodi was called "a real Italian woman, full to the overflowing of her heart with the wild, passionate action and melody of her delicious country."[40] At least some critics were fascinated by non-Anglo Saxon female performers. Like White, they ignored conventional standards of propriety in public discourse, even while marking opera's sexual content as a negative trait.

By 1860 many of the new operas had become repertoire staples and new terms of acceptance the norm. Opera's existence in New

York's social and cultural life had been clearly established. Its position was narrower than that of the old English operas in the theater; as time passed, opera competed with an ever-growing variety of public entertainment. Like any other commercial endeavor, operas such as *La traviata* were commodities, their success distinguishable from (if sometimes consonant with) critical approbation. The decline of great social, moral, and esthetic claims for opera created gaps in the city's public culture for other types of music to fill. The ideals of moral edification and critical approval were better served by musical performances that could be understood as "purest artistic efforts," removed not so much from the taint of the theater as from opera's inability to serve them. At concerts, especially those of Jenny Lind and the New York Philharmonic, audiences could develop a new, more strictly musical ideal on an esthetic foundation. Disassociating music from the problems of the theater and the world would help keep this ideal intact.

Seven

Opera and the "Higher Order of Composition"

*I*f opera was no longer recognizably lofty, music itself certainly was. And attempts to "prove [its] exclusive value . . . as the only one of the arts exempt from the trail of the serpent" continued apace.[1] In 1855 *Musical World* editor Richard Storrs Willis even claimed success in the political realm. His magazine was reaching important people in Washington — more than seventy members of Congress, the president, vice president, members of the cabinet, the Supreme Court, "and a score or more celebrities besides" were subscribers. "There is hope for this nation," he asserted. "The effect of this upon our national counsellors must be softening — tranquilizing — refining — harmonizing, . . . not even an excited Congressman can resist [music's] charms."[2] Willis's analysis notwithstanding, his facts testify to the high value still placed on music in American culture. Many still believed in its civilizing power. Purity of heart, tastes rendered simple and good, harmonious thoughts, holy sentiments of universal kindness and good will — these musical benefits had kept their hold on antebellum American society.[3]

The public's response to these ideals helps explain the success of Jenny Lind. The true inheritor of sentimental opera — the tradition of Amina and Amilie — was neither the Italian nor the English singer of the 1850s but Lind, who, by the time she arrived in New York in 1850, had given up singing opera roles entirely. P. T. Barnum's innovative marketing of Lind in the development of commercial entertainment is famous. Equally significant, however, is the way she kept alive — and used as selling points — all the old notions of music's moral value. While embodying the softening and refining attributes Willis claimed for music, her concerts also offered vocal music removed from a potentially corrupting dramatic and social setting. In this way, she mediated between opera and the largely nonverbal repertoire of orchestral concerts. Her moral purity anticipated the esthetic purity of music that would later receive the highest accolades.

Lind opened her two-year American tour in New York, arriving on the heels of the successful 1850 summer season of Italian opera at Castle Garden. Her repertoire consisted of four types of music: opera extracts, sacred music (usually from oratorio), balladry (largely English, Scottish, or Swedish), and virtuoso novelty pieces. Opera was prominent in her programs and even assumed pride of place at her debut; the first piece Lind sang on American soil was "Casta diva" from *Norma*. Yet Lind was nothing that an opera singer was supposed to be (fig. 7). She lacked glamour, prettiness, vanity, and arrogance. She was not Italian; in fact, her northern European origin was presented as a drawing card.[4] "Slight, maidenly," she was described as possessing an "intrinsic worth of heart and delicacy of mind, . . . a great and noble simplicity, combined with an ardent imagination."[5] She was an avowed Christian whose unwillingness to break the Sabbath to perform or even travel was publicized. Her decision to contribute much of her earnings to charity was likewise advertised, along with the recipients and amounts when she made good on her promise.

Lind was also famous for having given up the stage. For the religious press, she won attention and respect for this fact alone. Two New York religious papers, the *Observer* and the *Evangelist,* printed a view of opera, attributed to Lind, that distinguished between music itself and its use on the stage: "It was not till after much solicitation, that I consented [to appear in opera], and then, only on condition that I should control the stage, and, if possible, change its character. I always felt, as I do now, that music is divine, that it is from heaven, that there is no manner of sin or wrong in it, and that it should not be debased, nor made the instrument of evil. Music has a high and holy mission to perform, and we should not sing simply to amuse, but to purify, to elevate, to instruct." The commentator approved: "It was not till she visited Great Britain and France, that she became con-

Figure 7. Jenny Lind as Amina in Bellini's *La sonnambula,* sheet music cover for "The Sonnambulist's Song" (New York: William Hall, 1850). Note the "madwoman" hair flowing out from under her usual demure pageboy style.

vinced that the task she had undertaken [of reforming opera] was hopeless, and that she could do more for the art she loved so well by separating herself from the stage altogether. This she has done. She is no longer an opera singer. . . . She unhesitatingly expresses her belief that it is alike unfriendly to morals and to song, and opposes it by the influence of her name, her reputation, and her talents."[6]

Lind's disavowal of the stage was central to her promotion as a concert singer. Her European reputation would have sustained her in opera, but because no vocal recitalist had been marketed on such a grand scale she would need to attract people who did not go to concerts to succeed. Such individuals were assured that Lind, like Maria Garcia and Jane Shirreff before her, was not only the kind of singer but also the kind of woman they would care to patronize. Her reputed excellence, coupled with her disdain for the stage, confirmed the link between music and edification that had been frayed by the growth of the opera house. The idealized "mirror up to nature" had moved out of the theater and onto the concert stage. Personifying the connection between artistic and moral purity, she was "an admirable proof of the necessity of moral culture to the full development of the voice. Young declares an undevout astronomer mad; Miss Lind proves an impure and selfish singer impossible."[7]

This was the singer whose performances inspired some of the most rhapsodic prose the city had yet seen in print. "There was real sublimity in the scene, when Jenny Lind's voice, after one of her brilliant soarings into the highest heaven of melody, floated away into silence, and a hush as complete as that of death fell upon the house," wrote John Sullivan Dwight. He called her Castle Garden concerts "unequaled in moral grandeur."[8] The Beethovenite critic Hermann Saroni likened Lind's duet with two flutes by Meyerbeer to "a fairy web, through which the glorious tones of her voice peeped occasionally like some bright star."[9] Nathaniel P. Willis imagined Lind as a singer of sacred music only: "Had the divine music of Casta Diva . . . been the Lamentation of the Daughter of Jephtha, and had a background of religious reverence given to the singer its strong relief, while the six thousand listeners were gazing with moist eyes upon her, how immeasurably would not the effect of that mere Operatic music have been heightened?"[10]

The effect these writers described approaches the nineteenth-century ideal of emotional-religious reverence. Given what the audience knew about Lind, Willis was probably correct in asserting that the effect would have been even greater had she begun with a piece — one whose music was as "divine" as "Casta diva" — on a sacred text in English. With most of her operatic selections coming from unobjectionable operas (e.g., *The Magic Flute, I Puritani, L'elisir d'amore,* and *Der Freischütz*), it was indeed strange that she should begin with an excerpt from the problematic *Norma*. Willis noticed the irony: "Pure invocation to the Moon, the Norman Deity, as the first two stanzas are, the latter half of the solo is a passionate prayer of the erring Priestess to her unlawful love; and, to be sung truly, must be sung passionately, and with the cadences of love and sin." The second half could not be sung correctly "by a voice that had formed itself upon her life and character," and in fact, "on Jenny's lips, the devout purity and imploring worship and contrition, proper to the stanzas in which the Deity is addressed, are *continued throughout.*" In a literal sense, Lind could not be true to the music's original intent. But Willis rightly pointed out that the words could be ignored, allowing the listener to substitute a more worthy sentiment: "To those who listened without the thought of the words, it was delicious melody, and the voice of an angel — for, in its pathetic and half mournful sweetness, that passage, on such a voice, goes straight to the least expectant and least wakeful fountain of tears — but it was Jenny Lind, and not Norma."[11]

Although not central to Lind's appeal, the fact that it was she, and not Norma, singing "Casta diva" helps explain why she was acceptable to the American audience. As a character, Norma (or anyone else) would have projected a personality, volition, and an emotional life. Lind seems to have projected none of that, at least on stage. At her best, Lind performed "Casta diva" with technical perfection, allowing Bellini's music essentially to sing itself. No longer tainted with intimations of sexuality, "delicious melody" could come from "the voice of an angel." Indeed, the ethereal quality of Lind's voice probably hindered her in making a convincing interpretation of any passionate utterance. Thus it could inspire "moist eyes" in her audience, approaching the loss of rational control feared by critics of opera's emotional power but never quite reaching it. As Peter Buckley remarks, the hush over the crowds at Lind's concerts speaks to this quality. She seems to have been not quite human, but rather a more celestial being bringing music from another world.[12]

Jenny Lind sang operatic "gems" in their original languages, allowing her audience to hear "music from heaven," associate it with the pious Jenny Lind, and ignore (or remained ignorant of) its original setting. While spreading operatic music and reconfirming its appeal, she helped disassociate it from the theater—from plots and characters her audiences might find objectionable and from singers who no longer met conventional standards of feminine virtue. Moreover, in publicly rejecting the stage she told her listeners that the disassociation was conscious and morally based. In this way, she held up the distinction between controversial musical drama and inherently moral music.

With Lind, the power of music to move people in potentially dangerous ways was carefully reined in. R.S. Willis feared that "a suspicious fascination" in opera's music suggested "the Syrens from the Isle of Calypso [rather] than . . . the Muses of Mount Olympus."[13] With Lind, he need not have worried. Even compared with the sentimental heroines of the 1830s, her emotional range was narrow. Although characters of the 1830s were held to a strict ideal of femininity, they could at least give vent to despair or joy as their dramatic situations warranted. Holding to an even stricter ideal allowed Lind to offer operatic music without fear of debasement. The musical purity of her performances could reflect the purity, charity, and Christian virtue of the singer and assert their high place in American society. Through Lind, both commentators and audiences could use music to glorify a Victorian moral framework that seemed increasingly threatened by outside forces. She answered the fear that music's strong emotion would have an appeal of its own that would be independent of a moral message, for she was the moral message herself.

Jenny Lind was not the only performer to benefit from opera's loss of moral status. While Lind offered an analogy between pure music and a pure life, instrumental concerts offered purity of a different kind. By midcentury, orchestras such as the Philharmonic (1842) and the Germania Orchestra (1848) allowed New Yorkers to compare symphonic music and opera directly. Where the Philharmonic Society of 1824 had lasted only two years, the 1842 Philharmonic is the present-day ensemble. In his book *Philharmonic*, Howard Shanet has called the orchestra's early years unnecessarily German-oriented. Even granting the amount of orchestral music that Germans and Austrians composed, the Philharmonic's programming of more than 70 percent German works "exceeded the proportion that might be expected." Moreover, Shanet notes, although one would expect works by Beethoven and Mendelssohn to appear frequently, "the inclusion of a Gumbert, a Heinemeyer, or a Schindelmeisser, when equally talented American composers were clamoring for attention and being ignored" was greater cause for complaint.[14]

The Philharmonic was not yet the high-profile cultural institution it was later to be. In the middle of the nineteenth century it gave at most four concerts per year and sold tickets only to associate members and subscribers.[15] But its early success, indeed, its continued existence, speaks to a core of interest in German orchestral music in the city. Like Lind, orchestral music reined in some of emotional extremes found in opera, allowing music to convey seriousness and dignity in an atmosphere of social decorum and moral propriety. It offered elaborate structures along with complex harmony and counterpoint that stood in sharp contrast to the "suspicious fascination" of operatic melody. Unlike market-based opera, the symphony could seem (if not quite be) above the entrepreneurial fray. Without words or stories, it could not be considered crude or immoral, so its appropriateness for a polite audience was not questioned, and the kind of voyeurism possible at the opera had no object. It was comparatively inexpensive to produce, saving it from advertising ploys, interpreted as cheapening an art form through commercialism. Although early Philharmonic programs included vocal music, even operatic excerpts could be held up as pure art through concert performance, independent of economic constraints, moral controversy, or the dictates of fashion. As a writer for *Putnam's* magazine put it in 1853, "an audience . . . of those who truly enjoy and appreciate the best German music" had succeeded "the brief reign of fashion" at Philharmonic concerts.[16]

Interest in German orchestral music was matched by an increase in German opera. The first German opera in English adaptation had been Weber's *Der Freischütz,* performed in 1825 as the only German item in the eclectic repertoire of the English musical theater. Since then, periodic attempts had been made to explore other German works. In the 1830s, *The Magic Flute* and *Fidelio* were produced (both in English adaptation), and in 1845 a short-lived season in German was given at Palmo's to encouraging notices.[17] In 1850, for the first time since 1826, Mozart's *Don Giovanni* was finally produced complete and in Italian under Max Maretzek at the Astor Place Opera House.[18]

On terms current in midcentury New York, *Don Giovanni* was Italian opera after its language. But it was treated as if it were German. Moreover, its revival proved to be a watershed in the city's operatic life, opening the way for other non-Italian works such as *Der Freischütz* (1850), Meyerbeer's *Robert le diable* (1851) and *Le Prophète* (1853), *Le nozze di Figaro* (1858), Flotow's *Martha* (1859), and even Balfe's *The Bohemian Girl* (1859) and William Henry Fry's *Leonora* (1858), both translated into Italian from their English originals.[19] This expansion, along with the Philharmonic, fostered a new strain of music criticism in New York that continued to develop throughout the nineteenth century and into the twentieth.

While Verdi stood trial at the Astor Place and beyond, by the 1850s the publicity and commentary on *Don Giovanni* emphasized the value of a work by a great composer. In urging attendance, the *Herald* called the 1850 premiere "a great solemnity."[20] The German-born critic Hermann Saroni called the audience a "vast assemblage" and remarked, "We are gratified, because, if such Music be appreciated properly, a beneficent influence cannot fail to arise from it."[21] Another writer noted the respected English conductor George Loder playing bass at the performance and called the gesture "a voluntary homage to the name of Mozart."[22] A commentator on a later production felt inadequate even to comment on the opera: "What should we say of him [Mozart] that has not been said? How could a pen, now, add a single leaf to his ever-green laurels? But though we were unable adequately to praise him, we cannot help expressing our admiration whenever we are so fortunate as to witness *Don Giovanni*. What a wonderful composition is this opera!"[23] And finally, in reviewing a poor performance in 1855 a critic even used the word *canon*: "*Don Giovanni* is sacred ground. Mozart is canonized, and we cannot countenance the desecration, the wilful destruction of our musical idol."[24]

Imagine *"Don Pasquale* is sacred ground" and the difference becomes clear. Neither Bellini and Donizetti nor Verdi were presumed acceptable. The Italians, each in turn the creator of new works in the current musical idiom, had to prove themselves anew with each opera and were expected to have their day in the sun and die. One writer even used Rossini's eclipse by Verdi to note that "this experience can not but be gratifying to elevated musical taste, for if Rossini's operas, which contained at least some excellent music, have vanished in less than thirty years, there is some reason to believe that Verdi's musical and other horrors will die out in less time."[25]

At midcentury, then, German opera—and German music in general—was in the ascent. Its institution, like that of Italian opera, depended on audience-building and economic factors. Increased German immigration after midcentury contributed to its success. But so did the rapidly developing idea of a musical canon on essentially esthetic values, addressed not to Germans but to Americans. The canonic idea was not unique to New York. In fact, Boston, with its audiences less enthusiastic about opera and the theater, probably played a greater role.[26] The bases on which the canon was being established were more suited to concert than theatrical genres. These new critical bases included the sentimental ideal of music as amelioration. Saroni's comment on *Don Giovanni,* for example, repeats the by-now old saw that music brings a "beneficent influence" to refine and enlighten a people. But German music inspired a new set of premises for making such claims. The new critics no longer thought of music as "coming directly from the heart." Musical value was being transferred from supporting a verbal message to the style itself and the key player in its transmission from dramatic character to performer to composer.

This transference climaxed a long process. In the 1820s and 1830s a piece such as "Home, Sweet Home" could be appreciated for an unoffensive, lyric style and an emotional clarity that supported moral uplift. Even this early, however, a purer esthetic occasionally broke through the sentimental ideal. Italian opera had sometimes been called "rational and refined," free of the vulgar comic songs of the English tradition, pure and classical.[27] Even sentiment could be considered a hindrance to "pure taste." "Music first strikes the youthful mind," a commentator had written in 1833, "more from the sentiment it conveys, than from the love of the music itself. It is, in fact, the mere vehicle of some delightful passion, such as love, heroism or patriotism." Later, however, he explained, "The frequent recollection of the pleasing theme, however, is always attended by its brilliant accompaniment [i.e., setting], which in time becomes naturalized, and music begins to be loved for itself, and when that love is once established, the progress to the higher order of composition is easy and natural."[28]

In this context, "naturalized" meant something new. It no longer meant adaptation for a new audience as had occurred with opera in the 1830s. Instead, it expressed the hope that adaptation (i.e., simplification) would no longer be needed. Loving music "for itself" meant seeing it as universal, abandoning associations that might be helpful or even enjoyable ("such as love, heroism or patriotism") but were ultimately irrelevant to esthetic experience. Appreciation was to take work ("frequent recollection of the pleasing theme") in order to allow enjoyment of a more complex, "higher order" of music.

Yet music was not quite abstract — it was also a manifestation of its composer's creativity and style. That Verdi received more (and more negative) attention in the 1840s than had Rossini, Bellini, or Donizetti reflects not only his seeming use by a despised upper class at the Astor Place but also an increased critical focus on composers in general. The way was being paved for the ascent of German over Italian style and of German over Italian composers. As pure as this "higher order" of music was said to be, the Germans' ability to create it was linked to ideas of national character. In 1849, for example, differences between Germans and Italians, hence between their musical styles, were attributed to climate:

> The nations of the north, who live in the midst of frost, under a gloomy and silent sky, are less expansive and more thoughtful than those of a milder climate: they eagerly seek for strong emotions, and their concentrated passions require a vigorous harmony to excite them. They have, besides, few fine voices, and their languages are hard; hence, then, their preference of the effects of harmony.
>
> The inhabitants of the south are more sensible of the charms of melody; too happy, too indolent for thought, they content themselves with sensations entirely material. A pure and lively sky, smiling fields, picturesque views, and the sweetness of their languages, give birth to the light and joyous songs which they produce. Their barcaroles flow as softly as the gondola on the surface of the water.[29]

This interpretation was not meant to be pejorative, but it shows how much critical esteem Italians and their music had lost between 1825 and the middle of the century. No advocate of the Garcias would have called Italians indolent. Indeed, they had been called "children of harmony," praised for the very style trait here noted in German music.[30] Nor did they write "delicious" descriptions of Maria Garcia like those of later Italian singers. Rather, as Italian opera succeeded with a broad public, its style, along with its composers and performers, lost critical esteem relative to German art.

Germanophile critics preferred the elaborate and intricate over the simple and readily understood. Thus they cared more for harmony, texture, and orchestral color than melody, sentiment, or emotional impact. No longer valued for its unmediated qualities, scientific music was able to express itself without the aid of "impurities" such as words or an individual performer's contribution. Further, no longer merely a relief from everyday logical thinking and concerns, music offered abstract qualities that fostered the transfer of its value from sentiment, drama, or other temporal associations to the composer. As a commentator advised the singers about to perform *Don Giovanni* in 1850, "*Leave the music to make its own points.* Sing your music as it is written down for you in all its purity and perfect integrity. . . . It will be glory enough for you to have sung Mozart's music as he wrote it and as he intended it."[31]

The German canon brought new tasks for music critics. Because musical complexity was not readily understood, it depended on explanation. Hard music needed proselytizing on behalf of the music, its composers, and critical authority. In order to bother with a difficult repertoire, the public would need to accept its inherent superiority. In order to know which works to value most highly and why, it would also have to accept the idea of critical expertise.[32] This authoritarian stance was antithetical to the old theatrical mandate of pleasing the audience nightly, from the notion of the critic as the voice of the audience, and from the entrepreneurial principle of presenting what would sell. From this new perspective, the process begun when the Garcias' audience willingly tried out an unknown genre on the basis of reputed excellence was being completed.

Of these changes, probably the greatest was melody's loss of critical esteem. In abandoning melody, critics abandoned music's most obvious and accessible trait, one that audiences had come to love through opera. Melody expressed an individual singer's vocal quality, a trait remarked upon from the beginning and often considered a major communicative element. Despite the virtuosity often achieved onstage, melody linked the performance with something audience members could do themselves — sing. Melody also bore words, in turn the bearers of music's "lofty sentiments." With the decline of such sentiments in opera, music's value could no longer be derived from a melodic message. Although still important to opera's communicative ability, melody could no longer foster an elevated cultural position.

Thus the way was opened for a devaluation of communication. This critical process worked from two directions — a new emphasis on counterpoint and other sophisticated musical traits and a disparagement of audiences' ability to understand the music's most important elements. The new critical approach emphasized a "higher" level of understanding divorced from melody's ability to communicate to average music-lovers. It was matched by the growing negative approach to the audience already evident at the Astor Place. For example, a critic in 1858 called *Don Giovanni* unmelodic while chastising the opera's audience for failing to get anything else out of it:

> It will be determined one of these days whether *Don Giovanni* be really a popular Opera, or merely an antique work popular with managers because it enables them to play three *prima donnas* at one time instead of one. The four or five melodies which characterise and appetise the work for the public are spread over a fearful musical expanse, which *must* be uninteresting simply because none but a musician can understand its significance. Every act is a Salisbury plain of harmony, with the smallest possible Stonehenge of melody. The masses know nothing about counterpoint and are unmoved by its aural effect. They care less for orchestral figures, especially of the kind written by Mozart, which were of the most learned kind.[33]

In his disparagement, the critic was off the mark. *Don Giovanni* was Mozart's most popular opera. Regardless of critical judgments, managers were disinclined to mount pieces that had little chance of audience success. The notion of managers favoring an opera with a big cast is also faulty, contradicting the usual practice of spreading stars as thinly as possible over a season to save money and encourage repeat attendance. In fact, from the 1850 revival on, various Zerlinas charmed New Yorkers to the point where the opera gained a reputation for helping an unprofitable season break even. Clearly, the audience could hear the melodies that, along with other elements, delineated her character. But from this critic's perspective, to enjoy a charming character was to sell the work short. Zerlina mattered less than harmony, counterpoint, and "orchestral figures . . . of the most learned kind." Nor was it enough that the public flocked to *Don Giovanni* in droves. Because these "masses" were not musicians, they could not understand those aspects of the opera critics deemed most valuable. An old strain in criticism was coming to the fore. Years before, critics had treated opera's reception as a referendum on the public taste, urging attendance and chastising New Yorkers when a season was unsuccessful. By the 1850s, on the other hand, they had begun instead to chastise those who *had* come, asserting that they had done so for the wrong reasons.

The rise of the German instrumental tradition and the increasing distance between critics and audiences had their corollary in the process Lawrence Levine has called the "sacralization of culture."[34] Like the attempts to promote the Garcias in New York as high culture, the process of sacralization was led from above. This time, however, the leaders were critics and other members of an intellectual as opposed to a social elite. Joseph Mussulman has studied the writings of what he calls the "cultured generation" of magazine music critics from 1870 to 1900, men who had developed a taste for music seemingly independent of its social or entertainment values.[35] But believers in music as a set of sacred texts could be found earlier. In the 1840s these individuals—people whose respect for opera was based on its esthetic appeal—were contrasted with an elite bent only on showing off their wealth and social status. As the *Home Journal* had observed at the Astor Place in 1847, "a very few 'quiet' people took seats in the new opera-house with mere desire for music."[36]

These "quiet" people, not of the Upper Ten Thousand, included social satirists of the Astor Place Opera House and early critics of Verdi. In the 1850s such critics as George William Curtis and Donald Mitchell, both authors of city mysteries literature that mocked elites at the opera, joined what Matthew Arnold would call the cultural "Remnant." As members of the so-called thoughtful classes, critics hoped their vision of culture would set a tone for both the wealthy and the public at large.[37] Thus they recall New York's opera advocates of the 1820s who had promoted it as a source of civic pride. But the later writers represent another generation of musical reception. As social critics, their perspective was typically American, for they disparaged the "aristocratic" opera from a social position below the elite. Their authority as canonizers rested in part on this position. Ignoring the actual breadth of the opera audience, they took advantage of wealthy New Yorkers' noticeable presence at performances to dissociate themselves from the fashionable upper class. Thus they could hope to gain the ears of others who resented the wealthy as they did. By mocking the use of culture to flaunt one's social status, they could assure readers that their own assessments were based on purer motives.

These critics' hidden agenda, of course, was their own intellectual status.[38] As the writer of the comment on *Don Giovanni* assumed that the public could not understand the music, critics often accepted only a small portion of the opera audience as colleagues. This attitude was not the first effort to use music to confer status on a social group. Previous tries, however, had failed. The mercantile elite's attempt to dignify themselves through the opera house had been put down by the democracy. Creating an elite of virtue and respectability through sentimental opera had been undermined by morally questionable stories in the newer Italian style. The cultured critics' self-proclaimed identity as explicators of difficult texts was more successful, for the best critics could help readers who wanted to explore music's mysteries. But the terms of acceptance that canonizers advocated effectively removed music from the realm of cultural genres that mattered to the world beyond. If a large body of the public had no interest in either counterpoint or the critics who explained it, the effect on society was nil. Such ignorance fed the critical agenda of authority through distance from most segments of the public. Denying the right of audiences to choose the standard repertoire, they defined a minority opinion as a superior one.

Through the critics, Jacksonian-style disparagement of social elites at the Italian Opera House and the Astor Place continued as the century progressed. In them can be traced the heritage of the intellectual iconoclasts who had mocked Italian opera in Handel's London. Like Joseph Addison and his colleagues, New York critics wrote from the position of social outsiders criticizing an in-group. Thus they linked social and esthetic bases for judgment and to some extent misrepresented both. The major difference — and significant in terms of results — is that although eighteenth-century critics of opera advocated popular pieces such as *The Beggar's Opera,* their nineteenth-century New York counterparts were armed instead with the symphonies of Beethoven. Both groups were influential. Eighteenth-century critics sought to reduce music's status relative to literature and drama. Nineteenth-century New Yorkers, writing in a climate more favorable toward music, sought instead to reduce opera's status relative to the growing symphonic repertoire.

Both Levine and Mussulman have studied the simultaneous rise of sacralized culture and the German canon in the last third of the century. Looking back from 1900 and beyond, one can indeed link opera and orchestral music, as Levine does, placing them at the top of the cultural hierarchy. But looking back from 1860 exposes a different view, and a clear distinction between social and esthetic status. Opera was linked to an elegant social setting dominated by elites, if in fact available to others. But such socially "high" culture was not necessarily sacralized. Sacralization was — and is — first and foremost an attitude. And seeing a genre such as opera as socially elite, even aristocratic, is, if anything, an attitude of disrespect.

The institutional and repertoire developments that established Italian opera had begun in 1825. Although widely available and popular, opera failed nevertheless to earn a social, moral, or esthetic stamp of approval. In fact, Levine chronicles in great detail the successful sacralization of orchestral concerts and repertoire, yet the comments he quotes on opera show instead critics deprecating the works and performers as inferior and the audiences for liking it.[39] Opera presented the generic purity he sees as necessary for labeling a cultural creation sacred. It developed a decorous social ritual similar to that of concerts and presented a musical style still too current to exclude those who were not connoisseurs. Star values, glamour, and sex appeal were important, as were commercially based outreach efforts. Although critics had much to say about content and performance, the audience, by voting with its feet, played a role in maintaining a piece or company. Enthusiasm for a moving or virtuoso performance was still as important as decorum. Although some of the earlier operas were called edifying, the need to entertain, to please the audience, was still central to a work's success. Thus audiences still had a power antithetical to the ideal of sacralization, which mandated their rise to the occasion in supporting works deemed great and worthwhile by those more knowledgeable than they. Sacralization required a reversal in power between critic and audience that by the Civil War had not yet been achieved. Italian opera had only begun to leave open the

premiere position in New York's musical culture for German instrumental music — music "for itself."

◊   ◊   ◊

Ann Douglas says that in the 1840s Margaret Fuller "believed that
'art' was increasingly functioning in American culture as a diversion
from the pressing problem of the socio-economic order."[40] This function may have fit German instrumental music, but it was only partly
suited to opera. Whether serious or frivolous, optimistic or pessimis-
tic, highlighted or hidden, a social or sociopsychological vision appeared onstage in every work. After the War of 1812 an audience
gathered for a performance of *Love in a Village* could see the neat pit,
box, and gallery divisions of the auditorium presented reassuringly
onstage and enhanced by pleasant, unpretentious music. By the Civil
War, the social link between the stage and the house was not so clear.
Instead, performance of operas such as *La traviata* and *Rigoletto* shows
an audience willing to consider in a respectable public setting a new,
less comfortable "spirit of the age."

Although the two situations are not exactly parallel, in both cases
an opera codifies, somewhat idealizes, and then displays an artistic,
social, psychological, and sexual worldview. In *Love in a Village* the
presentation has been designed for palatability. The Verdi operas are
not so intended; they require greater emotional investment and willingness to take psychological risk. The foundations underlying New
Yorkers' acceptance of these new works in the 1850s are not self-
evident. On the one hand, one can imagine the modern Italian school
operas as catharsis, a way to bring the underside side of life and its
difficult issues out into the open with their impact rendered tolerable
and more profound by music. From this point of view, the succession
of opera houses, the elaborate social ritual, and the debates on opera's
social setting, politics, and economics bought New Yorkers time to
make peace with the repertoire. On the other hand, however, as the
operas aged they could become trite to the point of irrelevance —
essentially vehicles for powerful music, formulaic emotional response,
and a variety of star performers in well-known roles. And as Richard
Grant White's review of *Lucrezia Borgia* shows, they could also become
excuses for ethnically and sexually based voyeurism in fancy dress.

Elements of both interpretations were probably the case. Both are
based on the premise that culture codifies a view of society and fur-

ther, that music can enhance such codification but does not alter it. In this respect, *Love in a Village* and *La traviata* offer similar perspectives on music's place in culture and culture's place in society, for in both a musical style is consonant with a story and its underlying stable worldview. With *La traviata,* this consonance brought the assertion that Verdi's operas were "in accordance with the energy and velocity of our time." For the first time since before the Garcias' season, opera was being accepted without reference to reformist ideology. The genre had inspired its own redefinition.

This redefinition marks a full circle. Between *Love in a Village* and *La traviata* rose and fell the assertion that music could make society imitate culture rather than the reverse. By reforming the theater, by establishing the opera house with its polite social setting, by mounting "moral" stories enhanced by emotionally powerful melody focused on an elevated sentiment, and by appreciating Italian opera's "rational and refined" style, New Yorkers (as well as other Americans) could understand and use music as a reformist tool. The growth of musical activity of all sorts speaks to the power of their choice. As with religious revivals, reaching masses of people by speaking "from the heart" was a sure bet.

Much was achieved. Opera's success resulted from great effort by many over a long time, and civic pride was justified. But despite that success the reformist vision was not realized. The genre and its institutional setting were subjected to a variety of interpretations. Attempts to organize opera houses, thereby removing the genre from a theater seen as debased and corrupt, were taken as signs of either aristocratic exclusiveness or autocratic taste-setting by a self-proclaimed elite. An interest in opera was equated with fashion and disassociated from virtue. When public attention vacillated, audiences were accused of flocking to star singers only. The plots of most new operas from the 1840s on failed utterly to meet the ideal of the moral lesson; criticism of *Rigoletto* suggests that it strained New Yorkers' capacity to deal with sensitive issues in an operatic setting. From some quarters, the bel canto musical style was disparaged as meretricious and effete, while from others Verdi's direct, powerful music was criticized as vulgar. Finally, the ideological structure collapsed entirely; no longer sustainable by opera, the reformist ideal, expressed in intellectual and esthetic terms, was passed to German instrumental music.

New Yorkers ultimately learned from opera that music had no inherently positive value in and of itself. Its power could be unleashed for purposes considered immoral or subversive as well as those thought of as elevating. The kind of sentiment deemed conducive to virtue depended on both words and music. Middle-period Verdi established that value in music need not depend on its value as sentiment. This belief in turn opened the way for esthetically based evaluation in which an opera whose greatest musical success was a popular tune such as *Rigoletto*'s "La donna è mobile" could not compete on musical terms with the German symphonic canon. Belief in the canon's esthetic value allowed it to transcend the social, moral, and economic issues so prominent in Italian opera's climb to success and to replace opera as music's object of cultural aspiration. Italian opera could be considered socially "high" art, but it failed as an object of esthetic worship.

It was not claimed that the music of the canon spoke to the heart. Rather, its strengths were said to be the intellectual or scientific attributes of counterpoint and harmonic complexity and its greatest composers men already dead. The technically based understanding the newer critics advocated was a rational approach that answered old assertions that music was vapid and meaningless. It also kept music's emotional power at bay, implicitly calming any fear of emotional or sexual excess it might raise. German orchestral music spoke to a different set of human values than opera, which in the 1850s still consisted mainly of accessible works in a contemporary idiom. Lacking words, it was removed from associations with the world that texts provided. Thus it was a safer choice as a respected repertoire than vocal music of any type, whose words could call forth objection. But with safety came a loss of authority. As Mussulman shows, the canon was promoted through the end of the century as a way to smooth away the roughness of a boisterous, hard-edged civilization. This is a vague claim, perhaps the least one can say in advocating a valued cultural genre. Instrumental music spoke an abstract language whose purpose could not be easily inferred or explained. It was hard to claim that the music of the canon could persuade its audience not only to live more upright lives but also to find joy in doing so.

By the 1850s the last claim, made with vigor for such works as *La sonnambula,* was no longer being made for opera. No New Yorker regretted this loss in print; the closest is R. S. Willis's lament that opera cannot "prove the exclusive value of music as the only one of the arts exempt from the trail of the serpent."[41] But a loss it was; opera could

no longer take a place onstage alongside the "moral drama," helping
to improve society by improving culture.

The loss had its compensations, however. With opera's acceptance,
warts and all, Verdi could take a place onstage as part of a living
repertoire, as Shakespeare still did. Without a preconceived notion of
opera as "rational and refined," without the ideal of edification, New
Yorkers could begin to deal with the new style on new terms — terms
dependent on opera's acceptance as an American (democratic, entrepreneurial) institution and its disassociation with moral didacticism.
Canonized, opera could not have succeeded in New York, for the
esthetic terms on which a canon was being created were inconsistent
with what audiences saw, heard, and understood. The kind of connection the new Italian operas made with the world was not universally
hoped for. But by echoing the "energy and velocity of [its own] time,"
Verdi's operas allowed New Yorkers to confront issues that Victorian
tradition insisted they suppress. With that confrontation, musical culture could finally leave its mark on the "peculiarities of the age."

Notes

[Abbreviations used in the notes are spelled out on page 224.]

Preface

1. Quoted in Whitman, *New York Dissected*, 202.
2. Ibid., 202, emphasis added.
3. Ford Madox Ford, quoted in Douglas, *Terrible Honesty*, 9.
4. Broyles, *"Music of the Highest Class."*

Chapter 1: English Opera as Popular Culture

1. Park Theatre Leases, Astor Papers, NNHi.
2. *National Advocate*, November 23, 1823.
3. Levine, "William Shakespeare"; Levine, *Highbrow/Lowbrow*, ch. 1.
4. *Mirror*, August 7, 1830, 34.
5. Because no interior diagram of the Park exists, I have substituted one of Covent Garden from 1790. For schematic drawings of similar theaters, see Leacroft and Leacroft, *Theatre and Playhouse*, 100, and Tidworth, *Theatres*, 138.
6. *Evening Post*, September 2, 1821.
7. Undated advertisement, reprinted in the *New York Clipper*, ca. 1873, Scrapbook, NN-T, 36. The *Clipper* dates the advertisement 1823.
8. Gilfoyle, *City of Eros*, 109–12; see also Johnson, "That Guilty Third Tier"; Grimsted, *Melodrama Unveiled*, 55–56.
9. November 15, 1838, cited in Gilfoyle, *City of Eros*, 110.
10. Johnson, "That Guilty Third Tier," 579; Lawrence, *Resonances* 1:164–65.
11. Rinear, "William Mitchell's Management," 30; Grimsted, *Melodrama Unveiled*, 53–55; *Spirit of the Times*, February 18, 1832, 3; see also Walt Whitman's comments in chapter 5 of this volume.
12. *Mirror*, July 22, 1826, quoted in Shank, "The Bowery Theatre," 28, emphasis in the original.
13. Quoted from "a nineteenth-century gentleman," in Levine, "William Shakespeare," 45. On the gallery, see Grimsted, *Melodrama Unveiled*, 52–53.

14. Irving, *Letters of Jonathan Oldstyle,* 12.

15. Elias Dexter identified the individuals in 1868. His list is given in Buckley, " 'To the Opera House,' " 89–90, and Pessen, "The Wealthiest New Yorkers," 45.

16. Buckley, " 'To the Opera House,' " 91.

17. Ibid., 86–91.

18. Mates, *America's Musical Stage;* Sonneck, *Early Opera in America;* S. Porter, *With an Air Debonair;* Hoover, "Music in Eighteenth-Century American Theater." For performers, dates, and repertoire, see Porter, *With an Air Debonair,* Appendixes A and B; Odell, *Annals,* vols. 1–2; and Sonneck, *Early Opera in America.* For New York premieres of English and American musical theater pieces from 1800 to 1825, see Nelson, "First Italian Opera Season," 69–72.

19. Hume, "Multifarious Forms of Eighteenth-Century Comedy," 24; Fiske, *English Theatre Music,* 343–44. Both authors use dates from Van Lennep et al., eds., *The London Stage.*

20. Sheridan, *The Duenna,* act 1, scene 3.

21. Austern, " 'Sing Againe Syren' "; Leppert, *Music and Image,* chs. 3 and 7; on dance, see ch. 5.

22. Quoted in Leppert, *Music and Image,* 22; see also Ehrlich, *Music Profession in Britain,* 9.

23. Finney, "Ecstasy and Music"; Finney, " 'Organical Musick' and Ecstasy"; Cosgrove, "Affective Unities," 137–38; Scholes, *Puritans and Music,* chs. 14–15.

24. Ehrlich, *Music Profession in Britain,* 6; Fiske, "Music and Society," 4.

25. Leppert, *Music and Image,* 13–16.

26. R. Porter opens his account of eighteenth-century English society by evoking a "breezy, bigoted chauvinism" in which English insularity was taken as a virtue. *English Society in the Eighteenth Century,* 7.

27. *An Essay upon Publick Spirit,* quoted in Leppert, "Imagery, Musical Confrontation and Cultural Difference," 337. For similar commentary, see Hollander, *Untuning of the Sky,* 382–83 (Joseph Addison); Cosgrove, "Affective Unities," 143 (Alexander Pope); and Fiske, *English Theatre Music,* 48–53, 127–28.

28. Paulson, *Breaking and Remaking,* 155–56, 176–77.

29. Ibid., 176; see also Mellers, *Harmonious Meeting,* 269.

30. Paulson, *Breaking and Remaking,* 201–2.

31. Ibid., 175, 345n25.

32. On the Puritan critique, see McKay and Crawford, *William Billings of Boston,* 3–9; Silverman, *Cultural History,* 39–41, 195–97; Scholes, *Puritans and Music,* 268. On William Billings's apologia for psalmody, see DeJong, " 'Both Pleasure and Profit,' " 106–13.

33. On domestic music-making, see Silverman, *Cultural History*, 31–32; on concerts, see ibid., 37–38, 185–87, 469–76; Sonneck, *Early Concert Life in America*. On American gentility in general, see Bushman, "American High-Style."

34. Letter to Mercy Warren (1776), quoted in Bushman, "American High-Style," 355–56.

35. *Mirror*, March 9, 1833, 287, quoted in Hodge, *Yankee Theatre*, 18; Trollope, *Domestic Manners of the Americans*, 134; also quoted in Levine, "William Shakespeare," 43.

36. For Chesterfield's effect on colonial American social aspiration, see Bushman, "American High-Style," 353–55. On disparagement of music as a feminine accomplishment, see Tick, *American Women Composers*, chs. 2, 3.

37. Bushman, "American High-Style"; Wood, *The Radicalism of the American Revolution*, 119–20, 194–96, and passim.

38. On music as entertainment in the Early Republic, see Broyles, *"Music of the Highest Class,"* 17–19.

Chapter 2: Nature's New Mirror

1. Barish, *Anti-Theatrical Prejudice*.

2. For the eighteenth century, see Main, *The Social Structure of Revolutionary America*, 266; and Silverman, *Cultural History*, 65–67, 545–58. Both authors cite religious and journalistic sources. For the nineteenth century, see *Tribune*, August 16, 1844, September 30, 1847; Thomason, *Fashionable Amusements;* Cuyler, *Sermon;* and Buckley, *Christians and the Theatre*. Stowe is quoted in Grimsted, *Melodrama Unveiled*, 24.

3. Quoted in Barish, *Anti-Theatrical Prejudice*, 158.

4. Ibid., 163, emphasis in the original.

5. *Leviathan,* quoted in Barish, *Anti-Theatrical Prejudice*, 155; paraphrased in Agnew, *Worlds Apart*, 99.

6. Agnew, *Worlds Apart*, 138–43, quotation on 139.

7. Halttunen, *Confidence Men*, 33.

8. Ibid., 41–43. On confidence and theatricality, see Agnew, *Worlds Apart*, 195–203 (centered on Melville's novel *The Confidence Man*); Barish, *Anti-Theatrical Prejudice*, 311ff; and Reynolds, *Beneath the American Renaissance*, 300–301 and passim.

9. Davidge, *The Drama Defended*, 14.

10. Silverman, *Cultural History*, 546.

11. *Euterpeiad*, November 1, 1830, 116; *Mirror*, September 18, 1824, 161, April 1, 1826, 287, October 15, 1831, 115; *Critic*, November 22, 1828, 62, 64; *Herald*, December 28, 1836, October 9, 1840; *Knickerbocker*

10 (August 1837): 180; *Evening Post,* September 11, 1843; *Broadway Journal,* February 22, 1845, 120–21; *Holden's Dollar Magazine* 1 (April 1848): 250; Bellows, *The Relation of Public Amusements to Public Morality; Times,* April 20, 1857.

12. *Hamlet,* act 3, scene 2.

13. *American Monthly Magazine* 1 (June 1817): 138. On American moral criticism of this play, see Angotti, "American Dramatic Criticism," 116–17.

14. *Mirror,* August 18, 1838, 63; *New-Yorker,* November 19, 1836, 141; Angotti, "American Dramatic Criticism," 85–88.

15. *Evening Post,* October 29, 1817.

16. *Dramatic Mirror,* September 11, 1841, 39, November 27, 1841, 124-25; *Broadway Journal,* February 1, 1845, 74; *Tribune,* September 30, 1847, July 11, 1850; *Times,* October 25, 1853.

17. Quoted in Buckley, " 'To the Opera House,' " 130–31. For similar incidents involving other actors, see Grimsted, *Melodrama Unveiled,* 60–61.

18. Butler, *The American Lady,* 104. On audiences, see Buckley, " 'To the Opera House,' " chs. 2, 4; Grimsted, *Melodrama Unveiled,* ch. 3; Henneke, "The Playgoer in America," ch. 2; and Hodge, *Yankee Theatre,* ch. 1. On moral criticism, see Angotti, "American Dramatic Criticism," ch. 3; Buratti, *"The Spirit of the Times,"* ch. 3; and Salvaggio, "American Dramatic Criticism," ch. 3. On prostitution and theaters, see Gilfoyle, *City of Eros,* 18, 20, 67, 108–9, 110–11; and Johnson, "That Guilty Third Tier." On theater riots, see Gilje, *The Road to Mobocracy,* 246–53; and Weinbaum, *Mobs and Demagogues,* 37–39.

19. Hume, "Multifarious Forms of Eighteenth-Century Comedy," 11; see also Langford, *A Polite and Commercial People,* 466.

20. Hume, "Multifarious Forms of Eighteenth-Century Comedy," 7.

21. Bickerstaffe, *Love in a Village,* act 2, scene 10.

22. Other contemporary pieces with prominent nonsinging male leads are *The Slave* (Gambia), *The Libertine* (Bishop's arrangement of *Don Giovanni,* title character), *Guy Mannering* (title character), and *Rob Roy* (title character).

23. Grimsted, *Melodrama Unveiled,* 240–41; Shapiro, "Action Music"; Porter, *With an Air Debonair,* 44–50; Yellin, Introduction to Taylor, *The Aethiop,* xix–xxii.

24. On the star system, see S. Porter, *With an Air Debonair,* 14, 196–202.

25. *Mirror,* February 2, 1828, 239, quoted in Shank, "The Bowery Theatre," 232–33; *Ladies' Companion,* February 1841, 199; *Message Bird,* October 15, 1849, 103; *Musical World,* July 1, 1854, 97; Wood, *Personal Recollections of the Stage,* 391–98.

26. Bishop's *The Libertine,* an arrangement of *Don Giovanni,* had been performed before *The Barber of Seville.* It was done, however, with a non-singing male lead (Edmund Simpson as Don Giovanni in 1817). Likewise, Bishop's original arrangement of *The Barber of Seville* has a nonsinging Count Almaviva. For his American performances, however, Philipps added songs, none of which came from Rossini's opera. See Rossini, *The Barber of Seville.*

27. Arnold, *The Devil's Bridge.*

28. *Evening Post,* November 22, 1817.

29. Ibid.

30. Ibid.

31. Ibid.

32. No libretto was published for this production. The closest is a libretto from a London production of 1814, without prologue or epilogue. The cast list includes Incledon as Macheath. [Gay], *The Beggar's Opera.*

33. *National Advocate,* October 29, 1817; *Evening Post,* October 29, 1817; *American Monthly Magazine* 2 (November 1817): 62–63.

34. *National Advocate,* November 29, 1817; *Evening Post,* October 29, 1817; *American Monthly Magazine* 2 (November 1817): 62.

35. *National Advocate,* November 29, 1817.

36. *Evening Post,* October 29, 1817.

37. Ibid.

Chapter 3: Culture and Commerce

1. Ellis, "Pre-Revolutionary Culture and Capitalism," 169; see also Bender, *New York Intellect,* 55–58.

2. Quoted in Bender, *New York Intellect,* 56.

3. *Evening Post,* November 3, 5, 1825; *American,* November 5, 1825; Lamb, *History* 3:696–703; Wilson, *Memorial History* 3:319–31.

4. *American,* November 5, 1825.

5. Ryan, "The American Parade," 139–40.

6. *American,* November 5, 1825.

7. On the theater, opera, and art institutions as "ornaments," see *Albion,* May 13, 1826, 383.

8. Bender, *New York Intellect,* 54–56.

9. Ibid., 57–58, 75.

10. Ibid., 53; Lamb, *History* 3:688–91; Dixon R. Fox in *Dictionary of American Biography,* ed. Malone, vol. 2, pt. 2, 221–25.

11. Wilson, *Memorial History* 4:415–20; Lyman C. Newell in *Dictionary of American Biography,* ed. Malone, 7:69–71.

12. Webster, *American Dictionary* (1828), 2:n.p.

13. Quoted in Nelson, "First Italian Opera Season," 13; on Hardie, see ibid., 59, and Bender, *New York Intellect,* 59.

14. On Swindells, see Allwardt, "Sacred Music in New York," 132, and Lawrence, *Resonances,* 38. On the Philharmonic Board, see Shanet, *Philharmonic,* 49, 417n13. On the Philharmonic in general, see Lawrence, *Resonances,* xl–xliv, lii–liii, and passim.

15. Philharmonic bylaws summarized in the *Lyre,* August 1, 1824, 33–35.

16. "Musoeus" in *American,* November 15, 1825. Precisely how music could achieve these ends was only detailed in the 1830s; see chapter 4 in this volume.

17. The *Lyre,* June 1, 1824, opposite 1, and August 1, 1824, 33.

18. *American Monthly Magazine* 5 (April 1835): 158–59; *American Musical Journal* 1 (February 1835): 67.

19. Manuel Garcia, junior (1805–1906) never made a great career on stage, but he taught many operatic stars, including Jenny Lind. Maria Garcia (1808–36) was the first prima donna to duplicate her New York success in Europe. In 1826 she married Eugene Malibran, a French-born New York merchant, and was known in Europe as Maria Malibran. A third Garcia child, Pauline (1821–1910), was too young to perform in New York but later, as Pauline Viardot, made a major career, mostly in Paris.

20. *Harmonicon* 3 (October 1825): 191, 194. For variations on the basic star contract, see Printner, "William Warren's Financial Arrangements."

21. *American,* November 16, 1825.

22. *American,* February 25, 1826.

23. In the 1820s a box seat cost $1, a pit seat 50 cents, and a gallery seat 25 cents (*National Advocate,* September 1, 1823; *American,* January 13, 1827). The Park's prices during this period were rarely published; presumably, they rarely changed.

24. *Evening Post,* December 20, 1825.

25. *American,* November 16, 1825 (the Garcias' first advertisement).

26. Nelson, "First Italian Opera Season," 137–38, 279–80. The seasons' dates were November 29, 1825–March 11, 1826, March 14–May 20, 1826, May 23–June 24, 1826, June 27–July 24, 1826, July 26–August 11, 1826, and August 29–September 30, 1826.

27. *American,* November 16, 1825.

28. *American,* December 10, 1825. On price reductions in hard times to attract more spectators, see Odell, *Annals* 4:454 (on the Park), 626–27 (on the Bowery), and passim.

29. Mattfeld, *A Hundred Years,* 20, no source given.

30. *Mirror,* September 3, 1825, 47; *Evening Post,* November 30, 1825.

31. *Mirror,* October 22, 1825, 103.

32. *Literary Gazette,* November 12, 1825, 157. For similar criticisms, see the *American,* June 27, 1826, and Buckley, " 'To the Opera House,' " 252.

33. *American,* November 28, 1825, quoted in full in Lawrence, *Resonances,* xlvii–xlviii.

34. *Review and Athenaeum* 2 (February 1826): 231.

35. *American,* November 30, 1825, quoted in Nelson, "First Italian Opera Season," 140; Odell, *Annals* 3:183; Lawrence, *Resonances,* xlviii. See also the *Post,* November 30, 1825, quoted in Nelson, "First Italian Opera Season," 140.

36. *American,* November 30, 1825, quoted in Nelson, "First Italian Opera Season," 140, 153.

37. The Kean controversy and riot were reported widely. See the *Evening Post,* November 15–17, 1825; *American,* November 15–18, 1825; *National Advocate,* November 15–16, 1825; *Mirror,* November 19, 1825, 135; *Albion,* October 29, 1825, 159, and November 19, 1825, 183; and *Gazette,* November 15, 1825, reprinted in the *Commercial Advertiser* on the same date. This last account is reprinted in DeZego, "Edmund Kean in New York and Boston," along with excerpts from other press reports (508–17). See also Odell *Annals* 3:178–80; Weinbaum, *Mobs and Demagogues,* 42; and Fitzsimons, *Edmund Kean,* 206–7.

38. *Albion,* November 19, 1825, 183; *Mirror,* November 19, 1825, 35; excerpt in Odell, *Annals* 3:178.

39. *Evening Post,* November 30, 1825; see also *American,* February 27, 1826.

40. For complete performance dates and programs, see Nelson, "First Italian Opera Season," 316–20.

41. For eighteenth-century English social and moral concerns regarding this access, see Leppert, *Music and Image,* 56–66, including two *Barbiere di Siviglia*-style drawings of music lessons (64).

42. *Review and Athenaeum* 2 (December 1825): 79.

43. *American,* November 15, 1825.

44. Ryan, *Women in Public,* 27–28.

45. *Mirror,* February 7, 1824, quoted in Odell, *Annals* 3:101 (on Conway, see 3:99).

46. *American,* February 8, 1826.

47. Ibid., quoted in Odell, *Annals* 3:190, and Nelson, "First Italian Opera Season," 217.

48. *Review and Athenaeum* 2 (February 1826): 235.

49. "Philo Editor," *Evening Post,* March 7, 1826.

50. *Literary Gazette,* December 17, 1825, 239. For a similar argument, see the *Mirror,* October 20, 1827, 119.

51. *Literary Gazette,* December 17, 1825, 239.

52. *Literary Gazette,* December 3, 1825, 195–96.

53. *Mirror,* January 21, 1826, 207, emphasis in the original.

54. *Mirror,* February 4, 1826, 223, emphasis in the original.

55. *Literary Gazette,* December 17, 1825, 239.

56. *Review and Athenaeum* 2 (December 1825): 81.

57. *Evening Post,* November 30, December 6, 1825; *American,* November 30, 1825, January 5, February 8, 1826; *Review and Atheneum* 2 (December 1825): 81.

58. *American,* November 30, 1825.

59. *Literary Gazette,* December 17, 1825, 239.

60. *Literary Gazette,* April 8, 1826, 98.

61. *American,* April 7, 1826.

62. *American,* April 17, 1826.

63. *American,* November 30, 1825.

64. The sheet music for "Una voce poco fa" was published in New York by Dubois and Stodart in 1826.

65. On amateur performance of Italian bel canto in nineteenth-century America, see Hamm, *Yesterdays,* 76, 87–88.

66. *Review and Athenaeum* 2 (December 1825): 115.

67. Nelson, "First Italian Opera Season," 232; *American,* February 27, 1826.

68. *Literary Gazette,* August 26, 1826, 295.

69. *Review and Athenaeum* 2 (December 1825): 81, emphasis in the original.

70. *American,* November 30, 1825.

71. *Evening Post,* November 30, 1825.

72. *Albion,* February 17, 1827, 288; Shank, "The Bowery Theatre," 153, 156, 158. Maria Garcia was engaged twice more at $600 a night (*Albion,* February 10, 1827, 280).

73. *American,* February 5, 1827.

74. *American,* January 13, 1827; *Albion,* January 27, 1827, 264. See also *Mirror,* February 3, 1827, 223.

75. *American,* January 30, 1827; *National Advocate,* January 31, 1827.

76. *American,* October 30, 1827, reprinted in the *Mirror,* November 3, 1827, 135.

77. Ibid.

78. *National Advocate,* January 26, 1827.

79. *Albion,* November 3, 1827, 168.

80. *American,* August 12, September 30, October 2, 1826.

81. *Evening Post,* April 1, 1826.

82. In 1908 the Metropolitan Opera abandoned this system for a

company headed by a general manager on salary. Preston, comp. and ed., *Farewell to the Old House,* 16.

83. *Evening Post,* April 1, 1826.

Chapter 4: "Directly from the Heart"

1. Hamm, *Yesterdays,* 62.

2. *Literary Gazette,* December 17, 1825, 239.

3. Douglas, *Feminization of American Culture,* 110, 147–51, 158–59, 219, 290.

4. Tick, *American Women Composers,* 5; *American Monthly Magazine* 5 (April 1835): 158.

5. *Ladies' Companion* 1 (October 1834): 275; see also *Spirit of the Times,* February 18, 1832; *Knickerbocker* 5 (February 1835): 169; *American Monthly Magazine* 4 (August 1837): 135.

6. *Ladies' Companion* 1 (October 1834): 275.

7. Payne, *Clari;* Child, "The Beloved Tune," 116–25; "Address," 16; see also the *Mirror,* April 12, 1834, 326–27; *American Monthly Magazine* 4 (August 1837): 136–37. For similar examples in *Godey's Lady's Book,* see Koza, "Music and References to Music," 153–55.

8. "Prospects of the American Stage" and "Satire and Sentiment," both from *Arcturus* 2 (October 1841): 279–85, 304–9.

9. *Knickerbocker* 4 (October 1834): 286.

10. Reprinted in the *New York Clipper,* ca. 1872, Park Theatre Scrapbook, NN-T. The records also show daily income totals and comments about mitigating factors such as weather.

11. *The Barber of Seville,* arranged by Bishop.

12. See, for example, the facsimilie edition of Lacy's *Cinderella,* arranged from *Cenerentola* and other Rossini operas, ed. and with introduction by Graziano, in *Nineteenth-Century American Musical Theater,* ed. Root, vol. 3.

13. *American Monthly Magazine* 4 (August 1837): 137.

14. Elizabeth Austin sang *Cinderella,* Mary Ann Wood sang *La sonnambula,* and Jane Shirreff sang *Amilie.*

15. *Evening Post,* October 29, 1817.

16. Odell, *Annals* 6:243.

17. The term *true woman* comes from Welter's classic article, "The Cult of True Womanhood."

18. Bishop, "Away! Deceiver," in *The Barber of Seville* vocal score, 77–82.

19. See McClary, "Excess and Frame," 80–111.

20. On this change, see Budden, "Verdi and the Contemporary Italian Scene," 75–79.

21. *American Monthly Magazine* 4 (August 1837): 137, 135.

22. *American Monthly Magazine* 1 (March 1836): 317.

23. Ibid. See also *Knickerbocker* 6 (December 1835): 572–74, and comments on Jane Shirreff later in this chapter. The "nether mill-stone" refers to the heart of the "savage baron" Front-de-Boeuf in Scott, *Ivanhoe*, 324–25.

24. On this troupe of vocal stars, see Preston, *Opera on the Road*, ch. 2.

25. *Evening Star,* December 11, 1838, Jane Shirreff Collection Scrapbook, NN-T, 26.

26. *Courier and Enquirer,* December 11, 1838, Jane Shirreff Collection Scrapbook, NN-T, 27.

27. No newspaper source identified, Jane Shirreff Collection Scrapbook, NN-T, 17 reverse.

28. *Evening Star,* March 14, 1839, reprinted from *Philadelphia Star,* Jane Shirreff Collection Scrapbook, NN-T, 51.

29. *Evening Star,* October 15, 1838, Jane Shirreff Collection Scrapbook, NN-T, 7.

30. *Evening Star,* October 16, 1838, Jane Shirreff Collection Scrapbook, NN-T, 8.

31. *Spirit of the Times,* October 20, 1838, 281.

32. Ibid.

33. Ibid.

34. *Atlas,* October 21, 1838, Jane Shirreff Collection Scrapbook, NN-T, 10.

35. *Courier and Enquirer* (no date given), Jane Shirreff Collection Scrapbook, NN-T, 9.

36. *Courier and Enquirer,* October 16, 1838, Jane Shirreff Collection Scrapbook, NN-T, 9.

37. *Atlas,* October 21, 1838, Jane Shirreff Collection Scrapbook, NN-T, 10.

38. *Evening Post,* October 29, 1817.

39. *Star,* October 17, October 20, 1838, *Spirit of the Times,* October 20, 1838, 281, *Herald,* July 13, 1839, and *Atlas,* July 17, 1839, all in Jane Sherriff Collection Scrapbook, NN-T, 9, 10, 42, 43.

40. *American Monthly Magazine* 4 (August 1837): 134.

Chapter 5: The Failure That Flourished

1. Maretzek, *Crotchets,* 14.

2. Nash, *The Urban Crucible,* 7; Blumin, *Emergence of the Middle Class,* 26–27, 55–56.

3. Pessen, "The Wealthiest New Yorkers," 155, 161–64.

4. Pessen, "Philip Hone's Set." For more detail on the lives of these individuals, see Pessen, *Riches, Power and Wealth*.

5. *Evening Post*, March 17, 1834, emphasis in original.

6. *Evening Post*, November 1, 1834.

7. *Herald*, January 22, 1841. For a similar barb, see *Spirit of the Times*, July 7, 1832.

8. "The Old Bowery," quoted in Grimsted, *Melodrama Unveiled*, 55; see also McConachie, " 'Theatre of the Mob.' "

9. Gorn, " 'Good-Bye Boys' "; see also Buckley, " 'To the Opera House," ch. 4; McConachie, " 'Theatre of the Mob' "; Stansell, *City of Women*, 89–101 and passim; Stott, *Workers in the Metropolis*, chs. 8, 9; and Wilentz, *Chants Democratic*, 257–61, 300–301.

10. *Evening Post*, December 3, 1833.

11. *Mirror*, February 9, 1833, 254, June 8, 1833, 387, April 5, 1834, 319, and December 12, 1835, 191.

12. Trollope, *Domestic Manners of the Americans*, 300. Trollope lived in the United States from 1827 to 1830.

13. October 15, 1838, in Hone, *Diary* 1:348.

14. Buckley, " 'To the Opera House,' " 157.

15. For a list of Bowery productions from its opening in 1826 through 1836, see Shank, "The Bowery Theatre," 470–595.

16. *Figaro*, November 18–December 2, 1833.

17. *American Monthly Magazine*, 2 (January 1834): 350–51; *Mirror*, November 21, 1832, 167.

18. *American Monthly Magazine* 1 (May 1833): 191. On the Bowery's acoustics, see *Albion*, January 5, 1833, 7. On the Montresor company in New York, see Preston, *Opera on the Road*, 107–9.

19. Shareholder agreement, November 9, 1832. Association documents cited in the following notes are in the Manuscript Department, NNHi.

20. *Evening Post*, October 3, 8, 1832. By 1833 Da Ponte had fallen out with the association. In October he complained that he was not allowed to sell the librettos he had printed for Montresor at the new opera house, nor was his name even on the free list (*Post*, October 8, November 18, December 31, 1833). But in 1834 the association gave him a benefit (*Albion*, June 28, 1834, 207). See Da Ponte, "Storia incredibile ma vera," in *Memorie*, ed. Gambarin and Nicolini, 2:215–50; his open letter of complaint (1835) is given in Krehbiel, *Chapters of Opera*, 36–37. See also Da Ponte, *Memoirs of Lorenzo Da Ponte*, 491; FitzLyon, *The Libertine Librettist*, 271–76; Hodges, *Lorenzo Da Ponte*, 213–18; and Dizikes, *Opera in America*, 73–75.

21. Letter, March 9, 1833, Italian Opera Association Papers.

22. Minutes, December 11 and 19, 1832, September 24, 1833.

23. Minutes, February 24, 1834.

24. Articles of Association, March 9, 1833.

25. *Evening Post,* November 18, 1833.

26. Philip Hone's description of the drawing is given in Krehbiel, *Chapters of Opera,* 21.

27. *Evening Post,* November 18, 1833.

28. *Mirror,* December 28, 1833, 207.

29. Description from a leaflet by J. Mario Bragaldi, the artist, distributed "among the ladies in the private boxes" and reprinted in the *Evening Post,* November 19, 1833.

30. Association minutes, February 23, 1833, February 24, 1834.

31. *Evening Post,* November 8, 1833; description in *Albion,* November 16, 1833, 367; prices in *Evening Post,* November 12, 1833. No drawing of the interior is available.

32. Advertisements, *Evening Post,* November 10, 1834; *Courier and Enquirer,* November 10, 1834.

33. Six benefits were exempted from the free-ticket policy (Articles of Association).

34. *American Musical Journal* 1 (March 1835): 91.

35. Minutes, February 24, September 20, 1834.

36. *American Musical Journal* 1 (March 1835): 91.

37. *Ladies' Companion* 1 (July 1834): 152. For a similar comment, see *Courier and Enquirer,* February 4, 1834, quoted in Dizikes, *Opera in America,* 77.

38. *Albion,* May 16, 1835, 159.

39. Signed agreement, October 24, 1835, Italian Opera Association Papers.

40. Bond for sale, Italian Opera Association Papers.

41. Signatures of receipt in association minutes, December 20, 1836.

42. *Mirror,* December 28, 1833, 207; see also *American Monthly Magazine* 2 (December 1833): 278.

43. *Evening Post,* November 16, 1833, January 14, February 6, 1834.

44. *Spirit of the Times,* November 17, 1832.

45. See also *Mirror,* December 28, 1833, 207; Bender, *New York Intellect,* ch. 2, esp. 76–78.

46. November 11, 1835, in Hone, *Diary* 1:183, given in McConachie, "New York Operagoing," 183, and Lawrence, *Resonances,* 253; see also *American Musical Journal* 1 (July 1835): 89.

47. *American Musical Journal* 1 (July 1835): 189.

48. *American Musical Journal* 1 (October 1834): 18; *Ladies' Companion* 1 (July 1834): 153.

49. Association minutes, March 9, 1833.

50. *American Musical Journal* 1 (October 1834): 17.

51. *Mirror,* January 18, 1834, 231; *American Musical Journal* 1 (February 1835): 67.

52. On Palmo's, see Boromé, "Ferdinando Palmo"; Lawrence, *Resonances,* 250–67, 325–28, 415–18, 427–33, and passim; Krehbiel, *Chapters of Opera,* 38–45; Young, ed., *Documents of American Theatre History* 1:112–13; and Preston, *Opera on the Road,* 122–29.

53. There were, however, no Italian opera performances in 1846.

54. Undated clipping from the *Clipper,* ca. 1872, Scrapbook, NN-T.

55. Dickens, *American Notes,* 95.

56. *Evening Post,* September 15, 16, 20, 22, 23, 1843; *Herald,* September 18, 20, 22, 23, 28, 1843; Odell, *Annals* 4:694–95; Lawrence, *Resonances,* 216–18; Preston, *Opera on the Road,* 119–22.

57. *Herald,* February 5, 1844, quoted in Odell, *Annals* 5:50.

58. *Tribune,* February 1, 1844, quoted in Lawrence, *Resonances,* 253. The *Tribune* also reported that unaccompanied women would be denied admission.

59. *Anglo American,* February 10, 1844, 382.

60. *Anglo American,* March 9, 1844, 478.

61. Boromé, "Ferdinando Palmo," 69–70. Krehbiel (*Chapters of Opera,* 43) recounts this incident, incorrectly dating it January 25, 1845.

62. *Tribune,* December 26, 1844.

63. *Spirit of the Times,* April 3, 1847, 72, quoted from the *Express.*

64. On the 1847 Havana company, see Preston, *Opera on the Road,* 130–34; Lawrence, *Resonances,* 434–35, 438–46.

65. In [Bristed], *The Upper Ten Thousand,* Charles Astor Bristed credits Nathaniel Parker Willis of the *Mirror* and *Home Journal* with the term (289). According to Vera Lawrence, James Gordon Bennett of the *Herald* coined the term *codfish aristocracy,* which refers to the newer wealthy families' New England origin. For a cartoon of a codfish in a top hat, tails, and monocle, see Lawrence, *Resonances,* 578. On New Englanders versus old Knickerbockers in the city's elite, see Albion, *Rise of New York Port,* ch. 12.

66. *Albion,* November 27, 1847, 576.

67. *Democratic Review* 21 (December 1847): 564. On physical layout, decor, and management, see the *Courrier des États-Unis,* November 16, 1847, 261–62, translated in the *Herald,* November 23 and *Aristocratic Monitor,* November 27, 1847, 2.

68. The number of subscribers solicited was later lowered to 150. *Courrier des États-Unis,* February 11, 1847, 1148, May 6, 1847, 251.

69. *Courrier des États-Unis,* November 20, 1847, 277; *Tribune,* Novem-

ber 22, 1847. Conspicuously absent is any comment on the opera house opening from Walt Whitman in the *Brooklyn Eagle*. As a journalist, Whitman was on the free list for the theaters and Palmo's. He wrote admiringly of the Palmo's company and of Anna Bishop, whose English opera engagement competed with performances at the Astor Place. *Brooklyn Eagle*, February 13, March 13 (Palmo's), August 5 (Anna Bishop at the Park), and December 22, 1847 (Bishop at the Broadway).

70. Advertisement, *Courrier des États-Unis*, November 11, 1847, 248.

71. Ticket and handbill, 1848, Print Room Collection, NNHi.

72. Advertisement, *Tribune*, November 22, 1847.

73. *Herald*, November 27, 1847.

74. *Albion*, November 27, 1847, 576; see also *American Musical Times*, November 27, and *Age*, November 28, both reprinted in the *Herald*, December 1, 1847.

75. *Tribune*, November 25, 1847; see also *Home Journal*, November 27; *Atlas*, November 28, the latter reprinted in the *Herald*, December 1, 1847.

76. *Age*, November 28, 1847, quoted in Lawrence, *Resonances*, 456; see also the *Tribune* and *Herald*, December 6, 1847.

77. Advertisement, *Tribune*, December 3, 1847; reviews in *Tribune* and *Courier and Enquirer*, December 6, 1847.

78. *Albion*, March 4, 1848, 120; see also *Democratic Review* 22 (June 1848): 568–70.

79. Rinear, "William Mitchell's Management"; Rinear, "Mr. Mitchell, Mr. Macready."

80. Playbill, NNHi. Rinear consistently calls the play *Uproar House in Disaster Place*, citing a playbill at MH-T. Alternative titles were likely used.

81. Rinear, "William Mitchell's Management," 212; Rinear, "Mr. Mitchell, Mr. Macready," 16.

82. *Albion*, December 18, 1847, 612; *Spirit of the Times*, December 18, 1847, 512.

83. *Home Journal*, December 11, 1847, emphasis in original; see also *Times and Messenger*, November 14, 1847, translated in *Courrier des États-Unis*, November 16, 262, November 20, 1847, 277; *Herald*, November 20, 27, 29, December 1, 1847; *American Musical Times*, November 27, reprinted in the *Herald*, December 1, 1847.

84. *Herald*, December 13, 1847; *Times and Messenger*, November 28, reprinted in the *Herald*, December 1, 1847.

85. *Albion*, March 6, 1847, 120; see also *Democratic Review* 20 (April 1847): 376.

86. *Courier and Enquirer*, March 6 and 17, August 15, 1847 ("controlled abandon"); *American Whig Review* 5 (May 1847): 516. The term *ciaroscuro* is from the March 6 review by Richard Grant White.

87. *Albion,* March 6, 1847, 120; see also *Morning Express,* March 10, 1847; *Democratic Review* 20 (April 1847): 377; *American Whig Review* 5 (May 1847): 516; *Courier and Enquirer,* June 10, 1847.

88. *American Whig Review* 5 (May 1847): 516.

89. *Times and Messenger,* March 7, 1847.

90. *Albion,* November 27, 1847, 576; see also *Age,* November 28, 1847, reprinted in the *Herald,* December 1.

91. *Spirit of the Times,* May 6, 1848, 132.

92. *Democratic Review* 22 (May 1848): 473. The *Review* listed Mercadante's *Il giuramento,* Verdi's *Nabucco,* and Bellini's *Beatrice di Tenda* as the failures.

93. Wilentz, *Chants Democratic,* 359.

94. *Herald,* June 1, 1849, in an editorial entitled "Opera and Fashion."

95. Odell, *Annals* 6:160; Maretzek, *Crotchets,* 214.

96. Odell, *Annals* 6:244; *Bulletin of the Mercantile Library,* October, 1960, Astor Place Opera House clipping file, NN-T.

97. *Putnam's* 2 (July 1853): 113.

98. *Musical Review* 4 (June 1853): 91; see also the *Herald,* February 14, 1852; *Courrier des États-Unis,* December 11, 1854; *Democratic Review* 42 (November, 1858): 403.

99. Reprinted by the academy directors, May 1878, Theatre Collection, Museum of the City of New York.

100. On the history and uses of Castle Garden, see Andrews, *Iconography of the Battery.*

101. Ibid., 31–32.

102. Albion, *Rise of New York Port,* 43, 318–19.

103. Henry R. Conklin Papers, NNHi. Conklin was a contractor who worked on the Castle Garden renovation.

104. For history and description, see Lawrence, *Resonances,* 20–21.

105. *Courrier des États-Unis,* August 17, 1847, 617; Lawrence, *Resonances,* 421.

106. Maretzek, *Crotchets,* 157; Castle Garden receipt book, French and Heiser Papers, NNHi.

107. Castle Garden day book, July 25, August 12, September 6, 1850. For descriptions of well-attended opera performances, see *Saroni's,* July 13, 1850, 494; *Spirit of the Times,* July 20, 1850, 264; *Courrier des États-Unis,* August 1, 1850, 473, August 15, 1850, 515, August 17, 1850, 523, August 22, 1850, 533.

108. *Times,* January 20, 21, 1852. On "old prices," see the *Tribune,* January 15, 16, 21, 1852; *Herald,* January 16, 1852.

109. *Albion,* January 31, 1852, 56; see also the *Herald,* January 24, 1852.

110. *Times,* January 13, February 2, 1852; see also table 5 in this volume.

111. *Courier and Enquirer,* February 10, 1852.

112. *Saroni's,* January 24, 1852, 187, February 7, 1852, 214; *Times,* January 30, 1852; *Herald,* February 2, 3, 7, 14, 1852; *Courier and Enquirer,* February 4, 1852 ("people's opera"); *Tribune,* February 10, 14, 17 ("millennium of cheapness"), 20, March 5, 1852.

113. *Tribune,* February 20, 1852.

114. *Times,* February 21, 1852.

115. Advertisements, *Times,* January 3 and 10, 1853.

116. *Tribune,* February 20, 1852; see also the *Herald,* February 7, 17, 1852; *Saroni's,* February 14, 1852, 236, reprinted from *Courier and Enquirer* (no date given); *Musical Review,* April 27, 1854, 138.

117. *Herald,* February 14, 1852.

118. Act of Incorporation, April 10, 1852.

119. *Musical Review,* October 12, 1854, 353; *Herald,* October 3, 1854; *Courrier des États-Unis,* October 3, 1854; *Harper's* 10 (December 1854): 123.

120. *Musical Review,* September 14, 1854, 321.

121. *Home Journal,* October 21, 1854; see also *Democratic Review* 34 (November 1854): 463; *Courrier des États-Unis,* October 3, 1854.

122. *Putnam's* 3 (November 1854): 568; see also *Musical Review,* October 12, 1854, 353.

123. *Musical Review,* November 23, 1854, 402, emphasis in original.

124. *Musical Review,* April 27, 1854, 138, November 23, 1854, 402; *Democratic Review* 34 (December 1854): 550; *Harper's* 8 (May 1854): 695–96, 22 (March 1861): 413–14; *Courrier des États-Unis,* October 3, October 11, December 6, December 8, 1854; Maretzek, *Crotchets,* 334.

125. Starr, *Bamboula!* 240–41.

126. *Times,* October 18, 1858.

127. Advertisements, *Times,* October 20–December 7, 1858.

128. *Times,* October 18, 1858.

129. *Times,* October 14, 18, 20, 21, 26, 28, November 6, 1858; *Herald,* November 5, 1858.

130. *Courier and Enquirer,* October 14, 1858, reprinted in *Dwight's,* October 30, 1858, 244; *Leslie's,* October 30, 1858, 345, November 27, 1858, 408; *Spirit of the Times,* October 30, 1858, 456; *Albion,* October 23, 1858, 511–12, October 30, 1858, 523; *Times,* October 28, November 9, 1858.

131. *Times,* November 6 and 29, December 7, 1858.

132. *Times,* October 18, November 6, 1858; Odell, *Annals* 7:158–159.

133. *Herald,* December 8, 1858.

134. *Herald*, October 19, 1858.

135. *Spirit of the Times*, October 30, 1858, 456.

136. *Herald*, December 8, 1858.

137. Blumin, *Emergence of the Middle Class*, 146.

138. *Times*, December 9, 1858.

139. *Herald*, February 28, 1855.

140. Quoted in Gerould, ed., *American Melodrama*, 11.

141. Ibid., act 2, scene 1, 40, and act 4, scene 2, 63.

142. George G. Foster was a prolific writer of New York "city mysteries" literature. See also *The Lorgnette* (a periodical, 1850); Curtis, *The Potiphar Papers;* and *The Family of the Seisers*, ch. 17. The music periodicals sometimes took the same tack. See *Musical World*, February 1, 1850, 217; *Dwight's*, November 27, 1858, 276, December 11, 1858, 294.

143. *Life Illustrated*, November 10, 1855, 9, reprinted in Whitman, *New York Dissected*, 19–20.

144. *Broadway Journal*, February 22, 1845, 121; *Herald*, December 6, 1847; *Saroni's*, January 24, 1852, 187, February 7, 1852, 214; *Musical World*, May 28, 1853, 51; *Musical Review*, October 12, 1854, 354; *Harper's* 11 (July 1855): 269–71, 14 (December 1856): 127–28, and 14 (January 1857): 270–72.

145. *Times*, October 1, 1860.

146. *Times*, October 3, 1860.

147. *Musical Review*, October 16, 1858, 323.

Chapter 6: The New Italian Opera and Its Reception

1. *Albion*, January 5, 1850, 8.

2. *Times*, February 20, 1855.

3. *Musical Review*, March 1, 1855, 75.

4. *Evening Post*, February 24, 1855.

5. *Courrier des États-Unis*, February 21, 1855.

6. *Times*, February 20, 1855; see also *Musical Review*, March 1, 1855, 75.

7. *Tribune*, February 20, 1855.

8. *Evening Post*, February 20, 1855. On *Rigoletto*'s plot, see also the *Times*, February 19, 1855, 20, *Courrier des États-Unis*, February 19, 1855, *Herald*, February 20, 1855, *Tribune*, February 20, 1855, and *Evening Post*, February 20, 1855.

9. On melodrama as moral lesson, see Grimsted, *Melodrama Unveiled*, especially 241–48 on *Rosina Meadows*.

10. *Musical World*, February 24, 1855, 85–86.

11. *Musical World,* January 22, 1853, 54. The article is unsigned, but all substantial pieces not by Willis are either signed or identified as to their source.

12. Bellows, *Relation of Public Amusements to Public Morality,* 40; see also *Times,* March 20, 1857.

13. *Tribune,* March 19, 1856.

14. *Times,* March 18, 1856; see also *Tribune,* March 19, 1856.

15. *Times,* August 29, 1854.

16. *Albion,* March 22, 1856, 140.

17. *Albion,* January 24, 1857, 24. On Heron, see *Tribune,* January 23, 1857; *Times,* January 23, 1857; *Spirit of the Times,* January 31, 1857, 612; *Putnam's* 9 (March 1857): 334–35.

18. *Times,* December 4, 1856; *Albion,* October 22, 1856, 559.

19. "Trovator," *Dwight's,* December 13, 1856, 84.

20. *Musical Review,* December 13, 1856, 385.

21. *Musical World,* December 27, 1856.

22. *Courier and Enquirer,* quoted in *Dwight's,* December 13, 1856, 87.

23. "Raimond," *Albion,* December 6, 1856, 584. For critics tired of the morality issue, see the *Times* and *Post,* December 4, 1856; *Putnam's* 9 (January 1857): 111.

24. *Musical Review,* October 2, 1858, 308; *Herald,* October 14, 1858; *Albion,* October 23, 1858, 511; *Leslie's,* November 6, 1858, 358; *Times,* November 18, 1858.

25. "Trovator," *Dwight's,* October 30, 1858, 243.

26. *Atlas,* December 7, 1856.

27. *Leslie's,* October 30, 1858, 345.

28. *Musical Review,* May 2, 1857, 131, and November 14, 1857, 355; *Courrier des États-Unis,* December 18, 1854.

29. *Broadway Journal,* November 29, 1845, 318–19, reprinted in Whitman, *Uncollected Poetry and Prose,* 1:104–6. For Whitman on similar themes, see "Heart-Music and Art-Music," "Music That is Music," " 'True American' Singing," and "Music for the 'Natural Ear.' "

30. The Cheneys were among the popular touring family singing groups that followed the Hutchinsons of New Hampshire. As of the time of "Art-Singing," Whitman had heard the Cheneys but not the Hutchinsons.

31. *Life Illustrated,* November 10, 1855, 9, reprinted in Whitman, *New York Dissected,* 21–22. On opera and Whitman's poetry, see Faner, *Walt Whitman and Opera.*

32. *American Monthly Magazine* 4 (August 1837): 134.

33. *Albion,* October 23, 1858, 511.

34. On the *Courier*'s relationship with the Astor Place Opera House management, see Lawrence, *Resonances,* 457 and n48.

35. *Courier and Enquirer,* January 17, 1848.

36. Foster, *New York in Slices.*

37. Reynolds, *Beneath the American Renaissance,* ch. 6 and passim.

38. *Putnam's* 9 (January 1857): 8; see also Vance, *America's Rome;* Baker, *The Fortunate Pilgrims;* Douglas, *Feminization of American Culture,* 284; Levine, *Highbrow/Lowbrow,* 220.

39. *Home Journal,* January 16, 1847, 2.

40. *Musical World,* December 2, 1850, 546.

Chapter 7: Opera and the "Higher Order of Composition"

1. *Musical World,* February 24, 1855, 85–86.

2. *Musical World,* January 29, 1853, 65; for similar arguments, see *Musical World,* April 1, 1851, 17, May 1, 1851, 50–51, and August 1, 1851, 177; *Musical Review* 3 (August 1852): 116; Cuyler, *Sermon,* 10.

3. Paraphrased from *American Monthly Magazine* 1 (March 1836): 317.

4. *Observer,* September 28, 1850; Willis, *Memoranda of the Life of Jenny Lind,* 123; Levine, *Highbrow/Lowbrow,* 219.

5. Foster, *Memoir of Jenny Lind,* 3–4.

6. *Observer,* September 7, 1850, reprinted from the *Evangelist,* no date given.

7. *Evangelist,* September 12, 1850; see also Foster, *Memoir of Jenny Lind,* 58–59; Willis, *Memoranda of the Life of Jenny Lind,* 157–58. For the same idea without reference to Lind, see *Saroni's,* December 15, 1849, 131.

8. *Tribune,* quoted in Willis, *Memoranda of the Life of Jenny Lind,* 125.

9. *Saroni's,* September 14, 1850, 603.

10. Willis, *Memoranda of the Life of Jenny Lind,* 151.

11. Ibid., 150. "The latter half" refers to "Ah, bello a me ritorna," the intervening materal having been omitted. Program, September 11, 1850, Jenny Lind Collection, NNHi, emphasis in the original.

12. Buckley, " 'To the Opera House,' " 499–500, 535–37.

13. *Musical World,* January 22, 1853, 54.

14. Shanet, *Philharmonic,* 109–10.

15. Shanet, *Philharmonic,* 100, on subscription arrangements, see 106–7 and 125.

16. *Putnam's* 1 (April 1853): 468–69. On art versus fashion debates with regard to the Philharmonic, see Shanet, *Philharmonic,* 123–24.

17. *Tribune* (Margaret Fuller), December 11, 1845; *Broadway Journal,* December 22, 1845, 375, January 3, 1846, 407.

18. An 1840 production at the National Theatre may have been complete but in English. *Spirit of the Times,* December 12, 1840, 492.

19. The Meyerbeer operas were performed in Italian, the Flotow in German, and the Weber in Italian in 1850. A version of *Robert le diable* had been sung in English adaptation in 1834, possibly without any of Meyerbeer's music, and in French by a touring company in 1845. *Der Freischütz* had been sung in German at Palmo's in 1845. Mattfeld, *A Hundred Years of Grand Opera in New York,* 43, 53–54, 60, 63, 67, 71, 72.

20. *Herald,* January 29, 1850.

21. *Saroni's,* February 2, 1850, 218; see also November 10, 1849, 77, December 29, 1849, 158; *Sunday Mercury,* December 9, 1849; *Albion,* January 5, 1850, 8, February 2, 1850, 56; *Herald,* January 30, 1850; *Evening Mirror,* January 29, 1850, February 4, 1850; *Times and Messenger,* February 3, 1850.

22. *Message Bird,* February 15, 1850, 239; see also *Evening Mirror,* February 4, 1850.

23. *Musical World,* August 6, 1853, 210.

24. *Albion,* June 30, 1855, 307. For a similar comment, see *Musical Review,* April 4, 1857, 98–99.

25. *Musical Review,* October 2, 1858, 307.

26. Starr, *Bamboula!* chs. 10, 11; Broyles, *"Music of the Highest Class";* Saloman, *Beethoven's Symphonies and J. S. Dwight.*

27. *Albion,* November 10, 1832, 184; see also *American Monthly Magazine* 1 (May 1833): 191–92.

28. *Albion,* January 5, 1833, 7, see also November 10, 1832, 183–84; *Post,* February 6, 1834.

29. *Message Bird,* September 1, 1849, 37.

30. *American Monthly Magazine* 1 (May 1833): 191.

31. *Albion,* January 5, 1850, 8, emphasis in original.

32. *American Whig Review* 5 (May 1847): 516–17; *Saroni's,* July 6, 1850, 482; *Musical World,* August 1, 1851, 185–86; *Musical Review* 3 (August 1852): 114–15.

33. *Albion,* November 13, 1858, 547. For more disparagement of the public, see *Democratic Review* 42 (November 1858): 399–400; *Tribune,* November 10, 1858; *Times,* November 24, 1858.

34. Levine, *Highbrow/Lowbrow,* ch. 2.

35. Mussulman, *Music in the Cultured Generation.*

36. *Home Journal,* December 11, 1847.

37. *The Nation,* June 18, 1868, 487 ("The Organization of Culture"), quoted in Mussulman, *Music in the Cultured Generation,* 24–25. On the "Remnant," see 26–29; the term is from Matthew Arnold, *Culture and Anarchy.*

38. For a more detailed discussion of this issue see Ahlquist, "Mrs. Potiphar at the Opera."

39. See Levine, *Highbrow/Lowbrow,* 104–32 on orchestras, 101–3 on opera.

40. Douglas, *Feminization of American Culture,* 286.

41. *Musical World,* January 22, 1853, 54.

Bibliography

Unpublished material used in this study includes theater and opera house records, correspondence, playbills and programs, financial records, diaries, scrapbooks, clipping files, and iconography files. Two sources were especially valuable. One was the extensive Jane Shirreff Collection in the Billy Rose Theatre Collection, New York Public Library, which includes Shirreff's manuscript diary, account books, scrapbooks, clippings, and playbills covering her English and American careers. The other significant document repository was the New-York Historical Society, which holds the Italian Opera House papers as well as documents from Castle Garden and the Park Theatre (in the Astor Papers). The society also holds the manuscript diaries of nineteenth-century New York's best-known observers, Philip Hone and George Templeton Strong. The Harvard Theatre Collection has documents from the Bowery, Olympic, and National theaters and Seguin family correspondence. Other useful documents and ephemera may be found at the Folger Shakespeare Library, University of Michigan (Sanders Collection), Museum of the City of New York, New York Public Library (music and theater collections), and Free Library of Philadelphia. For more detail, see Ahlquist, "Opera, Theatre, and Audience."

The bibliography that follows includes scores and librettos for operas discussed in the text, including those given in musical examples. Many other nineteenth-century sources for the repertoire are available. Musical sources include sheet music editions, vocal scores, and some full scores, many at the Library of Congress or the New York Public Library. Also of great interest is the large Tams-Witmark Collection at the Mills Music Library, University of Wisconsin-Madison. Most of its scores and librettos are rare working copies from English opera troupes. Other important libretto and script holdings are the Edna Kuhn Loeb Music Library at Harvard University (Italian opera) and the Nisbet-Snyder Drama Collection at Northern Illinois University (English opera). The latter are catalogued in DuBois, *An Annotated Checklist of Prompt Books, 1800–1900, from the Nisbet-Snyder Drama Collection, Northern Illinois University Libraries.*

Except for John Gay, librettos and scores are listed under the name of the composer or musical compiler.

Library Abbreviations

DLC	Library of Congress, Music Division
ICN	Newberry Library, Chicago
IDeKN	Northern Illinois University, Founders Memorial Library, Rare Books/Special Collections, Nisbet-Snyder Drama Collection
MB	Boston Public Library
MH	Harvard University, Edna Kuhn Loeb Music Library
MWA	American Antiquarian Society, Worcester, Massachusetts
MiU	University of Michigan, Harlan Hatcher Graduate Library
MiU-C	University of Michigan, William L. Clements Library
MiU-M	University of Michigan, Music Library
NNHi	New-York Historical Society
NN	New York Public Library, Library of the Performing Arts, Music Collection
NN-T	New York Public Library, Library of the Performing Arts, Billy Rose Theatre Collection
PPSJ	St. Joseph's University, Philadelphia
PU	University of Pennsylvania, Van Pelt Library
WU	University of Wisconsin-Madison, Mills Music Library, Tams-Witmark Collection

Periodicals

Periodicals are listed by the short title used in the text; titles in parentheses are alternatives used by the same publication. Dates are given to distinguish among periodicals that have the same short title. All were published in New York unless otherwise stated.

Age
Albion
American
American Monthly Magazine (1817–19)
American Monthly Magazine (1833–38)
American Musical Journal
American Musical Times
American Whig Review
Anglo American
Arcturus

Aristocratic Monitor (*Monitor*)

Atlas

Broadway Journal

Brooklyn Eagle

Clipper

Commercial Advertiser

Courier and Enquirer

Courrier des États-Unis

Critic

Democratic Review (*United States Magazine and Democratic Review*)

Dramatic Mirror (New York and Philadelphia)

Dwight's Journal of Music (Boston)

Euterpeiad

Evangelist

Evening Post (*Post*)

Express (*Morning Express*)

Figaro

Harmonicon (London)

Harper's Monthly

Herald

Home Journal

Knickerbocker

Ladies' Companion

[Frank] Leslie's Illustrated Newspaper

Life Illustrated

Literary Gazette

Lorgnette

Lyre

Mirror

Musical Review (1838–39)

Musical Review (1850–73); (*American Monthly Musical Review, New York Musical Review and Choral Advocate, New York Musical Review and Gazette, Musical Review and Musical World*)

Musical World (*Message Bird, Journal of the Fine Arts, Musical World and Journal of the Fine Arts, Musical World and New York Musical Times,* and *New York Musical World*)

National Advocate

Observer

Opera Glass

Prompter

Putnam's Magazine

Review and Atheneum

Saroni's Musical Times (*Musical Times*)
Spirit of the Times
Sunday Mercury
Times
Times and Messenger
Tribune

Scores, Librettos, Books, and Other Sources

"Address." *American Musical Journal* 1 (October 1834): 16.

Agnew, Jean-Christophe. *Worlds Apart: The Market and the Theater in Anglo-American Thought, 1550–1750.* Cambridge: Cambridge University Press, 1986.

Ahlquist, Karen. "Mrs. Potiphar at the Opera: Satire, Idealism, and Cultural Authority in Post-Civil War New York." In *American Musical Life in Context and Practice*, 2: 1–21. Edited by Michael Saffle and James Heintze. New York: Garland, in press.

———. "Opera, Theatre, and Audience in Antebellum New York." Ph.D. diss., University of Michigan, 1991.

Albion, Robert G. *The Rise of New York Port.* 1939. Reprint, with Jennie Barnes Pope. Newton Abbot, Devon: David and Charles, 1970.

Allwardt, Anton P. "Sacred Music in New York, 1800–1850." S.M.D. diss., Union Theological Seminary, 1950.

Andrews, William Loring. *The Iconography of the Battery and Castle Garden.* New York: Scribner, 1901.

Angotti, Vincent L. "American Dramatic Criticism, 1800–1830." Ph.D. diss., University of Kansas, 1967.

Arne, Thomas Augustine, et al. *Love in a Village, a Comic Opera, as it is performed at the Theatre Royal Covent Garden.* Vocal score. London: I. Walsh [1763].

———. *Love in a Village.* Vocal score. London: J. Dale, n.d.

[———.] *Love in a Village. A Comic Opera. In Three Acts. By Isaac Bickerstaff.* Script. New York: David Longworth, 1817. IDeKN.

Arnold, Matthew. *Culture and Anarchy.* 1869. Reprint. Harmondsworth: Penguin Books, 1970.

Auber, Daniel Francois Esprit. *Fra Diavolo.* Libretto by Eugène Scribe. New York: Douglas, 1848 (Seguin company). MiU.

Austern, Linda Phyllis. " 'Sing againe Syren': The Female Musician and Sexual Enchantment in Elizabethan Life and Literature." *Renaissance Quarterly* 42 (Fall 1989): 420–88.

Baker, Paul R. *The Fortunate Pilgrims: Americans in Italy 1800–1860.* Cambridge: Harvard University Press, 1964.

Balfe, Michael William. *The Bohemian Girl.* Libretto by Alfred Bunn. New York: J. C. House, 1844 (Seguin cast). WU.

——. *The Bohemian Girl.* Vocal score. Edited by Max Spicker. New York: G. Schirmer, 1902. MiU-M.

Barish, Jonas. *The Anti-Theatrical Prejudice.* Berkeley: University of California Press, 1981.

Bellini, Vincenzo. *La sonnambula.* Vocal score. New York: G. Schirmer, n.d.

——. [*La sonnambula.* "Ah, non giunge."] "Ah! Don't Mingle." Philadelphia: George Willig, n.d.

——. *La sonnambula.* Libretto by Felice Romani. English adaptation by Samuel Beazley. Libretto from first English-language production, Drury Lane Theatre, London, 1833. Title page lacking. [London, 1833.] MH.

——. *Norma.* Vocal score. New York: G. Schirmer, n.d.

——. *Norma.* Libretto by Felice Romani. Translated by Alfredo Maggioni. New York: John Darcie, 1854. MH.

——. *Songs, Duetts, Recitative, &c. &c. in the Grand Opera of the Sonnambula.* . . . English libretto without spoken dialogue, music arranged by Henry Bishop. Boston: John H. Eastburn, 1835. DLC.

Bellows, Henry Whitney. *The Relation of Public Amusements to Public Morality, Especially of the Theatre to the Highest Interests of Humanity.* New York: C. S. Francis, 1857.

Bender, Thomas. *New York Intellect: A History of Intellectual Life in New York City, from 1750 to the Beginnings of Our Own Time.* New York: Alfred A. Knopf, 1988.

Bishop, Henry. *Clari.* Vocal score. London: Goulding, [1823]. DLC copy heavily annotated, including inserted songs and indicated deletions.

——. *Clari: or, The Maid of Milan.* Libretto by John Howard Payne. New York: Circulating Library and Dramatic Repository, 1823. MiU.

——. *Guy Mannering; or, The Gypsey's Prophecy; a Musical Play, in Three Acts.* Libretto by Daniel Terry. New York: David Longworth, 1816. MiU.

——. *The Libertine.* Opera after Mozart's *Don Giovanni.* Vocal score. London: Goulding, D'Almaine, Potter, [1817]. NN.

——. *The Slave.* Vocal score. London: Goulding, D'Almaine, Potter, [1816]. NN.

Blumin, Stuart M. *The Emergence of the Middle Class: Social Experience in the American City, 1760–1900.* Cambridge: Cambridge University Press, 1989.

Boromé, Joseph A. "Ferdinando Palmo: A Pioneer Impresario of Grand Opera in New York." *New York History* 45 (January 1964): 59–76.

[Bristed, Charles Astor.] *The Upper Ten Thousand: Sketches of American Society. By a New Yorker.* London: John W. Parker and Son, 1852.

Broyles, Michael. *"Music of the Highest Class": Elitism and Populism in Antebellum Boston.* New Haven: Yale University Press, 1992.

Buckley, James M. *Christians and the Theatre.* New York: Nelson and Phillips, 1876.

Buckley, Peter. " 'To the Opera House': Culture and Society in New York City, 1820–1860." Ph.D. diss., State University of New York at Stony Brook, 1984.

Budden, Julian. "Verdi and the Contemporary Italian Scene." In *The Verdi Companion,* 67–105. Edited by William Weaver and Martin Chusid. New York: W. W. Norton, 1979.

Buratti, David. "The *Spirit of the Times:* Its Theatrical Criticism and Theories as a Reflection of Cultural Attitudes." Ph.D. diss., Indiana University, 1977.

Bushman, Richard L. "American High-Style and Vernacular Culture." In *Colonial British America: Essays in the New History of the Early Modern Era,* 345–83. Edited by Jack P. Greene and J. R. Pole. Baltimore: Johns Hopkins University Press, 1984.

Butler, Charles. *The American Lady.* Philadelphia: Hogan and Thompson, 1836.

Child, Lydia Maria. "The Beloved Tune." In *Fact and Fiction: A Collection of Stories.* New York: C. S. Francis, 1846.

Cosgrove, Peter. "Affective Unities: The Esthetics of Music and Factional Instability in Eighteenth-Century England." *Eighteenth-Century Studies* 22 (Winter 1988–89): 133–55.

Curtis, George William. *The Potiphar Papers.* New York: G. P. Putnam, 1853.

Cuyler, T. L. *Sermon on Christian Recreation and Unchristian Amusement.* New York: E. D. Barker, 1858.

Da Ponte, Lorenzo. *Memorie.* 2 volumes. Edited by Giovanni Gambarin and Fausto Nicolini. Bari: Giuseppe Laterza and Sons, 1918.

———. *Memoirs of Lorenzo Da Ponte.* Translated by Elizabeth Abbott. Edited and annotated by Arthur Livingston. 1929. Reprint. New York: Da Capo, 1967.

Davidge, William. *The Drama Defended. Addressed, with Respect, to the Public Generally, and with Comiseration, to Messrs. the Rev. Strickland[,] T. L. Cuyler, &c. by William Davidge, Commedian.* New York: S. French, 1859.

De Jong, Mary Gosselink. " 'Both Pleasure and Profit': William Billings and the Uses of Music." *William and Mary Quarterly* 42 (January 1985): 104–16.

deZego, Frank. "Edmund Kean in New York and Boston: The 1820s." 2 volumes. Ph.D. diss., City University of New York, 1988.

Dickens, Charles. *American Notes for General Circulation.* 1842. Reprint. London: Oxford University Press, 1957.

Dizikes, John. *Opera in America: A Cultural History.* New Haven: Yale University Press, 1993.

Donizetti, Gaetano. *Lucrezia Borgia.* Vocal score. Paris: Latte, n.d. PU.

——. *Lucrezia Borgia.* Libretto by Felice Romani after Victor Hugo, *Lucrèce Borgia.* New York: Houel and Macoy, 1844 (Palmo's company). MH.

Douglas, Ann. *The Feminization of American Culture.* 1977. Reprint. New York: Anchor Press/Doubleday, 1988.

——. *Terrible Honesty: Mongrel Manhattan in the 1920s.* New York: Farrar, Straus, and Giroux, 1995.

DuBois, William R. *An Annotated Checklist of Prompt Books, 1800–1900, from the Nisbet-Snyder Drama Collection, Northern Illinois University Libraries.* Boston: G. K. Hall, 1973.

Dumas, Alexandre. *Camille.* Manuscript, adapted by Jean Davenport. NN-T.

——. *Camille.* Translated by Matilda Heron. New York: S. French, [1856]. MiU.

Ehrlich, Cyril. *The Music Profession in Britain since the Eighteenth Century: A Social History.* Oxford: Clarendon Press, 1985.

Ellis, Joseph. "Pre-Revolutionary Culture and Capitalism." *American Quarterly* 31 (Summer 1979): 169–86.

The Family of the Seisers. A Satirical Tale of the City of New-York. New York: J. M. Elliott, 1844.

Faner, Robert D. *Walt Whitman and Opera.* Philadelphia: University of Pennsylvania Press, 1951.

Finney, Gretchen L. "Ecstasy and Music in Seventeenth-Century England." *Journal of the History of Ideas* 7 (April 1947): 153–86.

——. " 'Organical Musick' and Ecstasy." *Journal of the History of Ideas* 7 (June 1947): 273–92.

Fiske, Roger. *English Theatre Music in the Eighteenth Century.* 2d ed. Oxford: Oxford University Press, 1986.

——. "Music and Society." In *Music in Britain: The Eighteenth Century,* 3–27. Edited by H. Diack Johnstone and Roger Fiske. Oxford: Blackwell Reference, 1990.

FitzLyon, April. *The Libertine Librettist: A Biography of Mozart's Librettist Lorenzo da Ponte.* New York: Abelard-Schuman, 1957.

Fitzsimons, Raymund. *Edmund Kean: Fire from Heaven.* London: Hamilton, 1976.

Foster, George G. *A Memoir of Jenny Lind: Compiled from the Most Authentic Sources.* New York: Dewitt and Davenport, 1850.

———. *New York in Slices, by an Experienced Carver.* New York: W. F. Burgess, 1849.

[Gay, John]. *The Beggar's Opera.* 1728. Reprint, facsimile edition with commentaries by Louis Kronenberger and Max Goberman. Larchmont: Argonaut Books, 1961.

———. *The Beggar's Opera.* Vocal score arranged by John Barnett. London: Chappell, n.d. DLC.

———. *The Beggar's Opera. The New English Drama . . . Edited by W. Oxberry.* London: W. Simplein and R. Marshall, 1818. MB.

Gerould, Daniel C., ed. *American Melodrama.* New York: Performing Arts Journal Publications, 1983.

Gilfoyle, Timothy J. *City of Eros: New York City, Prostitution, and the Commercialization of Sex, 1790–1920.* New York: W. W. Norton, 1992.

Gilje, Paul A. *The Road to Mobocracy: Popular Disorder in New York City, 1763–1834.* Chapel Hill: University of North Carolina Press, 1987.

Gorn, Elliott J. " 'Good-Bye Boys, I Die a True American': Homicide, Nativism, and Working-Class Culture in Antebellum New York City." *Journal of American History* 74 (September 1987): 388–410.

Grimsted, David. *Melodrama Unveiled: American Theater and Culture 1800–1850.* 2d ed. New foreword by Lawrence W. Levine. Berkeley: University of California Press, 1987.

Guerinot, J. V., and Rodney D. Jilg. *The Beggar's Opera.* Hamden: Archon Books, 1976.

Halttunen, Karen M. *Confidence Men and Painted Women: A Study of Middle-Class Culture in America, 1830–1870.* New Haven: Yale University Press, 1982.

Hamm, Charles. *Yesterdays: Popular Song in America.* New York: W. W. Norton, 1979.

Henderson, Mary C. *The City and the Theatre: New York Playhouses from Bowling Green to Times Square.* Clifton: James T. White, 1973.

Henneke, Ben Graf. "The Playgoer in America 1752–1952." Ph.D. diss., University of Illinois, 1956.

Hodge, Francis. *Yankee Theatre: The Image of America on the Stage, 1825–1850.* Austin: University of Texas Press, 1964.

Hodges, Sheila. *Lorenzo Da Ponte: The Life and Times of Mozart's Librettist.* London: Ceranada, 1985.

Hollander, John. *The Untuning of the Sky: Ideas of Music in English Poetry 1500–1700.* Princeton: Princeton University Press, 1961.

Holloway, Emory, and Ralph Adimari, eds. *New York Dissected: A Sheaf of*

Recently Discovered Newspaper Articles by the Author of Leaves of Grass. New York: Rufus Rockwell Wilson, 1936.

Hone, Philip. *The Diary of Philip Hone 1828–1851.* 2 volumes. Edited by Allan Nevins. New York: Dodd, Mead, 1927.

Hoover, Cynthia Adams. "Music in Eighteenth-Century American Theater." *American Music* 2 (Winter 1984): 6–18.

Horn, Charles, and John Braham. *The Devil's Bridge, an Operatic Romance in Three Acts. . . .* Vocal score. London: Goulding, D'Almaine, Potter, n.d. DLC.

———. *The Devil's Bridge, An Opera, in Three Acts. By Samuel James Arnold.* Philadelphia: Thomas H. Palmer, 1822. IDeKN.

Hoskins, Robert. "Theatre Music II." In *Music in Britain: The Eighteenth Century,* 261–312. Edited by H. Diack Johnstone and Roger Fiske. Oxford: Blackwell, 1990.

Hume, Robert D. "The Multifarious Forms of Eighteenth-Century Comedy." In *The Stage and the Page: London's "Whole Show" in the Eighteenth-Century Theatre,* 3–32. Edited by George Winchester Stone, Jr. Berkeley: University of California Press, 1981.

Irving, Washington. *Letters of Jonathan Oldstyle.* 1802–3. Reprint, edited by Bruce I. Granger and Martha Hartzog. Boston: Twayne, 1977.

Johnson, Claudia. "That Guilty Third Tier: Prostitution in Nineteenth-Century Theaters." *American Quarterly* 27 (December 1975): 575–84.

Johnstone, H. Diack, and Roger Fiske, eds. *Music in Britain: The Eighteenth Century.* Oxford: Blackwell, 1990.

Koza, Julia Eklund. "Music and References to Music in *Godey's Lady's Book,* 1830–77." Ph.D. diss., University of Minnesota, 1988.

Krehbiel, Henry E. *Chapters of Opera.* 3d ed. New York: Henry Holt, 1911.

Lamb, Martha. *History of the City of New York.* 2 volumes. New York: A. S. Barnes, 1877.

Langford, Paul. *A Polite and Commercial People: England, 1727–1783.* Oxford: Clarendon Press, 1989.

Lawrence, Vera Brodsky. *Strong on Music: The New York Music Scene in the Days of George Templeton Strong, 1836–1875.* Volume 1: *Resonances 1836–1850.* New York: Oxford University Press, 1988.

Leacroft, Richard, and Helen Leacroft. *Theatre and Playhouse: An Illustrated Survey of Theatre Building from Ancient Greece to the Present Day.* London: Methuen, 1984.

Leppert, Richard. "Imagery, Musical Confrontation and Cultural Difference in Early Eighteenth-Century London." *Early Music* 14 (August 1986): 323–45.

———. *Music and Image: Domesticity, Ideology and Socio-cultural Formation in*

Eighteenth-century England. Cambridge: Cambridge University Press, 1988.

Levine, Lawrence W. *Highbrow/Lowbrow: The Emergence of Cultural Hierarchy in America.* Cambridge: Harvard University Press, 1988.

———. "William Shakespeare and the American People: A Study in Cultural Transformation." *American Historical Review* 89 (February 1984): 34–66.

Linley, Thomas, and Thomas Linley II. *The Duenna.* Libretto by Richard Brinsley Sheridan. New York: Longworth, 1806. PU.

Main, Jackson Turner. *The Social Structure of Revolutionary America.* Princeton: Princeton University Press, 1965.

Malone, Dumas, ed. *Dictionary of American Biography.* 10 volumes. New York: Scribner, 1936.

Maretzek, Max. *Crotchets and Quavers.* New York: S. French, 1855.

Mates, Julian. *America's Musical Stage: Two Hundred Years of Musical Theatre.* Westport: Greenwood Press, 1985.

Mattfeld, Julius. *A Hundred Years of Grand Opera in New York, 1825–1925.* 1927. Reprint. New York: AMS Press, 1976.

McClary, Susan. "Excess and Frame: The Musical Representation of Madwomen." In *Feminine Endings: Music, Gender, and Sexuality,* 80–111. Minneapolis: University of Minnesota Press, 1991.

McConachie, Bruce A. "New York Operagoing, 1825–50: Creating an Elite Social Ritual." *American Music* 6 (Summer 1988): 181–92.

———. "'The Theatre of the Mob': Apocalyptic Melodrama and Preindustrial Riots in Antebellum New York." In *Theatre for Working-Class Audiences in the United States, 1830–1980,* 17–46. Edited by Bruce A. McConachie and Daniel Friedman. Westport: Greenwood Press, 1985.

McKay, David, and Richard Crawford. *William Billings of Boston: Eighteenth-Century Composer.* Princeton: Princeton University Press, 1975.

Mellers, Wilfrid. *Harmonious Meeting: A Study of the Relationship between English Music, Poetry and Theatre, c. 1600–1900.* London: Dennis Dobson, 1965.

Mozart, Wolfgang Amadeus. *Don Giovanni.* Full score. New York: Dover, 1974.

Mussulman, Joseph. *Music in the Cultured Generation: A Social History of Music in America, 1870–1900.* Evanston: Northwestern University Press, 1971.

Nash, Gary B. *The Urban Crucible: Social Change, Political Consciousness, and the Origins of the American Revolution.* Cambridge: Harvard University Press, 1979.

Nelson, Molly Sue. "The First Italian Opera Season in New York City: 1825–1826." Ph.D. diss., University of North Carolina, 1976.

Odell, George C. D. *Annals of the New York Stage.* 15 volumes. New York: Columbia University Press, 1927–49.

Paulson, Ronald. *Breaking and Remaking: Aesthetic Practice in England, 1700–1820.* New Brunswick: Rutgers University Press, 1989.

Pessen, Edward. "Philip Hone's Set: The Social World of the New York City Elite in the Age of Egalitarianism." *New-York Historical Society Quarterly* 56 (October 1972): 285–308.

———. *Riches, Power and Wealth before the Civil War.* Boston: D. C. Heath, 1973.

———. "The Wealthiest New Yorkers of the Jacksonian Era: A New List." *New-York Historical Society Quarterly* 54 (April 1970): 145–72.

Platt, Richard. "Theatre Music I." In *Music in Britain: The Eighteenth Century,* 96–158. Edited by H. Diack Johnstone and Roger Fiske. Oxford: Blackwell, 1991.

Porter, Roy. *English Society in the Eighteenth Century.* Revised edition. London: Penguin, 1991.

Porter, Susan L. *With an Air Debonair: Musical Theatre in America, 1785–1815.* Washington: Smithsonian Institution Press, 1991.

Preston, Katherine K. *Opera on the Road: Traveling Opera Troupes in the United States, 1825–1860.* Urbana: University of Illinois Press, 1993.

Preston, Stuart, comp. and ed. *Farewell to the Old House: The Metropolitan Opera House 1883–1966.* Garden City: Doubleday, 1966.

Printner, Calvin L. "William Warren's Financial Arrangements with Traveling Stars, 1805–1829." *Theatre Survey* 6 (November 1965): 83–90.

"Prospects of the American Stage." *Arcturus* 2 (October 1841): 279–85.

Reynolds, David S. *Beneath the American Renaissance: The Subversive Imagination in the Age of Emerson and Melville.* New York: Knopf, 1988.

Rinear, David L. "Mr. Mitchell, Mr. Macready, and the 'Uproar House in Disaster Place.'" *Theatre Southwest* 6 (February 1980): 12–18.

———. "William Mitchell's Management of the Olympic Theatre, 1839–1850." Ph.D. diss., Indiana University, 1971.

Rooke, William Michael. *Amilie, or The Love Test, Grand Romantic Opera. . . .* Vocal score. London: Duff and Hodgson; and Cramer, Addison and Beale, [1838]. DLC copy autographed by the composer.

———. *Amilie: or, The Love Test; a Grand Romantic Opera. . . .* Libretto by J. T. Haines. Baltimore: Joseph Robinson, [1839].

Root, Deane L. *American Popular Stage Music 1860–1880.* Ann Arbor: UMI Research Press, 1981.

Rosenwaike, Ira. *Population History of New York City.* Syracuse: Syracuse University Press, 1972.

Rossini, Gioachino. *Il barbiere di Siviglia.* Vocal score. Paris: Launer, n.d. PU.

——. *The Barber of Seville*. Arranged by Henry Bishop. Vocal score. London: Goulding, D'Almaine, Potter, n.d. DLC.

——. *Il barbiere di Siviglia*. Libretto by Cesare Sterbini after Pierre-Augustin Caron de Beaumarchais. Italian and English. New York: E. M. Murden, 1825 (Garcia company libretto). MiU-C.

——. *The Barber of Seville*. English prose by John Fawcett. Poetry by Daniel Terry. Prompt book. London: J. Roach, 1818. ICN.

——. *The Barber of Seville*. With additions by Thomas Philipps. Philadelphia: Carey and Lea, 1822. MH script annotated by Henry Placide.

——. *La Cenerentola*. Vocal score. Paris: Launer, n.d. PU.

——. *Cinderella*. Baltimore: Joseph Robinson, [1839] (Shirreff-Seguin cast). WU.

——. *Cinderella*. Adapted by M. Rophino Lacy. Edited with introduction by John Graziano. In *Nineteenth-Century American Musical Theater*, volume 3. General editor Deane L. Root. New York: Garland, 1994.

[——]. *The Maid of Judah*. Pastiche arranged after Walter Scott's *Ivanhoe* by Michael Rophino Lacy. Script. London: John Cumberland, n.d. PPSJ.

——. *Otello*. N.p.: Kalmus, n.d.

——. *Otello*. Libretto by Francesco Berio di Salza after William Shakespeare. Italian and English. New York: E. M. Murden, 1826 (Garcia company libretto). MH.

——. *Tancredi*. Vocal score. Paris: Pacini, n.d. DLC.

——. "Una voce poca fa." New York: Dubois and Stodart, [1826].

Ryan, Mary. "The American Parade: Representations of the Nineteenth-Century Social Order." In *The New Cultural History*, 131–53. Edited by Lynn Hunt. Berkeley: University of California Press, 1989.

——. *Women in Public: Between Banners and Ballots, 1825–1880*. Baltimore: Johns Hopkins University Press, 1990.

Saloman, Ora Frishberg. *Beethoven's Symphonies and J. S. Dwight: The Birth of American Music Criticism*. Boston: Northeastern University Press, 1995.

Salvaggio, Odette Carol. "American Dramatic Criticism, 1830–1860." Ph.D. diss., Florida State University, 1979.

"Satire and Sentiment." *Arcturus* 2 (October 1841): 304–9.

Saunders, George. *A Treatise on Theatres*. London: The author, 1790.

Scholes, Percy A. *The Puritans and Music in England and New England*. London: Oxford University Press, 1934.

Shanet, Howard. *Philharmonic: A History of New York's Orchestra*. Garden City: Doubleday, 1975.

Shank, Theodore. "The Bowery Theatre, 1826–1836." Ph.D. diss., Stanford University, 1956.

Shapiro, Anne Dhu. "Action Music in American Pantomime and Melo-drama, 1730–1913." *American Music* 2 (Winter 1984): 49–72.

Shield, William. *The Poor Soldier.* Vocal score with spoken dialogue edited by David McKay. In *Recent Researches in American Music,* volume 8. Madison: A-R Editions, 1978.

———. *The Poor Soldier.* Libretto by John O'Keeffe. London: John Cumberland, 1828. MiU.

Silverman, Kenneth. *A Cultural History of the American Revolution.* New York: Thomas Y. Crowell, 1976.

Sonneck, Oscar. *Early Concert Life in America.* Leipzig: Breitkopf and Haertel, 1907.

———. *Early Opera in America.* 1915. Reprint. New York: Benjamin Blom, 1963.

Stansell, Christine. *City of Women: Sex and Class in New York, 1789–1860.* Urbana: University of Illinois Press, 1987.

Starr, S. Frederick. *Bamboula! The Life and Times of Louis Moreau Gottschalk.* New York: Oxford University Press, 1995.

Stott, Richard B. *Workers in the Metropolis: Class, Ethnicity, and Youth in Antebellum New York City.* Ithaca: Cornell University Press, 1990.

Stratman, Carl J. *American Theatrical Periodicals, 1798–1967.* Durham: Duke University Press, 1970.

Taylor, Rayner. *The Aethiop* (1813). Libretto by William Diamond. Introduction and musical and orchestral reduction by Victor Fell Yellin. In *Early Melodrama in America,* volume 2. Series edited by Deane L. Root. New York: Garland, 1994.

Temperley, Nicholas. "The English Romantic Opera." *Victorian Studies* 9 (March 1966): 293–301.

———, ed. *The Romantic Age.* London: Athlone Press, 1981.

Tick, Judith. *American Women Composers before 1870.* Ann Arbor: UMI Research Press, 1983.

Tidworth, Simon. *Theatres: An Architectural and Cultural History.* New York: Praeger, 1973.

Thomason, D. R. *Fashionable Amusements.* New York: Jonathan Leavitt, 1831.

Trollope, Frances. *Domestic Manners of the Americans.* 1832. Reprint, with introduction by Joanna Trollope. London: Century Publishing, 1984.

Vance, William L. *America's Rome.* 2 volumes. New Haven: Yale University Press, 1989.

Van Lennep, W., E. L. Avery, A. H. Scouten, G. W. Stone, and C. B. Hogan, eds. *The London Stage, 1660–1800: A Calendar of Plays, Entertainments, and Afterpieces. . . .* 5 parts. Carbondale: Southern Illinois University Press, 1960–68.

Verdi, Giuseppe. *Ernani*. Libretto by Francesco Maria Piave. Italian and English. New York: Douglas, 1848. MH.

———. *I Lombardi*. Vocal score. Front matter lacking. Paris: Bureau Centrale de Musique, n.d. PU.

———. *I Lombardi*. Libretto by Temistocle Solera. Italian and English. New York: Douglas, 1848. MH.

———. "La donna è mobile." Boston: Ditson, 1853.

———. *Rigoletto*. Full score. Milan: Ricordi, 1964.

———. [*Rigoletto*.] "La donna e mobile." Sheet music. Boston: Ditson, 1853. MWA.

———. *Rigoletto*. Libretto by Francesco Maria Piave. Italian and English. New York: Breusig, 1859. MH.

———. *La traviata*. Libretto by Francesco Maria Piave. Italian and English. Front material lacking. [New York, 1858–59.] MH.

———. *La traviata*. Full score. Milan: Ricordi, n.d.

———. *Il trovatore*. Libretto by Salvatore Cammarano. Italian and English. New York: F. Rullman, 1857. MH.

Weaver, William, and Martin Chusid, eds. *The Verdi Companion*. New York: W. W. Norton, 1979.

Weinbaum, Paul O. *Mobs and Demagogues: The New York Response to Collective Violence in the Early Nineteenth Century*. Ann Arbor: UMI Research Press, 1979.

Welter, Barbara. "The Cult of True Womanhood, 1820–1860." *American Quarterly* 18, no. 2 (1966): 151–74.

White, Eric Walter. *A History of English Opera*. London: Faber and Faber, 1983.

———. *A Register of First Performances of English Operas*. London: Society for Theatre Research, 1983.

Whitman, Walt. "Heart-Music and Art-Music." *Brooklyn Eagle*, November 14, 1845.

———. "Music for the 'Natural Ear.' " *Brooklyn Eagle*, April 3, 1846.

———. "Music That is Music." *Brooklyn Eagle*, December 4, 1845.

———. *New York Dissected: A Sheaf of Recently Discovered Newspaper Articles by the Author of* Leaves of Grass. Introduction and Notes by Emory Holloway and Ralph Adimari. New York: Rufus Rockwell Wilson, 1936.

———. " 'True American' Singing." *Brooklyn Evening Star,* January 13, 1846.

———. *The Uncollected Poetry and Prose of Walt Whitman*. 2 volumes. Edited by Emory Holloway. Garden City: Doubleday, Page, 1921.

Wilentz, Sean. *Chants Democratic: New York City and the Rise of the American Working Class, 1788–1850*. New York: Oxford University Press, 1984.

Willis, Nathaniel Parker. *Memoranda of the Life of Jenny Lind.* Philadelphia: Peterson, 1851.

Wilson, James Grant. *The Memorial History of the City of New-York, from Its First Settlement to the Year 1892.* 4 volumes. New York: New York History Co., 1892.

Wood, William B. *Personal Recollections of the Stage, Embracing Notices of Actors, Authors, and Auditors, during a Period of Forty Years.* Philadelphia: Henry Carey Baird, 1855.

Young, William C., ed. *Documents of American Theatre History.* 2 volumes. Chicago: American Library Association, 1973.

Index

KAREN AHLQUIST is an assistant professor of music at the George Washington University in Washington, D.C. She has written for the *Journal of American History* and the *Journal of Musicological Research* and serves on the board of the Sonneck Society for American Music and the forthcoming journal *Women and Music*. She holds the Ph.D. degree from the University of Michigan.

Bluegrass Breakdown: The Making of the Old Southern Sound *Robert Cantwell*

Bluegrass: A History *Neil V. Rosenberg*

Music at the White House: A History of the American Spirit *Elise K. Kirk*

Red River Blues: The Blues Tradition in the Southeast *Bruce Bastin*

Good Friends and Bad Enemies: Robert Winslow Gordon and the Study of American Folksong *Debora Kodish*

Fiddlin' Georgia Crazy: Fiddlin' John Carson, His Real World, and the World of His Songs *Gene Wiggins*

America's Music: From the Pilgrims to the Present (Revised Third Edition) *Gilbert Chase*

Secular Music in Colonial Annapolis: The Tuesday Club, 1745–56 *John Barry Talley*

Bibliographical Handbook of American Music *D. W. Krummel*

Goin' to Kansas City *Nathan W. Pearson, Jr.*

"Susanna," "Jeanie," and "The Old Folks at Home": The Songs of Stephen C. Foster from His Time to Ours (Second Edition) *William W. Austin*

Songprints: The Musical Experience of Five Shoshone Women *Judith Vander*

"Happy in the Service of the Lord": Afro-American Gospel Quartets in Memphis *Kip Lornell*

Paul Hindemith in the United States *Luther Noss*

"My Song Is My Weapon": People's Songs, American Communism, and the Politics of Culture, 1930–50 *Robbie Lieberman*

Chosen Voices: The Story of the American Cantorate *Mark Slobin*

Theodore Thomas: America's Conductor and Builder of Orchestras, 1835–1905 *Ezra Schabas*

"The Whorehouse Bells Were Ringing" and Other Songs Cowboys Sing *Guy Logsdon*

Crazeology: The Autobiography of a Chicago Jazzman *Bud Freeman, as Told to Robert Wolf*

Discoursing Sweet Music: Brass Bands and Community Life in Turn-of-the-Century Pennsylvania *Kenneth Kreitner*

Mormonism and Music: A History *Michael Hicks*

Voices of the Jazz Age: Profiles of Eight Vintage Jazzmen *Chip Deffaa*